The Legacy of Wisdom

The Legacy of Wisdom

J W Nottage

Matador
9 Priory Business Park
Kibworth Beauchamp
Leicester LE8 0RX, UK
Tel: 0116 279 2299
Fax: 0116 279 2277
Email: books@troubador.co.uk
Web: www.troubador.co.uk/matador

ISBN 978 1848766 723

British Library Cataloguing in Publication Data.
A catalogue record for this book is available from the British Library.

All characters in this novel are entirely fictitious.
Any resemblance to any person, living or deceased, is purely coincidental.

Cover design and illustration by Tracey English

Typeset in 11pt Bembo by Troubador Publishing Ltd, Leicester, UK

Matador is an imprint of Troubador Publishing Ltd
Printed and bound in the UK by TJ International, Padstow, Cornwall

First Edition

To Geoffrey John Nottage, my dearly beloved Dad, a wise master and a kind, loving, trusting father and friend. Much missed and often remembered.

ACKNOWLEDGEMENTS

The life of a writer is, by its very nature, solitary, but a small band of wonderful people has supported me, and inspired me to keep going and complete a book which I felt had to be written in a time when all of us feel uncertain about the future.

Two people in particular have stuck with me on this journey.

Yvette 'Toots' Venables whose creative input and generosity helped mould this book into what I hope is something special. I couldn't have done it without her.

Fiona Wilson of Cameron Wilson who brought a vague cover idea to life and found a fabulous illustrator. Her publishing skills have been invaluable. I also couldn't have done this book without her.

My much loved mother Margaret Nottage.
The wise sage Robert Mitchell.
My soul mate Tyler Alexander.
David Tremayne.

Astrologer Frank Clifford, head of the London School of Astrology.
Allan and Jill Lowe – fantastic friends.
Astrologer Paul Mayo and his wife Sandra.
Jon Sandifer and Tony Holdsworth for advice on Feng Shui and energy.

Marcus Adey and Abi Holgate for fitness training.

Editors Melissa Marshall, Lisanne Radice, Kate Lyall-Grant and Jane Heller.

Jonathan Scull, Natalie Reeks and Anne-Marie Sproule of NatWest and Graham Morris and Stuart Chadwick of Wyatt, Morris, Golland & Co. They all kept my finances in order.

Steve and Londa of Swift Print Cirencester.

Claire Quiggan, Joy Walter, Adrian Stoddart, Danny Blyth, Annie McIntyre and Katrina Graham have kept me going. Doctor N. Agrawal and Doctor al Memar.

Peter Lederer, Chairman, The Gleneagles Hotel, for making Gleneagles so special.

My Oxford Creative Writing Group especially Lise-Lotte Lystrup and Dave Richardson, and also Symon, Rebecca, Otto, Rachel and Sam.

Jeremy Thompson, Terry Compton and Sarah Taylor of publishers Matador. Matador has been a much appreciated partner in this and their patience outstanding. This book has been 'about to be completed' for the last six months.

Here it is. I hope you enjoy it.

Quotes used in *The Legacy of Wisdom*

The Bible – various.

The Dead Sea Scrolls – various.

Hermetica by Brian P. Copenhaver – 'Let every nature in the Cosmos attend the hearing of the hymn.'

The Book of Enoch the Prophet by R.H. Charles – 'Wisdom Found no place where she might dwell.'

Winston Churchill – 'If you're going through Hell keep going.'

William Bryant – 'The summer morn is bright and fresh.'

Milton Berle – 'It's much better to be a could-be if you cannot be an are.'

James Pierpoint – Jingle Bells.

Chequers Inscription on the stained glass window in the long gallery.

1910 Holy Cross alumni dinner – 'And this is good old Boston.'

John Donne – 'Absence'

Alexander Graham Bell – 'When One Door Closes'

My spiritual journey and revelation started at The Gleneagles Hotel on 21st June 2010. It is continuing today as we face our moment of truth. We can get it right and fulfil our collective destiny or destroy ourselves. Like you, I want the human race to embrace redemption. Please make the journey with me.

Dan Adams. The Gleneagles Hotel. 27th December 2011.

CHAPTER ONE

Judea

June 68 AD

A flick of the wrist and the silver-tipped sword sliced through the intricate gold chain that encircled the young woman's slender ankle. It fell to the ground. She was free.

For a brief moment, she met the eyes of the man who had released her and smiled. Her gaze spoke of the unique understanding that existed between father and daughter. Silently, they clasped hands.

'The time has come,' he whispered. 'Sadly, I must now release you to make your own way in the world. I will meet you at darkness by the old stone road up by the sacred yew tree. You know where that is, don't you?'

'Yes, Father. I go to the end of the village road where we often walked on our nightly strolls. From there I continue on the long road west towards the sunset. When the sun is almost set I'll arrive at the sacred yew tree. If...' she paused, fighting to keep her emotions under control, 'if you don't come for me, I will hide in the cave by the tree until your good friend, Benjamin, the only one who knows of my existence here, comes to fetch me.' She held her father's hand tightly.

'Don't trust anyone else.' He pulled her close breathing in her light scent of juniper oil. He stroked her thick, dark hair soothingly. She felt so tiny and defenceless, hardly more than the child he used to amuse with his tales of great adventures.

Finally, he drew back, gazed at her one more time, then handed her a large bundle of scrolls and a round wooden ball with intricate markings on it which he'd been carrying in an old leather bag. 'Protect these with your life, my child.'

She nodded silently. Then she drew her dark cloak round her shoulders, slipped the documents and wooden ball into the deep hidden pockets of the cloak, and wrapped a long scarf round her head to hide her hair. She looked at him, regret reflected in her large, dark eyes, then wordlessly she turned, walked out of the house, and hurried across the courtyard.

He paused and watched Eschiva flee, feeling overcome with sorrow. It was the first time they would be apart in seventeen years as he had cared for her since her mother had died giving birth to her. He screwed his eyes up against the sun as he watched her disappear into the distance – a woman in the heart of a male-dominated sect. He had hidden her all these years, locked up in luxury, occasionally allowed out to walk with him late at night or before dawn, when the other members of the sect had been at private prayer. He knew if he hadn't guarded her closely, her inquisitive nature would have got her killed.

He turned away and sighed heavily. In one brief moment he had altered the course of history. But he had no choice. The most important secrets had to be taken out of the area. Chance was too risky when treachery came calling. The Romans, led by General Vespasian, would soon be here and they would ransack the place, leaving nothing untouched. Someone had betrayed their sect and told the Romans of their mysteries and their power.

The members of the Essene sect were disappearing into the rugged hills, taking their scrolls of leather and papyrus with them. They were heading for the caves high up above the settlement to hide their ancient secrets. Violent earthquakes and natural disasters had lately increased in intensity. God's punishment, the local people said, but Jacob knew differently. God did not seek to destroy mankind, but rather mankind, through its wilfulness against the laws of nature, caused its own destruction.

The old man walked to the centre of the courtyard and plucked a pomegranate from the tree, twisting it round and gently squeezing it in his hand as thoughts and images passed uninvited through his head. He remembered his initiation ceremony, the holy words, sacred music drifting through the night air, the seductive smell of incense as the elders had invoked the presence of the ancient deity to bless him. A long time later, the arrival of his soulmate, a wonderful union, a precious child and then sudden death leaving him bereft.

He breathed deeply and brushed his hand briefly across his eyes. The air was heavy with the scent of the desert. The sun was harsh and unforgiving, burning all it touched as it reached its apex in the sky. The people had been formed by their environment as shown in their lithe bodies and heavily lined dark brown faces. His people. His tribe.

'Jacob, my friend. Are you not escaping and seeking to protect our mysteries?'

He felt a hand on his shoulder. He turned round and looked into the face of his closest friend. He smiled.

'Benjamin, I was just coming to look for you. I have managed to send the Melchizedek Sacred Mysteries away to a safe place. They are with Eschiva. She will await me by the old yew tree, or if something happens to me, then I have told her you will come and find her, and lead her and our secrets to safety,' he said with a calmness he did not feel.

'Good. I will fulfil my promise and go and find her if you cannot.' Benjamin stared at him intently.

'Thank you. You are more than a friend, you are a brother. You are the only one who helped us when her mother died and we needed support. Whatever the future brings, if we are all to be scattered across the land, I am truly grateful for your friendship. I don't know how to repay you.' Jacob put his hand on his friend's arm.

'There is always a way to repay and be repaid,' the other man said quietly.

The silver flash of the dagger startled Jacob. He turned quickly to see if there was danger behind him. Then he gasped as Benjamin raised his hand and plunged the dagger into his neck. Blood spurted and fell to the dry sand, the stain slowly spreading.

Jacob cried out in pain and shock. The metallic taste of blood filled his mouth as he felt his life force ebb away. It was just as the old soothsayer had predicted: 'Your life will be taken in the name of friendship, not war.' His head spun. He sank to the ground, aware that his attacker had already fled.

He groaned and reached out in despair but nobody could save him. Betrayed by the only man who knew their secrets. As his mind faded away, he was left with an image of his beloved child surrounded by a gang of men, their faces filled with anger and a lust for revenge. Dear God, no.

'Eloi, Eloi, lama, sabachthani. My God, my God, why hast thou forsaken me?' he whispered as his blood stained the sand a deeper red.

As his spirit departed his body, a golden coin dropped from the palm of his hand and started to spin, gathering speed across the sand, spinning faster and faster, creating a vortex of power and mystery. A white light emanated from it, and, within the light, human shapes started to form as the secrets of mankind came to life.

Slowly, a man exuding a timeless aura walked towards the

crowd that was quickly gathering around the now lifeless body of the old man. He had long, flowing white hair, piercing green eyes and was wearing a long white robe and dark green cloak edged with thick gold braid. He was carrying a very old, black, leatherbound book, its cover embossed with ancient gold script. He held it up to the sky and suddenly a sweet soft song could be heard on the slight breeze from the mountains. The evocative sound wove its magic into the hearts of the group of men who stood in shock, gazing at the lifeless body of their much-treasured friend. The mysterious man had such a powerful presence that the people fell silent and parted to make a clearing for him. He looked around at the sorrowful crowd, pausing before he spoke.

'Betrayal from inside the family is the worst kind,' the man said slowly and with total command. 'You, who are the chosen ones, have abused the power granted to you and our friend has died. Sadly, you will learn this is not the path that leads to your rightful destiny. You have lived so long with the ancient wisdom and know the secrets of human existence, and yet it would seem you have learned nothing. You have thrown it away so carelessly. You must now ask yourselves some important questions. Will mankind live by the truth or choose to sacrifice his body for nothing? Will the human race take its rightful place with us in the heavens or deny its destiny? Will the good of the collective be denied for your individual desire for instant gratification? The choice will one day be made. However, for you, my beloved friends, it is too late. The mysteries will now be hidden again, this time for many centuries until the final battle will be fought. A battle not of swords, but of minds. The Lord speaks and the Lord comes to impart knowledge.' No one approached the man or questioned him. He was the beginning and the end. The alpha and the omega. He was Lord Melchizedek, the Prince of Light, from whom the Christ child and all the Prophets had been, or would in the future be, descended.

'"The Lord hath sworn and will not repent. Thou art a priest for ever after the order of Melchizedek." Psalm One hundred and ten,' One of the men in the crowd whispered.

As Lord Melchizedek faded slowly back into the white light, screams of torture and pain rent the air as the first battalion of Romans arrived. Death and destruction had come to stay. There was no way back.

CHAPTER TWO

Gleneagles Hotel

June 2010

Dan Adams sat bolt upright in bed, sweat dripping from his brow, his light brown hair sticking to his forehead, and his right arm twisted behind his back. A frisson of fear shot through his soul. The nightmare echoed in his mind. Torture, death, cries of pain, in some ancient place he didn't recognize. His breath was coming in shallow gasps as he felt the panic of the men who were trying to hide something... but what exactly?

He switched on the light, his heart still pumping hard and looked round the room. All seemed perfectly normal. He glanced towards the corner of the room where the faint outline of his Jack Russell moved with the regular rise and fall of deep breathing. Mr Big was clearly oblivious to his master's distress.

After a few minutes, Dan jumped out of bed, and paced around the room before flinging on a pair of sweatpants, grabbing a T-shirt and a light jumper and whistling quietly to the dog, who leapt up and followed him out of the room. Silently, they padded along the corridor, past the other rooms and out into the night. It was quiet, nearly 3 a.m. The bar at the Gleneagles Hotel was empty and peace reigned in slumbering Perthshire.

As Mr Big scampered around chasing imaginary rabbits,

Dan walked across the lawns, past the borders of lavender bushes, their heavenly scent hanging sweetly in the night air, and headed out towards the golf courses. Without really thinking, he ducked through the trees away from the road and strode along behind the famous King's Golf Course. On he marched, his long legs making big strides over the loose stone pathway that curved between the greens, past the houses that sat by the golf course, along the narrow cutting and past the silent road, which was a link to the local village of Auchterarder.

After a while, he made a sharp left turn through some farm buildings, the tractors and farm equipment lying quietly in the pre-dawn glow, and embarked on a gentle climb towards the hills.

'Come on Mr Big,' he called to the dog, who suddenly appeared over one of the small hillocks.

Finally, he stood at the top of the highest hill, straddled between the greens, the bunkers and the rough. Glancing straight ahead he looked at Glen Devon, and the majestic hills that were now covered in a gentle mist. Dawn was preparing to make a languid entrance, although in Scotland in June, night was but a casual visitor, the sky never completely dark, and never more so than on this new day, 21st of June 2010, the longest day of the year.

Dan leaned back and stared hard at the stars. He scanned the early-morning sky and saw the planet Venus. Then he let his gaze alight on the hills and their dark hues of ancient rock, which were slowly taking shape in the soft dawn light, their colours soon to change from grey to purple to green. If there was an omnipotent creator, and he wasn't at all sure there was, this was the place in the world where a divine presence would choose to live, he thought.

Dan loved this place. It was the scene of his childhood.

Born in America, the only child of an American father and an English mother, he had lived in Boston until he was nine years old. Every summer until then, thanks to a wealthy uncle, had been spent in Scotland at the Gleneagles Hotel, a place where his paternal grandfather had once excelled at golf, a game Dan had also become very good at. But, when he'd been nine years old his mother, Primrose, had upped sticks, left his father, Edward, and moved him to London. That had been the end of his childhood summers in Scotland.

After that he'd only seen his father twice, shadowy memories of a tall, upright and very sad man, who had been both familiar and estranged. Many times he had wanted to tell his father how much he loved him. But he hadn't. Then when he'd been fifteen years old his mother had, one day, announced that his father had died of an illness related to alcoholism. She had managed to look both sorry and mildly disdainful at the same time.

In time, teaching had taken over his life. He loved the challenges of being a head teacher at an inner London school, and he also loved the fact it gave him the freedom to spend a long weekend each year at this golfers' paradise.

He glanced over towards the thirteenth hole – Braid's Brawest – course designer James Braid's favourite hole. Closing his eyes, he recalled one of his finest moments on a golf course. His drive off the tee had been perfect, a good 280-yard hit, over the cross bunkers and into the middle of the fairway. He'd then pitched it perfectly on to the elevated green, and clipped the ball into the hole for a birdie and an entry into his list of all-time great play. That evening drinks had been on him.

'As William Bryant would say, "The summer morn is bright and fresh, the birds are darting by, as if they loved to breast the breeze, that sweeps the cool clear sky," but you, sir, seem preoccupied this summer morn. Is nature's great gift not moving you to joy and happiness?'

Dan spun round in shock as a soft Scottish brogue drifted into his senses. He came face to face with a shortish, rotund gentleman in a tweed jacket and waistcoat, cream shirt, pale lemon tie, and well-pressed light-brown flannel trousers. Very smart for the wee small hours of the morning.

'Where on earth did you appear from at this early hour?' he exclaimed as he stared at the strange little man, before recovering his usual polite manner.

'Oh sorry, dear chap, didn't mean to startle you. I was just passing by. Perkins is the name. I guess you're not from these parts?' the little man observed.

'No, I'm American by birth. Dan Adams is my name,' Dan said briefly. It was thirty years since he'd moved to England but he'd never lost his East Coast accent.

'Ah yes, the land of the free, although it has to be said that freedom always comes at a price.' The man smiled.

Dan raised his eyebrows, wondering briefly if he was still in the midst of his strange dream. A philosophical discussion certainly wasn't what he had in mind at this time of the morning on an uneasy stomach and with the after-effects of the strange nightmare still embedded in his mind.

'Oh yes, freedom of speech can get you in all sorts of trouble. Verbal incontinence is fatal, you know, much more deadly than pandemic 'flu.'The little man roared with laughter.

Despite the terrible joke, Dan found himself relaxing and laughing too as he turned back to gaze into the distance and allow the glorious view to slowly calm his turbulent mind.

'Well, sadly I can't stand around here all day...' he started, then stopped. The strange little man had vanished into thin air. Dan looked around but there was no sign of any human movement.

What the hell... was he going mad? He shook himself firmly and stared into the distance but there was nothing moving in the half-light. This wasn't possible. His own equilibrium must have been upset by the global meltdown and instability that was going on all around him.

'Bloody hell, get a grip,' he muttered to himself.

He was a dedicated teacher, a pragmatic dreamer, normally a man with both feet firmly on the ground. Now he was talking to strange little men on a Scottish hillside.

Dan pulled out a packet of battered cigarettes from the pocket of his sweatpants, lit one and inhaled deeply. It was a habit he couldn't quite break, especially in times of stress. And it had been stressful recently. He'd worked hard to change his school from a place where the local police were on speed dial to a place of academic achievement. He'd just got his first two pupils into Oxbridge, so he'd been shocked when seven of his teachers had resigned to follow different careers. Hot on the heels of this challenge had come the news that his budget was being cut by twenty per cent as he wasn't taking in enough 'statemented' children, children with special needs. And of course there was also the other problem to face. He kept putting it to the back of his mind, but soon he had to deal with it.

Far below him, a trail of smoke drifted upwards from the houses in the valley and, in the distance, a hawk swirled around looking for prey. As Dan gazed at the bird, the sun started its journey from its sleeping place in the east, a journey that was even more impressive when viewed from the top of a hill in the Scottish Highlands.

Calling Mr Big, he turned and ran across the golf course back to the hotel.

Hidden behind the tall pine trees that lined the golf course a woman observed him as he cantered off. Slight in build, dressed casually in a black jogging suit, and with her mane of chestnut hair tucked under a baseball cap, her stance suggested a benign female presence but her eyes spoke of her malicious intent. She had no intention of losing her quarry, hence the sophisticated tracking device she had put in place to follow his every move, which had alerted her to his presence on the golf course. In spite of her high professional standing and power, she had decided to involve herself personally in the finer details. At this stage nothing must be left to chance.

There had been a time when she'd thought they could be friends. But that was now out of the question. She was in control of the game, for now, and she intended to take full advantage of it.

Dan crossed back over the lawns which were covered in a light dew, reached the door to the hotel and then stopped. A shiver suddenly ran down his spine, intuition alerting him once more to danger. By his side, Mr Big growled quietly. Turning, he stared out towards the car park. It was silent, then he saw a tall, very thin figure, dressed unseasonably in a long, grey coat, slip between the trees. A few seconds later he heard a car door shut quietly and an engine start up. Straining his eyes, he saw a low, silver sports car edge its way through a narrow gap and head up the drive towards the hotel building. Overhead the hawk continued circling in the blue sky, its cry piercing the air.

He hesitated, took a deep breath and shook his head. Enough of this nonsense, he told himself sternly. Once inside, he walked briskly along the corridor to his room. After a quick shower, he hurriedly tidied up, flinging clothes back into the wardrobe and bath towels into the bath. Then he collected his wallet, tipped the contents of the ashtray into the waste bin and headed towards the Strathearn restaurant for an early breakfast, and some peace in which to read the morning papers, leaving Mr Big in the room.

As soon as he disappeared into the lift, a woman dressed in the uniform of a chambermaid, let herself into his room. Her long chestnut hair was now neatly tied back, her beautiful face devoid of any make-up.

Throwing a piece of meat to Mr Big, whose greed easily overcame his guard dog duties, she silently went over to the waste bin, put on a pair of disposable gloves, picked up three cigarette butts and carefully put them in a paper bag, which she then placed inside a plastic bag and sealed it.

A couple of minutes later she was outside, standing by the low silver sports car, which had drawn up by the rear entrance of the hotel.

'You know what to do.' She handed the sealed plastic bag to a thin, pale-faced man and then walked back to the hotel.

After quickly changing into jeans, she made her way to the restaurant. She was taking a risk but she had to see him again. The man who stood between her and her ambitious plans. She had to study him, his every move, and habit, however seemingly irrelevant. Surreptitiously, she glanced at the corner table where he was sitting reading the *The Independent*. Then she turned, dismissed the hovering waiter and walked quickly out of the restaurant.

CHAPTER THREE

Central London

4th July 2010

Independence Day. Dan strode along the street, smartly dressed and with a spring in his step. He was on his way to meet his best friend, Harry Bakhoum. Tonight was their annual dinner at Harry's London club. Dan had put the nightmare he'd had at Gleneagles behind him, although the problem of replacing seven good teachers was still very much ongoing, as was solving his other pressing, more personal, problem.

Glancing at his watch as he walked up the steps, Dan noted he was right on time – seven o'clock. He pushed open the door to the In and Out Club in St James's Square. Harry was waiting for him.

'Harry, great to see you and looking so well.' Dan grinned as they shook hands warmly. Egyptian by birth, but now living in Damascus, Harry was short and stocky, olive skinned and lively of mind. He had become more international as the years rolled by, and lost a lot of his Englishness, which he had clung on to so proudly when he and Dan had both formed a strong bond over their mutual unhappiness at boarding school. Harry's mother, Shakira Bakhoum, was the daughter of a wealthy and influential family who had been close confidants of President Sadat, and had needed protection after the Egyptian leader's assassination in 1981.

Dan had always thought, as a child, that it was far better to live under the cloud of an assassination attempt rather than with the shame of knowing your father had died an alcoholic.

'Come, we have much to catch up on.' Harry led the way to the bar. 'I see your friend Douglas is celebrating twenty years of marriage.' Harry waved a copy of *The Times* in front of Dan and smiled. On the front there was a picture of the British Prime Minister, Douglas Hamilton, with his ambitious, beautiful wife Fiona beaming at his side. Dan smiled. He had become friends with Douglas at university. Douglas had been a couple of years ahead of him doing an MA, but they'd shared a research tutor, and Dan had been very keen on Douglas's friend Anna Rossini, who had been doing a postgraduate course in pathology. It had been an odd friendship, the wealthy and urbane Hamilton and the down-to-earth, low-key Adams. Douglas always said that Dan was his conscience.

'Well, I guess we should toast a long and happy marriage.' Dan raised his glass. 'I haven't seen much of Douglas over the last few years since he became leader of the Conservative Party and then our PM. But good for him. A long marriage is more than we've managed, although hardly your fault that your wife became an enlightened lesbian and ran off with her female dentist.' Dan leaned forward and punched Harry lightly on the arm with a chuckle. Enough time had passed for Harry to be able to see the amusing side to it. 'As for me, well...' he trailed off. So far there had been no other love for him after Anna. Five happy years, at least for him, and then she'd just taken off and disappeared to follow her career. He'd dated a lot of women over the years but he had not, as yet, been tempted into marriage. Jenny, his current girlfriend was calm and easy to be with and he was at last enjoying passion without drama. He hadn't felt that for a long time. Early days, and for once he wasn't going to talk about her to anyone – not even Harry.

Harry studied Dan and wondered if he'd ever get over Anna. The problem with Dan was his intensity. Once his heart was captured it was captured forever and in Harry's experience this was not necessarily a recipe for happiness.

'I have news.' Harry leaned forward.

'You've met someone?' Dan enquired while he perused the menu.

'Good God, no, not that. I'm still enjoying the delights of batchelorhood in the sexual hothouse of the Damascene expat community. No, this is much more interesting, and of course highly confidential.' Harry's voice dropped to a whisper.

'The dig?' Dan stopped reading the menu and looked intently at Harry.

'Yes. We've found an ancient village, over four thousand years old, and we've discovered some documents there which are made of a kind of papyrus popular with the ancient scribes who worked in the scriptoria, the writing rooms, of the second century BC. We think the content of these documents was brought into Northern Syria by word of mouth, via a hierarchy of high priests, thousands of years before that.' Harry smiled.

'And what do they reveal?' Dan asked, registering the excitement in Harry's voice.

'It appears the people were much more sophisticated than previously thought. They weren't quite the robes and sandal-wearing tribal wanderers we thought they were. Society was very organized, very democratic and very advanced. Genetic research is finding that the tribes were interwoven with Europeans and Asians. People travelled and information spread. There are also,' he hesitated and lowered his voice, 'what would seem to be other documents that are linked to some of the most important discoveries over the last century, such as the Dead Sea scrolls. You'll remember from your theology degree that these were the documents that were discovered in 1947 in the caves around the Dead Sea in the Judaean desert. This was the place of the Qumran community where the Essenes, the sect of Christ, lived.' Harry paused and sipped his drink.

'Are you saying you've found documents as important as the Dead Sea scrolls? What's in them?' Dan demanded, his eyes widening in surprise.

'Well, it will take years to do a full translation, but from our preliminary analysis it would appear that the inner circle of this sect didn't disappear into thin air as previously thought but headed to Damascus. "I will exile the tabernacle of your king and the bases of your statues from my tent to Damascus,"' Harry quoted from the Dead Sea scrolls grinning from ear to ear.

Outside in the square the squeal of a London taxi braking hard could be heard, followed by shouting and then drunken laughter, but Dan and Harry were oblivious, immersed in their world of ancient discoveries. Finally, Dan found his voice.

'The ancient mysteries coming to life. I always wondered if there were more documents buried around the same time as the Dead Sea scrolls and the Gnostic Gospels. It seemed as if they were part of some vast ancient library not limited to what we have found so far. Tell me more.' He smiled, his unusual green eyes crinkling at the corners.

'The Dead Sea scrolls talk of a Teacher of Righteousness who led the Essenes from their supposed formation in the second century BC, although we believe a mystical sect had existed for many thousands of years before that. Anyway, we think this position was held by a series of men who knew the secrets of an ancient and mystical wisdom which, if understood correctly, would enable mankind to reach its true destiny. This ancient wisdom seems to form the core of the meaning of our lives, and in turn unlock how our lives resonate with the rest of the universe. I can't say more than that; we are only at the beginning of this enormous discovery, but I wanted to share it with you as I'd like you to come to the dig and help once the August heat is over and we resume our work. We need capable people we can trust,' Harry said, leaning back and grinning at his friend, 'and, although it's been a while since your degree, your language skills and theological knowledge, make you the perfect candidate.'

'Yeah, I know it's been a while since I did my degree, but the old brain is still in good working order as far as I can tell. How about I come out during half-term week in October? And what are your plans for releasing the documents to the external world? I remember the battles with the authorities to release the information contained within the Dead Sea scrolls and the Gnostic Gospels. It was years before they could even agree on the right form of translation and fifty years between discovery and publication. If this is the real deal we have to get the information out into the world,' Dan exclaimed excitedly.

'Quite, but my focus at present is on extracting the documents with minimal damage and storing them well to maintain their condition. We're a long way off full translation, and as you say, that will be a minefield. I'm sure it will be another battle to get agreement on the correct translation. Half-term would be a perfect time for you to come out.' Harry's expression grew sombre and he gently drummed his fingers against his glass.

'What are you concerned about?' Dan asked.

'There are undoubtedly people working against us,' Harry said so quietly that Dan had to bend his head towards him to catch his words. 'There is a clear warning in one of the documents relating to a wicked priest, a scoffer, a spouter of lies, who always works against the good of the wise masters. Rather colourful language, and could be a load of old tosh, as we have no absolute proof that this isn't just a bit of ancient spin, but we have experienced quite serious security problems.' Harry hesitated. 'We have discovered great hordes of beautiful artefacts, gold, jewels and much riches, a priceless patrimony. Well, a couple of weeks ago we had a major break-in – one of the guards was murdered – but they didn't take the gold or the jewels, they went for the documents. Fortunately, we had secured the most important ones in a special safe accessible by only two of us via visual and numerical identity, and they didn't gain entry, but they did take some general documents so it is a warning. We must all be careful. We don't have the luxury of free speech, careless words can be very dangerous.'

Dan frowned as he recalled the recent warning he'd been given about free speech. He told Harry about his meeting with the strange Mr Perkins in the Scottish hills.

'You'll be seeing pixies next! I doubt whether Mr Perkins had anything to do with our break-in, but thanks for the heads up.' Harry laughed breaking their serious mood. 'Now, let's go into dinner and have a good bottle of wine.'

The two friends went into the restaurant, sitting at one of the tables by the windows overlooking St James's Square gardens. Dan glanced at the vast paintings depicting various violent battle scenes and took a deep breath. He had to discuss his own personal dilemma with Harry. It had to be resolved once and for all.

'It's not pixies I'm having problems with but nightmares,' Dan paused.

Harry steepled his fingers and gazed at his friend. 'I sense your youthful indiscretions are coming back to haunt you,' he said. Dan's inner turmoil and self-doubt always heralded the same topic.

Dan nodded. He'd got into bad company when he was fifteen, joined a local gang that had robbed shops and stolen from local businesses. He'd been the lookout. They'd met up once a week, smoked cannabis and then gone on the rampage. It had all seemed so exciting at the time, then one of the shopkeepers had caught them during a robbery and been fatally injured and they'd all been arrested. He'd only avoided prison because his future stepfather was the local magistrate at the time, and he had pulled a few strings, citing the fact that Dan's father had just died and the boy was obviously suffering from grief, which of course he was. He'd been packed off to boarding school where he'd met Harry.

'You and Anna are the only ones who know, well, until now it seems. Some local hack came to interview me about the school's exam results, most improved problem children, etc. but right at the end of the interview she suddenly asked me if I thought honesty the best policy in all circumstances. I said yes, of course, but she kept pressing and referring to events that happened in nineteen eighty-six. I held firm and she didn't seem to have all the facts, but she is obviously on to something. I think I should come clean with the board of governors, and the local authority, it's time I faced this head on and cleared it once and for all,' Dan said firmly.

Harry nodded. 'It was a youthful folly, you weren't actually responsible for the poor man's death, you were very upset, not only on hearing of your father's death, but also your mother's impending marriage. Bloody woman was so ambitious she allowed your interests to take a back seat when she should have comforted you and stayed close, not dispatched you to boarding school like an unwanted parcel. I'm sure the board of governors will understand.'

'Going to boarding school turned out to be one of the best things that ever happened to me – I met you. However, back to the problem. I should have revealed it a long time ago. I went through checks when I became a teacher but my good old stepfather had carefully ensured all reference to my involvement with the gang had been erased. I work with children, it's very sensitive. You know how it's always hung over me like the sword of Damocles. It's time I stopped running away and faced up to whatever the consequences are. Time I took responsibility for my past. We can't always hide behind the curtain of psychological damage. No, I will call the chairman, or rather woman, of the board of governors and arrange a meeting,' Dan said with determination.

'Good decision. She seems to be ferocious but also very fair from what you've told me about her,' Harry said.

'Yes, I'll talk to her and maybe we can avoid involving the local authority although technically they should be involved,' Dan looked thoughtful. 'Right, that's settled then, I'll talk to the chairwoman first.' He relaxed and smiled again. He looked at Harry and felt the usual surge of contentment at having someone he could share his innermost thoughts and problems with. Their friendship was sacred.

Harry grinned. 'Enough of this solemn talk. Tonight we must drink a toast to America and her independence.' Harry raised his glass and they drank in companionable silence.

As soon as they finished their dinner, Harry headed off to Heathrow Airport to meet some colleagues at the Sofitel hotel where they were gathering before flying to the USA the next day for an international conference. When Harry had left, Dan decided to go for a walk before retrieving his car and heading home. He was just about to cross over Piccadilly when his thoughts were interrupted. A hundred yards in front of him he saw Anna, her long blonde hair swinging from side to side across her back as she walked quickly down Regent Street. He'd recognize that straight-backed, hurried walk anywhere.

'Hey, Anna,' he called out, but she didn't turn. Instead she just marched on. He followed her, quickening his pace, his eyes locked on her body. Just as he got within striking distance she turned abruptly and walked into a hotel entrance.

A few seconds later he pushed his way through the same revolving doors, but there was no sign of her. He made his way over to the reception desk.

'Can I help you, sir?' The receptionist stopped tapping at her computer and looked up.

'The woman with the long blonde hair... did you see where she went?' he blurted out before realizing how ridiculous it must sound. 'I mean... is a Miss Anna Rossini staying with you?'

The girl checked her computer, 'sorry, sir, there's no one of that name staying here.' She stepped back slightly from the desk. Was this some crazed stalker? Should she alert the night manager?

'Oh right, thank you.' Dan smiled. How stupid of him. She'd probably married by now and was using a different surname. It had been thirteen years since he'd last seen her. He was walking towards the exit past the business centre when he spotted a woman with long blonde hair standing up and talking animatedly into a mobile phone. She had her back to him. Grinning, he walked quietly up to her and put his hand lightly on her shoulder. The woman jumped in shock, turned around and shouted at Dan, 'What the hell are you doing? You nearly scared me to death!'

'Oh, I'm so sorry, I mistook you for someone else.' He backed hastily out of the room. It wasn't Anna. He made a quick exit before he made more of a fool of himself.

He walked back to the car deep in thought. He was thirty-nine years old, on the brink of hitting his forties. He'd been twenty-one years old when the sexy, sassy twenty-three year old Anna Rossini had blown into his life at Cambridge. He'd been bowled over. They'd shared the same zest for life, the same interests and the same sense of adventure. He grinned as he remembered the mad trip to the Middle East when they'd decided to cross over to the Golan Heights and nearly got arrested. But that was then and now it was time to grow up. He was indeed making a fool of himself.

Feeling the need for some familiar contact, he called his godson, Thomas, the son of his close female friend, Matilda, whom he'd also met at Cambridge and who had been a stalwart when Anna had disappeared from his life. Sadly, she had married a complete waste of space, who complained about everything and participated in nothing, which was why Dan didn't see much of them, but he loved Thomas.

Sixteen-year-old Thomas was camping in Wales.

'How's the school army training going?' Dan asked.

'Wet, tiring and tedious,' Thomas replied.

'So, on occasions, is life, and even my beloved Scotland is not without its potential for tedium,' Dan said, laughing.

'Scotland is not full of the Welsh, thank goodness,' Thomas snapped.

'Now, now, they aren't that bad,' Dan said soothingly.

'Rudest people I've ever met. You walk into a shop and they immediately start talking in a strange language, deliberately ignoring you and then they rip you off.'

'Oh, right, like being on Kensington High Street then.' Dan laughed again.

'No, Dan, it's like being in France without the great food and wine.' Thomas sighed.

'How's your mate Jack?' Dan changed the subject. He'd met Jack a few times and liked him, thought he was a good influence on Thomas.

'Off on a forty-mile night hike. I can't wait to get back at the end of the week. It's a bit weird here. Some odd people have set up camp along the road. They hang around trying to give out leaflets telling us to embrace God and await the dawn of the age of redemption, or something like that. Call themselves the Holy Trinity of Science, Religion and Philosophy,' Thomas said.

'Ignore them, probably the usual American wackos. Look forward to seeing you, and remember this is good for the soul,' Dan commented.

'Yeah, yeah, at least we go to the pub and watch the football,' Thomas said, sounding more cheerful suddenly.

'You're not drinking, I hope?' Dan said alarmed.

'Only to forget. Got to go, Jack has just turned up with a couple of cans of lager. Bye, Dan.' Thomas giggled and the phone line went dead.

Dan drove home and slumped in front of the telly watching reruns of *Have I Got News For You* with Mr Big curled up beside him.

Finally, at one o'clock, he went upstairs to bed. He undressed, and slid between the sheets, but sleep evaded him. Images of himself and Anna kept floating into his consciousness. Her brilliant blue eyes studying him intently, the way her body moved when she danced, undulating in perfect harmony to the music, and the way her tongue flicked slowly across her lips indicating pleasure. He could feel her long blonde hair brushing against his cheek, her distinctive perfume floating through the air. Where the hell was she now? Married? Children? He wished he knew.

CHAPTER FOUR

South Bank, London

August 2010

The slim, dark-haired man in his late thirties slipped quietly into the room and took his seat. He was late but with good reason. The others had arrived and were seated around the modern, oval, glass-topped table in a room with a magnificent view of the River Thames. As he opened his slim attaché case and pulled out a small, titanium-encased laptop computer, a heavyset grey-haired man in his late fifties stood up.

The Queen of England had apparently once said to her ex-butler, 'Be careful, there are forces out there beyond our control,' and she hadn't been wrong, the dark-haired man thought, as the older man made his way to the lectern.

'Welcome and thank you for coming today at such short notice. I know you are all busy people, which is why our usual chairperson is missing due to vital business overseas, but no matter, we are making great progress.' He cleared his throat, paused and then continued to speak in a clear, firm voice, the strong inflections of an East Coast American accent filling the air. 'Today is a great day, we have finally had confirmation that the key to unlocking our power is within our grasp. Let me recap and explain the new plan,' he said.

The Scientist, the Monsignor, the Judge, the Banker, the Linguist, who was absent today, the Philosopher and the Politician made up the inner chamber of the Holy Trinity of

Science, Religion and Philosophy, the world organization for a new era, superseding religion as the purveyor of truth and redemption. They had been biding their time, ever since they had discovered the presence of ancient wisdom and mystical knowledge in the lost texts of the old world.

It had long been decreed that the initial decades of the 21st century would see the new world plan unveiled and a new group provide the leadership and guidance that people sought in these troubled times. No one trusted the banks or the financial institutions any more, where often personal greed presided over common sense. The so-called establishment was becoming defunct, the people were rising against dictatorships, and government was weak, slain by the liberal left, who had wreaked more havoc on society than any conventional war. Theirs was a dangerous, insidious war where the self-righteous, who'd lost their moral compass in the haste to avoid retribution for any crime under any circumstance, imposed their views on society, often with disastrous consequences. In addition, conventional religion was not offering the people what they sought. Everyone felt at sea, unsure of their future; fear had replaced optimism, causing economic and personal inertia. Now the Holy Trinity planned to influence and control, manipulate and coerce, become a global power.

'Our spies tell us that work on the Syrian dig is progressing fast. Professor Harry Bakhoum is uncovering the ancient secrets. He thinks he outwitted us when he foiled our attempt to snatch the documents from the inner sanctum, but he is wrong. That was just a foil. We have infiltrated his organization at the highest level. As you know, thanks to Ms de Souza's painstaking work, we've known for some time of the existence of these documents and coins, which impart the secrets of mankind. We also, unlike Bakhoum and his team, at least to date, know of the existence of a mystical book, the Book of Eternal Wisdom, which imbues the leader with immense power.' The grey-haired man, known as the Scientist, nodded at a small, insignificant-looking woman with pale blue eyes and fine, wispy blonde hair. She was The Banker, Argentinian by birth, and the person in charge of the world's largest private equity group. Her decisions made or broke global companies and in some cases dictated a country's fortunes. Her plain looks belied her power and intelligence; her brilliant mind was unlocking the ancient codes which in time would reveal long-hidden secrets.

The Scientist's voice dropped to a whisper. 'This is the last chance for man to get his act together and fulfil his rightful destiny. The unrest and instability in the world is not happening by chance. If we don't snatch power, the human race will face annihilation again, and if that happens the power will slip past us, never to be recaptured. Earth will become just another planet, and lose its position at the centre of the universe. As you know, we are the planet designated to lead the fulfilment of the destiny of all life forces.'

'How do we proceed?' the Monsignor demanded. Known for his powers of persuasion and his superior academic intellect, the Italian was a man of huge influence within the Vatican. He had worked very hard to inveigle his way into the inner circle. After 9/11 he had been one of the main liaisons between the Americans and the rest of the world. His people were in place, all it needed was his word and the revolution to replace the existing structure of the Catholic Church would begin. They had pressed the start button once before, when John Paul I, Pope for only thirty-three days, had been sacrificed. But before the new Pope could be elected, they had abandoned their mission as someone within the highly influential American media had started to get on their trail, so they'd hastily disappeared underground. Now they had to plan their coup again and it wouldn't be so easy.

'We know there are seven mystical coins which resonate with the inner sanctum of secret documents, and that their powers are beginning to awaken, and as they come to life the mystical book also begins its journey back to earth. The question is not where is the book, but with whom is it aligned?' The man paused and five pairs of eyes looked at him. 'The answer is with the new Master of Destiny of the Order of Melchizedek. You will remember that the prophets have all been born of the Order of Melchizedek. However, fortunately for us, this new leader is unaware of his position so we can influence the process in our favour.'

'How do we know he is unaware of his position?' the Monsignor asked.

'I'll allow our colleague the Philosopher to explain.' The Scientist turned to the Philosopher, who slowly replaced the top on his Mont Blanc pen and looked at his colleagues.

'When the old leader dies, the new leader should be with him physically so the old one can transfer his power through a series of mystical rituals, which protect and empower the new one. We know the identity of the old leader and when he died this didn't happen, thanks to the intervention of our absent colleague. However, even though the new leader is unaware of his position, the Universal Power will still subject him to a series of tests to prove his worthiness. During the period of the tests his position will be made known to him,' the Philosopher explained.

'So it's easy. We just find this new leader, get rid of him and take over,' the Monsignor stated glibly.

The Philosopher closed his eyes and a pained expression came over his face. 'Not so easy, my friend. While the worth of the new leader is being tested, the Universal Power wants good to be done, it wants the human race to have a chance to choose the right person and redeem itself so it protects the new leader. The coins only dispense their power and divulge their secrets while the leader, whether he is aware of his situation or not, is alive, which means we have the tricky task of weakening him so he cannot harm us, while at the same time keeping him alive,' he said.

'Sounds like the perfect job for me.' The Judge smiled happily. He was especially gifted at destroying people without leaving any evidence. He hadn't been born to the privileges of a top public school education, instead he had used his cool, ruthless brilliance to fight his way to the top, leaving no trace of the mayhem he had often created to ensure he achieved his ambitions.

'"And so it shall be, from the father will come the son, and the son will carry the sword and take on the mantle, and his power will be all-encompassing,"' the Scientist quoted softly.

'I don't want to rain on anyone's parade but why are we expending our energy on weakening the new leader if the Universal Power is going to test him and he's going to lead us to this mystical book anyway?' the Judge asked impatiently. 'Why don't we just sit back and wait for him to lead us to it and then snatch power? Especially as we know...'

'Silence!' shouted the Scientist.

There was a buzz of discordant muttering around the room. 'We have agreed never to speak of our collective secret until we are sure we can win this battle. Words are powerful. We must be careful never to speak openly of this. Do not forget this essential truth of our existence. The golden coins and the documents will align themselves to the new leader in some way. We just have to keep one step ahead and snatch the power back at the time the mystical book is activated. We must stay in the game. We know the process of handing the power from the old Master to the new Master was corrupted nearly two thousand years ago when the mystical knowledge was being transported from Judaea to Damascus, and has been open to corruption at sensitive moments. We also know that many thousands of years before that, mankind fell from grace, causing us to lose some of our collective mystical gifts,' the Scientist finished quietly.

'I do hope you're not going to tell us that Eve gave Adam an apple and the snake took over the world, which is why thousands of years later the banking system went belly up and the world economy went into a nosedive. I haven't been hanging around for years to hear the same ridiculous fairy story.' The Judge raised his eyes to heaven.

'Let him speak,' said a quiet, commanding voice and everyone turned to the speaker, a small, slim man with a receding hairline and olive skin. The Politician, Abdullah Mustafa, was Iranian by birth but international by education and experience. At just thirty years old he was the youngest in the group, but his presence and demeanour spoke of an authority rarely earned in a lifetime.

'Thank you, Abdullah,' the Scientist said. 'If we are to embrace power and wealth, we must accept certain truths. The first is that many, many years ago there was a kind of Garden of Eden, a heaven on earth. The biblical explanation is very much simplified for the masses, but the Universal Power has without doubt made mankind the keeper of the Universal Secrets. We were to be the race that would, through evolution and wisdom, bring great fortune and gifts to the rest of the universe, but the Universal Power gave mankind a gift that was a double-edged sword.' The Scientist paused and looked at Abdullah.

'Free will,' the Politician said softly.

'Exactly, Abdullah. Mankind was given free will and he

repaid his masters by adopting a somewhat cavalier attitude to this precious gift, hence the mess we find ourselves in. You can imbue wisdom in mankind but you can't make him act on it.' The Scientist rubbed his tie pin absent-mindedly. It had a ceramic figure of a white stag on it. 'The Banker is working on breaking the code that will allow us to know the time of activation,' he added.

'You said this was the last time to get it right or the Universal Power would withdraw. If we interfere with the process won't the Universal Power make sure we are all destroyed?' the Philosopher enquired.

'The Universal Power is complex. It isn't just concerned about us on earth. The Universal Power wants what's good for the entire universe, which of course resonates to other multiverses that exist as well, so if we've understood the signs, and I very much hope we have, then if we snatch power in this final game, the Universal Power will recognize our organization as the leader of the earthly planet. This will give us access to the inner secrets of the Universal Council. We will lead the people to redemption and glory. And of course create great wealth and unimaginable power for ourselves.' The Scientist paused and smiled. 'However, if no one snatches power then, yes, we will all be destroyed. Great power is never left unclaimed in the universe.'

'And how do we know exactly what this power is apart from possible great wealth through the control of the people? It's all a bit nebulous. There's nothing wrong with feathering our own nests and taking advantage of the system, huge wealth and power can't be given to the ignorant masses, much better in the hands of the elite,' the Judge said tetchily. 'I don't want to focus my energy and talent on all of this only to find we've won peace, love and the art of giving, or whatever bollocks the so-called religious books teach us. I do not want to replace religious bullshit with more bullshit,' he added angrily.

'During his recent travels in Syria, Abdullah managed to obtain a gold coin,' the Scientist said. 'It is part of the set of mystical coins, which are linked to the Book of Eternal Wisdom. The coins contain secret messages. Abdullah and the Banker have managed to decode one of the most superficial. We cannot go any further as we cannot, at present, gain further access, but it will give you a glimpse of our new world. The prediction is on this memory stick. Read it. It will be destroyed after five minutes. Each of you has a role. Follow it. We will meet only when required. Remember, my friends, this is our time, our moment, we must be focused on our future. Now let me complete this briefing by showing you the human target.'

The Scientist clicked on one of his computer files and the screen was suddenly filled with a picture of Dan Adams, smiling, relaxed and walking into Braid House at the Gleneagles Hotel.

'May God's speed be with you all.' The Scientist handed each one of them a memory stick, shut his computer, put it in a slim, black leather case and, without saying another word, walked out of the room leaving the other five to read the message. The unholy crusade had begun.

CHAPTER FIVE

South London

September 2010

It was only seven a.m. but adrenalin was already pumping hard through his body as Dan fought to rescue his professional life. A cool breeze through the open window heralded the first hint of autumn after a welcome Indian summer, but there was an Arctic blast of disapproval to accompany it in the form of Mrs Dowling, the chair of the school governors.

'Well, I must say I am very shocked. You've always behaved with such restraint and decency. Not one bad word about you in seventeen years and now it would seem there was much that should have been discussed.' She pursed her lips and tapped her pen on the table. In the background an antique clock chimed the hour with laborious precision.

Surreptitiously, Dan wiped the palms of his hands on the sides of the chair. He had to maintain a cool front. His future was in the hands of this forbidding woman, known for her no-nonsense but fair attitude. She was studying a piece of paper, his interviewers' assessment at his original job interview.

Finally, she looked up and held his gaze. Neither of them blinked.

'I can only presume your grief at losing your father must have unbalanced you. Your actions were so out of character. A man died and that is a terrible thing to happen even if you weren't directly involved in his demise.' She bit her lip, wrestling with the dilemma, her moral compass swaying between accepting his regret and punishing him.

'Not a day has gone by when I haven't thought of that man and regretted our actions. I might not have killed him, in fact none of us actually killed him, he caught the gang members robbing his shop and went for them, tripping over and hitting his head on the corner of the counter, but we all felt responsible. I was sent to a tough boarding school to atone for my sins,' Dan said quietly.

'And how long after that did your mother remarry?' Mrs Dowling enquired.

'A month later.'

'Hmm.' Her pale blue eyes narrowed and she frowned. 'And of course it was your future stepfather who pulled the strings necessary to get you off the hook. Then you were dispatched to deal with your demons on your own...' She paused briefly. 'If I may be forthright, I would say your mother didn't appear to act in your best interests. It must have been hard for you being apart from your father only to find he'd died before you could really get to know him as an adult. That doesn't excuse you, of course, but it does explain some of the reasons. My worst sin was cheating at my English exam in the fourth-year exams, which of course I was punished for,' Mrs Dowling said in an uncharacteristic moment of self-revelation.

'I was lucky in that I met my best friend, Harry Bakhoum at boarding school, and his friendship pulled me through, made me decide to do something good with my life rather than descend into the bad ways of some of my peer group,' Dan explained.

'I'd be very upset to lose such a gifted head teacher as yourself, Dan. You've dedicated seventeen years, your entire professional life, to us. Your instinct for dealing with problem children and turning them into good students is unequalled, in my experience in education. I will talk to the other governors, including the local authority representative. We cannot lose you. We will deal with any media fallout from it, maybe turn this into a positive experience, a "look how you can turn your life around" example to the pupils. Yes, that's what we'll do,' she said half to herself, waving her right hand in the air, indicating that the meeting was over.

'Thank you. You won't regret giving me a second chance. I'll do whatever I need to prove my loyalty and my dedication.' Dan stood up and smiled, relief coursing through him. The school was his life. He'd been given a stay of execution.

'Don't celebrate too prematurely, I still have to speak to the other governors, although I expect they'll agree with me.' Mrs Dowling allowed herself a wry smile.

'Yes, yes of course.' Dan grinned. He wasn't going to screw up again. That was for sure, he thought as he headed back to his office.

CHAPTER SIX

Wimbledon, London SW19

September 2010

At six thirty that evening Dan was in his local pub in Wimbledon with Mr Big. Mrs Dowling had called him an hour ago to say the board of governors had all backed her proposal to give him another chance. Having enjoyed a much-needed cigarette, he was now looking forward to a pint and a pie. The only down side was that, to head off the journo who was trying to dig out the story, they wanted to organize an interview with one of the national papers to do a 'repent and survive' kind of story. He wasn't sure if he was ready to join the Jeremy Kyle generation but it looked as if he didn't have much choice.

Putting the *Evening Standard* to one side, he picked up his phone to call Jenny. They were still seeing each other in a low-key way, which was different from his usual burn and rush but felt a lot better. Mutual dog-walking had brought them together but it was her easygoing sunny nature which was strengthening the bonds between them. He was scrolling through his contacts list when he felt the intensity of someone staring at him.

'Hello, Dan, it's been a long time.' The familiar accent hit his senses like a firebomb. He dropped his phone and looked up sharply, shock coursing through his body. By his side, Mr Big shifted position and sat bolt upright.

'Anna! Bloody hell,' he gasped, 'So it was *you* I saw in Piccadilly in July.' He was aware that people were staring at him.

'No,' she looked confused. 'I only arrived back in London two days ago.' Then she grinned in that seductive, knowing way that always turned him on and slid into the seat opposite him.

Shit! He had to pinch himself. 'It's been thirteen years,' he managed to stutter. 'You just disappeared after you got that new job in Rome. What the hell happened?'

'Yes, yes, I'm sorry, I'm so very sorry.' She paused. 'It was a terrible, truly awful way to treat you and I don't expect understanding or forgiveness, but I just want to explain. Please give me a chance to do that, just a few minutes and then I'll disappear again if that's what you want. Certain things...' She hesitated, suddenly looking vulnerable, and he felt the old stirrings. He looked at her carefully. She was still as beautiful at forty-one as she had been at twenty-eight. Anna was a heady mix of Italian and Swedish, with the Swedish genes dominating her pale colouring and blue eyes, although her quixotic nature spoke of a strong Latin influence. Her skin was fresh and unlined and her eyes clear and bright, sparkling with an evocative combination of pure sex and keen intelligence. It was as though he'd seen her yesterday, except... there was a hardness round her mouth which hadn't been there before, a set look that spoke of unresolved conflict, along with a slightly unreadable quality in her eyes which he didn't recognize. His gaze automatically drifted to the third finger of her left hand – no ring.

'How did you find me?' Dan asked.

'Douglas said this was your favourite haunt, and although he hadn't seen you for ages, he'd been told you still hung out here, so I hung out here too as soon as I arrived back in

London,' she said, her Scandinavian accent becoming stronger, betraying her anxiety.

Douglas had never mentioned Anna after she'd exited Dan's life. Upset by her sudden departure and silence over the following months, Dan had been firm that he wanted to move on with his life. Douglas had kept his side of the bargain – until now.

'Well?' Dan said as Anna hesitated. 'Christ, it's been thirteen years. Why now?'

'It's the first time in thirteen years that I'm back working in the UK. I start work for the government soon. I'm still a pathologist, now professor of forensic pathology. As I'm back on your territory I wanted to see you, balance the books, so to speak, do what I should have done years ago. I didn't exactly go to Rome unencumbered.' She paused and bit her lip.

'Don't tell me, it was Mick wasn't it? Your very married Australian boss,' Dan said as it all suddenly fell into place. How could he have been so naive? The sudden business trips, the giggly phone calls, the new diet and fitness plan. A lovely thick gold necklace that had been '*a gift from my mother.*'

'Yes, it was Mick. It was such a cliché. Older married man lavishing gifts and attention on younger woman. I was swept away with the excitement. All so silly and reckless,' she said with tears in her eyes.

'For heaven's sake, I didn't realize we were the lead characters in a Mills and Boon reality show,' Dan said angrily before continuing, 'Cutting to the chase, what you're saying is you just got bored with me and Mr Money Bags came along and seduced you with exciting overseas trips and jewels.'

'I wasn't bored with you, just, well, we were in a bit of a rut, you content being a teacher and going off on those boys-only golf holidays, and me...'

'Developing your career, I thought, and anyway, you seemed to like the glamour of the occasional ProAm Celebrity Golf Tournaments I competed in, rubbing shoulders with the good and the great. I was a scratch player at the time! One of the best amateurs ever. You seemed so proud of me,' he almost shouted.

'I was, I... I was stupid, stupid, and when Mick dumped me a year into my Rome contract I didn't contact you as I was ashamed of myself, dumping a good man for such a shallow shit. Still, I'm not the first woman to fall into that trap! I had to find you when I came back to the UK just to say I've regretted what I did and not a day goes by when I don't wish I could turn back time,' she finished and stared at him.

'Well, one thing you can't do is turn back time. People move on. What did Douglas tell you?' Dan asked.

'Douglas wasn't very helpful at first, didn't say much, said he hadn't seen you for years and that he'd promised not to interfere as you wanted to move on. Then he suddenly changed. In fact, he'll be calling you soon, something about wanting you on an education advisory board.' She smiled again, noticing the inner confusion reflected in his eyes.

'I don't have time for his advisory board, although if he wants a realistic view of what is actually going on in education, I'll be happy to tell him. Seems like he's having some problems with it all. Anyway, do you want a drink?' he asked, changing the subject and trying to be civil.

'No, no thanks, I won't stay.' Anna got up and looked down at Mr Big. 'Nice dog, is he yours?'

'Yes, that's Mr Big, my faithful companion,' Dan said without a trace of irony.

'Goodbye, Dan.' And she was gone again, striding straight-backed through the crowded early-evening bar.

Before Anna reached the door, a woman with long chestnut hair got up from her seat in an alcove, strode out of the pub and walked quickly towards the car park, where a dark blue S-class Mercedes was waiting for her. The chauffeur held the door open for her and she got in, sat back and switched on her iPhone.

It was all going to plan.

CHAPTER SEVEN

Heathrow Airport

October 2010

Dan stood on the long, steep escalators as they glided up to the departures area. As the sun bounced off the steel sides, he felt as though he was being transported skywards towards some heavenly plane ride. 'This way for eternity,' the sign might have said. He smiled. He was finally on his way to Syria – Damascus – rather than the dig in the north of the country. Harry wanted him to see some of the documents that had been brought down from the site to the capital.

He felt a strong sense of relief to be getting away. His mind had been disturbed by the meeting with Anna last month. It had made him question his judgement. The issue of trust which was so important to him after the emotional turmoil of his childhood seemed to have got lost somewhere along the line and it bothered him. The meeting had also made him realize he still wanted her, could still be drawn back into her seductive web. She'd built up a brilliant career first in Rome and then in the USA, and now she was back in London. She'd phoned him once at school, asked if they could just be friends with no sex, but he'd sidestepped it, unwilling to be her stooge while she found her feet again. Maybe one day they could be friends, but not yet.

A couple of days after his meeting with Anna, Douglas had called him and asked him to go and see him when he got back from Syria. Needed his advice on education. Dan had explained he had his hands full with school, but Douglas had insisted, and when he'd explained about the opportunity to head up a new advisory board, Dan had to admit it sounded very interesting, the kind of new stimulation he relished. Douglas had also made it clear he didn't want to be piggy in the middle between him and Anna. Confusion and unpredictability had started to reign, and the tentacles of doubt which sometimes made their way into Dan's soul were never welcome guests. Thank God for Jenny. The more he saw her, the more he liked her. No dramas with her.

He made his way along the wide walkway by the shops, trying to avoid the bustle of people. Business people were striding about, clutching expensive briefcases and talking in clipped tones into their mobile phones: 'At airport, on time, about five, land eight, dinner nine, call you from car, yes, no, contract signed, Brussels tomorrow at seven,' and so on, a kind of international verbal shorthand. Couples were wandering around holding hands, sliding quietly into the new Victoria's Secrets airport shop, the promise of the weekend ahead written on their smiling faces.

Then came the families, mum, dad and two or three out-of-control kids, the fractious nuclear family on the move. Dan's friend from BA special services, Matt Underwood, materialized as previously arranged, and whisked him away into the tranquil atmosphere of the first class lounge.

As he sipped his second glass of very good Sauvignon Blanc sitting on the stool by the bar, a woman reached over to get a dish of nuts that were on the far side of the bar. She nearly knocked his drink over.

'Oh, so sorry,' she said, quickly stepping back.

'It's OK, no harm done.' He smiled and met her gaze briefly. As she moved away, the sunlight caught her short, fine blonde hair, creating a halo effect round her head. He shook his head and smiled. He wondered if he was now seeing angels.

Back at her seat the woman caught the eye of the man sitting opposite her. He gave an almost imperceptible nod. She'd just revealed the identity of the target. While in Syria he would find the right moment to perform his deed. He sat back, glad that the waiting was finally over.

CHAPTER EIGHT

Damascus

October 2010

As Dan walked off the plane in Damascus, a short stout man walked towards him smiling. He was dressed in a long white cotton *thobe*, the Arab male dress, and a red and white checkered *gutha* headdress, which was held in place with a black *agal*. Dan glanced at him, looked away and then looked again. It was Harry.

'*Salam Alaykum*. Peace be with you,' Harry said, smiling and holding out his arms in welcome.

'I didn't realize it was fancy dress,' Dan said, embracing his friend and laughing.

'This, my friend, is who I am.' Harry swept his hand over his outfit.

'Hmm, yes, well, peace be with you too.'

They made their way out of the airport and into Harry's air-conditioned jeep.

'I know it's strange to see me in traditional dress, but, believe me, it is better to blend in. We live in dangerous times,' Harry stated simply.

'Rubbish, it represents your ever-expanding girth and the fact that a long dress hides it better. Anyway, your father was British and a respected diplomat, so only half of you is of Middle Eastern descent.' Dan tapped Harry's protruding belly.

'That might be true, but it seems my mother's genetic

configuration is now becoming dominant. Anyway, I'll have you know that having given up alcohol I have lost almost five kilos in the last few weeks, and I intend to continue until I have lost at least another ten,' Harry said righteously.

'Well, good for you, a healthy body breeds a healthy mind, but could you just suspend all this do-gooder stuff for the week I'm here?' Dan said laughing again.

They arrived at Harry's house, which was deep in the old part of Damascus. It was a traditional house built around a central courtyard and a perfect example of the happy marriage between traditional craftsmanship and the comforts of the twenty-first century. There were old icons hanging on the walls of Dan's guest room, but all mod cons in the bathroom.

'Pomegranate juice?' Harry enquired as a girl appeared from the kitchen with a large jug and two glasses.

'Hmm, can't wait.' Dan grinned as he accepted the glass of juice as a sign of welcome.

'Don't worry, my friend, you're clearly going to be a pain if I refuse you good wine, so there is some vintage Bordeaux in my cabinet. For now let's go and enjoy the last of the sun.' They climbed the spiral staircase and walked on to the large roof terrace, on which was placed a low table, two sofas and two large chairs.

Dan sat in one of the chairs and raised his face to catch the last rays of sun. He breathed in the exotic scents of the ancient, mysterious city, thinking how good it felt to be here. The recent emotional turbulence linked to Anna was already slipping away.

'Things have changed here,' Harry remarked.

'In what way?' Dan asked.

'Attitudes are hardening. After many years of being blamed for facilitating the perceived evils in this part of the world, Syrians are sick of being regarded as Satan's children when all they want are the same things we all want: a safe home and a thriving economy. And they will fight for that whatever it takes,' Harry commented.

'Don't tell me I'm going to have to dress up myself?' Dan raised one eyebrow quizzically.

'Not this time,' Harry said. 'But the traditionalists are gaining power. One needs to be very careful when leaving Damascus, but as we're remaining here in the city, it will be fine.'

'OK, understood.'

'Now tell me what has been happening in your life. I can tell by your face that something is going on,' Harry stated.

Dan told Harry about his meeting with Mrs Dowling and also Anna's strange reappearance and request for friendship.

'Well, not something I could have predicted, but whoever understands a woman's mind has unlocked the secrets of life! My work had taken prime position in my heart by the time I got divorced so it was easy. But tell me, how do you feel?' Harry looked steadily at Dan. Anna had always had an unsettling effect on Harry. Nothing he could pinpoint, just a feeling that all was not as it seemed.

'To be honest, she's still sexy and gorgeous, but it's not the same. I don't want to rekindle a full-on relationship. I'm not the same man I was thirteen years ago. Anyway...' Dan blushed and decided to tell Harry about his prospective new love. 'I've met someone really nice. Nothing serious yet, but it could develop that way. I'll let you know if it does. Good God, I sound like some hormonal teenager!' he said laughing. 'I'm at a different point in my life, happy and secure in my job and settled where I live. It's time to put the ghost of Anna to rest.'

Harry shivered as he felt a chill run through his body. He quickly changed the subject.

'We are making excellent progress on the dig. Tomorrow

you'll meet Professor Zinohed here in Damascus, an extraordinary man. He's an expert on ancient religious cultures, a true religious historian – the best in the world. This is going to sound a bit weird but we think we've found the burial site of documents that contain ancient knowledge literally carried to us from the gods, from the eternal beings who guide and help us understand our destiny. They are known as the Masters of Destiny.'

'Whoa, slow down. Eternal beings? Masters of Destiny? What do you mean?' Dan wondered vaguely if Harry was working too hard and losing his marbles.

Harry smiled. 'You remember I mentioned the Teacher of Righteousness, as described in the Dead Sea scrolls, the man leading the Qumran community from about the second century BC? Well, it would seem that the Teacher of Righteousness was known by other more ancient cultures as the Master of Destiny. A man incarnated many times who was the holder of mystical knowledge – magic, alchemy, astronomy and astrology – it's all in our documents. It will take a lifetime to understand it all but tomorrow you will see some of the documents for the first time.' Harry beamed with delight.

'The Masters of Destiny?' Dan racked his brain, he'd heard that expression before. He closed his eyes. Memories of his childhood came flooding back.

He was running along the beach, trying to beat the waves as they crept up unexpectedly across the causeway. Later, when the rest of the family were in bed, he and his father had quietly left the hotel in Bamburgh, where they were staying on their way to Scotland, and gone to the beach where they lay on their backs on the sand and studied the heavens. His father had told him glorious stories of ancient civilizations who lived amongst the stars and who, long ago, visited earth to be among the human race, encouraging mankind to achieve great things and giving counsel to avoid destructive behaviour. Apparently, earth had once been the centre of the universe, a forum for the exchange of information and ideas, a powerful force in the magical well of Universal Power.

'Of course,' Dan said softly as he opened his eyes. 'Beings who could enter the human psyche and understand the way we think, and use this to advise and impart their wisdom, but the other side of this was their frustration that the human race had free will and just when they thought we were on the straight and narrow we went and screwed things up!'

Harry nodded remembering days spent on Wimbledon Common where Dan's mother lived, and where Harry had visited them in the school holidays. They'd ridden their bikes to the old oak tree, smoked cigarettes and Dan had talked about his holidays in Scotland, and related his father's potent and mystical stories.

'Dad spoke about how these so-called Masters of Destiny found it very hard to stand back and watch us make a mess of things, knowing that the consequences of our actions would leave our destiny unfulfilled for many generations. They couldn't interfere directly with mankind's choices; if they did, they would be destroyed themselves. I wonder when they decided to leave us be and return to wherever they came from,' Dan mused, remembering his father's presence and his distinctive aroma – a mixture of Imperial Leather soap and pipe tobacco.

'Who says they've disappeared?' Harry met Dan's gaze.

'Oh, come on, they're only fairy stories of an ancient age. I'm sure you'll unearth some interesting information, but don't expect me to believe the Masters of Destiny are walking amongst us today. And anyway, if they are here, how will it actually affect us? I'm fed up with reading books, however compulsive and thrilling they may be, that tell us Jesus was married, had a family and a bloodline and the Church has undertaken a massive cover-up to hide it all. So what? How does any of that actually affect my life or your life or any of us on a daily basis?' Dan snorted and turned his head. Suddenly he sensed his father's gentle presence, and felt himself slipping out of the present and into the past. He glanced at Harry but he was looking at the sunset and sipping his juice, unaware of what was happening. Dan closed his eyes as he drifted into another dimension.

'I'm so glad you remember the Masters of Destiny, but don't be so quick to write them off as fairy tales, my son. Many thousands of years ago, an advanced civilization inhabited this planet, ancient mystics such as Lord Melchizedek and Enoch came to us. They used the complex tool of reincarnation to illuminate successive generations until the human race was finally ready to fulfil its destiny. Then, just as nirvana was in sight, the human race went into self-destruct mode by enthusiastically embracing the seven deadly sins, and the opportunity was gone. The Great Flood wiped out most of them, but not all. There were a few survivors and they became the new Masters of Destiny, men like John the Baptist, and Jesus Christ, who was born into the Order of Melchizedek, and for over two thousand years they helped man develop from ignorant half-beast to...' Edward Adams paused. 'Well, I suppose man is still an ignorant half-beast!' He chuckled and his son Dan grinned to himself. He tried to focus his gaze on his father's face but he couldn't.

'What does this mean?' Dan asked, as images of his younger self being carried on his father's shoulders as they walked for miles in the Scottish hillsides swept through his mind.

Edward Adams didn't reply for, as quickly as he'd materialised, he faded silently from the scene and Dan's feeling of peace slipped away to be replaced by a strong sense of sadness.

'Right, let's go and explore the delights of Damascus.' Harry's voice brought Dan back to reality and he looked round. He shook himself, feeling shocked, but decided to keep silent. He had to keep a hold on his sanity. It had been a stressful few weeks, he told himself, visions and nightmares were just the brain trying to resolve problems. He'd always had strange dreams, even as a child.

Harry stood up, then paused and looked out over the rooftops. 'You know, this is still the same place it was thousands of years ago – a hot bed of intrigue and political power, and a centre of cultural exchange. I wish East and West could find a way to work in harmony. We could learn a lot from each other.'

Dan raised his eyebrows. 'What if Syria either refuses to let you bring the results of your dig into the open or uses the information to divide rather than unite?'

'I will die before that happens,' Harry said quietly as a light breeze arrived on the night air.

CHAPTER NINE

Damascus

October 2010

Professor Zinohed was exactly as Dan had imagined him to be. A man of medium height and medium build, with a full head of dark brown hair greying at the edges, a moustache and a neatly trimmed beard. He had very dark brown eyes, and a slightly unnerving stare, which gazed out at the world from behind thick black-framed glasses. He was older than Dan and Harry – probably in his late forties.

'Welcome to my overcrowded office. It's not really adequate but it's the best that the Museum of Antiquities can do. Come, do sit down.' Mumtaz Zinohed moved a couple of chairs to make room for Dan. Papers and strange-looking artefacts covered every surface.

'The government is keeping a close watch on us, but at the moment we're all getting on fine.' Harry said. 'They are giving us a lot of support because they are impressed with the huge hoard of priceless items we've found so far.'

'So you are giving the government the jewels and keeping the real patrimony of documents hidden, is that right?' Dan looked at them both.

'Exactly. Although we suffered that major break-in and attempt to take the most important documents, it would appear the government is not taking much notice of the old dusty ceramic jars and storage vessels. We still don't know who the perpetuators were. However, once the government people get bored with being knee deep in gold, they'll turn their attention to the other items, so by that time we need to have got them out and into the safe hands of our trusted coterie of international experts. We can't risk such an important discovery being locked up for years, or even centuries, because of arguments amongst government ministers.' Harry looked at Dan.

'Oh, I see. You want me to be the courier. I'm about to add international thief to my CV, am I?'

'Not really,' Harry said. 'We have a couple of government officials who are very helpful, so all the documents you carry will have the official seal indicating they can be transported out of the country, but we have to work quickly. As I've said before, you're the only person we can trust.'

'I'm intrigued. Can you show me the documents in question?' Dan could never deny Harry the help he needed. This discovery was his life, his entire raison d'etre.

'Of course. Put these on.' Harry handed Dan some white gloves and Professor Zinohed pulled down the blinds to eradicate the sunlight, turned off the fluorescent overhead lights and turned on several uplighters, which emitted a soft but penetrating glow. Then he walked towards the bookshelves, which were lined up along one wall, and gently pulled out a book, pushed a button and the wall opened to reveal a very large safe. The professor and Harry placed the palms of their hands on each of the pads on either side of the safe and then tapped in a series of numbers simultaneously into the two wall panels positioned on either side of the safe. The safe door slowly opened.

Dan watched in awe as the safe revealed a well-organized storage system housing what looked like thousands of documents. He gazed at it in wonder and felt a surge of excitement. It was truly impressive.

'We've worked day and night during the last couple of months to register and list all of these documents,' Harry explained.

'Good grief, how many of you did all this?' Dan asked.

'Just the two of us,' answered the professor. 'We gently removed each piece of paper and examined it, then dated and indexed it. There are nine hundred documents here, some in fragments and some whole. We managed to store about fifty a night, although some documents, like the Chief Priest's Holy Almanac, took us a week just to decipher the subject matter.'

'Which ones have you translated?'

'Just a few that we found irresistible. For the majority, we've only ascertained the subject matter and then placed it in the index. As you know, full translations will take many years. We'll need a group of the best international brains to undertake that demanding role. Our more urgent task is to take the documents from the dig and make them safe,' Professor Zinohed explained.

'My God, it must have been like this when the books of the Bible were discovered.' Dan let out a low whistle.

'Your instincts were right when we spoke in London,' Harry said. 'We believe that the Bible along with the Dead Sea scrolls and the Gnostic Gospels are in fact part of a vast universal library of world knowledge and wisdom. And not only Christian texts but also the great books of Judaism, Islam, Buddhism and Hinduism and other as yet unknown religions and sects which are all keepers of the ancient wisdom. However, from what we've seen to date, there appear to be seven precious documents which hold the key to unlocking information that will quite literally change the way we live, think and act.'

'Thousands of years ago the central documents were brought here to Syria for safekeeping,' the professor added, 'although we believe that the ancient scribes made copies that might be hidden in other places in the world. Apart from these seven key documents, there are thousands that deal with everyday life, along with stories handed down first verbally and then in the written word from generation to generation. They were probably sung by tribal elders who wished to impart wisdom to the youth of the day. We've found the gospel according to Mary, part of the Gnostic Gospels, which seems to give a fascinating insight into Jesus's early life, the lost years which we have until now no record of. But come, let me show you one of the most important documents. This is the Melchizedek Sacred Mysteries, the oldest document we've found.' Professor Zinohed gently picked up a very old, fragmented document with a pair of tweezers and placed it on a silk-lined book support. 'We've translated some of this document, it is the central part of the Trilogy of Inner Secrets which is the essence of the Book of Eternal Wisdom.' He turned to Dan.

'The Book of Eternal Wisdom?' Dan gazed at the old document, trying to make out words. He didn't recognize the language, although it could be a derivative of Sumerian, the language of ancient Sumer spoken in Southern Mesopotamia from about the fourth millennium BC.

'The Book of Eternal Wisdom is as old as time itself. It comes from the Universal Power, whom usually we call God, who at the beginning of all creation formed a blueprint for mankind. Through its predictive powers and its rich content of secrets and mystical knowledge, the Book of Eternal Wisdom has guided the human race through its layers of evolution and enabled us to take on the mantle of civilization.' Professor Zinohed paused then continued in a more urgent tone, 'From what we've read here, it is or was like the mystical Star of Bethlehem, in that its power was only active at predestined times, such as during a global crisis, under certain astronomical configurations, and when the leader, the Master of Destiny, was living amongst the human race. The Book would shut down if the various aspects were ignored and then the power would just slip away. We have no idea when it was last active or indeed if it will ever activate again, but we do know that the original Master of Destiny as stated in this document was Lord Melchizedek.'

Dan frowned. 'Why does that name keep ringing a bell?'

'Well, as a theology graduate it should do. Abraham paid homage to him in the Bible,' Harry said.

'I know, but apart from that...' Dan paused and bit his bottom lip as he frowned in concentration. 'Of course, he was the man in my nightmare when I was at Gleneagles. I dreamt of an ancient place in the desert, men running to hide documents, a man freeing his daughter before he was murdered... and Lord Melchizedek appearing with an old book which sang its messages.'

Professor Zinohed and Harry looked at Dan in stunned silence. 'How can you know already what we ourselves are only just discovering?' Harry asked.

'I have no idea. Maybe it really is just a coincidence. Don't forget my university thesis was on ancient religions and languages, and Lord Melchizedek is a very mystical figure in the Bible. He captures the imagination and exudes great power and mystery. Maybe under stress I was just conjuring up a strong paternal figure,' Dan said. 'I just don't know,' he added quietly, almost to himself.

'Maybe. It's possible,' said Professor Zinohed. 'We have to try and keep a grip on reality and not think everything has a special meaning. However, I've been looking at this document since yesterday and I have some more information about Lord Melchizedek. It would appear that he was our first great guide. The King of Spiritual Kings, who came to earth to save us from an eternity of misery. As you say, he was a man of immense wisdom and power, a man who came directly from the Universal Power. All of the great philosophies seem to emulate his sacred words. He lived for hundreds of years and reincarnated many times, until his body and his blood were transferred to man himself. The Book of Eternal Wisdom was gifted directly to man by Lord Melchizedek.

'We believe that the Book of Eternal Wisdom was the real gift that the Magi brought on their long journey to the Christ child. The documents appertaining to the journey of the Magi are part of the Inner Trilogy. We have yet to find the relevant passages but we believe there were other rituals they carried out on their journey. The Archangels protect and comfort mankind but the Magi are God's everlasting messengers and they anoint the Master of Destiny and his Council of Elders, which according to the Melchizedek Sacred Mysteries consists of six people. The Book of Eternal Wisdom is always protected by the Magi.'

'This is the central teaching of another document called the Chief Priest's Apothecary,' Harry interjected. 'We believe it explains how we can use the ninety per cent of the brain we don't understand to not only perform wondrous acts but also heal ourselves.' Harry carefully unfolded an old piece of papyrus.

Dan looked at it his head spinning. He recognized it as Avestan, the language of the Zoroastrian scriptures. He gazed at Harry and the professor in shock.

'Yes, Dan, we humans have the gift of healing ourselves from physical and mental illness, all we have to do is unlock the key and repeat the ancient rites,' Harry said, smiling. 'Once we understand these, each person, through his own power, can undergo a deep and personal transformation to complete well-being. It might take days, months, or years. A mild form of depression could be gone in a month or it might not shift for two years, while a person on the brink of suicide could feel the shift from despair in hours. That is the essential mystery. The process of transformation from sick body to whole body is personal to each individual. It's part of the individual's life journey,' Harry swept his hand across the documents. 'It's all here. Now enough, let us stop before your poor brain blows a fuse!'

Harry and Professor Zinohed started to put the documents back into their storage boxes.

'How old are these?' Dan asked.

'We think at least seven thousand years, but maybe much, much older than that,' Harry replied.

Dan looked startled.

'Indeed,' said Harry. 'The people who inhabited this planet thousands of years ago, or rather, the leaders who came to show us the way, owned knowledge that we haven't even begun to discover in the 21st century.'

Dan placed his hand on Harry's arm and grinned. 'What a wonderful discovery, the pinnacle of your life's work. It's like a scientist discovering the cure for a life-threatening disease. You must be so enthralled by it, sorting the difference between fact and fiction, reality and fantasy,' he said excitedly.

'I know, I know. I can't believe it myself, it's something one could only dream about and it's happening to me. Every day I wake up filled with a strong sense of purpose, which is wonderful. Look, before you go, I want to dazzle you with gold and silver.' Harry pulled open a deep, wide drawer and gently lifted a large, long object out of the depths. He carefully unwrapped it and placed it on the long table. Dan whistled with delight. It was a golden sword embedded with diamonds and precious stones.

'Go on, pick it up.' Harry laughed on seeing the wonder in his friend's eyes.

Dan gingerly picked up the sword. It was very heavy and he needed both hands to hold it. For one childish moment he felt like King Arthur with Excalibur; the power and beauty of the object was breathtaking.

Dan closed his eyes and felt the noise and heat of battle, the chaos of war. He could sense the danger, experience the threat of death and loss, and also feel the courage required in being prepared to lay down your life for a greater cause. 'How old is the sword?' he asked.

'We believe about four thousand years,' Harry replied.

'And we are also trying to understand the meaning of these.' The professor opened his hand and showed Dan a small coin with a circle and a complex set of squares on one side and a series of markings on the other.

Dan smiled. 'You're not going to believe this, but golden coins were part of my dream as well.'

'We do believe you. From what you've said today, the brain appears to act like a transmitter of information, so I now believe it's perfectly possible that in your dream you transposed the past into the future,' Harry said.

Professor Zinohed nodded. 'We don't know if the coins are a currency for goods, or whether they are a currency for secrets. If the latter, we have yet to unlock the mechanism for them to impart their knowledge.'

'Incredible,' Dan said softly, replacing the sword, which Harry then carefully wrapped up and replaced in the drawer.

A short while later, as Dan and Harry left the building, a tall, slim man with a balding head, dressed in traditional clothes and carrying a briefcase, walked out of the shadows and started following them. He was on strict orders to act with discretion and not draw attention to himself. He just had to make sure everything went to plan. Keeping to the shadows he remained hidden amongst the crowds.

CHAPTER TEN

Damascus

October 2010

'Have you ever seen one of these before?' Harry opened the palm of his hand and Dan picked up the small ceramic pin that Harry was holding. He studied it.

'It's an image of a white stag. Early Christians thought it symbolized Christ and his presence on earth, and that it held the key to mankind's redemption and glory. But it was around in pagan cultures long before that as a symbol of hope,' Dan said, looking at Harry.

'Quite. But what was it doing in my private room at the dig? It clearly isn't an ancient artefact. Made about fifty years ago, I would say.' Harry looked pensive. He and Dan were taking their usual walk around old Damascus to the Omayyad Mosque. As they stepped into the street, the sun was just appearing over the buildings, its bright rays lighting up the stone facades.

'Do you think it's linked to the intruders?' Dan asked.

'Undoubtedly, which makes me think they are some kind of religious or Christian scholars who somehow know what we have found. How could that be? We haven't told anyone about the secrets. Only three of us have security clearance at the highest level, me, Mumtaz and one other person who has worked with us on other sensitive projects for over ten years,' Harry said.

'Seems like someone has infiltrated your organization,' Dan stated.

'But how? It's not possible.' Harry frowned. 'Anyway, next time you must come with me to the dig. It's a day's travel to the site in northern Syria and I've got some places I want you to see along the way. Please plan a longer visit,' Harry added smiling, at Dan.

'That would be really good,' Dan said as they passed by an ancient building. He touched the stone, feeling reassured by its solidity.

'How about coming out for Christmas? It will be very cold but it would be good to spend more time with you. We've never spent the winter holidays together. Bring your new lady friend. I'll see if she's the one for you!' Harry laughed as they walked towards the magnificent mosque, where the head of John the Baptist was said to be buried.

'I don't want the poor girl frightened! But yes, let's plan on Christmas together. Give me more time to learn about the treasures from your dig, it makes my daily routine seem very boring.' Dan glanced at Harry. There was a zeal about Harry that was intoxicating.

They arrived at the mosque and walked inside. Dan had never been particularly religious but he always felt the presence of something greater than him inside these sacred buildings of prayer. He didn't understand it but it felt comforting. He looked around and noticed Harry praying silently and wondered when he'd made the conversion from agnostic to believer.

Afterwards they walked towards the souk.

'What if the Masters of Destiny really do continue to be among us today as our teachers and guides, trying to help us reach our destiny?' Harry mused as Dan paused outside the jewellery shop of Elias Karwashan.

'But *who* are they?' Dan asked. They walked into the Wedding Souk, and then past the stalls of abundant, multicoloured spices with their intoxicating aromas where Dan paused to buy some cinnamon, which he liked to sprinkle on his coffee.

'That, my friend, is a question I can't answer – yet. But I do feel that somehow they are accelerating their work on earth, in the vain hope they can save us from self-destruction yet again,' Harry stated. 'Come on, let's stop for some coffee.' They paused briefly to enjoy a short, sharp intake of caffeine, before continuing their exploration of Damascus.

As they walked along, Dan suddenly felt an all-encompassing sense of anticipation course through his veins, which was accompanied by a lovely feeling of calm and comfort. He felt as though he'd taken a pre-med sedative, the type they give you to forget about the scary bits of your forthcoming operation. He looked around. The houses were fading into the background, and the modern-day bustle had been replaced with people dressed simply in the manner of the first century. Some were leading donkeys laden high with goods purchased in the local market.

He felt his heart beat faster, but with excitement rather than fear. It was the same feeling he'd got as a child when unwrapping presents, a sweet feeling of happiness as he imagined the joys that awaited him.

He saw a group of people gathered in a square, which he seemed to know was near to the Madhat Basha Souq, by Straight Street. He walked towards the crowd and hovered on the outskirts. He tried to edge his way further in. As he peered over the shoulders of the people standing in front of him, his body was engulfed in a bright, heavenly white light, which seemed to emit pure goodness. The light was emanating from a man who was standing in the middle of the crowd and talking in a quiet but commanding voice. Dan stood observing the scene, breathing in the sweet, pure scent of the Damascus Rose, the red flowers of which had been scattered around the speaker. The man exuded benevolent power in its purest form. As Dan looked around he felt the high, buzzing energy that swirled about those present, connecting their thoughts, and linking their actions. It was creating harmony and the bond of goodwill between them all.

After a while, the crowd moved to form a clear pathway and Dan found himself standing in front of the man, whose piercing green eyes were the colour of rich, dark, glistening emeralds. The man smiled and placed his arm on Dan's shoulder. Dan felt a bolt of electricity shoot right through him, stimulating all his senses. He felt it transferring an infinite, intangible wisdom right to the centre of his being. The man was wearing a long white robe and a deep dark rich green cloak with a thick gold braid border. The bright, heavenly white light continued to encircle them, and Dan saw that within the light were thousands of stars. He felt a deep feeling of peace and serenity.

'Who are you?' Dan asked, although he already knew the answer. He had seen this man before, if only in his dreams and nightmares.

'I am the first and the last of all of you. We are all part of the same body,' the melodious voice said reassuringly.

Dan remained silent, looking intently at the man's face. It had an air of timeless wisdom, unlined, ageless and deeply calming. The man seemed unmoved by the throng of people forming and re-forming and trying to attract his attention.

'You will understand if you stop analysing and just embrace your thoughts and feelings. It is your destiny. We are the Masters but before we can use our powers we must first believe in them,' the man stated simply. 'As you know, I am

Lord Melchizedek. The Masters of Destiny were all born into my order and continue to be incarnated right to your day. Now you must be ready to take on the mantle. I can tell you that it will soon be yours and your role will be as the Redeemer, one of the most difficult roles we can assign anyone. May you be imbued with courage and wisdom, my dear son.' Lord Melchizedek leaned forward, kissed Dan on both cheeks and then he turned and slowly walked away, his footprints leaving their mark in the dusty street. At the far corner of the square, he paused, turned and raised his hand in acknowledgement. Then he was gone, leaving Dan standing alone, thoughts and feelings tumbling about his brain.

'And so, as you will understand, Professor Zinohed is the real hero of our dig. He's extraordinary, don't you think?' Harry said.

Dan started in surprise. Harry was at his side again, looking at him expectantly.

'Lord Melchizedek was talking to a crowd of people... incredibly powerful... white light dispensing benevolence and goodwill... he talked to me... told me I am a Master of Destiny... my role is tough but I have to work it out...' Dan gabbled away, his words falling out uncontained.

'Steady on. You're telling me that not only is Lord Melchizedek active but you are a Master of Destiny?' Harry stood stock still, his face frozen in shock. 'It can't be... can it?' he stammered almost to himself.

The two men remained silent for a few minutes each trying to digest what had happened.

'Ridiculous of course.' Dan finally pulled himself out of his reverie and attempted to smile. 'I'm not sure what's going on. I think I'm finally grieving for my father. Never did when he died. Was never allowed to. All this talk of ancient mysteries and Masters of Destiny is so like the stories my father told me as a child that it's clearly had a deep effect on me.'

'Maybe, but just because it seems far-fetched and completely mad doesn't mean it's not true. The reason I wondered whether the Masters of Destiny were active today was because Professor Zinohed and I have found evidence of higher beings...' Harry's voice tailed away. 'It would seem that our dig has activated some deep, secret ritual of wisdom and the Masters of Destiny really are active once more. Your vision seems to corroborate that theory. It's not necessarily the actions that shock me but the speed with which this whole process seems to be unfolding,' Harry said quietly. He glanced at Dan. His best friend. Kind. Enthusiastic. Hard-working. Responsible. A visionary in his field. Was he a Master of Destiny? Was it really plausible?

'Higher beings? What have you found? What do you mean?' Dan demanded.

'At the dig we put a certain combination of data into the computer and it, well, it produced something quite incredible, something not at all human, an interaction between man and another power – can't really explain it. Right now, it is beyond our comprehension, which is why we need the help of other experts.'

'Why now?' Dan turned to Harry.

'Because I believe now is our final chance to get it right. We embrace our destiny or we reject it. There will be no more chances. The human race is facing its moment of truth.'

'And if we reject our destiny?'

'Then all will be lost.' Harry gave Dan a sideways glance and marched on.

CHAPTER ELEVEN

Wimbledon, London SW19

October 2010

Dan could feel his heart thumping hard against his chest as he struggled to maintain control. He clenched and unclenched his fist, sweat forming on his brow, and then he buried his head in his hands in desperation. His humiliation was complete. It was all over the newspapers. His life. Or rather lies about his life. It was the destruction of all he held dear.

Finally, Dan stood up, walked over to the sitting-room window of his fifth-floor flat and stared out. Down below the headlines on the news-stand said 'Cuts worse than expected – the middle classes pay the price.' People were walking around in the cold air, going about their daily business – work, friends, love, the gym, travel – making plans, the normal things in life which had, without warning, been removed from his life.

He'd arrived back at Heathrow yesterday and been arrested, pulled aside in the customs hall in front of everyone. His suitcase had been emptied and then he'd been taken into a side room and strip-searched. They'd found cocaine hidden inside his jacket pocket – cocaine, for God's sake. He hadn't taken any drugs since his days as a troubled 15 year old when he'd smoked cannabis. It was a small amount, but the police were investigating further. He'd been charged and bailed. This would ruin his life. He could go to jail. His name would be on a register of people to watch. The only good thing was they'd let him keep the documents he'd brought back with him, basically because he had an official Syrian government signed letter, and they weren't much interested in looking at a bunch of old papyrus and copper scrolls. He'd hidden them in his small loft – fortunately he lived on the top floor.

He'd spent the rest of the day going over and over it all. Who had planted it in his jacket? And how? He'd been with Harry all the time. Who'd set him up and why? He'd tried to call Harry but he was back at the dig – crap mobile phone connection. Then he had wondered how he was going to get out of this with Mrs Dowling.

Well, that problem had been removed. Here it was on page 15 of *The Daily Telegraph:* 'Troubled Life of Award-Winning Young Headmaster'. All the details, even a shot of him walking out of the airport and a quote from customs, 'We never comment on individual cases,' which told everyone there was a case to answer. Even a quote from Jenny, 'I'm so shocked. The Dan I know would never do something like this. It must be a mistake. We'll get through this together.' What the fuck? How did she get involved in it all?

Mrs Dowling had, of course, rung early this morning, after one of her minions had alerted her to the fact that her prodigy had fallen flat on his face once again. 'I wish you'd told me you still had a drug problem, Dan. We could have worked it out together, maybe sent you to rehab, tried to find a way, but of course now, well, I have to say you're on suspension until we make a further decision. The local authority and the General Teacher's Council are all involved. It's a mess.'

Rehab? 'I don't have a drug problem. I'm innocent,' he had shouted, but it had sounded hollow, especially given his previous history.

Was it that easy for your whole life to unravel?

The phone rang.

'Dan, I'm so sorry. I know you would never risk your career like this.' Those familiar seductive tones. Anna, the only other person apart from Harry who had known about his previous scrape with the law.

'Well, you're one of the few people on this planet who believes in my innocence. It's such a mess. I've lost everything.' Dan suddenly felt overwhelmed by the situation. He was a broken man.

'You *are* innocent. We just have to work out how to prove it. I'm a scientist, proving the truth is not that difficult,' she said soothingly.

Dan started to relax. She'd always had this magic way of calming him. 'Thanks for the "we" but I have to sort this out on my own. It's my problem, not yours.'

'Nonsense. I'm on my way over,' she said briskly.

Half an hour later he saw a black BMW sports car draw up and Anna jumped out, dressed in jeans, and with her blonde hair pulled back in a ponytail.

He pressed the buzzer to open the outer door and a couple of minutes later she came bounding up the stairs. Five floors and hardly out of breath.

As soon as she saw him, she put her arms round him and drew him close. He smelt her familiar perfume and buried his face in the softness of her cashmere jumper. She felt so comforting, so safe.

Then she pulled back and held him at arm's length.

'You might think this is the end of the world, but it isn't. I remember when you flunked your exams, you thought it was the end of your dreams but it wasn't. You reclimbed that mountain and achieved a first, one of the top three students of your year. You can do it again,' she said quietly.

He smiled at the memory. They'd just met, he'd been head over heels in love, and he'd let his studies slip, failed his second year exams. That had been the wake-up call he'd needed to focus on achieving his full potential.

'This is a bit more final,' he said simply. 'Things seem to be constantly happening to me, and I don't mean in a good way. I have to get myself out of this crap.'

'Don't be so melodramatic, nothing is final. We can all recover from disaster. As Winston Churchill said "If you're going through hell, keep going."' Anna grinned

'What happens if you trip and fall flat on your face while going through hell?' He laughed for the first time since he'd been in Syria. 'Hey, let me make you some coffee and dig out the chocolate biscuits, only food I've got at the moment,' he headed to the kitchen and she followed him. 'Look, Bahlsen Choco Leibniz dark chocolate biscuits, you got me hooked on them.' He opened the biscuit tin and put a handful on a plain white china plate.

'If you trip and fall then you just get up and carry on moving forwards, it just takes a bit more time. Come on, you're tough.' She nudged him in the ribs, took a biscuit and studied him carefully for a minute. He did look knackered, as if he hadn't slept all night, which he probably hadn't, but there was still a steely look in his eye which always appeared in times of trouble. She reached over and took another chocolate biscuit. 'Bugger the diet.' She giggled and looked around 'Where's the dear little dog?'

'With his dog sitter. I've just got back from Damascus, as you read in the paper,' Dan replied. Mr Big was with Jenny. He'd collect him later and then have to go through endless explanations with her. He sighed. Jenny meant well. She was lovely, but... Oh God, there was always a but. This woman in front of him had just hijacked his emotions again.

'Things that happen in our lives are often inexplicable. God usually has a plan,' she mused as they sat on his sofa drinking coffee and eating more biscuits.

'What happened to the "only science has answers, God is just an illusion" lapsed Catholic girl I knew?' Dan raised his eyebrows in surprise.

'Life is what happened. Science finds the truth but I discovered I needed to believe in the mysterious and to believe that good could come out of pain. After Mick and I split, it finally hit me that I wanted the same things women all over the world want – love, marriage and babies. Life ticked by and I didn't meet anyone else so I may never have children. I've had to accept that but it hasn't been easy.'

'And so you thought you'd revisit the mug you dumped thirteen years previously, did you?' Dan raised his eyes to heaven.

'I finally understood how you must have felt when I just disappeared without even an explanation. I was incredibly selfish. I'm so sorry, Dan, please forgive me.'

'What do you want?' he asked, meeting her gaze.

'Like I said before, I just wanted to apologize to you. I've thought of nothing else since I knew I'd be coming back to England,' she said simply.

'I'm not a great lover of the unexpected. It's happened too often in my life, and it's not usually good unexpected. My parents' divorce. Losing Dad. One minute life is all safe and sound, the next it's shifting around as though I'm having a personal Richter scale nine earthquake. We can't return to how we were. Sorry but that's final.' Dan stood up and started to pace around.

'Stop making decisions when they aren't required. You need to trust that things will somehow turn out for the best. You never were much good at that,' Anna said ruefully.

'I have found that trust is rather overrated,' he snapped.

'Sometimes you have to think outside the box. Trust in faith,' she said.

'What?' he said looking at her. The cool, controlled Anna really was embracing religion? Surely not.

'I'm sure you find my change of attitude very strange after all my protestations that religion was nothing but mumbo-jumbo. But since I joined the Holy Trinity of Science, Religion and Philosophy, I have managed to come to terms with Mick leaving me and even forgive him,' she said calmly.

'The Holy Trinity...?' Where had he heard that name before? Thomas, his godson, on his rain-soaked week in Wales. 'I thought they were just a group of American wackos,' Dan said bluntly.

'Well, they are different and that always scares people, but to me they resonate with the truth,' Anna said stubbornly.

'And who would these madmen be exactly?'

'The group was started in the nineteen fifties by Doctor Peter Samuels and Professor Sally Thompson, academics who spent their life studying ancient manuscripts from old cultures to see if there were common links. When they died they left a legacy which brought a new order into being, spreading its reach on a global scale and offering people a more joyful life. People are fed up with weak, indecisive leadership and scandals,' she said firmly.

Dan frowned. They definitely sounded like a wacko happy clappy brigade even if he had to admit that not all religions and leaderships were bad. 'Hmm, I suppose the Pope's visit last month had a lot more of a spiritual effect than predicted. Crowds turned out and people seemed to feel a benevolent spirit lifting their hearts, so I'm not sure I'd write off conventional religion just yet,' Dan said, mildly, trying to present a more rational view.

'Yes, but the Pope's visit was just a moment in time. People need ongoing, consistent guidance in these troubled times. They need to hope that life is more than a constant, dull treadmill interspersed with global and personal disaster. Anyway, the Holy Trinity wants to empower people through knowledge. That has to be a good thing.' Anna continued to beat the drum of the recently converted.

'And who is the present leader of this new order?' Dan said looking sceptical.

'There's a central council. I haven't met all of them. I became involved through a well-respected judge, whom I met fairly recently in Washington. He spoke so much sense. He also introduced me to Oliver McManus, one of the world's leading criminal pathologists, who happened to be setting up a new unit in London, and he recruited me to head up part of it, and here I am, so you see it works.' Anna smiled, breaking the intensity.

'Just don't go all New Age on me.' Dan leaned back on the sofa and grinned at her. 'I always loved the strong, no-nonsense Anna.'

'And do you still love that Anna?' She gazed at him, smiling softly.

He leaned forward and took her face in his hands. 'It's been a long time, but right now it does feel good,' Dan said, kissing her lightly on the lips. She responded, pulling him close to her.

'You always were the mistress of seduction,' he whispered as she started to undo the buttons on his shirt, and run her hands lightly over his chest. He groaned and buried his face in her neck, breathing in the scent of her skin, warm and fresh and inviting.

She pulled off her jumper and slipped out of her jeans sliding her body under him. He closed his eyes and ran his hands over her soft skin, feeling the familiar curves of her slim waist and then moving up to play with her perfectly formed breasts, still firm, and not at all affected by the relentless effects of time. For years he'd played this scene over in his mind, imagined her head arched back in ecstasy. Now it was happening for real. He lifted his head to stare into her eyes.

'Don't stop,' she whispered running her hands over his stomach before playfully bending down, unzipping his trousers and flicking her tongue over his thighs. Pushing her back down against the sofa, he licked and teased her nipples and kissed her lightly tanned flat stomach, following the line down to her white lace thong, which he removed. She was as intoxicating as ever. 'Darling Anna,' he whispered as she pulled him inside her moving her hips slowly. Then she wrapped her legs tightly round his waist and he felt himself begin to lose control. Nothing was as good as this. Feeling Anna's cool demeanour melt into a hot flood of desire was exquisite. He felt her passion heighten as she started to reach orgasm, then he lost all control and heard himself cry out as he climaxed.

Afterwards, they lay in each other's arms, neither of them moving. Drips of perspiration ran down his face as his breathing slowly returned to normal. He looked at Anna, reaching his hand to her face to gently wipe away the tears that ran down her cheeks.

The next thing he heard was his front door opening. Christ, Jenny. She was the only one with a key, apart from his cleaner who was on holiday. He'd given Jenny the key in case she needed more food for Mr Big.

'Hang on,' he shouted out but it was too late. The sitting-room door opened and Jenny stood looking aghast at the scene before her. On the end of his lead Mr Big shot Dan a look of disdain and turned his back. Bloody hell. Dan tried to hide their naked bodies with cushions. His day probably couldn't get any worse.

Things happened rather quickly after that. Jenny shouted, threw a plate at him and then stormed off. Anna jumped to her feet in embarrassment and hurriedly got dressed, demanding to know why he hadn't told her he had another woman in his life.

'I hardly had a chance,' he said lamely.

Then she disappeared too. Mr Big sulked most of the day and at about four p.m. disappeared to visit his friend, next door's poodle.

Later that day, on the other side of London, the Scientist sat sipping a fine malt whisky, a sixteen-year-old Lagavulin, in a crystal glass. Outside, darkness had fallen, it was raining and the street lights were reflected in the puddles by the side of the road. His hand clutched the glass tightly. It was such a fine balance. Weaken but don't destroy. If they went too far, they would lose as much as the man they were weakening, but if they didn't go far enough then he would gain control – and they could never allow that to happen.

But it was so difficult to control things when human emotions were involved. They had unleashed the woman and it had worked – sort of. They hadn't reckoned on his present girlfriend turning up. That was the kind of thing you couldn't predict. The problem was they'd had to give the woman a very edited version of her role. She didn't and mustn't know the truth.

Sighing, he lifted up the phone and dialled. Almost instantly, the Linguist answered.

'Well?' she snapped.

'All fine, one minor hiccup but nothing we can't deal with,' he replied.

'Make sure it all goes smoothly. We can't afford any mistakes. The discoveries at the dig are going at a faster rate than we thought. I am flying out there soon. We'll meet when I get back. We might have to bring our plans forward,' she said, and then she was gone.

The Scientist twisted the glass idly in his hand, watching the drops of rain dribble down the window pane. That woman thought she was invincible, but there was a difference between divine right and invincibility. So far he had allowed her to run the show, but now it called for real leadership, and he was about to step up to take on the honour of greatness. Great riches and power awaited them. Already they had each made a cool quarter of a million on the currency markets when the message from the first layer of the coin's secrets had been decoded, giving them prior knowledge of the currency market movements. It hadn't been easy to access but they had managed to achieve it due to their final secret, and in any case, the information revealed was very superficial, imparting wealth but not knowledge. The real treasure was to come and he was going to make sure that by then he would be calling the shots. She was too emotional, had too much at stake. It called for a cool head and a cold heart and he had both.

Standing up, he switched off the table lamp, walked across the room and opened the door to the hallway. Tomorrow he would be delivering the Dimbleby Lecture – a great honour. Soon the world would skip to his tune. He would save it from destruction. He would be immortal. He would be a god.

Smiling, he made his way up the stairs to bed.

CHAPTER TWELVE

London and Syria

2010 and 1179

Dan walked through his front door, hung his coat on a hook and headed to the kitchen. He grabbed his favourite mug, the one with 'Jesus loves you but everyone else thinks you're an arsehole' written on it, and flicked the switch on the kettle.

He looked pale, tired and thin – he'd lost six kilos in weight. His career was over, he'd been forced to resign with immediate effect after the governors, the local authority and Uncle Tom Cobley and all had deemed his situation terminal, which it was. Anna had disappeared, apparently to give him space to decide who he wanted in his life, her or Jenny. As for Jenny, she wasn't returning his calls. Of course he'd never heard any more from Douglas about being on an education advisory board.

He absent-mindedly relit an old fag end took one puff then quickly stubbed it out – he was really, truly trying to give up – and ate a couple of chocolate biscuits – dinner. His diet was terrible these days. One good thing was he'd pulled himself out of the aimless jobless routine and was working in the kitchen of the local hotel, washing up and preparing vegetables. It was menial and badly paid and he didn't know how much longer he could continue to pay the mortgage, but it was brilliant in that he could walk out at the end of his shift and just leave it all behind him. It was the first time in his life he'd had a job like that, and it felt quite good, gave him time and space to regroup, think and plan his resurgence.

Harry had told him to come out to Syria immediately but he couldn't. He had to stay and face the music. He was waiting for his trial date.

He settled down on the sofa with his cup of coffee, into which he had poured a very generous measure of brandy. Mixing coffee with alcohol helped him ignore his growing dependence on the latter. It was late but he knew he wouldn't sleep. Insomnia had become another fixture in his life. He switched on the television, surfing the channels until he found an old crusader film starring Charlton Heston.

As the first battle scene got underway Dan's eyelids started to droop. He found himself drifting into a half-sleep, visions of the past flowing through his mind. After a while, he found himself standing on a rampart on top of what appeared to be a large crusader castle. A chill wind blew across the early evening sky making Dan shiver. He looked around and discovered he was walking amongst people dressed for medieval battle, although he appeared to be invisible to them. In front of him was an old man whom he followed down into the depths of the castle.

Down they went through a myriad of tight, narrow stone corridors, the steps and pathways worn and uneven. Sometimes they would come across a soldier who would turn and press himself against the wall to allow the old man past. Suddenly, the old man stopped outside a door.

Quickly checking to see if anyone was around, he put his face close to the keyhole and spoke softly. From the other side came a young man's voice.

The old man entered the room and the two men embraced. Father and son. An eternal bond in the perpetual regeneration of human life. The son was academically gifted and studying in isolation to be a high priest of the old order, but they both knew he had a higher calling than even that honour.

'The time has come. Go, I will meet you at the end of the Prophet's Way,' the old man whispered and the young man nodded.

'I will not let you down,' he said to his father, smiling.

The father smiled in return. Prophet's Way was their special place, where he had taught him to ride and control the Arab stallions he had grown to love. He had also instructed him in the wisdom of his knowledge handed down over thousands of years. It had been their secret. Later tonight when they met he would hand him the final precious artefact that he had to take on his long journey.

The old man watched him go, his eyes dark and dangerous behind hooded lids. It was as it had been a little over a thousand years previously in Judaea. As then, the documents had been marked for another destination. In one fluid movement he had, like his predecessor, altered the course of history – imposed mankind's will on God's overarching plan.

With Dan still following, the old mystic made his way once again through the endless corridors, through the stables, with their pungent smell of horses, past the kitchens, up the steps that divided the quarters of the ordinary soldier from those of their military leaders and then up the narrow, winding stone steps back to the top of the Crusader castle.

Finally, the old man was out in the open air again, high up on the ramparts. He walked slowly to the round stone table, wrapping his cloak tightly round his aching body to protect it from the biting cold. He sat down and waited patiently for the men and women who would soon join him.

By his side, Dan observed the scene, feeling strangely energized by the anticipation of what was to come. He breathed deeply and the sweet smell of lilies filled his nostrils. A servant boy holding a lighted candle approached the old man and placed a gold cup in front of him.

The old man smiled, recognizing it as the Gold Cup of the Chosen, only offered to those who belonged to the select group who had earned the right to place their lips on its holy rim. The servant boy filled it with a potent sweet red drink and the old man raised the cup and drank.

'With this cup I drink your wisdom that I might be free,' he mouthed silently to himself.

Sighing, he made an arch with his fingers, pressed them against his lips and contemplated the future. He was an old man now, his face lined by the ravages of time and his body scarred by the physical demands of the battlefield and the age-old struggle between the truth and free will.

After this meeting he would meet his son and after that he would make his way back to his home town of Maaloula, a small town between the Castle and Damascus where he would join the rest of his family and reconcile himself to his God, and wait for death to release him from this long and arduous journey. But before that there was one last act he had to participate in.

A slight movement at the top of the stairs indicated the appearance of his fellow council members. First to appear was a man, small of stature, slim of build, exuding a commanding presence and wearing a brown turban embossed with his personal gold crest. It was Saladin, the Kurdish Muslim military general who had taken over from Nur ad-Din. His fame as a ruthless military genius was tempered by his reputation for fair treatment of prisoners.

He gathered the old man in a warm embrace, his amber brown eyes dancing with enthusiasm and joy. 'Greetings, dear brother, I am so glad we are together again.'

The old man smiled. He had not had a choice. Tonight's meeting was part of their collective destiny.

As the others gathered at the table, more servant boys appeared bearing dishes of spiced lamb, followed by platters of rice and savoury delicacies wrapped in vine leaves, and bowls piled high with rich, succulent dates. Carafes of water and steaming jugs of the potent red, curious and lively drink the old man had drank previously, which the Arabs make from the fruit of the Bunn tree, accompanied the food. Far down in the depths of the castle, musicians were preparing to entertain the guests. Tonight there would be a feast, but first there would be the final meeting of this Master of Destiny and the Council of Elders.

Saladin took his place at the round table. He had personally chosen this table for the council and had it transferred from his residence. It represented the circle of life, the manifestation of their spiritual beliefs that mankind lived in a cycle of ever-changing information, ideas and secrets. From humble beliefs and knowledge, the circle, powered by a mystical hand, spun higher, evolving the human race to a superior state. At times when the circle had been broken, such as during the Age of the Great Flood, mankind had simply withdrawn into a shell and allowed darkness to envelop the world, but the light had never gone out entirely. During periods of darkness it glowed quietly within the soul, like an ember waiting to burst into flame again.

Dan, his presence still invisible, watched as the Imam of Damascus, a wise and fair man, slipped into his seat. Stephanie of Milly, a tall, dark-haired, handsome woman who had won the respect of the ruling male empire, greeted Joshua with a small bow and Saladin with a kiss.

As Stephanie sat down, her great friend Eleanor of Aquitaine appeared, with her saviour knights who had released her from her English prison. Eleanor had been married to two kings, and was mother of two future kings, King John, who would achieve fame through the Magna Carta, and Richard, her favourite, who would become known as the Lionheart. She was another strong-willed, powerful and courageous woman, whose wisdom and insight had kept alive the secrets of the East. As the two women greeted each other noisily and exuberantly, a very old woman, slight of build but with a commanding air, appeared at the top of the stairs and paused.

'Hildegard, welcome, welcome.' Saladin guided the woman to her seat at his right. She was Hildegard von Bingen, the German mystic and healer, a powerful purveyor of natural cures for diseases of the body, so powerful that she had cheated her own death the previous month to be here tonight.

In a fanfare of trumpets, the Master of the Castle, Roger de Moulins, appeared with his flag bearers who stood to one side.

Finally the old man, Joshua, the Master of Destiny, smiled and stood to address the gathered Council of Elders. As his words resonated in the cool night air, there were still three empty chairs at the table.

'Tonight, we will celebrate as our destinies are fulfilled through the mysteries of the Universal Power. Through this ancient rite, mankind's fate will be secure. Good food and fine music await but first we must drink a toast to our absent friends, those men and women who have protected and guided the truth over the centuries, and who continue to be with us in spirit.' Joshua raised his cup. 'This is the blood of life. We drink to our adversaries that they should be enlightened, and to our supporters that they should be gifted with the courage to embrace the truth.'

Standing off to one side, Dan felt an even greater sense of anticipation and curiosity fill his soul. He looked at Joshua who was once again seated and appeared deep in thought.

Dan found himself entering the old man's thoughts. Joshua was thinking of the Melchizedek Sacred Mysteries document with its description of the seven ages of man. It would be many years before the seventh and final age came – the Vitae Era, the Age of Life. The age when the human race would face its biggest challenge, to either accept the code of life or face self-destruction, but here, tonight, the conditions should be perfect for the Universal Power to reveal the final mystery, the seventh mystical secret.

Joshua looked in Dan's direction and nodded in recognition. Dan met his steady gaze, but to everyone else Dan remained invisible.

Saladin glanced at the sky, and saw Venus shining above him. Tonight it was the evening star, sometimes it was the morning star, always moving in its elegant double-horned pattern around the sun, and casting its mysteries on to its earthly counterpart. He breathed in the cold, scented night air that was rich with the fragrance of roses.

The time was right to delve into the ancient mysteries. It was after the nineteenth hour on 5th October 1179. A few weeks earlier the event which was the precursor to this meeting had taken place when Saladin had taken Jacob's Ford, the major tactical crossing of the Jordan River. This was a victory which would eventually lead to Jerusalem being retaken by Islam in 1187. It was, as always regarding the meetings of the Master of Destiny and his council, a key moment in history.

Joshua glanced around and shivered. Dan sensed that Joshua was infused with a strong sense of foreboding. Tonight should be the revelation that would take them to their destiny but the old man knew in his heart that something indefinable was meddling with their affairs. 'Please, God, let the covenant with mankind stay in place,' he whispered. But there was only silence. Man's fate was about to be revealed.

CHAPTER THIRTEEN

Krak des Chevaliers, Syria

12th October 1179

'Bring me the Board.' Joshua clapped his hands and a small, slight boy of about ten appeared holding a round wooden ball about the size of a very large tennis ball, which had intricate carvings all over its surface.

Dan peered closer at the small, perfectly carved human figures – baby, child, adolescent, adulthood in its various stages – dancing around the surface, their hands just touching. They looked like the representation of the seven ages of man. He gazed at the other engravings. There were clusters of what appeared to be stars and swirling clouds against a deep dark blue sky. He tried to imagine what they could signify. An image of the seven heavens, each one rising higher as man travelled on his journey of spiritual evolution, came to mind. There were also some very strange interweaved carvings, some encased in complicated latticework. He had no idea what they represented. The boy also held a small, red velvet bag which he opened to reveal seven golden coins, each one engraved with a circle within which were a series of complex squares, just like the one Professor Zinohed had shown him in Damascus.

Joshua placed the wooden ball carefully on a polished wooden plinth, and a small group of musicians gathered near and started to play a slow, deeply resonant musical beat on their drums. Then they began to chant an ancient poem, quietly at first then gathering in strength until its sweet aria filled the night air.

'"*Wisdom found no place where she might dwell; Then a dwelling place was assigned her in the Heavens.*

Wisdom went forth to make her dwelling among the children of men, And found no dwelling place; Wisdom returned to her place And took her seat among the angels.

And unrighteousness went forth from her chambers: Whom she sought not she found, And dwelt with them, As rain in a desert, And dew on a thirsty land."

As it is said in the book of the holy man, Enoch the Prophet.'

As the chant ended, the wooden ball slowly started to open and unfold like a bud turning into a bloom. An evocative white mist of heavy-scented incense drifted out of the ball and up into the night air, enfolding the group in a heavenly fog.

Out of the depths of time the ball transformed into a beautiful circular golden board, decorated with a plethora of paintings of beautiful flora and fauna. Its circumference covered the entire surface of the stone table. This was the Board of Destiny. The paintings came to life as a unicorn skipped across the surface, followed by a majestic golden eagle. Butterflies, their brightly coloured wings shimmering in the half-light, fluttered above the surface, while fish jumped out of the deep blue oceans. Buds more beautiful than could be imagined burst into flower in a celebration of glory. The Board was a living creation in all its powerful glory.

The Board was divided into twelve parts, like the houses of an astrological chart, with the first house sitting in the lower left-hand quarter, and the other numbers ascending in an anti-clockwise direction from one to twelve.

As the drumbeat continued, and the rich smell of incense transported the seven players into a trance-like state, the planets, and the moon, started to appear, each one accompanied by a pair of knights on horseback, one black and one white in each pair.

Stephanie of Milly spoke quietly. 'First to arrive is Mercury, the quicksilver communicator of the solar system, who takes up position in the playful fifth house, sitting nearest to the centre of the Board. Secondly, Venus, curvaceous and beautiful, takes position in the fourth house. The sun, bright, warm and luminous, arrives in a golden glow and also moves into the fifth house just behind Mercury. Mars follows, a red warrior, and heads to the eighth house.

'Gigantic Jupiter, the greater benefic, with its coloured bands clearly visible, moves into the ninth house. Now, the moon glides serenely into view and takes up residence in the seventh house. Saturn, the realist, follows the moon and settles into the second house. Ah,' she smiled, 'here is Uranus in the eleventh house.' She paused and the group watched silently as Neptune, surrounded by a swirl of blue clouds, made an elongated orbit and danced across the Board. 'Neptune is followed by Pluto, dark and mysterious, moving into the second house, a little way behind Saturn,' Stephanie intoned in a firm, clear voice.

Joshua sat silently contemplating the magical scene unfolding before his eyes. Even though these outer planets would not be discovered for many hundreds of years, every Master of Destiny knew not only of their existence but also of others that sustained life and knowledge,

Stephanie smiled as three more celestial spheres appeared, bodies of great influence. Tiny Ceres, the Great Mother, goddess of the harvest, moved curvaceously into the seventh house, while Athena, goddess of wisdom, appeared as an ice blue ball and headed for the sixth house. Nig-ba, planet of gifts, slowly appeared from the well and floated quietly to the outer reaches of the fourth house, behind all the other planets.

Joshua lifted his eyes to heaven and then froze in shock. Above him were only the stars, and the night sky. The celestial Archangels who protected the council during their sacred meetings were absent – Michael, Gabriel, Raphael, Uriel, Raguel, Sariel and Remiel were not to be seen. Why? It had never happened in previous meetings.

He tried to control his anxiety and focus on the revelation to come. For twenty years he and his six companions had been dreaming of the moment the Board would reveal its final mystery. This was not the time for fear or anxiety. Whatever was destined to be would be.

As the seductive wisps of incense continued to swirl round the group, three figures gradually materialized from the sky to fill the three waiting empty chairs. The Three Magi, their ethereal, ghostly bodies taking on human form, filled the space with power and light. Larvandad, Gushnasaph and Hormisdas, who were, according to the folklore of Saladin's people, the Zoroastrian mystics, were manifesting their presence through the shroud of timeless existence. Their presence was eternal, they were always present whenever the Master of Destiny and the Council of Elders met. Their benediction was necessary to imbue the Master with his powers. As they appeared, a very old, black and gold, leatherbound book holding thousands of ancient papyrus papers also slowly appeared – the Book of Eternal Wisdom.

The Board shimmered as the drumbeat increased in volume until it filled the air completely. At last the Earth appeared, teeming with life, which both nourished and depleted it, and locked in place directly above the central well. The players were ready, the game could begin.

'Imam, please start,' Joshua said. The mystical sequence always commenced on the command of the Imam of the Omayyad Mosque. Before the imams, it had been the Holy Man of Tikrit.

The Imam stood. He started repeating words that had been handed down from generation to generation for thousands of years from the original Holy Man long before the birth of Christ, even before the Great Flood, back to the time of the beautiful garden city of Eden.

'Oh, gracious Lord Melchizedek, by your leave may we know the secret of your mysteries? The mysteries that are yours should now, through your magnificent benevolence, also become ours.'

The Three Magi placed their hands on the Book of Eternal Wisdom, within whose pages was contained the destiny of mankind. However, unlike other predictive texts, the Book of Eternal Wisdom was a living work of art, changing and adapting according to man's actions. The key was to delve deep into the layers and discover the underlying blueprint created by the Universal Power.

Joshua looked at his council. The Board of Destiny and the Book of Eternal Wisdom only appeared intermittently throughout history, at times of great unrest and change. This was such a time. His previous anxiety dissipated as he felt the mood of anticipation flow through them all.

As the Three Magi linked their fingers with Joshua, Saladin and the Imam, the planets started to move to reflect the positions of the real planets in the night sky. As they moved, the other figures stayed in place. The seven coins started to spin above the Board. The Book of Eternal Wisdom opened and the pages began to turn, changing colour from blue to red to black to green to gold, at first in rapid succession, then more slowly until finally the pages stopped. As the final page was revealed, a soft voice could be heard singing quietly.

Joshua smiled. The Book of Eternal Wisdom never failed to lift his heart and captivate him with the force of its mystical power, and he was always surprised to hear the words sung in his own tribal language. That was the mystery of the book, each one of them heard the message in his or her own language.

Stephanie opened her eyes and said a quiet prayer to God. This was the final moment. The truth was to be revealed. She looked down, images were racing across the pages, a giant timeline of events in history. Finally, the jumbled images slowed, and into the light came the Three Magi, a shining light guiding them on their journey to visit the Christ child, before continuing to their final destination. Silence, a dark shape formed across the page, and then... Stephanie gasped and clasped her hand to her mouth as all colour drained from her face.

The book snapped shut, and the planets and figures all moved quickly back down the middle well, leaving a dark shadow weaving around the board until it, too, disappeared and the Board closed and turned once more into a round wooden ball. The Magi disappeared rapidly into the night sky, taking the Book of Eternal Wisdom with them.

Saladin jumped to his feet. 'A lie is transparent, but he who speaks a half-truth is more dangerous, for which half do you believe? And one of us is speaking a half-truth.'

'What do you mean?' The Imam turned to Saladin. 'It is written that the human race will be saved by the chosen ones, that's us, we are the same, nothing has changed. We are bound by our destiny and our religious beliefs.'

Saladin gave him a strange look. 'Religion is often the divider, not the peacemaker.'

'Pray, Madame, what horrors did you see in your vision?' Roger de Moulins looked exasperatedly at Stephanie of Milly, who held her head in her hands. Typical of a woman, hysteria at the key moment, he'd always known she'd be tricky. 'We have been told the holy men, the priests, would lead us to redemption and tonight we were to understand the meaning of their prophecy. What is different?'

'We are not all pure of heart. The black shadow of destruction will bring its torrid force to this earth. Redemption will be hard won, if indeed it can be won,' she said, looking up at the sky.

The dark power had attempted to intervene and take over. Someone had infiltrated the mystical sequence and used the power to destroy rather than build, Hildegard thought to herself.

Joshua met Saladin's gaze, and understood that all was lost, the purity of their collective spirit had been corrupted. Now the future depended on his strong-willed, brilliant but unpredictable son, Aziz. Tonight he would give him the Board of Destiny to take on his journey, while the Book of Eternal Wisdom would return to the Universe to await the right time for its next manifestation. Joshua rubbed his furrowed brow. It was as it had been a thousand years previously when Jacob's daughter, Eschiva, had been charged with protecting the inner secrets. In Judaea, so long ago, the Romans had discovered the key to unlocking some of their secrets, but the Universal Power had stepped in to prevent total destruction. The world had been given another chance, but betrayal had once more visited the chosen ones and tonight spelled the end of their power. The cycle would be repeated until the final act at some time in the long distant future. Then mankind would decide for the final time which path to take.

But before that time, Aziz had to deliver his gifts to their correct location. Joshua looked at his colleagues; someone was lying and he realized with great sadness that they would all die without discovering who had betrayed them and who was the true redeemer. The Universal Power had, long ago, challenged mankind to fulfil his true destiny, but just as it appeared within reach, the human race would press the button to self-destruction. Joshua wondered if the ancient wisdom would ever be absorbed fully into the collective soul of his immensely gifted but unpredictable fellow humans.

Dan awoke with a start, his heart thumping and his body feeling icy cold as the memory of the dark force that had interrupted the meeting chilled him. Mr Big was snoring by his side and the credits were running at the end of the film. He stood up and paced around the room. His father's stories. Harry's discoveries. What did they mean? And how did he fit into it all? Then he felt a surge of excitement and power course through his veins. The Book of Eternal Wisdom. He had seen it in all its glory! It existed. He had to tell Harry. Finally, he settled back down on the sofa, and picked up the remote control to switch off the television. Then he froze in shock. On the screen was written in bold letters: TIME WAITS FOR NO MAN, DAN ADAMS.

CHAPTER FOURTEEN

London

Early November 2010

'You're invited for the weekend. How about the thirteenth?' A deep, warm male voice enquired.

'Who? What?' Dan said sleepily as he tried to rouse himself from the deep slumber he'd fallen into after his strange vision the previous night.

'The weekend, you know the two days between Friday and Monday,' the voice said.

'Douglas! I didn't know you had my new number.' Dan had changed it only two days ago. He rubbed his eyes and automatically sat up straight. The British Prime Minister had that effect on people. Mr Big snorted grumpily, fell off the bed where he'd been sleeping, and landed unceremoniously on the floor.

'One of the perks of being PM is having access to any amount of information. I even have the delightful Michelle Obama's mobile number – impressive, don't you think?'

'But I'm a ruined drug user, failed teacher, and about to be sent to prison. What are you doing inviting me over for the weekend?' Dan blurted out.

'Rubbish, dear boy, you are far from ruined. Will explain all when I see you. Chequers. Arrive about four on Saturday. Smart casual. Looking forward to seeing you.' Douglas said brisk and businesslike. Then he was gone.

'What?... How?... Will...' Dan was left hanging in mid-air. How the hell was he suddenly unruined?

Replacing the phone on the bedside table, Dan rolled out of bed and headed to the kitchen to make a strong cup of coffee and feed the dog. His life was becoming more and more confusing. From washer-upper to houseguest at the PM's weekend haunt. More than bizarre.

Clutching a cup of coffee, he switched on his computer, then walked over to his CD player to put on a Simple Minds album. He allowed Jim Kerr's strong, expressive vocals to bring him back down to reality. Then he emailed Harry. He was hoping to return to Syria soon depending on his trial date.

Strange times. Last night I had the most odd, scary but also uplifting dream I've ever had. I saw the Book of Eternal Wisdom in action. Truly wondrous. The most mysterious sequence of events I have ever experienced. Even my overstimulated imagination couldn't have made it up. Can't wait to see you to explain more. Almost weirder, Douglas called. Has invited me to Chequers. Says I'm not ruined. What does it all mean? I am no longer certain of the boundaries between reality and fantasy. Am I finally going mad?

He pressed send. A couple of minutes later a loud ping announced Harry's reply.

I think your dream is some kind of cognitive recognition. Difficult to explain. Let's talk when we see each other. We have uncovered more of the city, completely intact with all the paraphernalia of daily life still visible: houses, furniture, cooking pots and utensils, baths, carts and strange wooden structures also used, we think, for transport. The library and temple await to be unearthed. We can trace the route through the city where the travellers and rich merchants brought their exotic and precious wares and goods from the Far East, some of which they would sell before continuing on their journey to Europe.

But proceed with caution, we have also unearthed warnings of a group intent on taking our patrimony so they can control the people through the knowledge it imparts. They don't appear to be the normal set of religious fanatics, in fact they might not be linked to religion at all, but they are clever people, people of great influence. BE CAREFUL. My guess is they are linked to the break-in and attempt to snatch the documents I spoke to you about. Insha'allah we are discovering the very root of our civilization. We have even discovered why the Mayan calendar ends in 2012.

Will explain when I next see you. Am driving back to the dig today and will be gone for ten days. Btw, in my view it's best to be completely mad or completely sane, it's halfway between the two that's the problem! Have satellite phone now. Will try and call. Allah alim. Harry.

The doorbell made Dan jump.

His godson Thomas was on the doorstep dressed in a smart blue wool suit complete with tie. What had happened to the torn jeans and funky T-shirt?

'A bit overdressed for a Thursday morning, and why aren't you at school studying for your exams?' Dan asked as Thomas walked in the door.

'Double study. I've been given permission to miss it so I can continue with the mission,' Thomas said seriously, sounding like a mini politician.

'Mission? What mission? You on another *Star Trek* reunion quest?' Dan enquired.

'*Star Trek*?' Thomas said dismissively. 'No, this is for the Holy Trinity of Science, Religion and Philosophy. It is the salvation of us all.'

'What?' Dan raised his eyebrows in surprise. The Holy Trinity was Anna's passion. Whoever they were, they were certainly having an effect.

'They hold the true secrets. Read about it.' Thomas gave Dan a booklet. On the front was a picture of the universe and the slogan: *Your Potential Is Our Future.*

'Do your parents know about this?' Dan enquired.

'Of course. They have joined as well. We all need to become members. Joining together is the only way to save the world and reach our true destiny. The eschatological force is nigh,' Thomas finished grandly.

'Ah, eschatology. So you think that the end of life as we know it is near, and we will embark on a day of judgement, and then a new messiah will come and save us? Well, you won't be the first or the last. By five hundred BC, Zoroastrianism had a fully developed prediction of the world ending in a huge fire. What do your new friends say about that?' Dan said.

'I knew you'd take the mickey, just because you studied it at Cambridge. It's real, you know,' Thomas said, patting Mr Big and sitting down on the sofa.

'Well, let's discuss it over tea. I guess if it keeps young people away from drugs and drink and focuses on creating good then it can't be all bad,' Dan said with a sigh and headed into the kitchen again. After Thomas had left, Dan picked up the booklet and flicked through it. He paused at the last page. There in all its glory was an image of a white stag: 'The Redeemer comes soon and through him we will be saved.'

Dan frowned as he remembered Harry showing him the small ceramic pin he'd found in his office at the dig. With Harry's warning about a renegade group on the loose, Dan's instincts were flagging up danger signs. He needed to discover more about the Holy Trinity.

CHAPTER FIFTEEN

Central London

November 2010

'Welcome and thank you for making the journey here today. I know everyone is busy and short of time so I'll be as brief as possible.' The Linguist was back in charge and stood on the podium at the front of the room addressing her colleagues, who were all present in front of her. She waited for complete silence, tapping her long, French-polished nails on the lectern. Her network of contacts was global and the main reason for the success of the Holy Trinity's infiltration at the highest level; all that remained was to give the signal and activate the power.

The Scientist sitting beside the General frowned and fidgeted. He had got used to being the designated leader of the group in her absence. Now she'd returned, charmed everyone and reclaimed her natural position. It just confirmed his previous thoughts that he had to make a move to claim the leadership for himself, with her as his right hand woman, of course. She had to be part of it, no question about that.

'I am delighted to report that all the elements for success are in place. As you know, we were successful in incorporating ourselves into the preparation of the new Master of Destiny through our DNA transfer at Gleneagles, when I retrieved the DNA of the new Master at the appointed time. We have overlaid our own profiles on to this so we have access to the process. The target is constantly monitored and his tests have started, controlled by the Universal Power, but with some help from us as well.' She smiled at the Banker whose contact had successfully planted cocaine on Dan Adams at Damascus Airport. Even better, they'd then manipulated the police and media and placed the blame on a disgruntled ex-pupil. Genius! 'However, we know that Dan Adams has to discover the location of the Book of Eternal Wisdom through his own endeavours. We also know from the clever work of the Philosopher that the Book of Eternal Wisdom will activate fully at the first meeting of the new Master of Destiny, around the beginning of April next year.'

'How exactly do we know this?' the Judge asked.

'According to the court astrologers who are constantly scanning the skies, the planets will be in perfect alignment at this time,' the Linguist explained.

'Court astrologers? Oh please do cut out the crap, do you think we're still in the Middle Ages?' The Judge sighed.

'Most royal families consult astrologers, they always have done and always will, they understand the power of the planets and their movements,' the Linguist said.

'Next April seems a long time away when we're enjoying such success with recruitment. Can't we hurry things along?' the Scientist enquired.

'We might live in a world of instant gratification but you'll have to learn patience if you wish to partake of the riches this book offers. It appears to resonate with a highly complex set of events which unfold at predestined times, so no, we can't "hurry it along",' the Linguist snapped, wondering if some of the people she had chosen were really up to the job.

'However, we do know that the Melchizedek Sacred Mysteries document, which is part of the Trilogy of Inner Secrets aligned to the Book of Eternal Wisdom, has been found, so the secrets will now be uncovered. This document is important and will help us to take power. It holds the secrets of controlling the people and keeping them in awe of the rulers. Also, we believe three or maybe four of the mystical coins have now been found on the site, in addition to our two which, unbeknown to the good professor, we have removed from the dig. We are trying to gain possession of the others. There are seven in total. I think we'll now find that certain secrets will be revealed, not the deepest secrets appertaining to our destiny, just useful titbits such as the pre-warning of the fluctuation of the currency markets, from which we all made a tidy sum. And with our DNA incorporated into the process, the coins should resonate with us, at least at the first level, although we'll need Dan Adams' energy to get beyond that. Anyway, we have our people at the dig, they are busy collating information and keeping close to the senior personnel. We will have the vital knowledge we need by the time the Book of Eternal Wisdom appears. Now, Monsignor, please explain the next part of our plan.' The Linguist deftly moved the meeting along.

'We have our man in place at the heart of the Vatican. When the Book of Eternal Wisdom becomes active, and we have taken control, then the Pope will be… removed,' said the Monsignor, carefully.

'And how will that be done? We don't want any fingerprints left which point to us,' the Banker said, her soft voice barely audible in the large room.

'The transfer of power will be seamless, our man is already accepted as favourite to be the new Pope. He is also privy to the other secrets, we'll call them the practical points of infallibility, which are hidden in the Vatican. The present Pope is elderly. A heart attack would not be unusual,' replied the Monsignor.

'We don't want any controversy as before,' snapped the Scientist.

'If you're referring to Pope John Paul I, I can tell you that we have learned our lessons. The mistakes of that will not be repeated,' the Monsignor said firmly. 'We all know what we have to do. We've sold ourselves and our promises well. We have millions of followers.'

'We have harnessed the power of the Internet to our cause,' the Philosopher interjected, 'especially through social marketing; and we are becoming stronger and stronger, reaching the far corners of the globe.'

'People are tired of empty promises, and the scandals of the Catholic Church, the intransigent position of Israel and the terrorist tactics of some of the more fundamentalist factions,' the Monsignor went on. 'They are following us like lambs to the slaughter. Our brain power harnessed to the support of the masses – an unstoppable combination! It's time for a new era and a new leadership which will share the truth.'

'Share? Now that's a new concept.' The Judge laughed.

'Share as defined and controlled by us of course.' The Linguist smiled at them all confidently. 'We will meet in one month and review our programme. As the secrets are revealed we must be ready to adapt and adopt. Time is on our side. Thank you, everyone.' With this, the Linguist swept from the room.

Abdullah Mustafa, the Politician, silent at the end of the table, smiled to himself. He knew that he who understood the complex dance of time understood life itself.

CHAPTER SIXTEEN

Chequers, Buckinghamshire, England

Mid-November 2010

'"This house of peace and ancient memories was given to England as a thank-offering for her deliverance in the great war of 1914-1918 as a place of rest and recreation for her Prime Ministers for ever."' Douglas read the words inscribed on the stained-glass window in the long gallery at Chequers. Then he turned to Dan. 'Right, the news.' Douglas spoke in his usual verbal shorthand. *Minimum words, maximum effect*, he called it. A tall, slim, handsome man in his early forties, the force of his personality as well as his ambitious wife had seen his meteoric rise to power. He had been blessed with a privileged background, but tragedy, in the form of the death of his twin brother, had brought compassion and intuition to what could have been an uncompromising character.

'I've been wondering why you'd invite me here when I am in disgrace,' Dan said, looking at his old friend.

'Your state of grace has been reinstated. An ex-pupil has admitted he organized it all. Apparently he is a big player in the criminal underworld. He got someone to follow you to Damascus and plant the small bag of cocaine in your jacket pocket at Damascus airport when you were on your way home. The police have confirmed it all,' Douglas said with no preamble.

'Who? H-h-how do you know? Why hasn't anyone told me?' Dan demanded, his mind doing a lightning recall of his movements at Damascus airport.

'I don't know the ex-pupil's name, but I do know you will be receiving an official explanation from the police in the next few days. I used my contacts to find out the truth and make sure your name was cleared. I also wanted to tell you personally as *The Sunday Times* is running the story soon, which will completely exonerate you, so I'm sure they'll be contacting you. You're free to enter the real world again.' Douglas was walking at breakneck speed through the corridors. Dan struggled to keep up.

'Instant redemption! Brilliant. Thanks. Big surprise. Need to digest it,' Dan said emulating Douglas's crisp way of speaking. 'Although I'm sure a bit of the mud will stick. You know the saying, "*No smoke without fire*,"' Dan added, feeling elated and anxious at the same time. Who hated him enough to do such a thing? And who had pushed Douglas to solve it?

'Anna saved you. I'm sure she'll tell you about it in due course,' Douglas said, as though reading his friend's mind. 'She always believed in you. Give her a chance. Now I need a favour.'

'Of course,' Dan said, his heart sinking slightly. Payback time. An eternity of having to canvass for the Tories in the most difficult marginal seats and be at Douglas's beck and call – and he wasn't even a paid-up member of the Conservative Party. Another thought dropped into his brain. Why was Anna trying to help him when the last time they'd seen each other had been somewhat embarrassing, to say the least?

'I need you to chair my new Board of Educational Progress. You know I mentioned it to you a while ago before...' Douglas paused. 'Anyway, Brian is causing havoc. I need a steady, experienced hand and you need a quick rehabilitation.

It will be good for both of us. What do you think?' Douglas stopped and turned to look at Dan expectantly.

Dan understood Douglas's dilemma. Brian Smith was the Minister for Education, a coalition compromise, a nod to the unions. He was neither gifted nor popular and in spite of the recent spending review, education was still a high priority.

'I thought I might try and get a job back in the state sector. You know how committed I am to a free and full education system for all,' Dan said firmly.

'Yes, quite. But rather than focus on one school you can ensure the standard of education is kept high for everyone. Give it a year. If you still want to go back to school after that you can. Deal?' Douglas asked hopefully.

'Deal.' Dan smiled. 'And thanks, I am very grateful.'

'Always glad when justice is done. How's Harry?' Douglas asked changing the subject in his characteristic abrupt manner.

'He's fine,' said Dan surprised by this line of questioning. Douglas had always thought Harry a bit of a dry bore on the few occasions they'd met each other. 'His dig in Syria is going well.'

'And what is the mood in Syria?' Douglas studied Dan carefully.

'I understand attitudes towards the West have hardened slightly. We probably need to build bridges, stop blaming them for problems they can't easily fix,' Dan said diplomatically.

'I agree and we are taking steps in that direction. I understand there is some very interesting information coming forth from the dig. Keep me up to date. Middle East visit coming up. Very important both diplomatically and economically. Your room is that way, by the Rembrandt,' Douglas said pointing back in the direction they had just come. 'See you at seven in the library,' He strode off leaving Dan feeling bemused, and wondering if he'd set off all the smoke alarms if he had a quick fag behind the very large and no doubt priceless Chinese vase that was at the end of the corridor. What the hell was life going to throw at him next?

CHAPTER SEVENTEEN

Chequers, Buckinghamshire, England

Mid-November 2010

Dan walked into the library at six thirty. He was deliberately early. He wanted to be the first to arrive. He didn't want any more shocks. He was beginning to feel like a passenger in a fighter jet, and the effect was causing him some motion sickness.

Drinks were laid out on the mahogany sideboard. He cast an eye over the superb collection of malt whiskies and poured himself a 30-year old Brora, sipped it slowly enjoying its exquisite taste and walked over to the antique writing desk. He sat in the chair and, on impulse, picked up a leaflet about the surrounding area.

A small golden coin dropped out and fell on to his lap. He picked it up and studied it carefully. It had a circle and a set of complex angles engraved on one side. It looked the same as the one Professor Zinohed had shown him in Damascus, and the ones he'd seen in the strange vision he'd experienced. He played with it for a few minutes, turning it in his hand and prodding it.

'Look at it from the other angle, turn it upside down and through one hundred and eighty degrees, press the sides together and you'll get your answer,' a female voice said to him. He looked up and caught sight of a tall, slender woman in the mirror on the wall behind him. She had long blonde hair, was dressed in a long blue velvet flowing dress and was wearing dangly silver earrings. She looked like a 1970s rock star. Michelle Phillips or Stevie Nicks in their glorious prime.

He turned round to face her but as suddenly as she had appeared, she had gone and the mirror was clear again. He noticed a small, wooden door to the right of the mirror. He walked over to it and opened it, peering round into a long corridor with plain cream-coloured painted walls. The staff quarters? He walked back into the library still holding the coin.

He sat twisting and turning the coin at various angles and pressing the sides. Suddenly it started to expand and move through different shades of gold, from a bright silver-white to deepest red. In the midst of these constantly changing colours, a white light slowly appeared in the centre and the entire coin morphed into a hologram of brilliant colour, shapes and textures. Faces appeared and disappeared, old, young, from different centuries, times and cultures. Then, slowly, the shimmering face of a man appeared, with intense eyes the colour of deepest emeralds. Dan was transfixed as a gentle, soothing voice sang to him.

'Seek not that which you know, but that which will bring you to your destiny. Jacob, Eschiva, Joshua and Aziz are a part of your destiny. Seek their truth and your crusade will become familiar to you. Open your mind to bring your past alive.'

Then the face slowly faded back into the bright lights and without further fanfare the coin returned to its original shape.

Dan sat in silence, his heart racing, as images passed through his mind of his father, of an old man, a young girl, father and daughter, father and son, united in the quest for the eternal truth. These strange apparitions were not getting any easier. He wondered, not for the first time, whether he should see a doctor. He poured himself another.

'Ah, might have guessed you'd already be into the malt, rather a good selection don't you think? Perks of being the PM.' Douglas strode into the room and marched over to the drinks table where he poured himself a very large 20 year old Auchroisk.

'So, who's the gorgeous blonde dressed in a long blue velvet dress that you've got hidden in your bookcases?' Dan asked, standing up and shaking himself back to reality.

'Fiona's away working on her thesis, so it must have been Anna. Didn't you recognize her?' Douglas looked at him strangely.

'Anna is here?' Dan said, taken aback. He did not want an awkward confrontation. 'Well, I think I'd have recognized her. This lady looked like a 1970s rock star.'

'Thought you'd be pleased Anna is here,' Douglas said. 'Anyway, maybe the girl was the Chequers resident ghost. Either that or the cook's daughter who sings in an Abba tribute band. Now, Brian is going to be here tonight so let me brief you on our Education policy.'

'Look, I'm really grateful to you and I'd be very happy to do a year for you as chair of the board, but I really do want to return to teaching after that. I didn't realize how much I missed it until I became a head teacher and admin took over my life. I hope you understand but I don't want to spend my life managing things,' Dan said firmly, saying what had been on his mind.

'Yes, yes. Whatever. Anyway, back to Brian, I really need you to bring him back to reality and stop these ridiculous left-of-field decisions he's making. Last week it was an annual free two-week adventure break for every pupil of every school so they can "bond" and develop their personalities. Christ, we're making stringent savings everywhere. How can we pay for adventure holidays when we're cutting back on welfare, trying to reform the NHS, and also cutting back on the number of police? It's a political disaster. Bloody Liberal Democrats, they seem intent on making this country a haven for second-rate spongers. I wish we could have secured a straight victory in the election.' Douglas paced around the room.

'Oh, I don't know, it would be a good idea. The pupils could all go to the Swiss mountains and enjoy a healthy, mind-strengthening experience,' Dan said, trying not to laugh.

'Very funny. Anyway, just bring some sanity to the proceedings, will you? I've read your speeches and admire the policy you implemented at your school, as does Brian, thank goodness. I've sat you together at dinner so you can talk.' Douglas finished his malt and refilled his glass.

'What's this?' Dan opened his palm to reveal the gold coin. 'I found it on the writing desk.'

'No idea, do you think it's real gold?' Douglas picked it up and studied it. 'It's got some strange markings on it.'

'I know, I've seen similar at Harry's dig. He's investigating them trying to understand what they mean,' Dan said.

'Then you should take it to show him, though God knows how it got here.' Douglas frowned.

The door opened and Anna strode into the room smiling.

'Anna. Welcome, welcome.' Douglas kissed her on both cheeks and led her by the hand towards Dan. He looked like the father of the bride about to give his daughter away, Dan thought to himself.

'I believe I have you to thank for saving me.' Dan approached her cautiously, wondering if she would take him to task again. But she took him by the hand, still smiling.

'You certainly do,' Douglas said. 'She kept badgering me until I called the police chief. He was loathe to get involved, said it was an open and shut case, would be going to court and to allow the process to go at its own pace. But Anna didn't give up, went to see him. He put an officer on it and sent the locals in who, as I said, discovered an ex-pupil with a grudge.'

'I can't imagine who.' Dan's mind shifted through all his problem ex-pupils.

'A chap called Paul Madison, according to the police,' Anna told him. 'A nasty, serious criminal. He told them you put him in jail, were responsible for his life of crime, and this was payback time. I managed to get most of the details from a friend who works on *The Sunday Times*, and is writing and researching the article at the moment.' She gazed at Dan noticing the grey flecks in his hair which gave him a statesmanlike air. He smiled and her heart missed a beat. He might have someone else in his life but she hadn't given up yet.

'Paul Madison – now it's all starting to make sense. I didn't put him in jail, he put himself there. Knifed one of the other pupils outside a kebab shop in Streatham. I noticed blood on his shoe the next day and called the police. It was the injured boy's blood. Bang to rights,' Dan explained.

'Sounds like you're well out of that den of iniquity of a school of yours. We can't risk our top teachers like this,' Douglas muttered.

'Violence and bribery have become major problems. The do-gooder brigade has made discipline almost impossible and teachers are vulnerable to manipulative and treacherous pupils, and their parents of course, that is if they have any parental presence at home,' Dan said, shaken that someone as unpleasant as Paul Madison could very nearly ruin his life so easily, so many years later.

'I intend to put a stop to the crime culture. We have been punishing the people who suffer rather than the criminals. It's wrong,' Douglas said firmly. Then he was off greeting his other guests.

'You saved my career. How can I thank you?' Dan said to

Anna, rubbing her arm gently. She met his gaze, her blue eyes twinkling with pleasure.

'I'm sure your lady friend keeps you happy,' she said with a hint of mockery in her voice.

'I haven't spoken to Jenny since she found us together. She refuses my calls, and when I went to see her she slammed the door shut. She even avoids me on the common, although Mr Big and her dog still run around together when they see each other,' Dan said candidly.

'Are you OK with that?'

'Yes, I think so. I've never been very good with the relationship thing,' Dan said ruefully.

'Well, I enjoyed our reunion – you were good at that,' she said flirtatiously, noting his familiar warm, open smile and kind, expressive eyes. Once again, she wondered how she could have walked away from him all those years ago. Mick had seemed so exciting – but their life had been built on sand, not the solid, steady love of a man like Dan. Regret might be a useless emotion but she still felt it.

'You always seem to run away from me,' Dan grinned.

'Running off all those years ago was my big mistake. But I didn't realize you had another woman in your life when we got together recently,' she said, placing her hand on his and squeezing it.

'It would appear I don't,' he said truthfully.

'Does that mean we can be friends again?' Her steady gaze met his.

'Must just come and say I'm so pleased Douglas sorted things out for you.' A man of about forty smiled at Dan. 'John Hodges. You saved my son from ruining his life,' he added, shaking Dan's hand.

'Excuse me,' Anna said and wandered away to join another group's conversation.

'Young Colin! How is he?' Dan asked. Colin Hodges had been a nightmare pupil, either causing trouble or playing truant until Dan had discovered he was suffering from his parents' bitter divorce, and living with a mother who was more interested in going out and having a good time than raising a son. Dan had discovered that he was close to his aunt so once Dan had sorted his daily transport to school, Colin had moved in with her and started to show his potential.

'He's just finished university. He got a two one. Fantastic!' John Hodges said proudly.

Dan smiled. John Hodges was a self-made billionaire, and friend of the Hamiltons. Made his fortune in property and trading commodities, and believed firmly in state education, which was why he had sent his son to St Saviour's. He was also very generous. Douglas must be looking for a large donation for one of his charities, Dan thought.

At eight dinner was announced. As they went into the dining room, lightning streaked through the garden, followed by a loud clap of thunder. The rain hammered on the mullion windows and bounced off the window sills. Dan hoped he'd remembered to close his car windows.

He was sitting between Brian and Anna, but the place opposite him was as yet unoccupied. The weather must have kept the final guest away.

In the midst of the dinner-party chatter and the sound of thunder, no one heard the voices in the hall but suddenly a butler entered and whispered something in Douglas's ear. He rose as a figure appeared behind the butler.

'Ah, our delayed guest, held up on the M25 in the unexpected storm. Welcome, Professor, good to have you here.' Douglas moved to greet the guest.

Into the room walked a heavyset man in his fifties with grey hair – the Scientist.

CHAPTER EIGHTEEN

Chequers, Buckinghamshire, England

Mid-November 2010

'Dan, I'd like to introduce you to Oliver McManus, one of the world's leading experts on solving the unsolvable – a real life American CSI. He's Anna's boss.' Douglas smiled as he gestured towards the Scientist.

'Good to meet you.' McManus held out his hand. Dan took it, noting McManus's accent – East Coast like his but more New York than Boston. He met the older man's gaze. It was cold, analytical and unnerving. Dan stared him down, feeling strangely unsettled by this new arrival.

'This is the man who brought me back to England,' Anna said with a grin and McManus winked at her. Dan noted the easy complicity between them.

'Anna is a much valued addition to our team, her expertise is unmatched,' McManus said.

Anna smiled. 'Oliver has changed my life in so many ways. I have to say I was getting bored in Washington, and then along he came offering me the most fantastic opportunity to join his specialist team in London. Every day is different and a challenge. It's just what I needed,' she said, glancing coquettishly at McManus.

The wind continued to howl outside, rattling the windows, and the night sky lit up angrily as the thunderstorm raged around the countryside. Dan finished his glass of red wine and the butler refilled his glass. He studied Oliver McManus, wondering what power he had to turn the cool, collected and eminently successful Anna into such an ardent admirer.

'Not sure if I'll ever get used to the English weather, all four seasons in a day, so unpredictable! Anna tells me you're a Boston boy. I'm from New York, born in Queens,' McManus said conversationally.

'I was born in the North End,' Dan said.

'Little Italy, marvellous part of Boston, great history. Do you go back often?' McManus enquired smoothly.

'No, not at all. My father died when I was fifteen. I've only been back a couple of times since then, passing through on my way to international teaching conferences. My father didn't have any relatives, or at least none left alive that I know of. He was...' Dan paused. 'He was a loner.' It sounded better than an alcoholic.

'Dan is head teacher of St Saviour's, South London, once one of the worst schools in Britain and now a huge success story,' Anna explained.

'I *was* headmaster of St Saviour's. Now I have another role.' Dan glanced at Brian. They hadn't had time to talk in depth yet.

'Dan has a very well-developed social conscience,' Anna observed.

'You make me sound like a sandal-wearing New Ager.' Dan laughed. 'I guess I like fair play, and I like to help develop talent to its full potential. Working with underprivileged kids floats my boat in that respect. It's tough and you have to be prepared to accept you can't change them all. Sometimes great potential will never blossom, but when we do achieve success it's hugely rewarding.' Dan smiled.

'Oliver is also dedicated to a very worthy cause,' Anna said, exchanging glances with the man sitting nearly opposite her. Dan saw him give her an almost imperceptible nod.

Anna lowered her voice, although everyone else at the table was involved in their own conversations. 'You remember I spoke to you about the Holy Trinity? Oliver is a member, even Douglas is intrigued and has given it his unofficial blessing.'

'Yes, I do remember, although with all the media and internet coverage on it I don't think you need to keep your voice down.' Since Thomas had first brought Dan's attention to the existence of the Holy Trinity, interest in the group had turned into a huge wave of endorsements from people whose lives it had apparently changed. There was even a BBC documentary planned.

'That is mainly speculation. We have much more interesting revelations than those mentioned in the media. We really believe this is the time when man has to follow his true path and face his final moment of truth.' Oliver McManus paused. 'We're not some strange sect locked away in the Arizona desert. All of us who sit on the inner council are involved in everyday life, or the conundrum of solving the problems of everyday life. We live life, and we feel it,' he said passionately, looking directly at Dan. He was taking a chance. But he was a risk-taker by nature. Loved to push the boundaries, which is why he'd got involved in the Holy Trinity. He had seen it develop from some slightly weird secret group into a global phenomenon. He'd seen the potential from the very beginning.

'The final moment of truth?' Dan said, remembering Harry's words in Damascus.

'Yes, we have to spread the word, get people working together, unlock our collective power. Come with me to my group meeting. It's not at all weird. It is held in a bishop's private residence, he actively approves. We discuss how to harness our collective power through prayer, so we can collect material and spiritual riches and improve each other's lives. It will change your outlook on life and give it meaning, and also make you rich – a great combination,' McManus said with an intense look on his face.

As Dan leaned over to pick up the salt he noticed McManus's cufflinks – they were decorated with a small ceramic image of a white stag. Dan shivered slightly, a sliver of danger flowing through his senses. Feels more like a coven than a church, he thought, but yes, he would go along, get involved. If these people were somehow interfering with Harry's dig then he could uncover their motives. He was certainly not going to shy away from this confrontation, whatever the cost.

CHAPTER NINETEEN

London

Early December 2010

Anna held Dan's hand as they crossed the road heading to the Church of the Holy Spirit in the heart of Mayfair. He guided her through the snow, which had arrived surprisingly early this year. She turned to him and smiled. Since the weekend at Chequers they'd rekindled their love affair, much to Douglas's delight, and they'd quickly become part of the PM's inner circle. He was already dropping hints about a spring wedding. 'Why wait at your ages?' he argued.

Dan loved Anna, he knew that he always would in some way, but after that initial rush of passion at his flat, it hadn't been the same. She'd changed, hardly surprising after all these years, and so had he. She was more detached, had put up barriers. He didn't yet know if what they had could be forever. Part of him missed Jenny but he wondered if he was just the kind of guy who always wanted what he couldn't have. At the moment he was enjoying the great sex and the intelligent company. Not a bad combination.

'Greetings. Welcome. Come in out of the cold.' A tall middle-aged man with an angular face opened the door of the imposing house next door to a large, well-appointed church and smiled at them.

'Bishop Martin, how lovely to see you. This is my boyfriend Dan Adams.' Anna said.

'New members are always welcome. Please, come through.' The bishop led the way into a big room at the back of the house. It looked out over the garden, which was lit up with carefully placed lights reflecting the gently falling snowflakes. Dan could hear the soft tinkling of water and saw a large fish pond to the right of the window. The muted chatter of about forty people filled the far end of the room, along with the clink of coffee cups.

Anna led the way to a table covered with a crisp, white linen table cloth, on which were placed cups, saucers, a pot of coffee, tea and a selection of what looked like home-made cakes and biscuits. Dan noted that all the attendees seemed to be well-heeled City people. Not a room full of hippy-dippy types.

After a few minutes, people started to take their seats. The room settled into silence as the bishop stood up and opened his arms.

'Let us pray that our collective spirit will hear the word of God and embrace His words into our hearts and souls. May the world be open to our love and compassion and may we integrate His will into our daily lives.' The bishop had a soft melodious voice.

So far, so conventional, Dan thought. As a child he'd been taken to church by his Catholic mother. He had enjoyed the rhythm and consistency of Mass. This wasn't dissimilar.

'The covenant made by the Father to us is unbreakable. The righteous ones will always be protected just as Noah and the chosen ones were allowed to form a new beginning after the Universal Power removed the unrighteous from our midst.'

Dan frowned. The Universal Power was an expression used by Harry and Professor Zinohed. It was a little too much of a coincidence to suppose that the Holy Trinity had plucked it out of the sky.

'We are nearing the time when, once again, the covenant

will see a new era, one in which we will be called upon to play our roles in fulfilling our lives here on earth. This time the war between the just and the unjust will be final. Our chance of redemption is finite. Our future is through the sacred documents taken to Damascus. We will be guided by the original heavenly prince of light, Lord Melchizedek, who will lead the way.'

Dan sat bolt upright. This was more than a coincidence; someone had definitely got information from the dig. Harry's instincts were correct. Anna gave him a reassuring look and squeezed his hand. He pulled away. Was she involved in all of this? And what exactly was it all?

'I am delighted to welcome one of our illustrious leaders to speak to us about the future and what each of us will be called upon to achieve.' The bishop smiled and Oliver McManus stepped out of the shadows and took centre stage. Dan raised his eyebrows. What was coming next?

'Welcome. Let me remind you of the precious words of the Father to his people, the Essenes, who kept his knowledge in their hearts and in their sacred scrolls for thousands of years so that we might be saved. '"All those who hold fast to the precepts contained in the Damascus Document, and who heed the voice of the Teacher and confess before God, and who have learned from the former judgements by which the members of the community were judged; who have listened to the voice of the Teacher, shall rejoice and their hearts shall be strong, and they shall prevail over all the sons of the earth."

'So it is written in the Dead Sea scrolls and so it shall be. But we are not just another religion promising much but delivering nothing. We do not ask you to give us your hard-earned money with nothing in return. We come and we make you rich both in corporeal and incorporeal ways. We teach you the tools to change your lives for the better, to make that fleeting feeling of happiness permanent, to achieve everything you desire, to enjoy happy relationships, to attain that which others say is impossible: to be rich, spiritually fulfilled and happy. To truly achieve heaven on earth as the scriptures promised us.' McManus paused and Dan noticed the group was looking sceptical.

McManus looked round the room. 'You are right to disbelieve my words. Just another jumped-up religious maniac promising the world. But I am the living proof. I was born into poverty and have attained riches and happiness beyond my wildest dreams. I am one of the world's leading experts on solving what many regard as unsolvable crimes, by using my knowledge of science and researching new ways of analyzing DNA and then using it to catch the perpetrators of crime. I am a scientist. I live by evidence not fancy words. In the beginning I, too, was sceptical. Then I started to listen to the truth and my life changed – my studies became easier. I acquired great material wealth, much more than could be expected of a someone even at the top of their profession like me. Like Midas, all I touched turned to gold. All I had to do was listen and understand the codes by which we live. However, we all need proof. Even doubting Thomas needed proof of Christ's existence after the resurrection. Let me give you proof.'

McManus opened the palm of his hand, revealing a small, gold coin. He held it up so everyone could see it. Then looking at Dan he walked over to him. 'We like to welcome our new guests by involving them personally with our power at their first meeting. Please open your hand.' Dan opened his hand and McManus placed the gold coin in his palm. 'Close your hand and feel the power in the coin.' McManus instructed. Dan closed his palm and felt a slight vibration of the coin. It seemed to resonate with him, just like the one at Chequers.

Then McManus quickly took it back and placed Dan's hand on his own. He turned the gold coin in his own hand, then still with Dan's hand on his, he squeezed it.

Suddenly, it started to expand and its boundaries melted away. The room was bathed in a golden light and, in the midst of this, figures could be seen forming and re-forming. A picture was slowly emerging as if from a negative.

All the people gathered in the room, apart from Dan who knew what was coming, gasped and cried out in shock and awe as they were enfolded in the mystical light. Several people looked frightened, some looked transfixed, while others raised their hands trying to touch the figures.

The picture came into stronger focus and Dan snatched his hand away and clenched the sides of the chair, wishing he hadn't fallen for McManus's cheap trick, getting him to hold the coin to tap into its energy, but making it look like McManus was the magician.

Then he gasped. At the centre was an old man and a young girl. The young girl was fleeing and the old man was looking at her disappearing figure – his beloved daughter escaping with the secrets. Then the old man was lying dead and a short while later his murderer was seen in the middle of the group, smiling and accepting the congratulations of the crowd. He was the new leader.

Dan wanted to shout, 'No, this is wrong. He is a murderer.' But no words came. Now he understood how the dark force had infiltrated the sacred sect. After Lord Melchizedek had left, the group had ignored his exhortations to fulfill their destiny and remained blind to the evil within their midst, allowing it to lead them away from spiritual evolution.

Slowly the image morphed into buildings and people of the present day. A sign appeared with a series of dates, 17th December 2010, 11th and 22nd February 2011 all stood out, then an image of the American flag and a mass of colours, blue and red indicating Democrat and Republican, with the red dominating. The Presidential seal was in the top left-hand corner. Dan saw it and started in shock. The eagle was facing the wrong way. Then the images faded.

McManus smiled at the stunned faces. 'This is our gift to you to become rich. You just have to understand it. That is your conundrum,' he said.

'Very fancy pyrotechnics and it seems to tell us that President Obama's home town of Chicago is electing a new mayor in February next year, and that the Republicans were successful in the mid-term elections. Not exactly a mind-blowing message,' someone shouted from the back. Everyone turned to stare at the person who could remain so unmoved by such a mysterious and wondrous glimpse into the future. People started muttering 'Throw him out, Take no notice', followed by 'Incredible,' 'life-changing,' and 'thank you, thank you', to McManus, who remained at the front of the room, smiling.

Dan tried to identify the cynic but couldn't see him for the sea of hands raised in the air, all demanding McManus's attention. McManus stood quietly waiting for silence.

'Embrace the unexpected for that is where your true destiny lies,' McManus said, and then he moved aside and the bishop stepped forward again.

'My friends, let us thank our esteemed friend, he has brought a great gift to us tonight. It is up to each individual to crack the code contained in this mystical vision. The Church stands at the crossroads and now we have to take the step to the next level. As St. Paul said to the Corinthians, "When I was a child, I spake as a child, I thought as a child: now that I am a man, I have put away childish things." We must leave behind our childish ways. It is the men and women of courage and strength who will lead us forwards. It will be painful but we must reject that which is comfortable and familiar and embrace the truth. I wish you all well in your journey and I wish you the true peace of everlasting knowledge.'

There was much chatter as the guests stood up. Most looked perplexed and some looked very shaken.

'I'll go and find Oliver and bring him over to us,' Anna whispered to Dan, but he knew McManus would have already left. Having used him to spin his magical trick, McManus wasn't going to hang around and have to explain himself or his group any further.

Dan frowned. So many unanswered questions. If he was the key to unlocking the future, it looked as if the Holy Trinity had already worked that out. In which case what was the next step? Looking around, he realized that no one seemed to have seen the reversed eagle on the presidential seal. The last time people had seen that was around the time of the assassination of J. F. Kennedy and the death of innocence. What was going to happen in the world in the next few months? He suddenly felt cold.

Pulling on his coat and wrapping his scarf firmly round his neck, Dan thought how glad he was that he was going to visit Harry the following week. He had no idea what all this meant, but he did know they were all in great danger. These people did not mean well, and they were becoming more and more influential. He knew that, whatever happened, he had to keep close to McManus to discover his master plan.

'He's gone. Had to dash to another meeting.' Anna had returned to his side.

Dan helped her on with her coat and smiled at her. Was she friend or foe? And what would happen when he found out? He wasn't in control of this game, just a participant who would either survive or die trying to discover the truth of what was really going on. As he turned to go out of the door, he felt a hand on his shoulder.

'Trust in your destiny,' came the soft, melodious, lightly accented voice of his father, along with the whisper of a breeze on his face. Dan knew he had no other choice.

CHAPTER TWENTY

Syria

Early December 2010

Dan escaped the heavy snow that had arrived with an Arctic wind and flew off to Syria to join Harry. As the plane had taken off, he had looked at the winter scene on the ground below and sighed. The cars and trains that had been caught up in the chaos in Scotland and the east of England seemed to represent the mood of the country – everyone was stuck, both physically and emotionally. Stuck in their houses and stuck in their lives.

'The Holy Trinity is now a powerful force,' Dan said to Harry as they drove out of Damascus in Harry's jeep. 'The biggest threat to mankind since we rejected the early Christian views of Gnosticism and the esoteric mysteries of our long distant past, and followed the path to disaster rather than redemption. This group not only want to hijack existing religion but also our hearts, minds and soul. You should have heard McManus, and more fool me for allowing him to use me for his cheap trick. I think you'll find the Holy Trinity of Science, Religion and Philosophy is the group you warned me to be careful about in your email.' Dan sighed heavily.

As they drove along, he pulled open the newspaper he'd brought with him from London. There was a small news item about the death of Cardinal Bennett, a vastly influential member of the Catholic Church in America and a confidant of the President, who had died peacefully in his sleep.

'One minute he is a fit seventy-five year old, the next he's dead, and the other day the number two in the Church of England Synod died suddenly, and no one seems to blink an eye. The problem is, the Holy Trinity is being very clever. Rather than hiding and plotting in secret, they are right out in the open. They are promising to turn the world economy from basket case to healthy growth by magic, rather than the tedium of restraint and hard work. As we're all high on anxiety, everyone is rushing to embrace their so-called spiritual materialism and solve their problems.

'Not only do they promise riches but they deliver them. I hear that there are groups in America that have made millions by playing the stock market using "ancient wisdom!"' Dan snorted. 'I wonder if the people from that group meeting have worked out the secret message in the presidential seal,' he added.

'Have you?' Harry asked.

'To some degree. I have no idea exactly what significance either the 17th of December holds or the 11th of February next year but the 22nd is the date of the elections for mayor of Chicago, although I don't think that is relevant. However, I think some aspect of their takeover bid will be made known on those dates. But it will be fairly low key. At first I thought the image of the eagle with his head the wrong way meant an act of terrorism, but I don't think so. I think it is the beginning of the death of life as we know it, something to do with technology and the way it will spread news of life-changing events. Cyber warfare, maybe. Some turning point for Obama, and a chance to make a killing if you read the markets,' Dan said, frowning.

'Yes, I agree they are dangerous and, more worryingly, are becoming a global phenomenon. I don't know how we stop them so maybe we have to approach things differently. Could we seek to infiltrate them and steer the ship? I mean, they seem to be making people rich and successful and fulfilling their dreams. They would appear to be a better alternative than some of the other despots and fanatics, as well as a better alternative than most world governments,' Harry said, glancing at Dan, who had an expression like stone. He had a very determined, focused look on his face, the head teacher look, something Harry rarely saw.

'Harry, get your head out of your intellectual backside. You're sounding like the misguided bunch who think serial killers just need a bit of understanding. No we can't work together and they would crush us before letting us "*steer the ship*," as you put it. You should have been at that meeting. They have access to your secrets and they are using them for their own ends. These people are killing to achieve their aims, of that I am now sure,' Dan snapped.

'Yes, yes, but we do need to keep close to them,' Harry said, a worried look on his face.

'I thought you were from the "Be careful, stay away, we're all doomed" camp. Look, just to be totally clear about them,' Dan rushed on. 'Anna arranged for us to have dinner with McManus. I asked McManus about the inner circle and what they wanted to achieve. He told me they wanted the greater good, but just because they wanted good for the world didn't mean they didn't want wealth for themselves. Fair enough. But he then said what a happy coincidence it was that he had met Anna and she had brought us all together. I asked him directly if he knew her before he'd interviewed her for the job. He said by reputation only, they'd never met. Anyway, he left his iPhone on the table when he went to the loo, and fortunately Anna chose that moment to go to the ladies so I took the opportunity to scroll down his contacts. He had her address and phone number from Washington, also her contacts from

Rome – that was thirteen years ago! And, wait for this, he had my address from five years ago and a summary of my daily routine. He must have transferred the details from an old address book. What the fuck is that about?'

'Hmm, I'm impressed. You're becoming quite the Inspector Morse. Is Anna part of it, do you think?' Harry asked quietly.

Dan shrugged but remained silent. It had been bothering him. Why had she suddenly pitched up after so long? Made such an obvious play for him? He had no option but to stay for the duration and find out, good or bad. He wasn't going to blink first on this one.

'If you ask me, it's about control and it's about power,' Harry stated without emotion. 'I was just musing aloud, wondering if we could muzzle them from within, but the answer is obviously no. Like you I am now convinced they are evil. We have the best security service in the Middle East at the dig, and yet someone is still managing to break our codes. I haven't got the proof yet but the Holy Trinity is the prime suspect. We don't know their exact end-game but I'm fast coming to the conclusion that this is a fight to the death. I'm determined that our secrets will be released to the wider world freely, and undiluted, and for all the human race to reap the benefit. Our future is in the balance.'

'I agree,' Dan frowned. 'But how do we fight an organization that most people seem to think is the means by which the human race will be saved?'

'Maybe we have some of the answers. We reckon they somehow have two of the seven sacred coins in their possession. You saw one of them and I've been told by a very trusted friend that someone linked to the Holy Trinity was talking about two magical coins. There were seven in your crusader castle dream and we now have four, including the one you brought with you from Chequers, so that leaves one undiscovered. That one will hold the secret of who wins this war and whether the human race will flourish or perish.'

'Yes, there were seven in my dream but the ritual was corrupted. How do we know there aren't more?' Dan said.

'Well, for now let's presume there are seven, so we need to find the seventh. I think that will tip the balance of power.'

They pulled off the main road and wound their way up a smaller road towards a large, tight cluster of houses behind which loomed the eastern slopes of the Al-Qalamoun mountains.

'This is Maaloula,' Harry said as they arrived outside the Mar Sarkis Monastery. They had started their journey just as the sun had risen and as Dan got out of the car he felt an icy cold wind whip through him but he also felt the first rays of the day's weak but welcome sun soothe his frazzled spirits.

'Come.' Grabbing his thick parka jacket, Harry led the way through the narrow entrance that had been carved out of a cave. They walked into a courtyard and then into the Church of St Serge. Dan gazed at the ancient golden icons which adorned the walls.

'OK, prepare for your first lesson on our history trail today.' Harry grinned. 'Maaloula is one of the oldest Christian communities. This convent and church were built sometime between AD 313 and 325, which was the date of the first ecumenical council of Nicea. Maaloula is linked to our destiny in some way. It is mentioned in the Melchizedek Sacred Mysteries. There is a pathway to our inner soul through some ritual of baptism and prayer, although I have yet to discover how it happens. Maaloula's Bishop Eutiches took part in the debates of the first ecumenical council and signed the creed.' Harry paused. '"I believe in one God,"' he recited quietly.

'And do you?' Dan asked his friend seriously.

'Yes, I do. Living with this wonderful discovery, I have to say I believe in one all-powerful God, and I never thought I'd say that.' Harry smiled. 'Remember my rantings at school about the stupid idiots being fed fairy stories every Sunday at chapel?'

'Yes, you got out of the services because you said your Islamic faith precluded it, while I spent most of my time trying to avoid the chapel because my mother insisted I should be an altar boy, saying it would look good on my CV, which I considered to be supremely pretentious.'

Harry laughed. 'She always was a terrible snob.'

' "And looking up to heaven, he sighed, and saith unto him, "*Ephphatha*, that is, *Be opened*." And his ears were opened, and the bond of his tongue was loosed, and he spake plain." I guess we just have to go out into the world and speak plain,' Dan said remembering the words of the gospel according to St Mark.

'Come, enough discussion, let's get some coffee to awaken our senses and you can tell me about the meetings you've chaired for the Board of Educational Progress. I expect Brian has kept you on your toes.' Harry led Dan to the little café by the church.

'A complete imbecile. Douglas should put someone else in charge and just tell these unions to get stuffed. I used to support the unions, still do as in most cases they've improved conditions for a lot of very hard working people, but some of them are returning to thuggery and bullying and I can't be doing with that. Meanwhile, I am trying to do my best to make sure the education system maintains a sensible structure. It's an uphill challenge but, as you know, I enjoy challenges!' Dan laughed. After a couple of shots of the thick, dark coffee they climbed back into the car and set off further north.

Not far behind them an almost identical jeep moved along the road at a steady pace. Inside, a woman with long chestnut hair adjusted her headscarf and smiled. She was enjoying this. It was a pity that death also had to play its part. There was still a small part of her that wished they could achieve their aims without the total destruction of her past.

CHAPTER TWENTY-ONE

Syria

Early December 2010

As they sped along the main road, Dan sorted through Harry's CD collection. It ranged from Mozart to the Arctic Monkeys. The Spice Girls? Disco Sensations of the 1970s? Dan grimaced. He selected the Rolling Stones – a compilation of their hits. 'Brown Sugar' filled the car.

'Oldies but goldies,' Dan said and sang along. Harry pulled a face.

'You always fancied yourself as a rock star. I remember you used to drive us all up the wall strumming a guitar every time there was a free period at school.'

'I could have been rich and famous by now. Anyway, where are you taking me?' Dan asked.

'On a deviation,' Harry replied enigmatically.

Two hours later Harry turned off at Homs towards Tartous. After another half an hour he turned right on to a minor road, which branched off in a northerly direction. A little way past the village of Shmiyseh, he turned left and took a steep mountainous road through an agricultural area. Dan looked at him questioningly.

Harry just smiled as they ascended the winding road. In the distance a great white fortress rose in front of them, sitting majestically on top of a hill and dominating the landscape. At last Harry pulled into an open area in front of the main eastern gate of the castle.

'Welcome to the Krak des Chevaliers,' Harry announced.

Dan gasped as his strange crusader dream came rushing back to him. 'I know it,' he said. 'I've been here before.'

'We haven't been here before, and you haven't been to Syria without me. It's probably like one of the castles you visited on your holiday a couple of years ago in the Cathar region of France,' Harry said logically.

'No, it's not. It's the place from my crusader castle dream. Come. I'll prove it to you.' Dan jumped out of the car, paid the entrance fee and headed up the steep cobbled slope, through the main entrance in one of the eastern towers and into the interior of the castle. As he entered, he felt a surge of recognition and strength wash away any doubts and fears.

Dan led the way through narrow passageways and through secret doors. Suddenly, he couldn't wait to show Harry some tangible evidence of his strange dreams.

As he walked through the castle, the corridors appeared to change and re-form. Around him old walls and battlements rose up and took on their twelfth century likeness.

Then, in front of him, the old man, Joshua, materialized. Dan could feel Joshua's urgency. The old man had to find his son before – well, before fate took him away. Moving with stealth, he entered a narrow corridor of doors, and he looked into each room through the small window in every door. Finally, he found the one he was looking for.

As the door opened, the young man turned, his face full of joy as he realized his father had come to see him. They embraced quickly, their time together brief. There was movement in the room above. Aziz was supposed to be a recluse during his studies.

'The time has come. Meet me at Prophet's Way,' Joshua whispered.

'I will not let you down,' Aziz said.

'Behind this door was a young man who was studying to be a high priest in the twelfth century,' Dan explained to Harry. 'Some aspects of Joshua and his son Aziz resonate with me. We share the same source, the same…' His mind struggled to elucidate his thoughts. 'Come,' he said and they ran up the steps and walked out on to the ramparts.

'I think it's time to talk again,' Harry said and sat down on one of the stone steps out of breath. He pulled out a large white handkerchief and wiped his brow. He had not intended to share his secret with Dan until they were safely ensconced at the dig.

'What do you mean?' Dan was still caught up in his dream. 'Look, here we are on the ramparts and ahead of us is the north-eastern part of the tower where the king's daughter lived,' Dan said and walked over to the outer wall. The wind was cold on his face.

Harry joined him and they gazed out over the plain of Al-Buqia. About twenty miles ahead of them was the Syrian coast, with the sea just visible, while closer in front of them was the beginning of the Lebanon and Alawiyeen mountain ranges. On three sides from the north, west and east, the castle was surrounded by very deep valleys, while the southern side of the castle was separated from the mountain by a moat. It was perfect as a place of refuge.

Restlessly, Dan continued his exploration. High up on the roof of the large wing overlooking a series of entrances to what appeared to be private chambers were the remains of a round stone table.

'Look, that's the table where the Master of Destiny, Joshua, met with the Council of Elders, who partook in a ceremony which involved what appeared to be the Book of Eternal Wisdom. It was activated by the opening of the Board of Destiny, the golden board I told you about from my dream, on which the planets appeared and settled into various houses to reflect their actual position on that night.'

'OK, I believe you,' Harry said. 'The presence of the Board of Destiny makes perfect sense, as the Book of Eternal Wisdom must be activated by certain astronomical alignments.' He coughed nervously, sat on one of the large stones that were scattered around and turned to meet Dan's gaze.

'I know you think I'm turning into some kind of fundamentalist nutcase with my traditional clothing and new belief in God, but suspend those thoughts and give some consideration to what I am going to tell you.' Harry took a deep breath. 'We have discovered a very, very old document, probably about five thousand years old. It was very hard to decipher but it appeared to be a birth chart, so Mumtaz spent all night trying to discover the date.'

'And?' Dan leaned forward.

'It is indeed a birth chart. It is the birth chart of a man born on 18th of February 1971 in Boston.'

'That's my place and date of birth! Why would some ancient scribe randomly choose my birth date thousands of years in the future?" Dan asked.

'I can't answer that yet, but it is your birth chart and it isn't a random choice, your name is in bold print at the top of the chart. And under your name is written the word "Redeemer" in a very ancient script,' Harry said quietly.

'Just as Lord Melchizedek said,' Dan whispered, trying to get to grips with his emotions which were once more jumping from excitement to fear and from acceptance to confusion, and then back through the range again. How the hell could he have some major role in getting mankind back on the straight and narrow? He was an ordinary Joe, a teacher, a man of the times, not exceptional… and yet? There was something deep within his soul which resonated with all of this. Something that made him feel that somehow, some way, it was all real. 'Has anyone studied the chart?' Dan found his voice again and looked at Harry.

'No, it is still with Mumtaz. I thought of waiting before telling you but things are running at such a pace I think you should know now,' Harry said calmly. 'I think that when we find the Book of Eternal Wisdom, and I say when not if, then we'll find the names and birth dates of all the Masters of Destiny.'

'And maybe information about their lives and the roles they played in the history of mankind,' Dan said, feeling an intangible strength flow through his body.

'The Book of Eternal Wisdom is the most precious gift God, or the Universal Power, has given us. Your presence on this earth has a purpose which brings...' Harry stopped and stared into the distance.

'Great responsibility,' Dan said simply.

'And great danger,' Harry added.

'All this makes me feel like I'm in the midst of an Indiana Jones film and that's just, well, a great adventure story but not reality, is it?' Dan said a little while later as they sat in the hotel opposite the Krak and ate lunch. He was back to giving all of this a massive reality check.

'Like I said, I think you should suspend your disbelief and go with the flow,' Harry said. 'I have come to the conclusion that great change is stimulated by some predestined force. It seems as if we are at the beginning of a new age, one in which we either take the path to fulfilment or self-destruct. For thousands of years astrologers have followed the path of the stars and there's no reason to think we can't also benefit from this knowledge. Next year Neptune will move into Pisces, and yes, that might sound like New Age gobbledy-gook, but it could herald the dawn of a more spiritual, telepathic and potentially unified time. But it may also denote secrets, subterfuge and deception.'

'So we really could be on the edge of great change,' Dan said almost to himself, allowing his intuition to guide his thoughts and tell his mind to accept it all for now and find the answers later.

Harry nodded. 'There seem to be seven ages of man, not just from individual birth to death but from the birth of civilization to the end, and my hunch, having been immersed in these sacred documents for some months, is that we're at the end of the sixth age and about to enter the seventh age, the Vitae Era, the Age of Life. The age when we have to prove we've learned life's lessons, and are ready to embrace our true destiny, or we'll just slip away into oblivion.'

Later, as they arrived in the northern Syrian town of Aleppo, Dan's mobile phone beeped, alerting him to the fact his godson Thomas's exam results were due. He went off to call him as soon as they arrived at the Jdayde Hotel in the Christian quarter of the town.

Much later after he and Harry had dined, Dan stood by himself outside the hotel, smoking – he still hadn't managed to give it up yet – and looked at the stars spread across a clear, night sky. He drew heavily on his cigarette and blew smoke rings into the cool night air. Thomas had passed all his exams. He was so proud of him, thought of him as his own son. More than ever he wished he'd had more time with his father. He felt sad that the only person who could really understand all of this was dead.

The cold night air made him shiver and he turned and walked back into the hotel. Once inside, he paused and gazed around for a minute before going to his room.

Sitting half-hidden in the bar of the hotel, the woman stared into the distance before she got up, wrapped her cashmere scarf round her neck, pushed open the hotel doors and headed out into the night. Like a spider she was weaving her web, all she had to do was make sure that no detail was left to chance. There was no room for mistakes and she worried about that, knew she wasn't immortal. What if...? Then she shook herself and walked back to her hotel. On the way she pulled her mobile out of her pocket and dialled. For once in her life she felt she needed some reassurance.

CHAPTER TWENTY-TWO

Syria

Early December 2010

The next morning Dan was woken at dawn by the call to prayer. He opened the shutters and looked out of the window. It was just light enough to see the citadel outlined in the distance, its reassuring presence looming in the pale dawn light. He breathed in the cold morning air, closed his eyes and let the sacred call fill his senses and calm his mind.

When he walked into the restaurant for breakfast, he found Harry already seated at a table by the window.

'How are you this morning? I have to say you look very fetching.' He smiled at Dan who was wearing a traditional dark brown *thobe* as they'd agreed it would be safer at the dig.

'I feel apprehensive and I look ridiculous.' Dan sat down opposite Harry and the waitress brought him a small cup of dark, bitter coffee. He downed it in one.

'Embrace your destiny,' Harry said, feeling a lot more optimistic than yesterday.

'Hmm, once I've figured out what it is, I will,' Dan replied.

'Instead of veering between highs and lows, why not find the middle road of acceptance? It might help you,' Harry said. 'I can't explain the mysteries of your birth chart and why it has been found at the dig, but then I haven't got a handy explanation for most of what's going on. I think we just have to keep a very open mind about things and apply a bit of lateral thinking.'

A short while later, they checked out, left the hotel and walked across the Sahet Al-Hatab Square, found Harry's jeep and headed in a westerly direction out of the city.

As the suburbs gave way to open countryside, the houses became scarcer and were replaced by fields of wheat, chickpea and barley, which flourished in the fertile soil of the north-western plains. The countryside was diverse and much lusher than Dan had thought it would be.

'There's an old Roman road not far from here, which travellers used to go from Aleppo to Antioch. There was constant trade between east and west in this region. Now, this is Kurdish country,' Harry said as they overtook a small van, which looked as if it had the entire family of five adults and four children sitting in the open back of it.

They drove on through Daret Ezzah, known as the Goat's Inn, before a ruined cathedral rose up on their left.

'This is Saint Simeon's Basilica,' Harry said as he pulled off the road.

'And who was he?' Dan enquired. 'Is this another part of your magical mystery tour, a kind of condensed guide to Syria?'

'Sort of. It's interesting, and full of symbols so I'd like you to see it. I have a few theories,' Harry said.

'I bet you do.' Dan smiled as Harry parked the car. They got out and walked up the path towards the basilica.

'After having performed a miracle, Saint Simeon got fed up with loads of people wanting to talk to him, or just stare at him, so he escaped the fuss and decided to live on a pillar for over forty years. The locals passed food up to him and his waste was transported via a quite sophisticated drainage system,' Harry explained as they reached the south wing, which marked the entrance to the basilica.

'Escaping the human race. Sensible chap.' Dan grinned.

'Look, here we have the signs of alpha and omega inscribed on the column.' Harry bent down and pointed out the carvings on the remains of a tall pillar. 'We believe this site is much older than first thought. The east wing is the main area of worship and it is exactly aligned to the east, indicating a religion that was already aware of the significance of direction and the power of the universe and the worlds beyond ours. And look, the three apses at the end of the east wing are on a higher level than the other wings. A rise in the floor level usually marks the iconostasis.'

'The point of divide between the divine and the human,' Dan said quietly, looking down at the ground and noting some complex markings carved in the join between the floor and the wall. They looked familiar. He bent down to inspect them more carefully. They were like the markings on the coin he had found at Chequers.

'Yes, the point where the human world would reach into the divine. We believe this basilica was much more than a church, it was a kind of portal, which connected man to other worlds and to God.' Harry looked at Dan intently.

'Those markings seem to be the same as the markings on the coin I brought with me from Chequers. Could this be the point where the human race communicated with the Masters of Destiny? My father used to talk to me about the merging of the different worlds, one divine and one human,' Dan said.

They walked round to the west wing and stood gazing over the valley and the Afrin plain. Once there had been a mini city around the monastery – inns, market stalls, tombs, a baptistery and the signs of a thriving community. Now it was a Byzantine ghost town, where the winds of its once lively past blew through the ruins.

'Excuse me, you dropped this,' a woman said. Dan looked round. Harry had wandered off back to the east wing and beside him was a woman with long chestnut hair and hazel eyes, which were looking at him intently. He noted her slight Parisian accent, which matched her chic but understated appearance. She was holding a small diary in her hand. He recognized it as his, it must have slipped out of the pocket of his *thobe*. He tapped the pocket – empty.

'Thanks, very kind of you,' Dan said, taking it and smiling.

'Oh, you're American but obviously a traditional Muslim, quite unusual,' she said, leaning on the wall.

'Err, yes,' Dan replied uneasily.

'Well, enjoy your day.' And she was gone, striding down the path, her hair moving gently from side to side and glinting in the sun. He frowned. It reminded him of Anna's hair. Different colour but same movement.

At the bottom of the path, the woman climbed back into her jeep. She'd picked up some useful information from his diary. Studying the map that was open on the passenger seat, she frowned, then put the jeep into gear and drove off.

'Right, ready for the next surprise?' Harry said when he returned to where he'd left Dan.

'Did you see that woman?' Dan demanded.

'Oh Lord, what is it about you? Even in the outback of northern Syria you manage to pick up women. Did she look like Jennifer Aniston? If so, I'll fight you for her. Never understood why Brad Pitt dumped her.' Harry laughed.

'No, more like Angelina Jolie,' Dan said.

'Oh dear, very scary. Come on, let's get going. I have one final stop on this tour of mystical places and then we'll go to the dig.' Dan followed him down the path.

CHAPTER TWENTY-THREE

Syria

Early December 2010

A little while later, after a twenty-minute bumpy ride along the rough road, Harry turned left down a track and brought the car to a halt under some trees. They climbed out. The sun had risen high and it was very warm, which was unusual for December, especially after the previous cold day.

'It's up that hill.' Harry led the way as they climbed up a twisty track.

Dan looked up and saw a large mound of earth on a hillock. It sat in calm supremacy of all it surveyed.

'This is Ain Dara, the holy of holies of the East.' Harry drank from his water bottle and pulled out his white handkerchief to wipe his sweating brow. 'The entrance to the dig is just on the other side of the hill, but I wanted you to see this sacred site first.'

Dan strode on, his eagerness winning over his inherent good manners as he left Harry to struggle along behind him. As he rounded the last corner, he was met by a very large, basalt stone lion marking the entrance.

Harry arrived a few minutes later, puffing. 'Well, as you can see, the facades of the stone animals which protect this site are blackened and in ruins. There were lions and sphinxes surrounding the inner temple area. This is the temple of the goddess Ishtar, the goddess of fertility. We believe there was an Aramean town here from the tenth century BC,' Harry explained, catching his breath and sitting down on a nearby rock.

'What happened to the facades?' Dan asked.

'The main theory is that they were destroyed by fire, during the seventh Century BC, but rebuilt in the fourth century, and prospered during the Roman period. However, it is said that the people who owned this site preferred to burn it down rather than reveal its secrets. It is a very sacred place. Ain Dara has many meanings in Arabic, it can mean a spring of water, and as you can see this site overlooks the Afrin River, or it can mean I as I am, I exist. We have yet to discover its exact meaning, but of course now we've discovered the riches that exist nearby, we can presume it was the place of worship for a very advanced civilization. Come, you can see the dig from the altar area.' Harry and Dan walked into the temple, following the imprint of large feet, which had been etched into stone at the entrance.

Finally, they stood by the altar staring down at the plains below and across to the Turkish mountain ranges. The Afrin River wound its way through the plains and at the base of the hill was the dig. Tents, temporary houses and offices, cars and archaeological implements were scattered over an area of about two square miles.

'And that, my friend, is my beloved child,' Harry said smiling as he swept his hand over the land where the dig was slowly revealing its precious secrets.

Dan stood and breathed in the sweetly scented air trying to identify its fragrance. Before him were the hills, which looked somehow familiar. He rubbed his eyes and then studied them again before realization hit him. It was like looking at Glen Devon, the hills up by Gleneagles, that same rolling, curvaceous gentleness, the feeling of protection and majesty. He smiled and lifted his face up towards the sun. Then he sat down next to Harry and paused to enjoy the peace of this holy site. There was an other-worldly feel to Ain Dara. He could imagine people worshipping at this altar, praying for good crops, plentiful rainfall and healing sun, and also praying for something else, something noble and divine. He stretched his mind back to his childhood.

Suddenly, he felt the slight rustle of a cool wind on his face, and his surroundings moved and changed as he was transported back many centuries. He opened his eyes and saw people kneeling in silent prayer in front of the altar where the statue of the goddess was placed. A man was moving through the crowd. People were whispering his name, 'Zoroaster, Zoroaster, Master, Master...' Here was the ancient mystic who had come from Persia to deliver his words of wisdom as a Master of Destiny.

The people were reading from parchment-bound books.

Dan drew nearer. *The Divine Way of the Universal Creator*, he read. It was a series of instructions on life.

- *Time is not your master. You are the master of your destiny.*
- *The eternal soul knows not what time is but she beats her wings to the slow pace of her unfolding spirit as it makes its journey in this life.*
- *Man measures the soul's earthly existence in time, but God measures it in destiny.*
- *When the soul completes its earthly cycle it will move on, not a minute before or a minute after, whether it be seconds, minutes, hours, days, months, years, it will always be perfectly aligned to the Universal Creator.*
- *Know eternal life through earthly experiences. They are the imprints of your universal journey.*
- *What is learned in this life will be taken forward to future lives, but transgressions will be magnified and honour demanded in each life until the lesson is learned.*

- *Receive the holy word in your heart, soul and mind. Repeat it a hundred times until the mind slows to receive the wisdom of the ancient masters.*
- *When the mind is slow and ready, then face the east, smile with happiness and the truth will be revealed.*
- *Your soul will recognize that which is true and it will resonate to the beat of the collective soul until brother will turn to brother and whisper, 'Now it is Known.'*

'Shall we go to the dig? I am looking forward to showing you more treasures.' Harry's voice broke the vision that was blissfully meandering around Dan's soul.

'This is a sacred portal,' Dan told Harry, energized by his latest insight. He described what he'd just seen.

Harry bit his lip and looked rather ill at ease. 'I think your induction as Master of Destiny is speeding up even more than I had previously thought.'

'These strange occurrences are indicative of something, of that I am now sure. I do believe that we are influenced by energy, and there is a new energy leading us to our destinies, both individual and collective. Do we choose our destiny?' Dan glanced at Harry.

'We do not have the luxury of choosing our destiny, it is imprinted into our souls. We can, of course, through free will choose to ignore it and remain unenlightened,' Harry said briefly. 'I must speak to Mumtaz tonight as he's working on a theory that the dark power is in control of the process rather than the Universal Power.'

'How can that be if the Universal Power is in charge of all that is in the universe?' Dan asked.

'I'm not sure it's as simple as that. Something seems to have happened in the past that corrupted this process,' Harry explained, looking worried.

Dan frowned as his mind went back to the crusader dream and the dark shadow that had spread over the Board.

'You would be tested anyway as the Universal Power has to know you're worthy, but if the process has been corrupted then I don't know how we get it back,' Harry said.

'We'll get it back when the Book of Eternal Wisdom appears,' Dan said, realization dawning that they could be ahead of the game by knowing when the Book of Eternal Wisdom would appear.

'I'm glad to hear you accept that the Book of Eternal Wisdom will appear.' Harry paused, deep in thought. 'And you're right. There is indeed a chance to beat whoever it is that's leading this dance. Come, let's go to the dig.'

As they reached the bottom of the hill, a man came to them offering small cups of sweet mint tea.

'*Shukran.* Thank you,' Harry said, accepting a cup.

Halfway along the road that traversed the flat plain, Harry turned right and they drove down a narrow track at the end of which was an iron gate beside a two-storey building. Four guards came out when their car approached.

'*Sa'eeda*,' Harry said to them. 'Come,' he said to Dan and they got out of the car. 'Place the palm of your hand on the pad.' Dan placed his hand flat on the pad that was by the side of the iron gate. It was linked to a central computer in Damascus, on which Harry had loaded Dan's palm prints, which he had taken during his last visit. Finally, after about twenty minutes, the guards received confirmation of Dan's identity and the red light blinked to green and the gate opened.

'We don't rely on the fallibility of humans,' Harry said, driving through. 'However, we still have some security issues.' They drew up beside a long, single-storey white building.

'This is the nerve centre of operations. Here are my office, my living quarters and my life. Each day we chart and file the discoveries carefully in a series of large books and also on a central computer. This computer is carefully encrypted, with only three people cleared for complete access, myself, Professor Zinohed and one other expert whom you'll soon meet. We often work through the night translating and referencing documents and preparing the priceless items of treasure for their journey to Damascus. We realize it's a race against time. I feel that at any time we could be shut down and then…' Harry's voice trailed away. He picked up his bag and led Dan into the building.

'This is your room.' He showed Dan into a small, simple but clean room, with a single bed, a small wardrobe, and a bedside table with a reading lamp on top of it. A low wooden door formed the entrance to the tiny shower room. 'Make yourself comfortable then we'll go and have lunch.'

When they walked into the large tent which had been erected on the far left of the main site, and which served as the site canteen, Dan felt at ease in his thobe for the first time. All the men were dressed traditionally and most of them had taken part in the pre-lunch prayers.

'Quite a fervent lot then?' Dan whispered to Harry.

'Yes, the traditionalists are the rulers here and they are keeping an eye on us, reporting what we do to the government ministry.'

The men stood and greeted Harry as he entered the room and he smiled as he made his way to a small table at the far left-hand corner. Three places had been laid, and there was a basket of Arabic bread in the centre surrounded by a selection of mezze.

Dan didn't have long to wonder who the third place was for. A very large, dark-skinned man of middle years approached and bowed. 'Your guest is here, Mr Harry.'

'Thank you, please show her in.' Harry smiled at the man.

In walked the woman who had rescued Dan's diary at St Simeon's Monastery. Dan looked surprised. The woman smiled.

'Well, well, we meet again. I should have guessed you were something to do with this dig. Hello, I'm Angelica Duval.' She held out her hand and Dan shook it. There was a murmur around the room. The men recognized her, although a woman in their midst was not altogether welcome.

'Have you two met?' Harry looked quizzical.

'Briefly, at Saint Simeon's Monastery. This is the woman I told you about,' Dan said, a feeling of unease passing through him.

'Oh, good, good. Angelica is the worldwide expert on very ancient languages. She can read Phoenician, Proto-Sinaitic script, Old Hebrew, Avestan, Aramaic and translate Egyptian hieroglyphs as fast as you and I can read *The Times*. She is here to help us translate our discoveries, having just arrived from the United States. She is the third person allowed access to the ancient documents and has worked with us for many years translating various ancient manuscripts. I have also arranged for you to have special access to the documents while you are here. Angelica, do sit down.' Harry indicated the third place at the table.

'Thanks. I'm looking forward to getting down to work. So tell me, Dan, what is your role here?'

'I'm not sure if I have a set role. Harry and I are old friends, he's seen me through some difficult times recently and I'm here to see what has so captured his imagination and help out where I can,' Dan said, meeting Angelica's gaze.

'Dan is my family,' Harry stated. 'We're like blood brothers, together in good times and bad, simple as that. He's a gifted linguist so a valuable addition to our team.' He dipped his bread into the bowl of soup which had been placed in front of him.

'When can I have access to your latest discoveries?' Angelica turned her gaze from Dan to Harry.

'This afternoon. As soon as the archaeologists retire for

their afternoon siesta we can go to my quarters and study the documents that I haven't got round to indexing yet.' Harry clapped his hands and a servant boy appeared with jugs of coffee and trays of sweetmeats.

'Are you from the Lyon region of France?' Dan turned his attention back to Angelica.

'Oh, you are a gifted linguist! I thought I'd lost my regional accent a long time ago. I've been living an international life for over thirty years.' She laughed but clearly didn't want to elaborate further.

After lunch Harry led them on to the site where a man was waiting in another jeep, to show them around. 'This is our site foreman,' he said, as he handed Angelica a long scarf.

She smiled. 'I presume this is to placate local sensibilities rather than just keep the sun off my head?' She placed the long black scarf over her head and swung both ends over her shoulders so her head, hair and shoulders were covered.

'My men are rather traditional,' Harry said to her.

'I don't mind, that's why I'm wearing this long dress. I hope it is acceptable, it's certainly not designed to fan the flames of desire.' She laughed, hitched up the hem of her dress and jumped into the back of the jeep.

It was a long tour as Harry wanted to be briefed on all aspects of the dig, new discoveries, changes in the topography, the mood of the workers and of course the progress they were making in uncovering ancient buildings. 'This is the main temple,' Harry said as they approached a large ruined building. The jeep stopped and they got out. Harry led the way past a series of coloured pegs in the ground and into the inner area. 'It is aligned to the holy site at Ain Dara, but we're not exactly sure how, whether by location or spiritual presence.'

'Have you found any more documents?' Angelica asked Harry.

'A new batch was found in the far north-west corner of the site. Strange, I've been looking in the far right-hand side of the dig but found nothing,' Harry said and then, as he saw Dan's look of confusion, he quickly explained. 'I found an old piece of parchment indicating the site of hidden secrets to be in the far right-hand side of the site. Well, I didn't find anything there but the archaeologists have uncovered another series of underground grottoes which actually go under the river. It's extraordinary. These people were very advanced engineers, they could have built the Channel Tunnel thousands of years before we developed the necessary skills.'

'And given the French more years to maraud unopposed through the lovely English countryside? Not a good idea!' Dan said provocatively and gave a sideways glance towards Angelica who looked vaguely irritated by his childish teasing. 'So, which one is your favourite ancient language?' Dan took on a more serious tone.

'It depends on your definition of language. Communication between humans has been present for many, many thousands of years, maybe hundreds of thousands. We have communicated by sign language and through drawings, which you can see in caves throughout the world. But of course the earliest form of sophisticated language was not spoken, but then you'd know that.' Angelica looked at Dan.

He did indeed know that. Mankind had once communicated through music, and the structure and form of music held many secrets which modern man was only just beginning to understand. He had studied the language of music at a postgraduate course. It had been fascinating... his mind drifted to the Book of Eternal Wisdom and its soft, evocative songs of life and destiny.

'Are you remembering the music of life?' Angelica was studying him. He looked away. Did she know about the Book of Eternal Wisdom? He had to admit he was irritated by her prissy, self-righteous attitude, but maybe he was also hacked off to discover there was a third person involved. He had hoped it would just be him and Harry delving through the treasure and sharing memories and thoughts that he hadn't been able to express through their email exchange.

'Let's go and see our new arrivals,' Harry suggested. Lost in his world of ancient artefacts and oblivious to Dan's growing irritation, they climbed back into the jeep and drove back to Harry's quarters. The site was silent as everyone had returned to their rooms for a siesta. The action would recommence at four.

Harry led his little party through his office and down a long corridor, off which a series of doors led to rooms full of treasures, yet to be analyzed.

Finally, Harry paused outside a door and unlocked it. Inside, about a dozen ceramic jars were lined up, the contents of which were waiting to be extracted.

'Good heavens, this is the biggest haul yet,' he exclaimed. 'I must call Mumtaz, we'll have to arrange for transportation of the jars to Damascus. Let's work on making them secure for travel as soon as possible.' Harry bit his lip and leaned over to study the jars.

'What about the seven key documents you mentioned?' Angelica asked Harry.

'We have five of them in Damascus, two are still to be found. They could be amongst these.'

They put on protective white suits and hats and then Harry led the way into a large, windowless room which had a series of dials on the wall to regulate the climate and the lighting to allow old documents to be studied without the danger of further damage.

Angelica crossed over to a bench, put on a pair of white

cotton gloves and opened a drawer of instruments. Then she picked up a document with a pair of tweezers and laid it carefully on a piece of silk.

'This is Avestan, an old Iranian language.' Angelica bent forward with a magnifying glass and studied the words before her. The document had been partly translated. 'It's a song about the wonders of life and the gifts God delivered in the form of the natural wonders of the world. Birds, trees, flowers, all the various types of flora and fauna are celebrated in this Song of Life. It tells of the complex relationships between man and animal life on planet earth.'

'We have found many documents like this,' Harry said as Angelica finished reading. 'I think they are part of the series of teachings which make up the philosophy of this ancient race. Let me read you my favourite.' He pulled open a drawer and took out a very slim, black tube, out of which he teased a copper scroll. He read it aloud.

My life is your life and your life is my life and our lives dance to the eternal song of joy but your life is yours and yours to celebrate. Dance to the words of Lord Melchizedek, which he spake to you and you alone. These words are your shining light and these words will give you the strength to know that which is to be done. And then many blessings will be yours, my beloved child.

Harry smiled. 'The words never fail to cheer me.' He paused. 'One day I hope to have time to delve into the wonders of all these writings and musings but right now we're trying to understand the key documents. You remember I mentioned the Mayan calendar end-of-world predictions?' Harry looked at Dan.

'Yes, you said you'd explain the meaning of it,' Dan said.

'Here is the document which refers to both the Mayan calendar and Crystal Skulls, which some people think hold the ancient wisdom that will predict the future.' Harry gently placed a very old piece of papyrus on another silk-lined wooden block. 'This document contains a very complex mathematical code that I sent to CERN in Switzerland, and they decoded it. They couldn't interpret the meaning but Professor Zinohed thinks it relates to the appearance of a planet which is referred to as the home planet of earth.'

'The home of the Masters of Destiny?' Dan asked as Angelica looked on silently.

'We think so,' Harry grinned. 'This planet has an orbit of about 3600 years and would seem to coincide with the Mayan Calendar's end on the 21st of December 2012, when it will once again be very close to earth. It would appear that rather than the end of the world, it is the start of a new era. An era that will be the gateway to other forms of consciousness, other forms of being. It's a transition from one world age to another, which we can make difficult for ourselves or easy, depending on whether we embrace a new way of thinking and acting or fight against it. If we make it difficult then, yes, it could be the end of the world. Up to us to use our free will in a positive manner.'

'Do the skulls hold magic properties?' Angelica's eyes glistened in the half-light.

'We're not sure. The original skull became an icon for many people around the world, a symbol of future worlds. It became a phenomenon and its owner travelled all around the world. I am told there are twelve real ones in total, one discovered in 1881, is in the British Museum, one is in Paris. Personally, we believe they are beautiful pieces of art work but the real secrets are in…'

'The Book of Eternal Wisdom.' Angelica finished for him. 'Any further evidence of where it could be?' she pressed on.

Dan raised his eyebrows. So she did know of the existence of the Book of Eternal Wisdom.

'Yes, it seems as if it is close to becoming active once more,' Harry said briefly.

'Mr Harry, Professor Mumtaz is on the phone,' Harry's chief assistant interrupted them.

Divine intervention, Dan thought, not wishing to share all their secret thoughts and theories with this woman.

'So let's continue.' Angelica smiled at Dan as Harry left the room.

An hour later an excited Harry burst into the room. 'Good news. I spoke to Mumtaz. He has made great progress and discovered the place where the seventh coin is likely to be hidden. Mumtaz has also discovered more about the Book of Eternal Wisdom. He finally has the proof of how the original highly civilized race lived on this earth and details of the wisdom and secrets they kept. He thinks the Masters had a very, very advanced computer type system that could connect with other beings in the universe, and communicate thoughts, ideas and facts. These beings could be contacted through earthly portals, and immense power and knowledge came to us through them and through their mystical instruments of enlightenment, the Board of Destiny and the Book of Eternal Wisdom. So you were right, Dan, there is a Board of Destiny as well as the Book of Eternal Wisdom. And...' He paused for effect.

'Well?' Angelica snapped.

'Mumtaz has found the location of the Book of Eternal Wisdom. Apparently, the location is also stated in one of the key documents here. The Book of Eternal Wisdom is now lying in a place safe and secure and will soon be ready to come alive once more. However, it will only come alive in the presence of the new Master on his own, without the Magi and the council, then it will return whence it came and await the call of The Magi.'

Dan smiled, remembering his dream in which the Book of Eternal Wisdom appeared with the Magi at the meeting of the Master of Destiny and his council.

'We will discover the location when we meet in Damascus on Thursday, as my conversation with Mumtaz was interrupted by someone arriving at his office. Oh, the joy!' Harry clapped his hands in delight.

After dinner, Angelica pleaded jet lag and disappeared to her room. At last Dan and Harry were alone. They wrapped up in puffa jackets, took two canvas chairs and sat outside under the starlit sky with cups of coffee to warm them against the chill of the night. Dan lit a cigarette, eliciting a glance of disapproval from Harry.

'You don't seem entirely at ease with our lady expert,' Harry commented.

'Maybe I'm just put out that I haven't got you to myself. I was hoping we'd have some boys' time together,' Dan replied.

'We've just had two days travelling together and we'll have plenty of time to relive our youth. Angelica is very good at her job and has been vetted by every agency on earth,' Harry said firmly.

'Quite,' Dan said, frowning.

'Well, I'm heading to bed, my friend. See you in the morning.' Harry yawned and stood up.

'Give me a knock and I'll join you for breakfast,' Dan said.

'Good night.' Harry turned to walk into the building but then hesitated. 'Oh, by the way, I'll ask Angelica to look at your birth chart when we return to Damascus and see if she can decipher the words and the meaning.'

Dan sighed. He didn't want Angelica Duval anywhere near his birth chart. He leaned back and looked at the stars thoughtfully. They shone back at him, their mysteries hidden deep. Then he stood up to go back to his room. As he did so he glanced up and saw Angelica Duval studying him from her bedroom window. She hastily turned away but not before he'd noted the look of triumph in her eyes. For a brief moment he felt as though he was living in a John Le Carre novel – maybe *The Night Manager*, where Jonathan Pine, a former soldier, penetrates Roper's inner circle. He quickly headed to his bedroom and locked the door behind him.

CHAPTER TWENTY-FOUR

Syria

Early December 2010

The next morning the sun appeared again, lifting the spirits of the workers. When Harry and Dan arrived in the laboratory, they found Angelica poring over more documents and making notes. Occasionally, she would sigh or mutter over a particular series of words.

'What's new?' Dan asked.

'As Harry has already said, these documents are clearly the work of a very advanced people. The messages of day-to-day life could apply to our world today. Mankind starts a new society with an altruistic view of the world, then greed and ego take over and it's all lost again. That's a message we've seen for thousands of years but what's new are the documents of healing, ritual and destiny. We are close to finding the answers to our beginning and... to our end.' She turned towards Dan, her eyes narrowing as she studied him.

He was clearly intelligent, and also charming and talented. In very different circumstances they could have worked together. Since her marriage had broken up seven years ago she'd been on her own, her life dedicated to the interests of the Holy Trinity. Recently she had begun to feel lonely, an emptiness that could not be eradicated by hard work, which was her usual default setting. She hated to admit it, but there was an empty part of her which was not satisfied any more by power. She needed a friend and she preferred the company of men to women. Maybe when this was all over… She stole another glance at Dan before shaking herself back to reality.

Dan peered over Angelica's shoulder. His translating skills felt pretty rusty, but looking at the lines of script, he could soon feel his old knack returning as he made sense of the lines and curves.

'What language is this?' He pointed at another document that Angelica had placed to one side.

'Oh, that's not so interesting. It's in Old Hebrew and talks about the life of an obscure priest, who seemed to spend all his time locked in a tiny room chanting one word, but no one ever found out why.' She avoided his gaze.

Dan raised an eyebrow and remained silent. It was not written in Old Hebrew at all. He had recognized the script as Phoenician, similar to Old Hebrew but existing about one hundred years earlier. He studied the linear, abstract lines and wondered why Angelica was lying to him. She had clearly underestimated him. He was still rusty in some languages but Phoenician had been one of his specialities, although few people knew that as he had written his thesis on Sumerian.

'That sounds pretty boring. Are you accompanying Harry to Damascus?' Dan said evenly not betraying his knowledge.

'Yes. I want to spend some time with Mumtaz, find out his thoughts on these documents and also meet some experts from the antiquities department of the museum. Harry is going to introduce me.'

Harry walked back into the room. 'Angelica, would you mind going to talk to Lars Hansen, he's the Scandinavian expert on religious artefacts. He's found a chalice with some script on it and he wants to date it. You'll find his knowledge fascinating.' Harry smiled at her.

For a moment Angelica looked as if she was going to protest, but then she meekly put down her tools, removed her cotton gloves and disappeared to the anteroom to remove her white protective suit and hat.

Damn, that was a key document, she mused as she straightened her dress. Had she made a mistake lying to Dan? He might know it was Phoenician. She would be back as quickly as possible.

'She just lied to me. Said this was Old Hebrew when it's clearly Phoenician.' Dan turned to Harry as soon as Angelica had left the room.

'Old Hebrew and Phoenician are very similar, easy mistake to make, especially when you've been looking at documents for five hours without a break. She was up at four, you know, filing and dating all of this. Don't be so sensitive.' Harry clapped Dan on the back and left the room.

He sighed and bent further over the document. There was something… He scratched his head. This wasn't a boring document about some reclusive priest. This was a fragment of the central part of a document about The Book of Eternal Wisdom.

He started to read.

A Golden Book, imparting ancient wisdom. The Final Age will arrive amongst much global turmoil, wars, financial instability, a collapse of the old ways. But remember, what you perceive as frightening is an opportunity to change and achieve true fulfilment. Leave behind the false gods and embrace the new, for what is worse, dying clinging to the old ways or walking along an unfamiliar road leading to a new dawn? That is your individual decision. We can tell you that Dan Adams will feel the power when the Book is activated. Be patient, your time is near.

His name. The final confirmation. He looked more intently at the page. It had been torn but there was a co-ordinate: 40° 22'N 18° 10'E. He hastily scribbled it down.

'Just thought I'd come back and secure the documents.'

Dan jumped. Angelica had crept up behind him.

'That was quick,' he said, noticing that she was red in the face, with perspiration glistening on her forehead. She had obviously been running.

'Yes, it wasn't difficult. Now I'll just put this away.' She tried to take over from Dan.

'Don't worry, I'll do it.' Dan carefully picked up the fragment with a pair of tweezers and replaced it in a slim box. Then he placed the box in a special safe which had been designated to hold the key documents, and he locked it.

As he did so, Angelica gave him a strange look, before turning on her heel and marching out of the door. Dan frowned. Angelica Duval was unnerving but she was soon forgotten as Harry suddenly appeared in the doorway of the room, sweating profusely, his eyes wide with shock.

'Oh God, oh God! Terrible news... I can't believe it... why?' He was struggling for breath, gasping and clutching his chest as beads of perspiration ran down his forehead. He looked as if he was going to have a heart attack. Dan got up quickly and put his arm round his friend's shoulders.

'What the hell has happened? Calm down. Come, sit down and catch your breath.' Dan rushed into the bathroom and returned with a wet towel which he gently placed on Harry's forehead.

'Mumtaz... dead... he's been murdered... Oh God, how terrible... what a disaster... what a tragedy... such a good man... a dedicated and kind human being... his family...' Harry let out a sharp cry and sank back in the chair. Dan sat down on the sofa beside him.

'What? Professor Zinohed is dead? How? When?' Dan demanded, his own face ashen with shock. 'And what's happened to your precious documents?

Harry took a couple of deep breaths and started to talk

more calmly. 'One of Mumtaz's assistants has just arrived, having driven here all night, he wouldn't ring me in case the phone was being bugged. Last night Mumtaz Zinohed was murdered. He was found this morning with his throat cut and the knife left like a stake through his heart. The office has been ransacked. No idea if the documents are still there or not. Oh God, all is lost. What shall we do?'

Dan put his head in his hands. He felt his breath coming in short gasps. It was a disaster. But he had to stay strong for Harry.

Dan calmed down and took control. 'It's terrible, truly awful and unthinkable but we can't do anything for Mumtaz now. But we need to know if they were after the gold and precious jewels or the coins and documents. Who's in charge down there?'

'The authorities.' Harry mopped at his face distractedly.

'Right. We need to return to Damascus and find out what's going on. What are the police doing exactly?' Dan stood up and paced around the room. He felt better when he was on the move.

'They've called in the secret service and it's now all sealed off. We won't be able to get access,' Harry said.

'Don't you believe it! Get your faithful troupe together and we'll go in. There must be a way. Now let's finish getting these documents ready and get on the road, we don't have any time to lose.' Dan ran to his room, grabbed his bag and flung his clothes inside. Then he went to Harry's quarters and packed his bag for him.

Within an hour Dan and Harry were on the road back to Aleppo from where they would head to Damascus, on the main road from the north to the south. Angelica Duval had been left to deal with extracting the documents from the ceramic pots and preparing them for removal to Turkey, as the

Turkish border was only a couple of hours' drive away. With Harry in a state of shock there hadn't been a chance for Dan to express his further doubts about Angelica. They'd had no choice but to involve her. They hadn't time to do it all themselves. But Dan had ensured that the key documents were hidden in the car with him and Harry. It might be risky taking them to what now appeared to be enemy territory, but there was no alternative.

The journey was long and mostly silent. Harry lay back in the passenger seat looking pale and wiping his brow at regular intervals while Dan tried to negotiate the roads without getting them, and their precious cargo, wiped out by kamikaze drivers.

At last, six hours later, they reached the outskirts of Damascus. Dan drove straight to the Al Mamlouka Hotel. He'd phoned them en route and booked two rooms. The owner, May, was an old friend of Harry's and had been only too pleased to help. They would go round to Professor Zinohed's office under the cover of darkness, accompanied by the professor's two cousins who were, according to Harry, both very senior members of the Syrian secret services.

May met them at the great oak doors to the entrance of the hotel.

'Come, everything is ready for you. I have put you in our best rooms which occupy all of the top floor so you will be private.' She led them up the stone steps to the courtyard where two waiters appeared holding trays of steaming mint tea and savoury pastries.

An hour later two small stocky men arrived with a small battalion of aides. They were Professor Zinohed's cousins, accompanied by their underlings, who were milling around talking into mobile phones and chewing tobacco. Dan raised his eyebrows. This wasn't exactly Scotland Yard but it was the best they could do under the circumstances.

The small group set off down the small alleyways and passages that comprised the old part of Damascus. Dan recognized an area they had passed through only a couple of days previously. It was dark and the shadows seemed to flicker and waver against the stone walls, making it appear as if they were being followed. Secrets and lies seemed to whisper around the enclosed spaces and encompass them in a parallel universe, where murder and mayhem came visiting like malevolent guests at a wedding feast.

As soon as they drew near Professor Zinohed's office, two other men slipped out of the shadows and joined them and they all slowed to a walk. Mr Elwi, Mumtaz's eldest cousin, was at the head of the group and he approached the uniformed man who was standing by the entrance to the building. There was a quick exchange of words, and then Mr Elwi turned and waved them in. They all ducked under the red tape that had been placed round the building and walked through the door and along a corridor.

A few minutes later they walked into Professor Zinohed's tiny office. Dan looked around. There were signs of a struggle and pools of blood on the floor. The whole place smelt of death.

Harry glanced at Dan and then walked to the bookcase. 'You take the other side,' he said. Then he gently pulled out a book and pressed a button and the bookcase swung aside to reveal the safe. He handed a piece of paper to Dan on which he'd written a series of numbers. 'We need to punch them in simultaneously, so on the count of three. One... two... three.' Both Harry and Dan punched in the numbers and the safe swung open.

'Thank God.' Harry breathed a sigh of relief as he saw that nothing appeared to have been disturbed within the safe. Then he crouched down and grabbed a couple of long thin metal tubes from deep inside. 'Come, we have enough time to save the key documents.' Harry searched through the filing system and then located the documents and very carefully placed them in the metal tubes. Then he opened a drawer and found hundreds of coins. He sighed, looking desperate. 'How the hell do we know which are the mystical ones?'

Dan immediately dumped them all on the table and started to sort through them, searching for the markings. An hour later he'd located three and put them safely into a tiny purse. If the Holy Trinity had two and one was as yet unlocated, then where was their fourth one? Was it the one he had brought back from Chequers? If so, where was it?

'Be careful, my friend,' Harry said with tears in his eyes.

'If I'm the Master of Destiny then I must be invincible.' Dan tried to laugh.

'Not with the dark power in control.'

'Dark power or no dark power, I'm going to discover the truth, starting with Anna. I need to know if she is caught up with the Holy Trinity by chance or by design,' Dan said firmly.

Harry looked away. He did not have proof but he feared it was the latter.

'What's this?' Dan asked Harry, picking up a small, scrappy piece of paper that had been left inside the safe, and handed it to Harry. The writing was faint and spidery. Harry read what was written.

'*The Holy Trinity is to be feared. They are taking control of the key positions. They must be stopped. Absolute power corrupts absolutely. Dan must unlock the code and take over at the precise moment the Book of Eternal Wisdom becomes active again. He MUST be present. Imperative to know.*

'The rest is too faded to read, but it's Mumtaz's writing. He must have been trying to warn us.'

Dan looked at Harry. 'Stop them? How? They have woven their way into the heart of Western society. They count bishops, judges, scientists and MPs as their supporters. Even the PM supports them, thinks they're good for morale, that they're providing moral and religious leadership where there was a void. I wish someone would give us a clue as to how we can stop them.' Dan looked at Harry who seemed to have aged greatly in the last twenty-four hours. Dan put his hand on his friend's shoulder. He had to get him through this.

Harry stood deep in thought, still clutching the piece of paper. Then he looked up. 'We have to discredit them, of course. Be one step ahead, find the location of the Book of Eternal Wisdom and win the game. There are no short cuts. We have to prove our worth – and you, my friend are very worthy,' he said, looking more confident.

'Rest assured that I will fight to the death to make sure these people do not take over our world,' Dan said softly, his striking green eyes shining in the half-light. 'Come with me to London. It's too dangerous here.' But, even as he said it, Dan knew Harry would never leave his life's work behind.

Harry just shook his head, tears rolling down his cheeks. 'Please protect the documents, they are my life's work, but remember they are not more important than your life, nothing is more important than that.' Harry and Dan hugged each other then Dan stood back and smiled.

'I understand. Please be careful. Don't trust Angelica. She lied about the content of one of the key documents.' Dan gripped Harry by the shoulders.

'Dan, I've told you, she was jet-lagged and made a mistake, which is the first one she's made so far. She is trustworthy. Focus on keeping safe.'

Dan nodded. He'd deal with Angelica himself. Harry was on overload.

Dan made his way to the airport for the early-morning flight. Terror had once again set up camp in his soul, but there was also another feeling – conviction that all would be well.

Just as he was making his way to the departure lounge to board the plane, having shown his signed letters authorising the removal of the documents and been waved through customs, a small rotund man approached him. The tweed jacket and brown flannel trousers had been replaced with a tartan *thobe* and a white headdress.

Dan did a double take. 'Mr Perkins...What the hell?' He said shaken by the sudden appearance of the little man who he'd first seen in the Scottish Highlands.

'I presume you meant to pack this in your bags,' Mr Perkins said in his Scottish brogue, handing Dan a short metal tube.

'What is it?' Dan said as he took it, his hands shaking slightly. Please let there be no more weird shocks and strange visions, he thought.

'Your birth chart, of course, vital to unlocking your eternal myth.' Mr Perkins smiled. 'And here's your golden coin from Chequers as well.'

Dan took the coin. 'It's not actually my coin, and how did it disappear when I brought it here? And what is my eternal myth?' he demanded.

'Your eternal myth is given to you at the time of your birth, your destiny, your own unique journey handed to you as your soul travels through the heavens on its way to earth. Up to you to solve the puzzle and discover the blueprint. As for the golden coin, it is also part of your journey.' And with that Mr Perkins turned and left.

As the plane took off, Dan looked down at the city of Damascus and from somewhere deep within his being he felt peace envelop him, replacing his previous anxiety. He knew with inexplicable conviction that he no longer had to fear death. When it came it would not be the destruction of his body, soul and mind but just the dissolution of its parts. He smiled and closed his eyes. No one could destroy his essence. His will. His soul. His being.

CHAPTER TWENTY-FIVE

Istanbul, Turkey

Early December 2010

In her palace suite at the Kempinski Hotel in Istanbul, Angelica Duval sat in a trance, the pupils of her eyes dilated in wonder. In her hands she held a small wooden ball. It had intricate carvings all over it, some of which were inlaid with tiny precious stones – diamonds, rubies, sapphires and emeralds. She turned it round, looking at the small figures with their linked hands and the mysterious symbols that were interspersed between the figures. She felt giddy with anticipation. Its value wasn't contained in the precious stones, its value was immeasurable and its power infinite. For in her hands she held the Board of Destiny.

Just as Harry had said, it had been hidden in the far right corner of the dig. She had driven out there after Harry and Dan had left for Damascus and spent the afternoon digging. With both of them gone no one dared challenge her – she was one of only three people given the highest clearance. And she knew time was against her, had felt Dan's antagonism and mistrust. She had to be careful, she didn't want to risk being removed from the dig.

After two hours, just when she had been on the point of giving up, she'd felt something hard beneath the ground. She had got down on her hands and knees and pushed the earth out of the way. Eventually she had uncovered what looked like a copper box, turned green with age. Of course it had been locked so she had put it into her jeep along with the other documents that had been placed in her safe keeping and headed for the Turkish border.

Once in Istanbul she'd found a master locksmith, but even he'd had problems unlocking it. A day it had taken him. She hadn't let it out of her sight. Unlocking it was easy but then click – it would be locked again in an instant, so quickly that she didn't have time to jam it open. The call to prayer had begun and the locksmith had looked at her regretfully and said he must go. She'd pleaded with him to give it one more go and he had, and this time it had remained unlocked for an instant longer – time for her to pull it open. There before her had been a small wooden ball, its intricate carvings, obviously the work of supremely gifted craftsmen.

Five minutes later she had walked out of the workshop, leaving the locksmith dying, a pool of blood forming like a halo around his head.

Now it was hers. One half of the holy grail which would unlock the mysteries of human existence.

She carefully replaced it in the box, its lock now permanently disabled, and walked over to the window. Pulling her silk wrap tighter round her body, she leaned forward and felt the cool of the windowpane on her forehead. She stared out at the Bosphorous. She hadn't yet called Oliver McManus or any other members of the inner circle. She wanted to savour this time alone with the object of her desires. She could hardly contain her excitement. Total victory for her and The Holy Trinity was just a matter of time.

Now all she needed was the Book of Eternal Wisdom and only Dan Adams could lead her to that. Ah yes, Dan Adams. She'd been following his life for a long time. She knew material gain and personal power were not important to him. And the short time they'd spent together had confirmed her view of him as a man of morals. She slowly shook her head. He'd made her feel second-rate – not for the first time in her life – and she didn't like the feeling. She rarely questioned her right to rule or play God and hated to be confronted with people who made her feel otherwise. She breathed deeply. They were entering the most crucial part of the plan. She had to remain calm.

CHAPTER TWENTY-SIX

London and Sussex

December 2010

Dan breathed a huge sigh of relief as he walked back into his flat in Wimbledon and felt the comforting presence of the familiar. Mr Big was still at the kennels so silence greeted his entry. He flicked on the central heating and turned up the thermostat. The flat was freezing.

Then he headed to the kitchen, made a cup of coffee, lit a cigarette and pondered the question of what to do about the precious documents. For the time being they'd have to go in the loft – along with the others – and he'd have to wait until Harry gave him further instructions. Dan had called Harry on his way home from the airport but the line had been terrible, and they'd been cut off.

Dan had just finished placing the metal tubes in the loft and was heading to his study to deal with his post when the outer doorbell buzzed.

He looked on the video screen – it was Anna.

He pressed the button to open the door.

'Hi, couldn't wait until tonight so thought I'd come over and see how you and Harry got on,' she said as she wrapped her arms round him and hugged him.

He hugged her back and then held her at arm's length, studying her face, searching for any hidden expression. He had to confront her, find out if she was working with the Holy Trinity to get access to the secrets of the dig.

'What's wrong?' she asked, meeting his gaze.

'Let's have a coffee,' he said, avoiding her question.

'Yes please. I brought cake – lemon drizzle, your favourite, and homemade.' She put a cake tin on the side table. Dan smiled. In spite of her high-flying ambitions, she'd always been an excellent cook. But today he was going to keep a cool head.

He made the coffee, grabbed a couple of plates and she put a large slice of cake on each one. Then they headed to the sitting room. He took a deep breath. Might as well get it over and done with.

'Anna, your friends at the Holy Trinity are not what they seem,' he started. Then he explained everything that had happened, ending with the murder of Professor Zinohed.

When he finished Anna was silent, her face white but her expression set. 'But it doesn't make any sense, they aren't milking us all for money, they are improving our lives. How can it be? Oliver cannot know of this… this renegade faction who are working against the common good.' She spat out these last words.

Dan sighed. 'Oliver is the central player in all of this.'

'No, Dan, it's all conjecture. You haven't given me facts, just your own thoughts and feelings,' she said stubbornly.

'What about the emblem of the white stag in Harry's private office?' Dan snapped. 'And what about the gold coin, or two, they seem to have nicked?'

'Oh, for heaven's sake, Dan, it's hardly surprising that the Holy Trinity not only know about the dig but are actually involved in it. Everyone in academia knows about it even though gaining access is very difficult. It's the centre of very important discoveries of treasure and mysterious documents. One of the archaeologists probably gave the Holy Trinity the coin privately to see if they could assess its secrets using their esoteric knowledge.'

'Then why not declare their presence at the dig? Harry has no idea which of his trusted advisers are members. And who murdered Professor Zinohed?' Dan challenged.

'Certainly not the Holy Trinity, they are *not* murderers. How dare you!' Anna shouted, her eyes glistening with tears.

'You're just the same as ever!' Dan shouted back. 'When we were at university, you'd never admit you could be taken in by people. You always had to be perfect.'

'And you're as naïve and gullible as ever, always believing your friends. How do you even know Harry is a good guy? Just because he's your friend doesn't mean he's on the right side.' And with that she gathered her coat and stormed out, slamming the door behind her.

Dan leaned back on the sofa, placed his hands behind his head and looked at the ceiling. Another grand screw-up, and he was no nearer to the truth. He had no idea whether Anna was covering up her knowledge or was unaware of the dark side of this organization.

Wearily, he stood up and stretched his aching muscles. Another problem to sort out and one he was going to have to tackle head on without letting his emotions take over. Thank God he hadn't told Anna that some of the precious documents were hidden in his loft. He lit another cigarette and headed back to the kitchen to make yet another cup of coffee, this time laced with a good slug of Baileys.

Later that day with Mr Big asleep at his feet, twitching in his doggy dreams, Dan started to open his post and check his emails, the usual junk mail, taxi service cards and discount leaflets from the local pizza house, along with the ever present bills, but at the bottom of the pile was a postcard from Jenny: 'Juliet and I are in Spain. Remembered you asked me about travelling with dogs. Pet passport brilliant, you should take Mr Big on holiday. Kind regards, Jenny.' Not exactly affectionate but maybe it indicated a thaw in her disdain for him. He wondered if Juliet the dog was enjoying the delights of Spain as well.

Oh good, an email from Brian's office signing off on the educational Charter he'd created and sent to him for comment. Douglas would be pleased.

Underneath the postcard was an official-looking embossed cream envelope. On the back was printed the name of a company of attorneys based in Boston, USA, his town of birth. Dan studied it for a few minutes before opening it.

Dear Mr Adams,

I am Edward Adams' attorney acting on his behalf in sorting out his estate.

His estate? He'd been dead over twenty years! The USA must be in a bad state if it took in excess of twenty years to contact a member of the deceased's family, Dan thought, irritated.

As you are your father's only beneficiary in his last will and testament, I would appreciate it if you could contact me at my office so we can discuss this matter further. I apologize for the delay in contacting you but can assure you we worked at best possible speed to locate you after Mr Adams' death in June of this year.

What the fuck? Dan pushed away his half-eaten piece of cake. There must be some mistake.

He immediately called the American attorney, who went through various security questions to verify his identity and even then was as cagey as hell, insisting Dan would have to come and see him in Boston.

'I will but it's not easy for me to take time off at such short notice, I have commitments. Can't you just clear this up on the phone and tell me you've got the wrong person? This man who died in June is not my father. He can't be, he died twenty-four years ago.' Dan rubbed his throbbing forehead with his index fingers.

'It is, of course, always possible a mistake has been made, sir, but highly unlikely. Due to the nature of this case and the fact our senior partner was a close friend of the man in question, and executor of the will, we have carried out unusually expensive and detailed traces to locate you.'

'Sorry if I'm sounding ungrateful, life's been very complicated in the last few months. Could I ring you back?' Dan asked.

'Yes, of course, take your time, there's no rush,' the man said calmly.

Dan replaced the phone, stood up and looked out of his study window towards the back gate where the underground car park was situated. From there he looked towards the common. The trees were bare, their naked branches lightly covered in snow, preparing to withstand what was already a harsh winter. Beyond that, people were bustling about, their faces hidden from the biting cold which had arrived again last night on the north wind.

There was only one person who could clear this up. His mother. He hadn't spoken to her for ages. They'd had a big falling-out a few years ago when she'd told him two days before Christmas that 'the family', meaning her husband's kids, had decided to gather in Ireland at the last minute, and it was only going to be his stepfather's family. It had been a rejection too far.

He glanced at his watch. It was nearly five o'clock. He could make it down to Sussex in time for supper, not that he expected food, but it was likely she and her elderly husband would be at home. He decided to surprise her rather than give her any warning.

Bundling Mr Big into his car, he headed towards the A23. As he drove through the worsening weather, trying to avoid the black ice on the roads, he attempted to think of all possible explanations. Maybe his father had only died a few months ago, but someone had convinced his mother he had died twenty-four years ago. Perhaps it was what his father had wanted, a complete break from the woman who had caused him pain and a chance for his son to adjust to a new life without being pulled in different directions – the unhappy product of different cultures.

As he drove out of the London suburbs and the high density of housing gave way to open countryside, he talked himself back into the land of the rational. After all, there had to be some logical explanation for this latest shock.

After nearly two hours, in pitch darkness, he turned off the main road and made his way towards his mother's house, which was near Lewes. After ten miles of winding country lanes, he arrived at a T-junction, turned right, headed up an even narrower country lane and then swung left through a pair of gateposts with large stone lions regally guarding the entrance.

He followed the long, lit, tree-lined driveway and finally arrived at the enormous stone fountain in front of the seventeenth century Grade I listed house. In spite of his apprehension he smiled. It was all very *Brideshead Revisited*. He half expected Sebastian Flyte to come tripping down the steps to greet him. His aristocratic stepfather had four children, each one more obnoxious than the last. The eldest, Albert, now sixty-six years old, lived in Ireland, having inherited his own mother's 400-acre farm, which he'd converted to an organic goldmine. The second child, Penelope, had married a rich Bolivian playboy, and lived a life of constant movement travelling between Paris, Monaco, New York and Bolivia. Ruth, a sixty-year-old hippy, lived on a commune somewhere in Norway, and the baby of the family, Leopold, who must be about fifty, led a dissolute life in the south of France.

Dan glanced at the bare rose bushes now slumbering in the

flower beds, took a deep breath and rang the bell. It echoed around the house and suddenly Dan felt like a young schoolboy again, returning to this forbidding house for the holidays, forced to live by his mother's archaic rules and her fear of upsetting her wealthy but emotionally distant husband. The young Dan had sort of understood that his mother couldn't afford to lose another source of material comfort, but it had been a hard, cold, cheerless existence for him. Silence greeted the bell, and his heart dropped as he wondered if his mother was out.

Then he heard footsteps and the door was opened not by his mother but by a woman dressed in a long flowing skirt and a dirty white T-shirt, her long hair pulled back from her face.

'Ruth?' Dan asked.

'Dan!' She flung her arms round him and Dan caught the slight whiff of body odour. He drew back, unused to displays of affection from any member of his stepfamily.

'Come in, Dad's really ill, the doctor's with him, looks like it might be pneumonia. Your mother's upstairs with him. How are you? You look great, it's been ages,' she gabbled away.

Oh God, did this mean the rest of the odious bunch were all here? He stepped inside the house, noticing the strong smell of wood polish and the faint but distinctive smell of old age.

'The clan's arriving later tonight,' Ruth said, answering his silent question.

His mother appeared on the stairs, looking pale and anxious.

'Good grief, Dan, what on earth are...?' Primrose visibly pulled herself together. Life had been tough these last few years and she realized she missed her only child. Her husband's antipathy towards him had always ruled her life. 'How did you know?' she asked.

'Know what?' Dan asked, noticing with some shock how

much his mother had aged since he'd seen her. She was only sixty-two, twenty-five years younger than her husband, but her face was heavily lined and her hair almost completely white. She looked thin and uncared for. In spite of his own distress he felt sorrow that the once vibrant woman had been lost.

'How did you know that Tobias is seriously unwell? It looks like he'll have to be admitted to hospital. He's not expected to...' Primrose turned away, tears filling her eyes.

Dan thought quickly. He should really just get in the car and drive back to London and address this another time, but damn it, he had to know the truth.

'I'm sorry, Mother, I didn't realize Tobias was unwell, but I need a few minutes of your time to resolve something important,' Dan said calmly.

'That's not possible. We can give you a light supper but I'll have to accompany Tobias to hospital.'

'It will only take five minutes. Please.' Dan hated begging, but he needed her to tell him the truth.

'Very well. Ruth, would you mind bringing me a glass of water and a paracetamol? I'm getting one of my headaches.' She led the way into the dining room where she sat down at the head of the table. 'Well, what is it that's so important? Are you OK?' She looked momentarily worried.

'All fine. This is... well, it's difficult...' He just had to spit it out. 'I had a letter from an attorney in Boston, he said Dad died in June... this year. I know that's ridiculous, he died twenty four years ago, but why would they contact me now?'

His mother looked away and a brief look of guilt crept over her once handsome face. Dan gasped. Her expression said it all.

'But why?' he shouted, as Ruth came running in holding his mother's glass of water and a packet of paracetamol.

'What's going on? The shouting will distress Dad.' She shot Dan a filthy look.

'I'm sorry, please leave us, I won't raise my voice again,' Dan said, trying to maintain control. Noticing Dan's shocked expression, Ruth left them to it.

Primrose stood up and walked over to the French windows and gazed out at the pitch-black garden.

'You have to understand, it was very complicated. I'd just met Tobias when you were a teenager and your father was causing problems, which was irritating Tobias.' Primrose bit her bottom lip.

'Who didn't want me anyway!' Dan hissed.

'That's not true. Tobias took care of your problems when you were struggling with the divorce, and he didn't want your father making matters worse. It was affecting things between us.' She ran her hands shakily through her hair.

'So, you mean to tell me that you pretended my father had died just because it was threatening your cushy lifestyle. That's all you've ever cared about, your own welfare. You found your pot of gold when you met poor, lonely widower Tobias, so you sacrificed my love and need for my father on the altar of your own selfish desires.' Dan was pale and shaking. 'I remember the day you told me Dad had died. You managed to look upset and concerned. What an act! How could you?' he hissed at her.

'There are a lot of reasons we did it. Your father was a very complex person, he had many secrets and an odd lifestyle. He wasn't a good influence. I intended to tell you the truth that he was still alive when you finished university, but by then you were building your own life, had met Anna, were doing well. I didn't want to unsettle you.' Primrose turned to her son and walked towards him. She placed her hand on Dan's shoulder, her eyes pleading forgiveness, but he shrugged it off.

'It was for the best,' she said firmly.

'You are an absolute bitch,' he spat out, his face contorted with anger.

'Whatever you say, you'll always be my son and I hope one day you'll understand it really was the only decision I could have made.' She tried to put her hand on his but he snatched it away. She turned away to hide her tears. It had to be this way. There had been no other choice.

'I never want to see you again.'

And, with that, Dan stormed out of the house, climbed in his car and roared off down the drive with Mr Big staring out of the window in the back seat.

Watching him go, tears ran down Primrose's face. There was one secret she'd promised never to reveal and, whatever it cost, it was a secret that would go to the grave with her. She wiped her face with her white lace handkerchief, blew her nose, then walked back up the stairs to her sick husband.

As he was speeding down the driveway, Dan's mobile phone rang. He ignored it and drove unseeingly along the country lane, flooring the accelerator. After sliding on some ice and narrowly missing a delivery van, he pulled over, buried his head in his hands, burst into tears and then banged his hands hard on the steering wheel.

He felt the dark fingers of betrayal wrap tightly round his heart. His mother had known all this time that his beloved father was alive, and his beloved father had chosen, *chosen*, not to get in touch not even when he was an adult. All the empty years when his father could have been involved in his life, offered much needed advice, shared good times with him. Why? What had happened to make his father, who had been so loving when he'd been a child, turn his back on his only son? Then another thought came into his head. Maybe his father had remarried and had another family? No, the attorney had said that he was the only heir to his estate.

Had Edward Adams remained in Boston for the rest of his

life? Or had he wandered about from one place to the next, alcohol his only companion and happiness just an illusion? Dan's mind reeled with unanswered questions. He thought back to his recent visions of his father as a loving, caring man. He'd catch the first flight he could to Boston.

When he neared London he stopped at a service station to fill up with petrol and picked up an *Evening Standard*. He flipped through it in the queue to pay and gasped. It was on page five. Education Minister dumps Board of Educational Progress and turns the education system upside down.

He read on, skipping over the paragraphs, until he found a quote from Douglas which made his blood run cold: 'While I am committed to a modern and innovative education programme, I fully support my education minister in his decision to dissolve the Board of Educational Progress. It is clear we need to make additional cuts in the budget. I am sure education will flourish in Brian's hands. I confirm that the money saved from dissolving this organization and the immediate cancellation of the considerable fees involved will be put into the government education trust, and go towards practical help for disadvantaged children.'

For the third time that day, Dan felt betrayed. Fuck Douglas. Like most politicians, he'd left his integrity at the ballot box. Whatever it took to retain the power of his office he'd do it; he'd sacrificed friendship and loyalty without a second thought. What had happened to his need to keep Brian on a tight leash?

With the board appointment gone he didn't have any income to pay the mortgage. However, he did have his freedom. He would go back to teaching, once he returned from Boston. But first he would spend the last bit of his savings discovering the truth about his father.

His phone rang again. It was Douglas.

'I need to talk to you about the board, so sorry I couldn't ring you before, just been on the phone to Obama for two hours. Fairly hellish, as you can imagine,' Douglas said in his usual brisk manner.

'Well, it's too fucking late. I've just read all about it in The Evening Standard. Couldn't you control Brian? Do I have to be regularly humiliated in the media?' Dan said angrily.

'Calm down. I'll get the spin doctors to quieten the media. Come to Chequers in a few weeks, we'll find something else for you to do. If I don't, Anna will be on my case again,' Douglas said, trying to lighten the mood.

'I don't need your charity. Push off and stop interfering in my life,' Dan snapped and ended the call. Then he switched off the phone and spent the rest of the drive home chain-smoking with memories of his father drifting in and out of his mind.

CHAPTER TWENTY-SEVEN

London Suburbs

December 2010

Anna hurried out of the lab building, her heart beating fast, pale with shock. The icy wind numbed her facial muscles, and turned her hands blue with cold. She tried to pull her scarf up to cover her face but she couldn't find it. Damn, she must have dropped it.

Oh God, Dan had been right and she'd helped his enemies plan his death. She was about to be instrumental in the demise of her soulmate. Kind, wonderful, loving and gifted Dan. The man whose heart she'd so carelessly chucked away once before and who was now facing certain destruction. Why had she dismissed his concerns?

She was a bone-headed idiot. A poor excuse for a human being, more concerned with outward signs of success than the hidden inner ones, which brought that wonderful elusive feeling of contentment. She had to get to him before it was too late. She had to warn him. She had to reach him before they did. If she didn't then her life would be pointless.

It was early on Sunday morning and she'd gone into the lab. Some results from a previous autopsy were puzzling her and she wanted absolute peace and quiet to think. They weren't conforming to past patterns. That was odd in itself as the tests had been exactly the same as those done previously. Even the standard controls were the same. So why the difference?

She'd arrived about ten and no one had been around. Well, with thick snow and ice blanketing most of the country it wasn't surprising. She'd had the place to herself – or so she'd thought. However, walking past Oliver's office, she'd noticed his light on and two shadows, their backs towards her, outlined through the opaque glass. Usually she would have walked on, returned later when he'd been on his own to discuss their work. But something made her hesitate. Made her stop and eavesdrop. She'd listened hidden by the side of the door.

'We cannot risk the reputation of the Holy Trinity. We have the support of many of the world's leaders and we have our people in position ready to take over. Do not take risks,' Oliver was saying.

'We aren't taking risks but we need to move this up a level. We have to be certain we snatch power at the time of activation of the Book of Eternal Wisdom. That means we have to keep pressure on Dan,' a woman replied.

Anna had felt a cold shiver of apprehension. Dan. Why were they discussing him? Oliver had talked about him sometimes when they'd exchanged views on love and romance. Oliver McManus had just gone through a nasty divorce but he'd seemed thrilled that she'd hooked up with Dan again and keen to know all about him.

'We've found the Board of Destiny, we're in control but we can't push him too far too quickly. We can't throw it all away at this stage,' Oliver said.

'*I* found the Board of Destiny and *I* am in control, you'd do well to remember that, Oliver.' The woman had a smooth, very lightly accented voice.

'We cannot afford mistakes, not at this juncture. We have the code to unlock the secrets, and once we have the power of the Book of Eternal Wisdom, that power cannot be broken again. Then you can have your revenge, though God knows why you need to pursue that line when you'll have all the power you could possibly desire. Adams could be useful in recruiting more people to our cause,' Oliver said.

'Once we have the power he will be of no more use to us. He will be eliminated, as agreed. Don't go soft on me now,' she snapped.

'But he's —'

'No buts, Oliver. End of discussion.'

Anna had turned and fled the building. The car park was just ahead. As she reached into her pocket for her car keys, she lost her footing on a patch of ice and the world went spinning.

'Poking your nose into other people's business is not good for your health. The lady boss hates interference,' a male voice said behind her.

Anna tried to sit up, her head sore from bumping it on the ground. A very short stocky man, of indeterminate age, with crewcut light-brown hair was standing over her. 'I demand to know what's going on,' she blurted out without thinking, her mind confused by the knock to her head.

'That's not up to me, but security is, and the boss is on her way,' the man said.

Anna was trying to get to her feet when a woman with long chestnut-coloured hair strode up to them. She looked at Anna coldly. 'So you want to know the truth do you? I'll give you a short summary. Dan Adams is at present the key to our power and glory. He is aligned to the Book of Eternal Wisdom, not that you know what that is, but as well as infusing wisdom on its leader, it offers the opportunity for unimaginable power, wealth and immortality. You can't begin to imagine. Immortality! And you most definitely are not going to get in our way,' she said, as Anna fought to remain conscious.

Without a word the woman handed something to the man and walked away. The man smiled, raised his arm and jabbed a syringe into Anna's neck. She collapsed back, twitching slightly before becoming totally inert. Her breathing became ragged then stopped. The man looked at his watch. Five minutes passed then Anna emitted an almost imperceptible groan as her soul departed from her body. She was lost for ever to this world.

CHAPTER TWENTY-EIGHT

Boston, USA

December 2010

Dan walked briskly down Newbury Street, past the smart designer boutiques and the bookstores and on towards his destination, Beacon Hill.

He was finally back in the land of his birth, and it felt glorious. He lifted his face up towards the sky and sniffed the air – the same air that had filled his lungs for the first time nearly forty years ago in a small maternity hospital just a few miles from where he was now.

He'd spoken to Harry before he left London. It had been brief, Harry had sounded distracted and tense, but he'd asked Dan to contact some people in Boston, experts on deciphering ancient documents.

'At Harvard, there is a group of world experts on the Pharaonic Era, the Mycenean Era and the development of Mesopotamia. Please take the documents you have and leave them with them. Stay in the Old Bostonian Hotel in Back Bay. I hope to be able to join you soon,' he'd said enigmatically before adding that Angelica had stored all her documents safely and was continuing to make important discoveries while translating them. Dan had been about to enquire where she was and to voice his doubts again when Harry had abruptly said that he had to go to an urgent appointment and ended the call. Dan hadn't even had time to tell him the reason he was going to Boston.

Dan sensed his father's presence at every corner, felt the strong grip of his hand as they had crossed the road to walk into Boston Common. Part of him felt happy at the memories but he was still very hurt that his father hadn't contacted him.

Boston was a compact city, easy to move around in and also enticing – academia, culture and sport all wrapped up in one package. He reached Beacon Street, glanced at the Ritz-Carlton and paused. His mother had insisted this was the only place she would take tea with her friends. He could recall his father patiently putting quarters into a china piggybank, and when he'd asked what he was saving for, he'd replied drily, 'This is your mother's Boston Tea Party fund.'

Dan was on his way to meet Geoffrey S. Lowell, his father's legal representative and he was, unusually, meeting him at his house not at his office. The documents were safely stashed in the suitcase he had with him. Safest place for them was with his father's lawyer until he could contact Harry's Harvard group of experts.

'And this is good old Boston. The home of the bean and the cod. Where the Lowells talk to the Cabots and the Cabots talk only to God.' He tried to remember the famous rhyme as he strode through the moneyed and stylish neighbourhood of Beacon Hill, in which elegance and good manners were praised above nearly everything else.

He arrived outside 5 Katherine Millicent Avenue slightly out of breath. He stopped for a few seconds and then pressed the bell. He closed his eyes, feeling anticipation course through his veins. He was about to uncover the secrets of his past. He hoped they wouldn't disappoint.

An elderly man of about eighty opened the door.

'Mr Lowell? I'm Dan Adams.' Dan smiled and held out his hand.

'Welcome.' The old man smiled in return and invited him in.

Dan stepped into the elegant house and followed Mr Lowell into a small reception room at the rear of the house. The old gentleman was immaculately dressed in a formal white shirt, with a patterned silk cravat, dark brown cashmere waistcoat, and tailored brown twill trousers. His dark brown shoes were highly polished.

'Thank you for coming to see me. May I offer you a cup of coffee or tea?' Mr Lowell asked.

'I'd love a cup of coffee, please.'

Mr Lowell nodded and rang a small bell. A grey-haired woman appeared dressed in a blue wool dress, over which she wore a white apron. She had a white lace cap on her head. It all seemed rather surreal. Dan felt as if he'd dropped into a different century again.

'My wife, Margaret, always insisted on running the house on a formal basis. She was a Cabot, from one of Boston's oldest families, and as such lived by a very rigid set of rules,' Mr Lowell explained.

Dan wondered briefly if she spoke only to God.

'I know the letter we sent you must have been a great surprise to you. Your father was my dearest friend for the last thirty years of his life, so I knew he had not had any contact with you for many years after his ex-wife...' He paused. 'Well, after his ex-wife decided a complete break was necessary.'

Dan wondered how his poverty-stricken father had managed to have such an influential best friend.

'Your father was an unusual man,' Mr Lowell went on. 'When your mother set her new husband's lawyers on him to stop him having contact with you, he decided to accept it, as a long drawn-out court case would have been distressing for you. He knew that it was his destiny and yours that you would be parted. He also had to accept the lies about him being an alcoholic. It was all a terrible sacrifice for him.' Mr Lowell looked down briefly.

'It was a terrible sacrifice for me, Mr Lowell. Why didn't he try and contact me when I came of age?

Mr Lowell shifted in his seat. 'He put his own wishes aside for you which hurt him greatly as he had a great love for you. However, it was made clear that contact with you would be detrimental to your equilibrium. He was also given this.' Mr Lowell produced two sheets of paper and handed them to Dan.

Dan recognized them at once. It was a short essay he'd written on his summer holiday, the first holiday in England, and it had been full of his anger at his father. He buried his head in his hands and fought to compose himself as waves of despair flowed over him. 'But I was a child. I adored my father. I was only nine when my mother dragged me back to England. I found myself in a cold, harsh climate in a school run by archaic rules and suddenly without my father and his wondrous tales of mystery and fantasy. I was angry he wasn't there but I never stopped loving him,' Dan said.

'And it is those wondrous tales that have brought us together today. Your father has a rich heritage, Dan, richer than you can imagine. But I must let him tell you his story from beyond the grave.' Mr Lowell picked up a remote control and pressed a button.

White wavy lines appeared on the TV screen and then a title that said simply 'My Life'.

After a few seconds Dan's father's face appeared on the screen like a ghost from the past. He was old, but his eyes were still bright and inquisitive and his wide, trusting smile lit up the screen.

'My dearest Dan, finally we are communicating even though I have departed from this world. There are many things

I want to say to you, which I didn't have the chance to say during my life, but what is life but a brief interlude in the eternal glory of the universal kingdom?' The voice was clear and strong.

'Life is rarely how we imagine it to be, but that is the power of fate, so I say to you, do not be alarmed by the twists and turns of your life. It is part of your eternal myth. Everyone has an eternal myth. It is the conundrum that was imprinted in your soul at the time of your birth. To realise your personal destiny you need to solve it. By fulfilling yourself, you will help to fulfil the world.'

Dan smiled at the screen, remembering the words of Scottish Mr Perkins, as he felt his father return to life.

'I can prepare you to embrace the journey to find your eternal myth but I cannot tell you what it is, my son, for it is your personal journey. What I can do is tell you about my eternal myth and the legacy I have left you to help you discover yours.

'Where shall we begin? Do you remember the stories I used to tell you? The star people and how they came to earth to help us? Well, they weren't stories but powerful messages from the Universal Power. But first, let's go right back to the beginning when the earth was starting its journey to be the host of intelligent life. The Universal Power wanted to see if this intelligent life could, with guidance, fulfil its destiny and by fulfilling its own destiny help to fulfil the destiny of the universe. It was a kind of living laboratory, and into this living laboratory came the Masters of Destiny, the men who would guide man. Lord Melchizedek was the original Master, the Teacher of Righteousness, the eternal Universal Power for good and benevolence in the world. The Master from whom all Masters such as Enoch, John the Baptist and Jesus would descend from their sacred home planet, to teach us their wisdom and guide us in their ways. Some Masters lived high-profile lives and led the people by their example, but some led quiet, uneventful lives, protecting the secrets for later generations to bring out into the open. But of course things rarely go to plan, especially when you give man free will, that most double-edged sword, which has often brought greed, envy and self-absorption to the fore.

'At various times in the history of the world, the Masters have been actively trying to guide the people back on to the right path, and sometimes it has worked, as seen by our magnificent achievements in the arts, science and philosophy, but often at the height of achievement man's dark side has appeared again, and he has destroyed everything.

'But the Masters have persisted in the quest for success. They are chosen long before birth. I was one, a silent, quiet keeper of the secrets. My life was uneventful. I made many mistakes, mistakes which I hope will not affect the desired outcome. But my greatest achievement was you, my son. I understand you are destined to be the last remaining Master of Destiny of this era, there are no others at this present time on this planet. Your destiny is yours to find, and you can reject your calling or you can embrace it. You have the potential to be one of the great Masters, but there is also the danger of failure and then...' a look of pain passed over Edward Adams' face,' ... well, then all will be lost as the Universal Power will find another way of guiding the universe.

'Geoffrey has a letter for you and some documents. This will confirm the location of the Book of Eternal Wisdom. You will know by now that the Book of Eternal Wisdom is the ancient mystical book that holds the secrets of life, which change according to man's free will. The real challenge is to reach down and discover the blueprint of life, which the Universal Power imprinted in it at the beginning of time. If you can understand this then you will understand man's true destiny and how to avoid the mistakes of the past. The Board of Destiny will also appear, to guide you to the meaning of the Book of Eternal Wisdom through the wisdom of the planets and the stars. The Book of Eternal Wisdom only activates at certain times in the history of man; it didn't during my time, but it will during yours.

'Harry's dig is unearthing the ancient secrets. Keep them safe and share them only with the chosen experts, who will be guided to you. Harry is your truest friend, and you are his. Treasure this bond; you will achieve great things together.

'Please don't be alarmed by this, for you have been given the gifts of character to deal with the challenges. You will slowly discover the potential of your gifts in your birth chart. Now...' his father paused and his face changed and he looked sad, 'we have been apart for so many years, years in which you weren't even aware that I was still alive, and for that I'm truly sorry. I want you to know I loved you very much, dear son, and I have followed your life from afar. I have celebrated your successes, and I have mourned your hardships. I know my death will be hard for you, especially as it will bring with it the shock that I've been alive all these years and did not get in contact with you. It's easy for me to say but do not dwell on my absence in your life, know that my love for you was the most important thing in my life, but we could not meet. Do not seek to blame your mother, she acted in a way she considered correct, but it was my pain and part of your life's lessons that we could not be together. Accept it and know that we have an everlasting bond that will never be broken. I know you will have other traumas to live through when I'm gone, but you have courage and integrity and compassion in your soul, and those three gifts will give you the strength to overcome what life throws at you. And although I am no longer on the earth plane, I will never be far away from you, my son. Life ends but love never does.' Edward's smile filled the screen.

Then the picture faded and the screen returned to its wavy white lines.

Dan sat in silence digesting his father's words. A myriad of emotions was pouring through his soul. Sadness, regret, guilt, pride, love, wonder, along with the sharp pain of loss. Finally, he stood up. 'Do you mind if I get some fresh air?' he asked Mr Lowell, who smiled wordlessly and opened the French windows that led to his garden. He watched as Dan walked down the garden path and hoped loneliness wouldn't be his destiny as it had been Edward's.

Dan walked amongst the trees, their bare branches waving in the wind. He reached up and touched them as he contemplated his future and allowed his mind to go back to his father's mystical stories.

'Help me, Dad,' he said, softly, as he looked up at the cold, clear blue sky. He strode quietly to the bottom of the garden and stood in silent contemplation. He wished he had the courage to trust and totally embrace this unknown destiny. Then he heard a soft voice whisper to him.

'Remember this, dear Dan. It's much better to be a could-be if you cannot be an are; because a could-be is a maybe who is reaching for a star. And believe me when I say, it is much better to be a has-been than a might-have-been, as a might-have-been has never been, but a has-been was once an are. You are going to be an are, no doubt about that.'

Milton Berle's saying always made Dan smile. The voice faded and he turned and walked back to the house. 'Where is my father buried?' he asked Mr Lowell.

'He requested that he be cremated and his ashes given to you so you could decide where his last resting place should be.

I have them in my safe, along with all the paperwork. I'm quite happy to keep them until you are ready to make a decision,' Mr Lowell replied.

Dan nodded.

'Here is the letter and also the documents your father left you.' Mr Lowell handed Dan a large white envelope. 'And this is also for you.' Mr Lowell indicated a brown cardboard box that was sitting under the window. 'It contains his possessions, he wanted you to have them. Please feel free to read the letter and look at his possessions in the privacy of your hotel room and call me with any questions. I am here any time you need me.' He handed Dan a card with his private phone numbers on it.

'Would you look after this for me please? It contains some important documents,' Dan said without further explanation indicating his suitcase.

Mr Lowell nodded, smiled and took the case.

'Thank you.' Dan took the envelope, the DVD and the cardboard box and left the house. He felt dazed, totally disconnected from reality, not sure where to go or what to do.

A light rain had started to fall. Dan placed his raincoat carefully over the box to keep its contents dry, then he set off down the road, deep in thought.

As he watched Dan walk down the street, Geoffrey Lovell sighed. There was one last secret that Edward had made him promise would never be revealed. If it became known it could destroy everything.

CHAPTER TWENTY-NINE

Boston, USA

December 2010

When Dan arrived back at the hotel, the receptionist handed him a message: 'I'm on my way, arrive tomorrow. Love Harry.'

Dan breathed a sigh of relief. All would be well once Harry was here.

He went up to his room, opened his father's letter and read it.

My dear Dan,

Your life is full of the promise of fulfilment if you choose to use your special gifts. There is no doubt that your path will be difficult and full of challenges but the hardships will dissolve when and if you obtain that which is rightfully yours. Meanwhile, here is something of mine, which is now yours from the Masters to their sons and daughters. Almost two thousand years ago a brave young girl from Judaea travelled many hundreds of miles, against the odds and defying her father's enemies, to this sacred place where the final mystery is to be found, the location of which you are about to discover. Her father was the last truly great Master, and she managed to avoid her enemies and arrive safely at this sacred place. After that, the dark power of the liars infiltrated our secret sect, so hundreds of years later another master, Joshua, lost his only son, Aziz, in a terrible way, betrayed and annihilated by his enemies.

There is a hidden memorial to all of them in the garden of this sacred place. Underneath it you will find your golden treasure – it will start to reveal its secrets when the time is right. I used to travel to this place as a child when my parents were... well, when they were living apart. Although they never divorced, they found it difficult to live together so every summer my mother took me to this lovely, rich and fertile land, and we would eat, swim and laugh together with not a care in the world.

Have patience, my son, and live in peace with yourself. And please stop smoking, it's bad for your health.

'Per ardua ad adstra.'
Your loving
Dad.

Dan smiled and closed his eyes as his mind rolled back the years to his childhood. His father had not been a fussy man but he had always been particular about diet and health. He'd hated smoking, although he'd had nothing against that other great vice alcohol, even though Dan could never remember his father being drunk. Then Dan laughed out loud. He realized he'd only smoked as rebellion against his absent father. He didn't need it any more.

He read the letter again. He had family, family whose roots seemed to go back thousands of years. With the letter was an old map, and a photograph of a group of people outside an impressive-looking whitewashed house. It was a U-shape built round a mosaic tiled courtyard, in the centre of which was a very ornate fountain. On the map was written a set of coordinates, 40° 22'N 18° 10'E.

His mind flashed back to the document Angelica had been studying at the dig. The coordinates were the same. He was sure of it. He tried to connect his laptop to the internet but the connection was down. Damn. He'd have to go to the reference library tomorrow.

He sat on the bed and started to go through the box of his father's possessions. Eighty-three years and an entire life distilled into an ordinary cardboard box. Tears ran down his face as he carefully picked up each item, many of which held such bittersweet memories for him.

He found the old blue felt fish that he'd made for his father when he'd been five and the wonky wooden boat which had never quite floated but which had been assigned pride of place in the bathroom beside his mother's exquisite Lalique glass collection. Then there was his maths exercise book, the one in which the teacher had written, 'Excellent. Dan shows a grasp of mathematics way beyond his young age.' There were his school reports, the certificate he'd won for being top of his class in Religious Studies, and his ballroom dancing class report in which the teacher had written, 'Dan seems to have two left feet, but this is mitigated by his kind heart.'

There were pictures of his father and a young Dan. Dan picked up one and took it over to the desk lamp so he could study it in detail. It showed his father probably in his late forties with a small Dan on his lap. They were sitting on a riverboat on the Charles River. It was clearly summer as the sun was beaming down and dancing on the water, forming crystals of light. Dan was leaning back into his father's chest and laughing – a picture of joy and happiness.

Also in the box was his father's birth certificate, 18th February 1927. So he had been born on his father's forty-fourth birthday. He also found his parents' marriage certificate, dated 21st March 1968, and his death certificate, 21st June 2010.

Right at the bottom of the box he found the rent book for an apartment in the north end of Boston, the Italian quarter. His father had lived there ever since Dan had been taken away from him.

Finally, he opened an official-looking letter, written in Latin. Dan studied it carefully and started to translate it.

After an hour of deciphering, Dan leapt up in surprise. The

location of the place his father had referred to in his letter was described here. It appeared that he now owned a house in Italy, somewhere in the south near a town called Lecce. He paced the room, impatient to tell Harry. Finally, he left the hotel and spent the night walking around the city, his mind full of strange images, shapes and dreams. From somewhere at the back of his mind, a voice said, 'Dan Hesiod Adams, heal thyself, and heal the world.'

Dan was sipping a very strong, black coffee when Harry walked through the hotel restaurant door. The two men hugged.

'Great to see you. Loads to tell you,' Dan blurted out.

'So have I,' Harry said, ordering fried eggs, beef sausages, bacon and hash browns. 'I've been under house arrest since the day after you left. The authorities discovered documents had been taken out of the country – they weren't best pleased,' he explained.

'Why didn't you tell me before? And how did you escape?' Dan asked with a worried expression on his face.

'I couldn't tell you as they listened to everything. In the end we reached, shall we say, a compromise. The Syrians are clever, they realized there's not much kudos to be had from making the most important discovery of ancient documents and artefacts ever made if you can't sing it to the world and use it as currency. We can't do that without the right experts to help us. So they let me out to meet with the good Professor Teddy Maitland at Harvard and gave me their blessing to proceed with unravelling the mysteries contained within them. Of course they will have sent a couple of secret service guys to tail me, but I can handle that. I've made an appointment with the professor for ten o'clock this morning. What have you been up to? Where are the documents?'

Dan told Harry about his meeting with Geoffrey Lowell where he'd left the documents for safekeeping, and his discovery that his father had only died a few months ago, and he appeared to have a house in a place called Lecce in Italy. Harry was shocked.

'Good grief. It's all more complicated than even I thought. But you now do have to let go and trust. "When one door closes, another opens; but we often look so long and so regretfully upon the closed door that we do not see the one which has opened for us." So said Alexander Graham Bell. Take his advice, it's so much easier to go through the open door than bang in vain on the closed one. Have courage to go into the unknown and stop clinging to the unsatisfactory,' Harry said firmly. 'Look, sorry to gabble on but we don't have much time on our own before…'

'Hello, not late, am I?' a female voice said. Dan looked up straight into the almond-shaped eyes of Angelica Duval. Damn, why did this woman always insist on turning up just when he needed Harry on his own?

'It made sense for Angelica to join us with her documents and for us to go to see Teddy together,' Harry explained.

'I see,' Dan said shortly, and got up to pour himself another cup of coffee, wondering how he could get rid of her. He paused. Maybe he should just quiz her, see if she was on their side or not. Harry could be right and she'd just made a mistake. Paranoia mustn't be allowed to get in the way of the truth.

At the table Angelica watched him. Fool if he thought he was going to escape from her. Her contact here, who was under strict instructions not to let Dan out of his sight, had already told her of his visit to Geoffrey Lowell, Edward Adams' friend, and some of the secrets he'd revealed. All she had to do was bide her time, which was perhaps the hardest part of all.

After breakfast Dan left Harry and Angelica and slipped

back to Mr Lowell's house to retrieve the documents so they could take them to Professor Maitland.

Teddy Maitland was as different to Professor Zinohed as it is possible to be. Large and expansive, he was a body in perpetual motion, talking quickly and using his hands to make salient points. He and Harry had been friends for years, having studied together in the U.S.

'A great discovery, Harry,' he said. 'I've been following your progress on the web. It's not been easy as the powers that be have been pretty determined to keep it as quiet as possible, but recently things seemed to have opened up a lot more.'

Dan, Angelica and Harry settled themselves on high stools and peered into light monitors to view the documents.

'We've discovered a treasure trove that will take your breath away and we need your skills to help us unlock it,' Harry told him. 'I've finally been given approval for you to go ahead and help us translate and record the documents. And, most importantly, the government has also provided a budget.'

'Good, good, so let's get down to work.' Teddy leaned over to study the documents.

'There are many other documents still in Syria but this new agreement with Syria means we can open up channels of direct communication,' Harry said, smiling.

They spent the rest of the day in Teddy Maitland's offices. Every modern and high-tech aid to research and decoding languages was there.

'How do we know these aren't just nice fairy stories?' Teddy Maitland suddenly said. 'Just like, in my view, most of the Bible stories.'

'Actually modern science is proving a lot of the Bible stories to be true,' Harry replied. 'The parting of the Red Sea, which allowed the escape of the Israelites from the Egyptians, could have been facilitated by a freak storm which occurred around that time. And the flood happened about five thousand six hundred years BC, during a warming period in the earth's temperature, when the melting glaciers caused an onrush of seawater from the Mediterranean. It cascaded through the straits of the Bosphorus in Turkey to the Black Sea, transforming it from a freshwater lake to a vast saltwater sea. As recently as 1997, Colombia University geologists William Ryan and Walter Pitman claimed that ten cubic miles of water poured through each day, and the deluge continued for at least three hundred days. So Noah could well have built his ark and waited for the waters to abate. Their findings are backed by carbon dating and sonar imaging, although there is also some evidence to the contrary. Myth or reality? I like to think there is substance to it all.'

'What about the resurrection of Lazurus? Don't tell me that's true?' Dan asked with a smile

'Well, you might not believe it but in 2008 the heart of an American woman stopped beating three times, and she was clinically dead for seventeen hours. Ten minutes after her life support system was shut down, she woke up. So science can once again be found to explain what we usually consider to be inexplicable. Even the destruction of Sodom and Gomorrah has its truth in notes made by a Sumerian astronomer observing an asteroid. When the symbols were decoded, scientists pinpointed the time to slightly before dawn on the 29th of June 3123 years BC. So be careful before you mock,' Harry said.

'So it's science not God in the driving seat, is it?' Angelica asked.

'Science can explain a lot but not everything. We know how babies are conceived but the reasons for the precise moment of conception in the human body remains a mystery. Synchronicity, when rational things combine to create the irrational resonates to its own beat. I believe these things are the work of the Universal Power, God's, work,' Harry said quietly.

'I guess we're only just beginning to understand those things that ancient civilizations understood and respected,' Dan observed. 'Anyway, we're living history right now as the recent extremes in weather are showing us. We have no idea what nature can throw at us. England is shivering under piles of snow as the Gulf Stream seems to have got knocked south by a vicious Arctic weather system. Who knows what's to come?'

'Ever the optimist, I see,' Harry said, laughing. 'Now, let's go and grab some lunch.'

Teddy took them to a small Italian restaurant where they relaxed and talked about their lives. Angelica fixed her gaze on Dan.

'You were born in Boston, weren't you?' she said to him.

'Yes,' he replied.

'How long did you live here?' she asked and he felt her eyes probing him, making him feel uncomfortable.

'Until I was nine and my mother decided to return to England. Harry and I met at boarding school when we were both fifteen. What about you?' He decided to turn the tables on her.

'I was born in Nice, south of France. My parents never married but my father was devoted to my mother. I was lucky, I had a very close relationship with my father. Did you with yours?' she enquired.

'I had a very happy childhood until we returned to England. My father has always been important in my life,' he said, evading the question.

'And what else is important in your life, Dan?' she asked, smiling.

'Many things. Teaching is my passion, although I guess like

most people I'd like to have a family before I get too much older,' Dan replied with honesty.

'Do you have a family, Teddy?' he asked the American professor.

'Oh yes, a highly complicated one. Three ex-wives, nine children and chaos at Christmas!' Teddy Maitland laughed.

Dan thought of Anna; he hadn't spoken to her since their argument. It was unfinished business. Was she for or against him? He had to know. He'd just discovered what withholding information could do to a person's life and he wasn't going to allow that to happen again.

Angelica smiled, then got up and walked over to the French doors that led out on to the restaurant terrace, and looked out over the Charles River. Anna Rossini had just made things so much easier for them than Angelica had anticipated. She turned back to look at Dan. Nice man. Shame really. But it was too late to re-write the battle plan now.

'Anyone fancy a coffee?' she asked brightly as she returned to the table.

Dan looked at her and frowned. There was definitely something about her he didn't trust. Then it came to him. She wasn't a team player. She always gave the impression that she was privy to some big secret none of them knew about, and she wasn't about to share it. Strange really, considering they were the ones with the secrets. What did she know that they didn't?

CHAPTER THIRTY

London

December 2010

Two human-shaped outlines could be seen on the video screen by his front door. Dan hesitated. It was 3.30 a.m. in the morning. A little too early even for the Jehovah's Witnesses brigade. He yawned. He'd only got back from the USA the previous day.

Jingle bells, jingle bells, jingle all the way, oh what fun it is to ride in a one-horse open sleigh, Oh jingle bells, jingle bells, jingle all the way...

His irritating doorbell – an early Christmas present from Thomas – rang again.

He pressed the speaker button and shouted into it. 'Who is it?' Behind him Mr Big growled, irritated at having been woken up.

'Police,' came the reply.

He pressed the buzzer to open the outer door and then opened his flat door a fraction, keeping the chain on. Two uniformed policemen appeared and showed him their warrant cards.

'Good morning, sir, sorry to disturb you at this hour. I'm Sergeant Ellis, and this is Constable Hampton, may we come in please?'

Shit! Now what? Dan locked Mr Big in the kitchen and opened the door.

The older of the two men was a carbon copy of a children's book policeman, short, plump, bushy eyebrows, his kindly face heavily lined by years of chasing criminals and confronting the unpleasant aspects of life. By his side was a young, nervous-looking officer who looked barely older than Thomas.

'Would you like some tea?' Dan said automatically, as though entertaining officers of the law at this time of the night was a normal everyday occurrence. He spied a packet of mints and stuffed one quickly in his mouth as he led the two men into his sitting room.

The sergeant cleared his throat. He hated this part of his duties, imparting bad news in the middle of the night, calling round on some soul who was peacefully asleep and in a few words turning their world upside down.

'I believe you knew Anna Agnetha Rossini?'

'Yes,' Dan replied. What had she done? Dan moved to the edge of the armchair.

'I'm afraid I have some bad news. There has been an accident,' the sergeant said softly.

'What's happened?' Dan said in alarm.

'I'm afraid she's in the morgue, sir,' the sergeant said.

Dan relaxed and smiled. Sergeant Ellis looked perplexed. This wasn't the usual reaction to a fiancee's death. Anna Rossini had been a good friend of the PM, and he'd been told she and this Dan Adams were to be married, only a matter of time before they announced their engagement. Could Adams be hiding something? Even then the sergeant would expect him to try and cover it up. Just what he needed, some nutter to haunt him after a straight fourteen hours on duty.

'Well, of course she is. She's a pathologist,' Dan said as though talking to a very slow child. 'It's her job.' His brain was befuddled with sleep and jet lag and he couldn't understand why he was being told the obvious.

The sergeant nodded and the constable scampered off towards the kitchen to make tea. As soon as he opened the door, Mr Big shot out barking.

'No sir, sadly she is in the morgue on... a more permanent basis than in her capacity as a pathologist.'

All colour drained from Dan's face as the policeman's words started to spin round his brain. He fought to control his emotions, his heart beating wildly as waves of shock engulfed him. The pain. The horror. It couldn't be true. God, he'd never spoken to her after their argument. This couldn't be happening. From somewhere in the distance he heard the young police officer cough. As the reality hit him, he stuffed his fist into his mouth to try and stop himself from screaming. Anna was dead. NO, NO, NOT POSSIBLE, his brain shouted to him.

'How?' Dan's voice was barely a whisper, his face ashen.

'We don't know all the details, the crime squad is at her house now. We think she's been dead for a few days. I am truly sorry but we need to ask you a few questions,' Sergeant Ellis said in an apologetic voice.

Dan clutched his head to try and stop the insistent thumping that was beginning to form into a blinding headache. Tears seeped through his fingers. Anna, a brilliant mind, one of the country's top pathologists, a solver of complex deaths. Dead. NO. Suddenly he couldn't breathe at all, his chest felt constricted as though the air was being forced out of it, it felt tight, a vice gripping him in its unrelenting clutches. He was going to have a heart attack, his heart was going to just split apart from grief.

Then it struck him. The Holy Trinity! Had she confronted them? Had he, Dan, sent her to her death?

Why did everyone he cared about die?

'I last saw her a few weeks ago. We had an argument but I don't understand...' Tears flowed silently down his cheeks. He tried to stem them by blinking hard. He wasn't going to tell the police about the Holy Trinity. He'd confront McManus first.

The older man stood up and crossed over to the armchair and put his hand on Dan's shoulder. 'I know you've had a hell of a shock but please try and think of anything that could help us. It's very important.'

The truth of the matter was that the sergeant had no idea what was going on. The chief inspector had called him personally to ask him to go round and talk to Dan Adams.

All the CI had said was, 'The heavies are involved, I need you to show we're on the ball. We have pressure on us from on high, and I mean PM high.' That meant the secret services as well as the PM's office, and his role was to gather information from this man in very stressful circumstances. The sergeant sighed and rubbed his forehead.

'I'm sorry, I can't help you,' Dan whispered.

'We understand, sir, we'll call round another time. Here's my number. If you remember anything...anything at all, however insignificant, please ring me.'

'How did she die?' Dan asked. He had to know.

'We don't know. A post mortem is being carried out. It's... well, it's rather baffling, so I understand,' the sergeant said.

Long after they'd gone, Dan lit a cigarette, ignoring his late father's pleas, and sat in the chair with his head in his hands, images and words going round and round in his head. As he sat there, night became dawn and finally day. Disaster had visited him again. He felt bereft, guilty, responsible. All optimism and hope had left his heart. He didn't think he would ever heal from this.

After many hours with Mr Big huddled close to him, Dan stood up and walked over to the window. He was now certain that the Holy Trinity had had a part in Anna's death. He would confront McManus as soon as possible and discover the truth. He no longer cared if he lived or died; he would fight this to the end. It was a fight for survival, him or them.

CHAPTER THIRTY-ONE

London

December 2010

'I made some cup cakes.' Jenny was standing at the door holding a cake tin in one had and her dog's lead in the other. Mr Big was jumping about, happy to see Juliet.

'You're so kind after...' his voice cracked.

'Please forget about that. You've just lost the woman you loved. You need support and comfort. I just wanted to say how sorry I am for you.'

'Please, come in.' She walked into his flat and put the cake tin on his table.

'I guess you read about it in the papers, the mysterious death of a top pathologist, motive and mode of death unknown.'

Jenny nodded.

'Tea?' he asked rummaging round for some plates and wondering, as welcome as it was, why women seemed to think life's disasters could be eased by a cup cake.

'Sounds good,' she replied, smiling.

They sat for two hours just talking, with no mention of their break-up. He felt easy in her company. When she'd gone, he sighed. He'd forgotten what a lovely, calm person she was, as well as loyal. He was beginning to appreciate consistency and loyalty in the female form. He hoped one day they could be good friends. He needed friends around him right now as he faced the toughest fight of his life.

Later that day, Dan took the gold coin out of his desk, the one he'd found at Chequers and taken to Syria, where it had disappeared to reappear with Mr Perkins. He'd kept it as Mr Perkins had told him it was part of his journey.

He turned it through 180 degrees and then pressed the sides. Almost immediately a hologram formed, endless bright colours swirling around and drawing him deeper and deeper inside. Suddenly, he found himself inside the expanding white light, floating weightlessly. Images spun round him, forming, dissolving and then re-forming.

Edward Adams' face materialized through the mist of light, his intense blue eyes locked on his son and he smiled at Dan.

'Continue with your journey. Distraction is not an option, my son.'

'Life is complicated, Dad. Much more so than I ever imagined. Anna died and I have to discover why. I can't just go on pursuing my own interests ignoring the events that shape the world we live in and affect those we love,' Dan said.

'We are composed of soul, body and mind and you already know that death is not the destruction of these parts but only the dissolution, so the soul is immortal and therefore will continue. Take comfort from that fact. But we all have a destiny to fulfil whilst inhabiting our mortal body. Go in pursuit of yours. Humans will insist on acting on information that is rarely complete. Patience! Remember time is relative to the dimension in which you live, you should not chain yourself to the vagaries of time. Find your true path and follow the rhythm of your soul.'

'Well, as you have the big picture, Dad, maybe you can share some of it with me,' Dan said, fed up with playing games.

'I can only share that which is agreed,' Edward Adams said firmly.

'Agreed by whom?' Dan asked.

'Dan, patience. I've told you that you must solve your eternal myth on your own and uncover that which is yours to know through your own endeavours. I, we, cannot interfere. If you fail then it will be because of your inability to transcend the challenges life throws at you. But if you win, then your prize will be the redemption of humanity.'

'Quite frankly, from what I've seen I'm not sure if I want to be part of redeeming humanity. It seems to be in a right mess. You can't tell me there isn't another race in the universe that is a bit more compliant and intelligent than us,' Dan said.

'Oh, there are many races, but the race we hail from has the most potential. That is the conundrum. Our reason to exist is not taking the easy option of accepting that which is perfect and worshipping it. Rather, it is taking that which is imperfect and making it whole. You cannot begin to understand the real potential of mankind. We need to unleash that potential for the entire universe to evolve,' Edward Adams said earnestly.

'And if we don't?' Dan asked, meeting his father's direct gaze.

'I'm not privy to the solution to that universal disaster. I guess it would be the end of life as we know it, not only on earth but everywhere, or maybe the Universal Power will switch focus to a more compliant race, but, anyway, please follow your path and have courage, for you can achieve glory, unlike me. I... well, I did not fulfil my destiny, but you are our last hope.' Then he was gone.

Dan found himself spinning round gently and then falling out of the wonderful light of the hologram and landing with a gentle bump on the sofa. Mr Big, who was just trotting into the sitting room having finished his supper, backed hastily out of the room, bolted through his dog flap and headed over the fire escape.

Dan shook his head and stared into space. Then he stood

up and paced around the room for hours, going over and over his conversation with his father. If mankind was facing its critical moment, and if he could make a difference to the final outcome of the battle for survival, then he had to try and unlock the codes contained in Harry's documents. He had to understand the information that was being imparted to him.

But prior to that, destiny or no destiny, he owed it to Anna to discover how she had died.

On the Saturday before Christmas Dan made his way to a meeting with Oliver McManus. As he walked through the crowds of late-night shoppers he thought how ironic it was that buying presents for their loved ones made people so bad-tempered. Peace and goodwill to all men. He sighed. That morning he had done his usual sweep through the news websites. A small item had caught his eye. Yesterday, an unemployed university graduate, Tunisian Mohammed Bouazizi, had set himself alight in protest at his unfair treatment by officials who had confiscated his fruit and veg vendor stand. After years of struggling he'd had enough. Dear God, the desperation, Dan thought, as the crowds continued to flow past him. The complete lack of hope in any kind of future. What the hell was the world coming to? From the sheer horror expressed by several prominent Tunisian commentators, Dan had the feeling this was the start of something much bigger. The date, 17th December 2010, had appeared in the hologram of the golden coin at the meeting of the Holy Trinity. It was a warning.

Dan walked into the restaurant at precisely 7 p.m. Oliver McManus was already waiting for him. Dan noticed he was looking strangely ill at ease. His usual sangfroid had departed him. He was slugging back what looked like a large Scotch on the rocks, a Johnnie Walker black label, judging by the hovering waiter clutching the bottle. He had stubble on his chin and dark bags under his eyes.

'Drink?' McManus enquired as soon as he saw Dan.

'Thanks. A small Talisker,' Dan said, deciding to stick with one of his all-time favourite malt whiskies. Mind you, this was business not pleasure. He intended to remain sober.

'I'm so sorry. So unexpected. Such a loss,' McManus babbled away as the maitre d' showed them to their table.

'Have they discovered what happened to Anna yet?' Dan demanded as soon as they sat down.

'No, it's a mystery. We've called in Professor Bernard Hall, the expert in investigating matters of this kind. He worked on the Gareth Williams case, you know – the MI6 spy found dead in a holdall in his bath in his apartment in Pimlico?'

'I don't think there's ever been a satisfactory explanation of that so I wouldn't call that much of a success story in terms of discovering the truth,' Dan snapped.

McManus bit his lip. 'I think you'll find MI6 know more than they are prepared to say.'

'So what do you know about Anna?' Dan asked.

'We were working together as normal and then she took three days off to visit her mother in Sweden. When she didn't turn up for work after the visit we raised the alarm.'

'Come on, Oliver, don't play the innocent and tell me that you and the other members of the coven at the Holy Trinity weren't using Anna to get to me,' Dan said, his anger barely contained.

McManus shifted uncomfortably, his hands tensing round his glass of whisky. 'I admit we used Anna to keep a close eye on you, but nothing more. I promise you that. She had no idea of your importance, she just thought we were keen to get you on board to help us. We had nothing to do with her death,' McManus said sincerely. He really had no idea how she had died. He loosened his tie. He was feeling very nervous. He looked at Dan. Gone was the slightly diffident, charming man he'd met at Chequers. In his place was a determined and angry man who had no fear for his own safety. He could see why Anna had been so besotted with him.

'Look, you'd better come clean with me,' Dan said forcefully. 'I know I'm part of all this. I seem to be the one chosen to lead us out of the mess mankind has got itself into. God knows how or why, but there it is. I have no idea how it is going to manifest itself. I don't plan on spending all my life chasing secrets. In fact, I intend to return to teaching in the New Year, and allow the rest to unfold in its own good time, but I do know that my way of life is not in any way similar to your way of life. You seem hell bent on stopping me or anyone close to me from uncovering the secrets which somehow hold great power.'

McManus hesitated. He could continue to deny or he could explain, get Dan on their side, harness their resources. It was a long shot but it was worth a try. 'The secrets hold immense power, Dan. You could be part of it. I know you have an important role to play. If you joined us we could rule the world. Think about it. You could fulfil any role you wanted,' McManus said, genuinely hoping Dan would agree. If he did agree, he'd personally make sure Angelica was kept in check.

'Now you're reminding me of the devil tempting Christ in the wilderness. And if that's too trite and religious then, to put it plainly, you're full of shit. You kill people who get in your way, and you like to control people, not to mention the fact that you're chasing the secrets of Professor Harry Bakhoum's dig, which are some of the most important discoveries in the history of mankind. You want to get your hands on them. You're running some kind of warped holy crusade to put people in the right places of influence so when the time comes you can just flick the switch and hey presto you'll be the new ruling world order. A new solution for a new era.'

'A new world order, encompassing all religious groups, to take us forward to a new way of life. Who's to say we are wrong?' McManus asked earnestly. 'Sometimes you have to take a hard line. Think of the holy crusades and the violence carried out in the name of Christ. But can you say that everything done in the name of religion has been wrong? Look at all the good they've also done. The people who were saved. The hope for a better life kept alive over thousands of years. It is the same with us. We want to bring good things to people, help them fulfil their lives, but people need control, they need to be led. You have no idea of the power we can hold when we unlock these secrets. Life is no longer black and white. It's changing. Regimes will fall, the world will become unstable. We offer hope. It's not good versus bad but the enlightened versus the unenlightened.'

'Is Angelica Duval part of your set-up?' Dan asked.

'Never heard of her,' McManus said quickly.

Too quickly, thought Dan. 'Don't lie to me, Oliver. I repeat the question: do you know Angelica Duval?' He leaned forward.

'No I don't,' McManus said, this time meeting Dan's gaze. The first course arrived. Smoked salmon for Dan. Asparagus for McManus, who carefully dissected it before consuming it.

'Like St. Peter I'll give you one more chance. Is Angelica Duval a leading light in the Holy Trinity of Science, Religion and Philosophy?' Dan demanded.

'She is not. Who is she?' McManus said, unsettled by Dan's continued interrogation. It had been agreed that Angelica would stay out of the public eye. He felt the power shift away from him in this confrontation.

'That's what I'm going to find out along with solving the

mystery of Anna's death. And don't think you can frighten me away. I've experienced some life-changing events. I've looked in the mirror and seen the devil staring back. I've beaten him and seen goodness and kindness replace him, and I've held onto that as my inspiration. You can't fuck with my mind any more, and quite frankly I don't care if you kill me because somehow we are linked and I think if you kill me, you'll kill your own dream. I'll take a chance that you won't end my life – at least not yet,' Dan said.

'How is Professor Bakhoum getting on? I hear the Syrian authorities have opened up channels to international experts. We look forward to hearing more,' McManus said tightly as he fought to wrestle back control.

'Cut to the chase. You're after the Book of Eternal Wisdom and the Board of Destiny, and you need all seven mystical golden coins to activate it,' Dan said, looking at him sharply.

'How do you know we haven't already secured them, either physically or metaphysically?' McManus had recovered his composure as the main course arrived – fish for Dan, beef for McManus. A glass of red wine for Dan, the rest of the bottle for McManus.

'I know you haven't got all the gold coins and I don't believe you have got either the Board of Destiny or the Book of Eternal Wisdom or you wouldn't be trying to make deals. You need me for something, of that I'm certain. And be very sure that I will find out the truth about what happened to Anna,' Dan snapped.

'You'd be well advised to take up my offer and work with us rather than against us, Dan,' McManus said, his eyes narrowing. Dan noticed McManus's hands were shaking slightly.

'Don't threaten me, Oliver. As I've already told you, you don't frighten me at all, and if I discover you had anything to do with Anna's death, then be very afraid.' Dan finished his dinner and stood up. 'No point in making polite conversation. I don't think we have anything further to say to each other. I'm sure we'll meet again.' He strode to the door, leaving McManus to pay the bill.

Sooner than you think, McManus thought as he watched Dan's straight-backed figure exit the restaurant. He sighed then sat back and took a large gulp of Lagavulin, one of his favourite malts. Something was bothering him. Something from the morning he and Angelica had met at his lab. It was lurking at the back of his mind. He closed his eyes and swirled the antique gold coloured liquid around the glass. Suddenly, he opened his eyes and sat bolt upright. Of course! Why hadn't he remembered it before? A small detail but vitally important. Damn, it proved beyond all doubt... It was time to call a full meeting of the Holy Trinity. He and Angelica had been working on their own, as agreed, but now the other members had to be involved. He stood up abruptly, paid the bill and left the restaurant.

He hailed a cab just as it started snowing heavily again. His life's work was in peril. He hoped the situation could be salvaged. If not it would all be over – forever. There would be no redemption and no glory. It was unthinkable.

CHAPTER THIRTY-TWO

40/30, The Gherkin City of London

20th December 2010

Oliver McManus was the first to arrive. A light lunch awaited them with bottles of soft drinks stacked up neatly in the small fridge. A large, oval, glass-topped table dominated the room. He walked over to the large picture windows. It was a spectacular view. The city was still deep in snow. Ice was hanging off the buildings and far below people walked gingerly along the treacherous pavements. McManus glanced up at the sky which was unusually silent due to the cancellation of flights at both Heathrow and Gatwick. The extreme weather conditions had created a scene straight out of Charles Dickens, all it needed was Scrooge to appear and the picture would be complete. He sighed. The British really didn't cope at all well with snow. He picked up the *Daily Telegraph*, 'Frozen Britain' was the headline, minus twenty degrees in places. He gazed into the distance. This was a view of their empire. Unless they completely fucked it up of course. He walked over to the table and poured himself an orange juice.

Next to arrive was Angelica. She marched into the room, high heels, smart suit, hair in a chignon, a killer combination of elegance, energy and confidence – but not for long.

'Drink?' McManus asked her.

'Sparkling water, ice and lemon,' she replied, her eyes studying him.

'I remembered something from our discussion in my lab that Sunday morning a couple of weeks ago.' McManus paused, placing his glass of orange juice carefully on a coaster at the head of the table. He was claiming leadership, a move not lost on Angelica who raised one eyebrow and stared at him.

'And what did you remember, Oliver?' Angelica's cold humourless eyes looked at him. She walked over to the window, turning her back on him.

'When I arrived there was a small vial of suxamethonium in the lab ready for the daily collection. When I left the lab, it wasn't there and it definitely hadn't been collected yet. Outside in the corridor a woman's scarf was lying on the floor. It had a distinctive perfume. Anna's perfume. Perhaps you can explain all of that.' Oliver McManus stared at her.

'Really, Oliver, you're not living in an episode of *Spooks*. This is real life. You must have, for once, been mistaken about the suxamethonium. You did seem distracted by some unusual results in one of Anna's test groups. And it must have been my scarf. As for Anna's perfume, it was so strong I'm surprised you couldn't smell it all over the building. It's no big deal. Do get a grip,' she replied coolly.

'I rarely make a mistake of that magnitude. Suxamethonium is a potent drug, a depolarising muscle relaxant and hard to detect. Without adequate intubation it will kill someone in a few minutes,' McManus said.

Angelica turned to meet his gaze. 'Your point is?'

'My point is Anna is dead and we can't find a cause. Do I advise the leading pathologist to look for suxamethonium?' McManus moved towards her. She stood her ground.

'Tell them what you want, Oliver. It's of no concern to me.'

'Angelica, we agreed Anna would be useful to keep us close to Adams. We did not agree to eliminate her,' Oliver said, feeling like a small schoolboy as he always did when challenging Angelica.

'And what do you think we would have done with her after Adams had been dealt with?' Angelica asked him.

'I still don't necessarily agree he should be "dealt with" as you so elegantly put it. He could be a useful member of our group,' McManus said defiantly.

'He would be a constant thorn in our sides with his do-gooder attitude, another wishy-washy liberal, just what the world doesn't need. You seem to forget that I am the leader of the Holy Trinity of Science, Religion and Philosophy and I make the final decisions. In any case, we cannot achieve our ultimate aim without me as leader.'

And we quite possibly can't exist with you, McManus thought.

'Do I detect discord?' Roger Pendleton, the Judge, walked into the room carrying a slim briefcase.

'Not at all. Just a friendly discussion,' Angelica said, smiling.

Giovanni Barbarelli, the Monsignor, Beatris de Souza, the Banker, Kent Briggs, the Philosopher and owner of the largest media group in the world, all arrived a few minutes later. Finally, Abdullah Mustafa, the Politician walked in.

Angelica took her place in the middle of the oval table.

'We've decided to emulate the positions of the British Cabinet Office today with the leader sitting amongst his cabinet, and the most important members sitting next to the leader,' she said, smiling and looking at Oliver McManus who was now isolated at the head of the table.

She swept her eyes across the room. The crème de la crème of global influence. Oliver had been her original partner in this venture. Together they had plotted and planned, developed their contacts and placed the recruits in positions of power, ready to take over once Angelica gave the word. But he was the one she had doubts about – and if he caused trouble then he would have to go.

However, it would for the most part be a bloodless coup. They had built up so much support over the last few years as people sought answers on how to build their lives on solid ground.

They were fed up with being fed horror stories in the media – which was carefully manipulated by Kent – that made danger appear in every aspect of their lives. Eat the wrong food and you'd die of a heart attack or cancer; drink too much and you were a goner; do something completely outrageous like fly on a plane and you'd be blown up and be consigned to an early grave. You couldn't even put your life savings in a bank any more without the danger of losing it all in the next financial crash. In addition, more tax, more hardship, more job losses, more unrest, more need for security and safety. The world governments were impotent, racked by indecision, corruption, greed or just plain stupidity.

The Holy Trinity had offered a way to work towards a better life. They'd fed tit-bits to the masses from the secret ancient knowledge at their weekly sermons and the people were making money and enriching themselves spiritually. They'd created a global family. Even if you travelled to the outer reaches of Alaska you could find the Holy Trinity.

Now the last piece was about to slot into place – and she was about to share it with her partners.

'Welcome. Today I have great news to share with you.' She rose and looked round the table. Six pairs of eyes stared right back.

'I have found the location of the Book of Eternal Wisdom, and also the exact date when it will appear. The information was contained on a very ancient piece of papyrus at the dig. I have coordinates, and the date of the first meeting of the new Master of Destiny is the 3rd of April 2011. We must prepare carefully.'

'Does Adams have this information?' the Judge enquired.

'He was at the dig and looking at the same piece of paper but it is not certain if he understood the significance or not. He certainly does not have our knowledge of the inner workings of the process. We are ahead of him,' Angelica said smoothly.

'And of course we have one piece of information which he is totally unaware of – the element of surprise is always important in battle,' the Politician commented quietly.

'Are its present location and the place of activation the same?' McManus enquired.

'Good point, Oliver. We don't know. This is our next quest.'

'So why don't we ask our oracle?' the Politician said.

'You mean one of our two golden coins?' Angelica replied.

'Exactly.'

'The problem is knowing which coin has that information. If we ask the coins an inappropriate question they will shut down. We only have one chance,' Angelica explained. 'You know perfectly well that we only have *very* limited access to the coins due to our, well, due to our special position, shall we say.'

'I think I have another way,' the Politician said. 'Give me a little more time to work on it.'

'Very well,' said Angelica. 'Now to more mundane matters of the management of our meetings. The Church of Scotland has offered us its main meeting house for the major prayer festival in Aberdeen…'

At the end of the table McManus studied his colleagues. Were they at the edge of a new dawn? Or staring into the abyss of disaster? Until recently he wouldn't have given disaster head space, but he had the feeling Adams was going to prove to be a more able adversary than they'd previously thought. Angelica didn't know about his meeting with Adams. Her arrogance worried him; it could lead to her downfall but he damn well wasn't going to let it be his.

CHAPTER THIRTY-THREE

New Year, Scotland and Italy

January 2011

Dan stared out at the snow-capped hills of Glen Devon. Winter was in the midst of its white, icy glory. A touch of magic unless you were actually trying to travel anywhere. It had taken him all the previous day to get to Gleneagles. Flights delayed, car hire erratic and roads blocked. But he'd made it in time to celebrate Hogmanay. He'd always promised himself Hogmanay at his spiritual home, so he'd recklessly spent the rest of his savings and here he was. He'd been for an early morning brisk walk, followed by a breakfast of scrambled eggs and smoked salmon. Now the entertainment was about to begin.

Smiling, he patted Mr Big, who was looking smart in a tartan bow tie, and headed downstairs to The Orchil Room. The day was starting with fortune telling. Somewhat off-beat and quite ironic really considering all the twists and turns of 2010. If the fortune-teller was any good she'd be running out of the door after five minutes tuning in to his vibes. He breathed in the scent of burning logs and mulled wine that drifted by in the grand hall and smiled. It felt good to be back even if it was only for two days.

He had decided not to fly to Syria and spend Christmas with Harry as they'd previously discussed. Dan loved Harry like a brother but he needed some time alone before he went to see his father's legacy – the house in Italy. He'd asked Harry to check the coordinates on the document to see if they tallied with his father's coordinates for his property. He'd said he'd work on it urgently.

On Christmas Day Dan had found himself, surprisingly, at dawn Mass at St Simon's Church in Putney – where Thomas's parents had got married and he'd been best man. Father Quinlan had given a thought-provoking Christmas sermon. It had been about changing our reference points, building the foundations for lasting happiness through getting involved in communities, and re-engaging with that most basic building block in human existence, the family. He also spoke about learning to accept that contentment could arrive in unexpected ways, and, like Christmas presents, was not always what you hoped for but often what you didn't know you needed.

A few days into the New Year, the day after his return from Gleneagles, Dan flew to Italy and travelled to the town of Lecce, in Puglia, Southern Italy, another port of call on the road to discover his roots. Armed with an address and a map, Dan headed to via Augusto Imperatore, to the offices of the man who could tell him the exact location of his father's house. Halfway along the street he found the building he was looking for. He climbed up five flights of narrow stairs and knocked on the door.

'Avanti,' a man's voice said.

Dan entered the office and a short, smartly dressed, very lively-looking man stood to greet him, smiling warmly.

'Ah, you must be Mr Adams, how nice to meet you. Come and let me get you a coffee. I have some good news for you,' Dottor Rossi said in excellent English and bustled about, taking Dan's coat and ordering coffee from his secretary.

Dan sat down and gazed around the office. It was piled high with papers and boxes. He frowned, feeling some trepidation. He hoped Dottor Rossi would produce the right documents for the right house – it all looked a bit chaotic.

'Let me show you where your property is.' Dottor Rossi spread a large map out in front of him. 'I have studied the copies of the documents you sent me and found the exact location of the house using your coordinates and the details in the legal documents. It is here in a place called Frassanito, near Borgagne.' He pointed to a point on the map that was quite a way south-east of Lecce near the sea.

'I have also visited the site,' he added.

'And?' Dan asked expectantly.

'It isn't quite in its original condition, but there is potential.' Rossi rubbed his nose distractedly. 'Anyway, very good news. I have checked with the council office and your documents are in order.'

'Is anyone living in the house?' Dan asked.

'No, no, as I said it's not exactly, how do you say, er what's the word? Ah yes, *shipshape* at present, but I'm sure it will be soon,' Rossi said vaguely.

Dan breathed a sigh of relief. At least there weren't any locals to evict.

'Now we'll go to see it,' Rossi said, finishing his coffee and grabbing his coat.

They drove for over an hour towards Otranto before finally turning off the main road and heading towards a town that was perched on a hill a few miles away. Halfway up the hill Rossi turned off and made his way towards an old iron gate. He opened it and they drove through a very large olive grove.

'This is your land – all of it,' Rossi said, waving his hand expansively.

Dan saw hundreds of olive trees, interspersed with lemon and fig trees, all looking very well looked after. Someone was obviously tending to them.

Dan smiled, feeling anticipation and excitement flow through him. This was all his, this land of his ancestors. It was a new beginning. He closed his eyes and breathed in the sweet scent of his land. Then he suddenly felt a sharp twinge of intense regret – Anna would never see it. He bit his lip. He was no further forward in finding out the cause of her death, not yet, but determination and tenacity were his hallmarks; he wouldn't be defeated.

He'd seen Jenny again. They'd had tea and yet more cake at the Windmill restaurant on Wimbledon Common. It had been very relaxing, nothing more, nothing less, but their friendship was enjoyable, trust was being rebuilt and Mr Big had gone to stay with her while Dan was in Italy.

Dan and Dottor Rossi drove up a long incline and the tension of expectation within Dan grew. He looked at the old photograph which he'd brought with him. The land and lie of the trees was the same. They were in the right place.

At the top of the incline, Rossi stopped the car, climbed out, and walked over to what looked like a very large pile of stones. By the side of it was a small barn-like structure.

'Outbuildings?' Dan looked quizzical.

'Not quite, although with a bit of tender loving care this pile of stones could once again create the splendour of the original house.' Rossi smiled hesitantly. 'The small barn over there was built about ten years ago by the locals, so they had somewhere to shelter during the harvest. This land is very fertile, you are very lucky, it produces the best olive oil in the area, not to mention wine, lemons, figs and some very specialist herbs that are used in the local kitchens.' Rossi continued in his singsong voice. 'The olive harvest took place in November and the locals are here every day processing it, but today they have left us alone. They have the right to harvest it under a local law which specifies that if fertile land is left for more than a year and its produce left to rot, it can be tended and harvested by local families until the owner claims his rights.'

'The house has gone,' Dan said, sitting on a rock and feeling the bitter taste of disappointment as he looked at the old ruin that had once been such a beautiful house. He felt gutted that his dream of a lovely family home had been dashed. He didn't have the money to rebuild it. He studied the photograph from his inside pocket. 'What a shame, it was once so beautiful,' he whispered, his hand gently caressing the picture.

'And it could be again. You can rebuild a house but you can't make fertile land from rock! Rejoice, my friend, you have nothing to be sad about, you have won the lottery with this lovely land. People have been fighting over it for the last sixty years, about the time the house has lain empty and dormant,' Rossi said, spreading his arms wide to encompass all the land.

The eternal optimist, Dan thought, smiling. 'Maybe one day when I've got the money,' he said. 'How come the house had been empty for so long?'

'I don't know its very early history but one of the locals told me that a young woman came here in about 1927 with a young baby and returned every year until the 1950s, when they disappeared and never came back. Since then no one has lived here. I presume if this house belonged to your father, then this lady must have been your grandmother. It was destroyed by an earthquake in 1989,' Rossi explained.

'I didn't think earthquakes were usual in this part of Italy,' Dan said mildly.

'They aren't very usual but, like the heavy snowfall this winter, they sometimes occur unexpectedly.'

Dan got up and went for a walk. He stood at the top of a small mound of earth. The land extended as far as his eye could see. It was indeed rich and fertile. The red mud was sticking to his shoes. He found a stone and sat down. He reached down, picked up some of the earth and lifted it up to his nose. He breathed in deeply, savouring the strong smell of minerals and base elements. It felt reassuring.

"'In my father's house are many mansions; if it were not so, I would have told you; for I go to prepare a place for you. And if I go and prepare a place for you, I come again, and will receive you unto myself; that where I am, there ye may be also,'" he whispered to himself, quoting from the gospel according to St John. One day he would rebuild this house and make it the focal point of the community again. He wondered if the woman with the young baby had indeed been his grandmother. He'd never met her. He knew very little about her. She'd died before Dan had been born and his father had never really mentioned his family, apart from the fact that his parents had separated shortly after he'd been born.

He stood up and made his way back to the car where Rossi was waiting for him.

'Quite a surprise, *non*?' Rossi asked, smiling.

Dan nodded but said nothing, and they drove off back down the hill. Just before he lost sight of it, Dan turned and looked back. Aside from the simple matter of the lack of an actual house, the site was perfect. Dan looked up to the sky and said a silent thank you to his father.

'Now we'll go and meet the people in your local town of Borgagne,' said Rossi. 'We need to make friends with the mayor so, when you have money, you can rebuild the grand house that was once there.'

Dan took in the sights, sounds and smells of southern Italy. It appeared to be more like Greece and North Africa than the lush valleys of Tuscany or Umbria. It was simpler, less sophisticated but, nevertheless, happy in its own skin.

Suddenly out of nowhere a picture entered his mind of the old man he'd seen in his dream at the Krak des Chevaliers, and his son, Aziz, whom he'd sent away with his secrets. Where did he go? What happened to the secrets he was carrying? Were they part of Harry's discovery in Syria? And what had happened to the Board of Destiny and the Book of Eternal Wisdom after that last fateful meeting at the Krak des Chevaliers?

'Here we are in Borgagne. Now let's go and meet the mayor. You can just drop in at certain times of the day.' Rossi parked his car in the square, a short distance away from the open-air fruit and vegetable market, and they walked over to the council offices. 'The mayor will issue the permissions for you to rebuild your house so he is a very important person, and one to keep on your side,' Rossi said, smiling.

'Yes, quite.' Dan had no intention of rubbing him up the wrong way. He'd heard about Italian politics and knew if you wanted to get anything done in this part of the world you had to make friends with the people in power.

They were shown into a large room with an ornate carved ceiling and a very large mahogany desk.

'*Il Sindaco e in arrivo*,' the young secretary said and left the room. Next minute a glamorous, full-bosomed woman of about forty with a head full of what looked like expensive blonde highlights swept into the room and smiled. Dan assumed she was one of the mayor's underlings.

'*Buongiorno, sono il Sindaco, Maria Elena di Tiggiano*,' she said, introducing herself.

Christ, this was the mayor, thought Dan thinking of the matronly members of the British cabinet. He glanced at the good dottore who was also looking surprised. Obviously the mayor of Lecce was a more traditional male version.

The mayor indicated that they should each take one of the two chairs in front of her desk and she settled herself into her imposing throne. Her face was a vision of perfection from the carefully applied bronze lip gloss to the grey eyeliner that highlighted her startlingly clear blue eyes. Well, thought Dan, as Rossi and the mayor engaged in conversation, time to switch on the charm.

'I am very pleased to own land in such a beautiful place. I look forward to rebuilding it and recreating its original splendour,' he said in Italian, summoning up his GCSE vocabulary. Italian hadn't been one of his chosen languages, but its Latin roots meant it wasn't very difficult for him to pick up.

'We're also happy to have you here, but unfortunately, when you're ready, we can only give permission for you to build a house of a maximum of eighty square metres,' she replied in English. '*Purtroppo*,' she added in Italian. Unfortunately.

Dan recognized the Italian.

'Why is that?' he asked, overwhelmed by a desire to rebuild his family house. It might take him years to raise the funds but he wouldn't roll over and let a bunch of bureaucrats run roughshod over him. He pulled the photograph of the old house out of his jacket pocket and handed it to the mayor. 'This is my father's house, I wish to rebuild it, exactly as it was,' he said firmly.

The mayor looked at the picture and smiled. '*Bella casa*. My father knew the woman who lived there. She had a small child – Edward. He and my father were good friends.'

'He was my father,' Dan said, a smile replacing his irritation.

It transpired that her father had indeed known Dan's father, in fact they were almost the same age, they'd been friends until one day in 1953 he and his mother had disappeared and they'd never heard from them again. The mayor's father had tried hard to find his friend.

'*Purtroppo*, I'm sorry,' she said and stood up.

'But…' he started. However, it was obvious that the audience was over.

'Well?' Dan said to Rossi as soon as they were walking down the steps towards the exit.

'Beautiful woman,' Rossi said, placing the thumb and forefinger of his right hand together and blowing an imaginary kiss.

Dan frowned in irritation. 'Yes, yes, but how do we get her to agree to increase the square footage?'

'It will be tough. You have hundreds of very old olive trees, some of the oldest in southern Italy and none of them can be cut down,' Rossi said.

'I don't want to cut them down but there's plenty of room at the top for a large house. What's the real problem?' Dan demanded.

'Patience, my friend, Rome was not built in a day. We'll need to conquer this part of paradise in a different way.' Rossi backed the car out of the parking space and headed back to Lecce.

As they drove away, the mayor stood watching them from the floor-to-ceiling double windows. Behind her a male figure appeared.

'*Bene, bene*, Maria Elena. You did well,' he said.

She turned to the man. '*Spero di si*, Marco.' *I hope so.* She sighed and turned away from the window. They had to protect the income of the local community and the land they'd spoken about was very profitable for them, so she couldn't just let it return unchallenged into the hands of a stranger. But she felt guilty. Dan Adams had seemed like a good man, and there weren't too many of those around.

CHAPTER THIRTY-FOUR

Boston, USA

January 2011

Harry had flown back to Boston to work with Teddy again as soon as he'd been able to leave the dig for a few days early in the New Year. There was a massive cover-up going on over Professor Zinohed's death, with the government insisting it was linked to opportunist robbers. Harry was certain the Holy Trinity had been involved, but they had powerful contacts everywhere, and he'd been warned off asking awkward questions in no uncertain terms. He'd had to back off or risk the future of the dig, and he knew Mumtaz Zinohed would not want their work to be compromised. The good news was that although the Middle East was beginning to rumble to the sound of discontent, the Syrian government had been true to their word and had put a budget in place so international experts could work on the documents.

After two days of sorting through the hundreds of documents that now flowed between Syria and the USA, out of the blue came the breakthrough they had been searching for. Harry had always expected a fanfare of trumpets to sound but instead it had just appeared on a fairly dull, grey, January day.

'Hey, come and look at this. The computer has just spat out some interesting info.' Teddy was smiling and waving his hands about.

'What?' Harry hurried over.

'The document that Professor Zinohed found and placed in a special box for us to translate contains a secret code. It's aligned to the very ancient document, the one Dan talked about, that describes the Book of Eternal Wisdom. Both documents give a set of the same coordinates that Dan asked you to check.'

'And?'

'They are 40° 22'N, 18° 10'E.' Teddy fed the coordinates into Google Earth on his laptop. 'It's a place near Lecce in southern Italy.'

'Well, I'll be damned, that's where Dan is right now. Dan's father had a house near there, which Dan has gone to find. It would of course be entirely logical for it to be there,' Harry said.

'What?' Teddy said.

'Something very important,' Harry said mysteriously. Although he trusted Teddy implicitly, he still kept their relationship on a "need to know" basis. 'I need to get over there and make sure Dan is aware of this,' Harry said.

'Where did you say he is?' Teddy asked.

'In a place called Frassanito, near Borgagne, not too far from Lecce. That must be it! It all makes sense.' Harry shouted, forgetting his previous reticence to share information.

'Hey, cool down, man, no idea what you're talking about but remember you're a rational scientist not Tom Cruise on a secret mission. Call the guy and tell him whatever you need to. You don't have to go over there, you're needed here.'

'Oh, believe me, Teddy, I do need to be there. This is the high point of everything we've been working on. I must be present. No choice. It's amazing, incredible, fantastic – all the best things you can imagine all happening at once. A new all-encompassing religion for a new future,' Harry said, his face wreathed in smiles.

'Hmm, good for you, you can tell me about it some time, but don't forget religion has started most wars on this planet,' Teddy pointed out.

'That hasn't escaped my notice, which is why the rational world of science still thrills me.' Harry replied, logging on to a travel site to book his flight. His life's work was about to culminate in the most important discovery for thousands of years.

CHAPTER THIRTY-FIVE

Southern Italy

Early January 2011

Oliver McManus and Angelica Duval flew to Rome and then on to southern Italy on a dreary, cold January day. They headed to Lecce in a hire car. They'd thought they had time, but the news that Dan Adams was in Italy had prompted the inner circle of the Holy Trinity to vote unanimously that Oliver and Angelica should go.

However, the air was heavy with tension. McManus had ordered a new post-mortem on Anna to see if there was evidence of suxamethonium in her body. Of course there was – a dead body produces it anyway as it decomposes. One of the ways to prove whether or not the body has been poisoned with it before death is to perform a post-mortem on a body of similar decomposition to see if the levels are the same. Not easy. Angelica had of course refused to discuss the matter.

This was a key moment for the organization. They had to stay together at least until Dan Adams had been dealt with, one way or another. Oliver had to support Angelica, there was no other choice. If he didn't, their plans would be blown apart and he'd worked too hard for that to happen. Adams would have to be sacrificed.

Meanwhile, Dan was trying to communicate with the locals who had turned up on his land to continue their production of olive oil. There were about twenty of them. They weren't very cooperative. It wasn't a good start.

At 11 a.m. an old white Mercedes drew up and a man climbed out and walked towards him.

'My name's Marco and I think it's time for a chat,' the man said in near perfect English, putting his arm round Dan's shoulder and leading him away from the others and over to a group of lemon trees. 'I understand this was your father's house, although he only visited here each summer. My father remembers him well, the cleverest child around, spoke three languages, English, Italian and the language of his mother.'

'Who are you? How did you know my father and my grandmother?' Dan asked.

'My family have lived in this area for hundreds of years. My father is an historian and records our personal history and that of the region. He has passed this knowledge on to my brothers and me. He went to summer kindergarten with your father and the mayor's father and they all spent every summer together until one day, when he was a young man, he never came back,' Marco replied.

'And what was the language of his mother?' Dan said, eager to learn more about his paternal family.

'She appeared to be the perfect English lady but her first language wasn't English, it was Arabic. She was a very private person, with few friends,' Marco said.

Dan was silent. His grandmother was of Arab descent! He suddenly felt a huge urge to laugh. He could imagine his stuck-up English mother being very unamused by this. She had always thought Delia Adams was Edward's mother, but she must have been his stepmother. What happened? Why did his father never discuss it?

'Your father was my father's best friend. He missed him so much. Spoke about him constantly. Was always wondering what he was doing and where he was, even if he was still alive. Did he marry? Was he happy? My father would love to meet you,' Marco said.

'And I'd like to meet him. I'd love to know what my real grandmother was like,' Dan said, sincerely.

'According to my father, your grandmother, Alima, was an amazing woman – strong, feisty, fearless, and very protective of her only child,' Marco said. 'Anyway, suddenly the community found this magnificent house abandoned. It has a fascinating history, all researched by my father. It's said that an Arab boy built it in the twelfth century, in memory of his young uncle who was murdered while escaping his country with his family secrets. He found his peace in this beautiful place.' Marco paused and smiled. 'I don't know if all of that is true but we Italians love a story involving family secrets. We are great romantics. In any case, what is true is that the house was built around the time of the crusades, but a few hundred years later it passed out of the Arab boy's family and became the summer house of one of our most important mystical poets, a man known for his interest in the metaphysical. As such it attracted the *bella gente* and was the centre point of our culture for many years. But when the poet died, they all drifted away.'

'Then what happened?' Dan demanded, enthralled by the ancient stories.

'Well, one day many years later, one of the descendants of the Arab boy returned and bought it. The locals tell of wonderful parties and strange events, which took place at certain times of the year. There are said to be secrets buried around here, but as you can see they must have either been destroyed by the earthquake or not been here in the first place as there's nothing left of the place,' Marco said, looking around. 'Anyway, when Alima departed, it was abandoned and as a close knit community we felt abandoned as well, so a local family moved in and kept it in reasonable repair, until the earthquake destroyed it. We have all benefited from its abundant produce. It's the most fertile land in the area. We've sold the olive oil, the lemons, the figs and the rare herbs to international traders. Ten years ago we won an award for the best wine in the region. We now have wine schools and cookery schools in the area which carry the name of this land – *La Terra dei Sogni*, the Land of Dreams,' Marco explained.

Dan could see where all this was heading. The locals were pissed off that some foreigner had waltzed along to remove their very lucrative trade. 'So none of you is exactly pleased to see me,' he said.

'That's not our way, we're a friendly people. We like to welcome strangers into our homes and our hearts, but we would like to enter into a commercial agreement with you to continue our trade. The annual income from the land and related products is in excess of two million euros,' Marco said, looking at Dan closely.

Dan's eyes widened. Two million euros! Even sharing the income left him a life-changing amount. He could rebuild his house! God, his life was spinning on a sixpence – again.

'Well, we can discuss the detail, but there is one condition – that I can rebuild the house exactly as it was,' he said, swallowing hard and trying to keep calm and rational.

'I can't see that being a problem. The mayor is very understanding,' Marco said.

Dan hadn't noticed.

'In fact, she is on her way to look at the property and discuss it with you now.' Marco smiled.

Dan looked up as an Alfa Romeo came into view. The mayor emerged, looking as immaculate as ever. She smiled at them but, before walking over to join them, she flipped open the boot and changed into a pair of what looked like brand-new wellington boots.

'A lovely lady, no?' Marco smiled again. Dan nodded in agreement, although to him she'd only be lovely when she'd agreed he could rebuild his house to the original size.

'*Cara,*' Marco called to her and walked towards her. They spoke in Italian and Maria Elena nodded and smiled at Dan. It seemed that a truce had been called and his house plans were acceptable.

Later on, once he was alone on his land, Dan walked around its many acres, getting to know the contours and the feel of the earth beneath his feet. It was his and miraculously it seemed his finances were once more on a secure footing. Life was, indeed, mysterious.

He'd almost decided to call it a day when on impulse he walked over to the ruin. There was only one wall still standing. What had once been the interior of the building was overgrown with foliage. Dan closed his eyes and tried to imagine it as it had been, the large rooms furnished with rare items from the four corners of the world, the exotic people, the meetings and the parties. The poets and writers gathering here to seek inspiration, relaxing under the trees, enjoying the fresh produce – abundant fruit and vegetables, lemons, figs, almonds, pistachios and glorious wine. What a wonderful life.

The scent of lemons drifted through the air and then a sound, a sweet singing. Dan opened his eyes. He thought he was dreaming but he wasn't, the sound drifted through the late afternoon air, soothing and comforting him. It reminded him of the King's College chapel at Cambridge and the sacred music that had been a love of Anna's. She'd introduced him to the Sunday evening services and the music had never failed to calm his soul and ease his anxieties. He looked around. It appeared to be coming from somewhere below his feet.

He knelt down and started to part the grass and twigs, looking for a hole or some kind of opening, but he found only earth. As the singing became louder, he got up and moved around. Then kneeling down again he parted the grass and found a large iron ring. He pulled it and a hidden trapdoor swung open, revealing a large compartment. He gasped. His heart started beating very fast, and beads of sweat appeared on his brow. He felt a shiver of anticipation ripple through his body.

The sound was now very loud, a wonderful Gregorian chant of ancient times and ancient mysteries being sung in Latin. Was he having another vision? He bent down and peered inside the compartment. He saw a wooden box with a small plaque on it. On it was inscribed, 'In Memory of Jacob, Eschiva, Joshua and Aziz'. He pulled the wooden box out. He tried to open it but there didn't seem to be a lock or any way of getting inside it. He looked all round it, over the sides and underneath, but nothing. It appeared to have been hermetically sealed. He sat down and ran his hands over the wooden box wondering what to do next as he watched the sun begin to sink behind the low hills. As he sat in silent contemplation, the mysterious box suddenly started to open of its own accord. As the top swung open, a brilliant golden light spilled out, illuminating everything around it. Dan shielded his eyes. Inside he saw that the box was lined with what looked like pure gold. Nestled in the middle of the box was a very old black and gold book. Its pages were turning and changing colour. It was coming to life. Its songs were drifting lyrically into the gathering darkness. The language changed from Latin to English: 'For I am free, so the ancient ritual must begin again. Gather the chosen ones and share my secrets. The new leader is once more with us and the power of destiny is ours.' There was a pause in the music and a man's voice could be heard. 'But someone is speaking a half-truth, the most dangerous lie of all, for how do you tell which part is the lie and which the truth?'

Then the singing started again, loud and full of vitality and hope: 'But those times have gone and you my friend are the truth, the light and the redeemer.'

Dan sat back, open-mouthed in astonishment, his entire soul pulsating to the beat of the magical song. The Book of Eternal Wisdom. It was here in his possession. It was as it always had been and always would be. The dance to the mysterious rhythm of that ancient conundrum of time.

CHAPTER THIRTY-SIX

Southern Italy

Early January 2011

As he sat in awed silence, Dan suddenly heard a shout and looked up in alarm. He saw Harry striding towards him, his outline clear in the last rays of the setting sun. He was wearing a Panama hat and waving.

'Harry, what the hell are you doing here? I thought you were babysitting your beloved documents in Boston with Teddy.' Dan was astonished. What else was going to happen on this strangest of days?

'I was.' Harry was puffing as he walked up the slight incline before stopping to embrace his friend. 'Let me catch my breath. All the taxi drivers seem to be maniacs in this country.' Harry walked towards the old ruin to sit down. As he neared it he suddenly stopped dead.

'It's here... it's as we thought... oh, my God... I never thought I'd be...' he fell to his knees.

'I just found it, or rather it found me,' Dan said quietly, looking at Harry as he gently caressed the cover of the Book of Eternal Wisdom which was now closed.

'We must be careful, danger is upon us, my friend,' Harry gasped.

'It's too late for any caution now,' came another voice. Harry and Dan spun round. Oliver McManus stood behind them. He was holding a gun, which he was pointing at Dan.

Angelica was by his side. They had parked their hire car by the gate.

'So, the treacherous duo has pitched up at last. The liar and his sidekick, the odious Miss Duval,' Dan spat out. Harry stood there pale and speechless.

'Depends how you define treacherous,' McManus said coolly.

'I define it by its consequences and I'd say you two have caused quite a bit of unpleasantness in the last few months, although I should have been on to that sooner. Should have got final proof of Miss Duval's treachery. A stupid adversary is no fun at all,' Dan replied before turning and casually sitting down again on a piece of rock. He felt no fear at all.

McManus didn't flinch. 'I have certain regrets myself. I've enjoyed your company enormously. Under different circumstances we could have been friends, even partners in our belief for a better world, but I realize that is not possible,' he said, and flicked the safety catch of the gun.

'Angelica? No! Oh God.' Harry had suddenly found his voice. 'I've allowed a traitor into the inner sanctum,' he cried, looking extremely distressed.

'Oh well, you're in good company. Jesus Christ made the same mistake with Judas,' Angelica said, her voice icy.

Harry stumbled towards McManus. 'I know you can't shoot Dan or you'll destroy the power of the Book of Eternal Wisdom. It's written in one of our documents: "He that destroys the leader will destroy the oracle that speaks."'

'But I can shoot you, and you're getting on my nerves.' McManus turned his gun on Harry. Quick as a flash Dan flung himself on top of Harry.

'Go on then, take the risk of killing me and losing your precious prize,' Dan gasped.

McManus kept his gun steady, pointing it at both of them. 'Sadly for you I have information that has changed the way this game is going to be played. Who is to say that you, Dan Adams, are the new leader?'

'Dan's father and my documents say so,' Harry spluttered. 'Dan is the new Master of Destiny of the Holy Order of Lord Melchizedek. He is the son and only child of Edward Adams, who one of our key documents referred to as the silent keeper of the secrets, but who sullied the purity of his purpose.'

Angelica walked over to peer inside the box in which the Book of Eternal Wisdom was now lying silently. Her eyes devoured it in anticipation of what was to come.

'Well, your presence seems to have removed whatever power the book has, and what do you mean my father sullied the purity of his purpose?' Dan said to Harry, while still protecting him with the weight of his prostrate body.

'It would appear that your family is tainted,' McManus sneered, 'so don't be too sure of your destiny. The Book of Eternal Wisdom will fully awaken when the new Master of Destiny takes his rightful place, and that, my friend, is not you.'

Harry groaned and tried to move. 'Oh, for fuck's sake get off me, Dan, I can hardly breathe.' Harry pushed Dan off him and staggered to his feet, spitting earth out of his mouth and brushing his creased and dirty trousers.

'Stop!' Dan shouted. 'Do not kill Harry and deny the world the benefits of his knowledge.'

'Oh, do stop playing cops and robbers and let's get to the point. The new Master of Destiny is not who you imagine it to be,' Angelica stated simply.

'If it's not me, who is it?' Dan asked.

'You're looking at the new leader.' McManus shouted, his voice filling the cool evening air causing the leaves to rustle.

Dan looked momentarily confused. 'You?'

'No, her.' McManus jerked his gun towards Angelica.

'How the hell do you work that one out?' Harry

exclaimed. 'The leader has to be the child of the old leader.'
Then he froze as he remembered the words: 'sullied the purity
of his purpose.'

'Exactly.' McManus looked triumphant as he saw the
shocked expression on Harry's face. He returned his gaze to
Dan. 'Do I have to spell it out?'

Dan was staring hard at Angelica. 'Are you saying she's my
sister?' He looked horrified.

'Your father is my father, although our mothers are
different, so yes, I am indeed your sister,' Angelica said simply.

'Impossible,' Dan spat out furiously.

'Not at all. I was born in Nice on the 1st of August 1971.
My father was present at the birth, Edward Warren Delaney
Adams. My mother was Elisabeth Sanchin, a descendant of the
Mahmouds, the ancient mystics from Syria. It was destined that
I should be the new leader, not you. The leader only has to be
of the bloodline, legitimacy is irrelevant.'

'This is preposterous.' Dan shouted, confident that his
father would have told him about this in the DVD he'd made
for him in Boston. It couldn't be true.

'Your mother didn't find out until you were nine years old,
which was when she left Edward, taking you back to England.
When you were fifteen and wanted to go and live in Boston
with your father to avoid living with your future stepfather,
she told you your father had died. Between them your mother
and your stepfather threatened your father so he stayed away
from you. It was all so simple. Call your mother and ask her.'
Angelica handed Dan her phone.

He looked at it and hesitated. They still hadn't spoken since
the night he'd confronted her. He'd heard that Tobias had died
but he hadn't attended the funeral. He looked at Harry who
nodded, so he quickly punched in the numbers.

'Mum, it's me,' he said hesitantly.

'Dan... I... how are you?' Primrose sounded tired and somehow beaten.

'Fine, but more importantly, how are you?' he asked.

'Beginning to understand how hard loneliness is... I am so...' She paused and McManus raised his eyebrows, looking impatient.

'Mum, please don't ask why but I need to ask you something important,' Dan said in a low voice.

'Ask me anything you like, I have decided that there is no room for secrets in our lives any more.' Her voice sounded stronger.

'Have I got a half-sister?' Dan blurted out.

There was a long silence on the other end of the phone, and Dan wondered if she'd hung up. Finally, he heard her sigh.

'So you've found her?' she said softly.

'Maybe. Is Angelica Duval her name? Is that the woman?' Dan's voice was barely a whisper. It was one more betrayal, the shattering of the high esteem in which he'd once held his father.

'She wasn't called that when I found out about her. But then I was so shocked that I was hardly paying attention to her name. She was born in August 1971 in Nice. That was what really hurt, it was only five months after you. That other woman was pregnant when I was pregnant.'

'Mum, I'm so sorry, why didn't you tell me before?' Dan asked.

'I made a promise to my own parents, who were thoroughly appalled by it all, never to tell you, but when you reached fifteen and wanted to go and live in Boston, Tobias and I had to take action to prevent it. I couldn't bear for you to be hurt by the man you worshipped. And if you're wondering why your father didn't tell you later, he agreed never to taint your life with his betrayal,' Primrose said quietly.

McManus waved the gun. 'OK, cut the emotional crap and end the call,' he said firmly.

'Are you really OK?' his mother said, her voice sounding worried. 'Who's with you?'

'No one, I'm fine. I've got to go. I'll call later… and Mum, I love you, I really do,' Dan whispered.

'Oh how touching, a rapprochement with the woman you've spent most of your adult life hating.' McManus smiled.

Dan handed the phone back to Angelica. He remained silent even though his mind was in turmoil. Angelica Duval was his half-sister. He couldn't believe his father had committed such a betrayal of his destiny, and in doing so had destroyed his family life. All these years he'd deified him and he walked with feet of clay.

'And we have something else to help us,' Angelica said, interrupting Dan's confused and painful thoughts. She opened her hands and held them out towards Dan. She was holding a small wooden ball with intricate carvings on it. 'The Board of Destiny,' she said, smiling. 'Or at least it will be when we discover its activation mechanism. Now we've got the Book of Eternal Wisdom, we are unstoppable.'

Dan stared at the exquisite carvings, his mind going back to his Krak des Chevaliers dream: the tiny figures representing the seven ages of man; the clusters of what appeared to be stars and swirling clouds against a deep blue sky; the strange interweaved carvings, some encased in complicated latticework, the precious jewels interspersed around them.

'How did you find the Board of Destiny?' Harry demanded.

'Easy. I found it protected in a copper safe in the far right-hand corner of the site by the white rock, a location I found when I was spying on your emails. I just had to find a gifted locksmith in Istanbul and it was mine.'

'You killed Mumtaz,' Harry said, with venom in his voice.

'Couldn't be helped,' Angelica snapped.

Dan stepped forward. 'From what I've understood during my strange encounters with the mysterious forces that appear to emanate from the Book of Eternal Wisdom, the Universal Power wishes the human race to fulfil its destiny. The Master of Destiny is supposed to be a force for the good, a benevolent guide who is here to help us even when we refuse to listen. If this is the case, it would preclude either of you pitiful examples of humanity from being a Master of Destiny.'

'Enough! Your precious father was a common adulterer, hardly a prize example of a superhuman force,' McManus snapped.

Dan walked towards Angelica.

'Stop,' McManus shouted.

Dan kept walking, his eyes never leaving those of his evil sister. She had to be stopped.

Then suddenly, as McManus pulled the trigger of his gun, a dense fog circled the group, making it impossible to see beyond a few centimetres. Dan heard McManus cursing and felt the air from a bullet narrowly missing his skull. This was the end.

CHAPTER THIRTY-SEVEN

Southern Italy

Early January 2011

Out of the mist, three figures slowly emerged, descending from the sky to the ground. One had long white hair, one short red hair and one dark, wavy hair. They were wearing long, silver cloaks made from silk and cashmere, and woven with precious stones – diamonds, sapphires, rubies and emeralds. They seemed to shimmer, dipping in and out of focus, and they exuded a sense of calm, soft benevolence.

Dan was entranced. Just as he'd recognized the Board of Destiny from his dream, so he recognized these magical figures and felt soothed by a feeling of intense peace.

'As Dan knows, we are the ancient mystics, the Magi, Larvandad, Gushnasaph and Hormisdas, and we bring to you the same gifts we brought to the Christ child, and to all the other Masters we've encountered on our long journey. We come to…'

'Save us?' Harry interrupted.

'Our motive is not to save but to reveal the truth and bless the one who would be the true leader. It appears that there is confusion over this matter. It must be resolved so the Universal Power can be certain justice is being done. Since the sacred ceremony was corrupted in the early years of the Common Era and also in 1179 by the conniving of the dark forces with the Council of Elders, the process of anointing the new leader has been vulnerable to external forces at a critical point. This critical point is at the time of the old Master's death. If the challenger to the new leader obtained his or her DNA, then they could snatch control of the series of tests that would be set for the new leader to prove his worth. And that is what you did, isn't it, Angelica?' The Magi extended their long, elegant fingers and summoned Angelica to the circle.

Angelica gazed straight ahead. How did Dan know these strange men? She suddenly felt fear. She couldn't lose this battle.

'My intentions were honourable, believe me.' Angelica looked at the Magi. 'I just wanted to be in control of the tests to protect my dear brother. He isn't as strong as me. So, yes, I was indeed at Gleneagles the night our father died, and managed to obtain your DNA, Dan, from the cigarette butts you left, so I could invoke the power of the universe and take control. I knew I was your half-sister so I knew if I was present at the appearance of the Book of Eternal Wisdom, then, as the daughter of the last Master, I could also be under consideration as the new leader. After all, my character is more suited....' Angelica tailed off and looked at the Magi again.

'You are not speaking the whole truth, child. We are all-seeing and all-knowing. We are sent to look into human hearts and see the truth in a person's soul. You should never underestimate the Universal Power,' the Magi explained in unison. 'As you have understood, this is the final moment of truth for the human race. After thousands of years of guidance and support the Universal Power has decreed that mankind must overcome the unpredictable nature of the great gift of free will and embrace its higher purpose.'

'And if we don't?' Dan asked. 'What will happen to us all then?' He felt calm. He was not privy to the greater knowledge of the mystics. His journey into the realms of the supernatural and the mysterious had been through his recent dreams and visions, but he knew he had nothing to fear.

'Mankind will exit from the Greater Council, which is the council of the representatives of the chosen ones of the universe. All the other intelligences are on the right path to fulfil their destinies, which means that the universe lives on, but earth remains our problem child. We will, regretfully, have to leave you all to the destiny you choose to follow,' Larvandad answered him.

'I'm surprised you've tried to help and guide us for so long without giving up,' Harry stated from the sidelines.

'Earth is the favoured and much beloved son of the Universal Power, and the one planet which, if it reached high into its spiritual potential, could lead all the others. Your potential is boundless and all-encompassing. It is a potential that could inspire and enthrall the other intelligences. However, as you know, with great gifts come great challenges and the twenty-first century is your moment to prove you can overcome these challenges and dig deep into your souls for the good of the collective, rather than the good of the individual. We are here to ensure the will of the universe is done. Then, dear earthlings, it is up to you.' The air shimmered and crackled as the Magi paused to allow their words to sink in.

'It's true that the new Master of Destiny is the child of Edward Adams, but Mr Adams did not quite follow his sacred path, and in exercising his free will he created a situation of... confusion,' the dark-haired Hormisdas explained.

'Neither of you stayed with your father for the length of time required of a Master to teach his heir the ways of the mystics. You were both the victim of his actions. You, Dan, lost contact when your mother returned to England, and you, Angelica, lost contact with your father when your mother ran off with another man, James Duval,' red haired Gushnasaph stated.

Dan looked at Angelica. Had she lived with his father when he'd gone to live in England?

The Magi smiled benignly. 'It's time for the person involved to tell you himself.'

Out of the mists, the outline of a face appeared, fuzzy and indistinct at first, then gradually gaining focus – the thinning grey hair, a long mournful face, intense blue eyes and a dazzling smile. It was Edward Adams.

Dan remained rooted to the spot; as much as he loved his father he felt the bitter taste of betrayal. Angelica, however, rushed forward. 'Dad, I miss you so much,' she cried, trying to touch his face.

'Ah, Angelica, you have disappointed me with your ruthless quest for power and wealth. I'd hoped you had better qualities, you showed such promise, a first-class honours degree, and awards for your brilliance in translating ancient languages. And your dedication to the Holy Trinity has been most impressive. Even if you had selfish desires in the beginning, this organization could have evolved into the saving grace of the human race, but instead it has become an unwieldy receptacle by which the few may gain personal power and immense wealth. I thought you'd already been discounted as the next Master of Destiny, although of course the final decision on that does not rest with me. Your brother also shares your linguistic talents, but at least he has used them for the higher good of his pupils. He has also shown much courage and fortitude, especially during the last year when he has been tested and has more than risen to the physical and spiritual demands made of him. He is a good man, and has great leadership qualities. I'm sorry to see you become so bitter and full of hate,' Edward Adams said sadly.

'I followed your example, Father, and took what was mine and sought to turn it into gold. I have achieved much that I am proud of, even with your inconsistent presence in my life, and I know I can take on your legacy,' Angelica said, meeting her father's gaze.

'You're right to admonish me; in following my heart I betrayed both of you for which I am truly sorry. You, Dan, my firstborn and the child I loved so much, were torn away from me because of my adultery with a woman I felt was my soulmate, who in turn left me for another man, thereby placing both my beloved children in an emotional vortex. I lost both of you through my own selfish desires and I also failed to realise my destiny, forced as I was to lead a lonely, contemplative existence for the rest of my life.'

Dan stepped forward and raised his hand tentatively towards his father's face. 'I wish you'd told me I had a sister, it would have explained why my mother bolted back to England. Yes, I am angry and I do feel betrayed but above all I'm sad that we lost precious years living separate lives when we could have been together. I have missed you so much. Whichever of us is to take over your legacy, I hope these past sins will be forgiven and we will walk towards our future with courage and compassion. It is indeed time for us to work for the greater good of all.'

'It was Dan's birth chart we found amongst the documents,' Harry suddenly blurted out. 'So he must be the new leader.'

'We also have Angelica's birth chart,' Hormisdas said, and he held up two birth charts. 'There are two charts to indicate the possibility of two leaders as all the children of a deceased Master are to be considered as rightful heirs, but only the leader with a strong and truthful heart can be the right one.'

'Dan, draw nearer please.' Gushnasaph said.

'Was it you who engineered the disasters in my life?' Dan asked, looking at the Magi.

Larvandad spoke quietly. 'The new leader has to survive a

series of tests, but as I've explained, in this instance they were not in our control. In any case, our role is not to treat the lives of the human race like a game of chess, our role is to ensure that justice is done and the gifts of leadership are given to the chosen one.' He held his hand up, indicating the contest was about to begin.

The mist cleared and a central dais appeared in the middle of the circle, its edges clearly defined by a fine golden thread. Dan stood on the dais and the three Magi placed frankincense and myrrh on a tablet of gold. The smoke from the incense drifted into the evening air, enfolding the group in its seductive scent.

The Magi stood together, their outlines shimmering, the jewels woven into their cloaks radiating beams of hypnotic light around their ethereal bodies. They spoke as one.

'Dan Hesiod Adams, you stand before us today in your role as potential leader. We see from your birth chart that as your soul travelled through the heavens on its journey to earth, the planets it visited gave you the gifts of vision, compassion and courage in your quest to seek the truth, as well as loyalty and empathy for the plight of your fellow man. But you must dig deep into your soul and find immense fortitude and understanding before you can realize your true potential. To help us in our quest to discover the true leader please answer this question: from whom will you seek the wisdom of leadership?'

Dan felt a sudden surge of power, like electricity, flow through his body. His fingers tingled and his head spun momentarily, as a feeling of certainty and courage cleared away the indecision and fear of the past. He felt the ground solid and safe beneath his feet. He was finally grounded in the sure knowledge of his own abilities.

'From the past Masters who are within and around me at all times. They know the truth of the imprint of my soul, my past sins and my future achievements. Nothing can be hidden from the soul of the collective wisdom,' he answered.

The Magi nodded and indicated Dan should stand back so Angelica could step forward.

'Angelica, you are charismatic and have natural leadership qualities which could have been nurtured into becoming a leader of the world.'

'What do you mean "could have?"' Angelica demanded.

'Do not question us and do not speak unless we request it!' the Magi said. 'We will continue. Your penetrating intelligence and strength of purpose are the qualities enjoyed by great kings and leaders. However, you have not placed any limits on your ruthless desire for power and material gain. You must prove to us that you can change.' Hormisdas glanced at Angelica's birth chart. 'You were born with a 'void of course Moon' in your chart, when the Moon has made its last major aspect to other planets and is stepping into another astrological sign. It is the chart of the potentially great who will only achieve their destiny through hard work and by changing their inner character. Most do not achieve greatness. You will only be redeemed if you confess your sins with a true intent to show remorse and embrace the good within you.'

Angelica stepped up to the dais. She felt very nervous as for her there was no surge of power and inner knowledge.

'Please reveal to those gathered here your dark secrets,' the Magi commanded.

Angelica thought quickly. She looked at McManus, who was standing uneasily at the edge of the group. He was to blame. His constant questioning of their plans had brought about disaster.

'You are right, some dark acts have been committed under my watch. I should have been more vigilant in choosing the people close to me. I feel ashamed that the gentle and wise

Professor Zinohed died. We were trying to get information from him and he had a heart attack and died. I did not intend that to happen. It just couldn't be helped. We wanted to extract information from him, but he was not... cooperative.' Angelica tried to look contrite. Dan felt sickened by what was obviously fake guilt.

'*Liar*! He died from having his throat cut. You've already admitted you were responsible. When I accused you of killing poor Mumtaz, you replied that "it couldn't be helped,"' Harry shouted. How could he have been so easily taken in by this evil woman? He was as guilty as she of his close friend's murder. If he'd seen through her, his friend would still be alive. He felt tears of shame fill his eyes.

Seeing his distress, Dan walked over to Harry and put his arm round him.

'*Silence!*' the Magi raised their voices. 'Angelica, we know everything and see everything. We know that Professor Zinohed died, as Harry has described, from having his throat cut. Do you not understand that *nothing* goes unnoticed? Now, what else do you have to tell us? *You must be truthful.*'

'Believe me, I am sorry people died, but it wasn't my fault. My heart has always wanted the best, but sometimes the demands of leadership were such that human mistakes were made. My biggest error was in choosing the wrong people as my confidants.' Angelica felt panic as she desperately fought her biggest battle.

McManus shifted uneasily but remained silent. He knew what was coming. The blame game – Angelica's favourite pastime.

'Who else did you kill?' Dan asked.

Larvandad held up his hand for silence.

'I am truly sorry,' Angelica said quickly, hanging her head, her heart beating wildly.

Dan snorted in disgust.

The Magi looked at Angelica expectantly. 'Now, Angelica Duval, there is one death we should discuss, isn't there?' Gushnasaph asked, his deep brown eyes boring into her soul.

Angelica closed her eyes. No, not that, even she had tried hard to block it all out.

'We're waiting, Angelica.' The shimmering cloaks of the Magi seemed to have taken on an even greater luminosity, filling the evening darkness with thousands of magical lights. Dan put his hand over his eyes, which were beginning to hurt from the blinding brightness.

'I… I saw the person who killed Anna, I should have stopped them.'

'*Liar, Liar*, you were responsible!' the Magi shouted, their voices so loud it felt as though the ground was shaking. They held up their hands and bolts of electricity shot out and headed towards Angelica. '*Tell the truth*. It is time to reveal yourself in full,' they demanded.

Angelica cried out as strands of her beautiful chestnut hair – her crowning glory – started falling to the ground, in a slow, almost graceful dance. Her hands flew to her head in a desperate attempt to halt this awful act. 'No, no, please stop, please stop it *now*!' she shouted as clumps of hair fell from her scalp.

'We cannot stop that which has been started, we are not the ones destroying you, that is not our doing. Your soul was asked to reveal itself and the process has begun,' the Magi said.

Dan, Harry and McManus looked on in horror.

'Please don't do this to me,' she wept. 'It wasn't me; I didn't kill Anna Rossini.'

'Dear earth child, why are you so insistent on self-destruction? Why can't you understand that we don't come here to destroy but to hear the truth? Your deeds have already been documented; there is no point in lying any more. You must understand that lying to the Universal Power destroys the soul. It unleashes the poison within to destroy that which it feeds off.'

Angelica gave an animal-like cry and pulled her hands from her head and stared at them. A look of sheer terror crossed her once lovely face. Her fingers had started to turn in against one another, twisting and curling into her palms. The skin was peeling away, revealing the red raw sinew and bones below. She screamed, a sound of such intense pain that Dan closed his eyes and turned his head away.

'I-I-I will confess, please, please stop this now. I can't take this pain,' she sobbed.

'Tell us,' the Magi said quietly.

'It's true I... I... I k-k-killed Anna Rossini,' she stuttered, as she bent over to try and grab at the clumps of hair that lay on the ground in a vain attempt at preserving her dignity. The few strands of hair that were left on her head had turned a shade of iron grey.

There was a sharp intake of breath from Dan, Harry and McManus. The Magi remained immobile.

'Please, I b-b-b-eg you, let me explain, I d-d-didn't kill her myself.' Her words were almost inaudible as her physical body continued its disintegration.

'Explain,' the Magi demanded.

'We h-h-had to k-k-keep Anna close to Dan. We... we k-k-knew that Dan was aligned to the Book of Eternal Wisdom. She f-f-fell for our religious ideals, we st-st-steered her towards an exciting new job with Oliver... rekindled her romance with Dan... all fell into place... s-so easy,' she said, trying to access every ounce of energy. She had to stop this torture. She tried to smile, look convincing, but it was grotesque as her once lovely face had become wax-like in colour and etched with deep lines. She looked old and haggard, the poison of her evil life oozing from every pore.

At that moment Dan strode forward with a thunderous look on his face but the Magi raised their hands and he stopped dead in his tracks.

Angelica tried to straighten herself but she bent over again as the pain intensified. She fought to breathe to complete her confession, 'It was g-g-going well... managed to entrap him into attending the m-m-meeting... we would put on a show... it c-ca-caused Anna to row with Dan... he suspicious of us... she t-t-t-turns up at the lab Sunday... overheard Oliver and m-m-me di-discussing Dan's elim-elimination,' she gasped, her strength diminishing fast. 'I c-c-c-can't carry on,' she said, weeping, her tears falling down her ageing face.

'You must complete your confession,' the Magi demanded.

'Oh God, help me.' Angelica clutched her stomach as intense pain whipped through her again. 'Finish this,' she said to herself. 'Do it, don't let them see you are weak. It will end soon. Courage.' She pulled herself up as far as she could. 'I-I-I was having her f-f-followed, monitoring calls... I k-knew she was there... Oliver kept supply of su-suxamethonium...' She stopped, her breathing erratic and weak.

'And I believed in the Holy Trinity as much as I believed in Dan and his inherent goodness, which is why I was confused by his sudden antipathy towards them.' Out of nowhere Anna appeared, walking slowly towards the group, her long blonde hair swinging from side to side. She smiled and opened her arms to Dan.

'Oh my God, Anna. How can I have doubted you?' Dan ran to her and enfolded her in his arms, surprised to feel her body solid and warm. The boundaries between death and life seemed to dissolve as the power of the Magi flowed through the group.

'I'm so sorry I doubted you about the motives of the Holy Trinity. You were right. I was wrong. It is built on the desire for power and control, and of course the stockpiling of immense personal wealth.' She paused and looked around, smiling at the Magi and nodding at Harry, who was transfixed. 'I'm also sorry you have suffered for my foolishness.' Anna took Dan's face in her hands and gently caressed it. He felt his eyes well with tears. He stepped back, a feeling of deep loss filling his heart.

'You believed it was for the greater good and for the good of me,' he whispered.

'Yes, but I was blinded by a tarnished prize. I involved you in something that was wrong,' she said, gently touching his face.

Angelica, who was now crouching on the ground, peered up at McManus, hatred filling her ravaged face. Calling upon her inner demons, she turned to Anna. 'You w-w-would have told Dan about our plans. We couldn't allow that... y-y-you had to die... interfering too much, he...' she spat out the word, looking at McManus, 'didn't know y-y-you were there that morning... he w-w-would have killed you himself.' A sneer formed on Angelica's thin withered lips.

Total fear was enveloping McManus's body; he had to distance himself from this mad woman. 'I would never have killed Anna,' he yelled at her. 'You know that, don't try and put the blame on me. I always told you that your killing spree would end in disaster. We had such influence and power and you ruined it by crushing everyone who dared to get in your way. You were out of control.' He looked at the Magi, hoping they would believe him and leave him alone.

Dan took Anna in his arms again, smelling the slight but distinct scent of her favourite perfume.

'I would have died instead of you,' he whispered.

A blood-curdling scream emanated from Angelica. They

turned to look at her, and the sight made them all cry out in shock and horror.

'I have confessed… you must stop,' she shrieked with the last of her strength.

The Magi were standing still, their arms raised, pointing at her, their power forcing her demons to flee in the face of their omnipotent strength.

It was too late for her. She made one last high-pitched animal sound that further chilled the bones of everyone present. The stench of her warped life filled the air as her skin and bones dissipated into the night. Suddenly, with a small final whimper she was gone, vapourized into the bowels of an everlasting hell.

As she disappeared, Oliver McManus shouted in pain. His flesh, too, was dissolving, exposing his bones and sinews. His face contorted in agony and overwhelming fear as the forces of retribution claimed him as well. In a few seconds he too had disappeared.

As soon as they had both gone, Anna smiled and hugged a shocked and pale Dan. 'You must embrace your destiny. If you listen to those sent to guide you, you will give mankind the chance of fulfilling his collective destiny. You must focus on this. Happiness awaits you, dear Dan. I wish you a glorious life lived with the joy of the eternal wisdom of the Masters.' Then she slowly rose into the night sky, together with Edward Adams. Just before the two figures disappeared they paused and waved, their souls heading into the outer heavens.

Dan stood quite still, gazing up at them as they vanished from view. Although still shocked to the core by the night's events, he knew Anna would be safe, and he hoped his father would be forgiven by the Universal Power. He breathed deeply and suddenly the feeling of courage and peace he'd felt earlier returned to form a permanent base in his soul. Anna would remain in his heart forever but now he did, indeed, have to embrace his future.

Harry walked towards him. 'And so it was written, from the father comes the son, and from him the path to greatness,' he said quietly.

Dan smiled at Harry and turned to the Magi, questions already forming in his head.

'Everything will unfold in its own time,' they said.

'How long will that be?' Dan tried to press them.

'Time is relative and unreliable. What time are you in and what time do we think we're in? Are we in fact on our way to visit the infant Christ at the beginning of the previous new era, or are we embarking on a journey into the fourth millennium? Time is what you think it is. God's will is done only when it is the right time to do it. Blessings to you both.' And with that the Magi departed, their dazzling presence slowly fading into the dark night.

As they disappeared, Dan walked over to the box. The Book of Eternal Wisdom had gone. He glanced over to where Angelica had been holding the Board of Destiny. That too had gone.

Then Dan and Harry stood for a long time staring silently up into the star-filled sky. It was 6th January – Epiphany. The celebration of the arrival of the Magi to pay homage to the Christ child. Arriving or departing? Past or present? Or even future? What was time? The stars were spread in a blaze of glory across the inky blackness. As they stood there, each one lost in thought, a very low hum could be heard.

As one, Dan and Harry turned round. Walking towards them was a man of timeless presence. He had long white hair that illuminated his face and framed his penetrating emerald-green eyes. He wore a long, white robe, over which was a rich dark green cloak bordered with a gold braid, and on his face was a benevolent smile. He was encircled in an intense white light and the stars suddenly appeared to be chasing each other skittishly around the night sky, playing happily with each other and emitting short, bright bolts of dazzling energy. The man held his arms open in welcome, and thousands of smiling faces surrounded him. Dan recognized him at once from his vision in Damascus. This was Lord Melchizedek, the original Master of Destiny. His legacy was about to be revealed.

CHAPTER THIRTY-EIGHT

The Qumran Community near Jerusalem

5400 BC

'Welcome, welcome.' Lord Melchizedek embraced Dan warmly. 'And welcome to you, dear friend,' he said, smiling at Harry, before turning back to Dan. 'I come to take you on a journey.' He looked at Harry and smiled again. 'Please excuse us for a while.' Then he held out his hand to Dan who took it. As their fingers locked he felt the same surge of electrical force that he'd felt when the Magi had arrived. He found himself rising from the ground. He looked down to see Harry staring up at him. He felt weightless, as though gravity didn't exist. Cool winds rushed past him as they travelled through different climates and time zones and he lost all track of time. Images floated through his mind, people in different forms of dress living in mountains, villages, cities and towns. Wars, tempests, celebrations, weddings, family events, musical gatherings and other examples of human life all sped by in a kind of cinematic montage until he felt himself gradually slow down.

He glanced down, and his feet were planted firmly back on the ground. He looked up and the sky was a brilliant blue, the sun beating down on the landscape. Dan gazed around, trying to adjust to his new surroundings. He rubbed his eyes. The area around him was rugged and rocky, a barren and harsh landscape seemingly bereft of any signs of civilization. In front of him Lord Melchizedek was walking towards a large gate, which had been carved out of stone. Dan followed him.

They walked through the gate together. Dan stopped and stared in astonishment. In the middle of this desert was a thriving community. Men and a few women were bustling around going about their daily business. Traders were standing or sitting in the shade, laughing and chatting, selling household wares and tending succulent dates, which were drying on wooden slats. They all smiled and nodded when they saw Lord Melchizedek approaching. He raised his hand in greeting.

Dan frowned. He recognized this place. His nightmare at Gleneagles. Men rushing about preserving the ancient wisdom.

They walked on towards an imposing building which was located in the centre of the community. As they approached, a very tall, slim man wearing a long white robe appeared and ran towards Lord Melchizedek. When he'd reached him, he placed his hands on the wise man's shoulders and bent his head in homage. The sage briefly touched the top of the man's head in blessing and the young man smiled at Dan.

'Samuel, please meet Dan Adams. He is beginning his journey and has much to learn,' Lord Melchizedek explained.

'Welcome, Dan, welcome. This is the temple, please come with me,' Samuel said, indicating the building before them and leading him towards it. The three of them walked inside.

There were many rooms around a large central hall. 'Our place of worship,' Lord Melchizedek said.

'Where are we?' Dan asked him.

'I have brought you home to Qumran in the year 5400 BC. My kingdom of Jerusalem is near but this is my spiritual home, the place of my people and where the wisdom of all time is kept. Come.' Lord Melchizedek led Dan into a large room where there were rows of benches. In front of each bench was a desk where a scribe was busily writing on parchment, his brow furrowed in concentration.

Dan turned to his master, who explained.

'These men are copying the sacred scrolls so that the wisdom will be preserved forever. One day you will know them as the Dead Sea scrolls, which will be discovered in the caves that surround this area, and they are also carefully copying the Melchizedek Sacred Mysteries, which, as you know, will be found in another location. We will be gone from this area, but not from this world,' Lord Melchizedek told him.

'Sadly, some documents will have been lost by the time you get to hear of them, and some will be in translation for a very long time, their information held back by those who wish to control the people, while some will still be waiting to be discovered. We left many documents here but our inner secrets were transferred to Syria and your friend Harry is discovering their wisdom. In your lifetime all the information will be found. We are preserving our knowledge but we can't guarantee that people will act on it. Your job will be to bring light to documents that have not been released to the general public, and lead the experts to uncover those that are still to be found.'

'Is the Book of Eternal Wisdom now active?' Dan asked.

'The Book of Eternal Wisdom is the focal point of our patrimony. It is the testament to the power of the universe to bring salvation to its people. Listen to it. It will come to life fully again on the 3rd of April 2011. Uncover the hidden secrets and discover the blueprint of the destiny of the human race. It is your role to bring about redemption, or...' Lord Melchizedek paused.

'Or what?' Dan enquired.

'You already know this is the final moment of truth for the

human race. I don't need to explain further at this point.' Lord Melchizedek walked out of the scribes' room and led Dan into another room. Inside were three men, the Magi, the ancient astrologers of the East, who'd just been in Italy with him. They were studying charts and reading from scrolls, on which were written a series of what looked like highly complex calculations.

'As it is in heaven, so it shall be on earth,' Lord Melchizedek said quietly. 'The movement of the planets influences us all, yet how many of us understand or even accept this simple fact?'

'Apart from reading their horoscopes, I think most people have little understanding of the movements of the planets,' Dan admitted.

'Ah yes, the fortune tellers of the modern era, often just cheap tricks for a society built on instant gratification. Astronomy and astrology are not easy routes to discover your future. They are tools to uncover the messages of the heavens. Soon you will understand the eternal link that unites you to the activation of the Book of Eternal Wisdom. Not now but soon.'

'How will I understand?' Dan asked.

'Your power will come to life as you study the intricacies and meaning of your birth chart. You must experience it, act on it as your deepest instincts indicate. It's up to you to crack the code of your eternal myth.'

'But could you give me a few hints please? I feel I'm groping around in the dark.'

'Lose the need for instant gratification and learn to trust. You would not be chosen as the redeemer if you did not have the qualities to succeed. We, your guides, have faith in you,' the ancient mystic said.

'Who are you and where do you come from?' Dan asked.

'We are everywhere, in all of you if you choose to

recognize us.' Lord Melchizedek leaned over to pick up a gold coin that had just been placed in a silk-lined box by the Magi. 'As you have discovered, these coins dissolve the boundaries of your reality with the reality of other worlds. But they also have a series of messages on many levels, which resonate with the Book of Eternal Wisdom. Think of it as complex telemetry. Now you can only access the first layer but as you travel along life's path you will also unlock the code to multiple layers, each one taking you nearer to the core of your eternal myth, and thereby closer to solving the collective myth of the human race. But live it, don't overthink it.'

'Are there seven mystical, active gold coins?'

Lord Melchizedek smiled. 'There is an eighth coin, but it is not the time for it to be revealed to you, its power and mysteries are too strong for you at present. Beware of those who try and access its power. Once it is in play, it resonates to its own beat. We don't know when that might be, and we cannot control it, only you can do that. It is part of the human mystery to understand and access it for the collective good, but believe me, you don't want to face that challenge yet. Learn to deal with what you have and deal with what will be presented to you when you need to. And don't be seduced by fool's gold. Learn from the forthcoming collapse of the old ways in the Middle East, along with the overwhelming rise of anxiety which is causing such inertia amongst your leaders. You need to find courage, strength, conviction and teach the joys of self-sacrifice – it's a hard role we've assigned you. Learn the lessons of events such as the financial collapse of 2008, an event planted years previously in the souls of those seeking to build empires on sand and sell things that didn't exist.'

'Don't we all trade in ideas that didn't exist before we made them reality?' Dan suggested.

'Ideas created with a sound basis bring about the alchemy

of human progress but ideas based on a complex web of illusion will not reap rewards. It's a rule of universal physics. And that's the end of the first lesson.' Lord Melchizedek smiled.

Dan felt the ground move beneath him, followed by a sensation of the boundaries of reality shifting once again.

Then he felt himself travel back through the hologram of human life – births, anniversaries, weddings and funerals, good times of celebration and sad times of remembrance – all part of the human condition, he thought, as the earth and stars shifted position and he moved towards his own timeframe.

When Dan opened his eyes again, he found himself back on his land in Italy. Feeling dazed, his thoughts in turmoil, he sat for a few minutes by the outbuildings before making his way over to his car. He opened the door to find Harry sitting in the driver's seat, looking agitated.

'Where have you been? Who was that? I can't believe... my God, so much to take in... the confirmation of the ancient wisdom... the Book of Eternal Wisdom in all its glory... McManus and Angelica, and me such a fool to trust her... what have I done?' Harry gabbled, looking flushed and as usual wiping his brow.

'Calm down. First of all, you mustn't blame yourself for trusting Angelica. She came with eminent references and although I didn't trust her, that was no reason for you to just discard her talents.' Dan spoke slowly as he tried to adjust back to reality, or what he perceived as reality. His mind was still re-playing his recent journey back in time. Or was it forward in time? Were the ancient mysteries part of the past or the future?

Harry drove off and they sat in silence for a few minutes, until finally, as they made their way along the roads, the silhouettes of rocks and bushes faintly visible in the darkness, Dan recounted his journey.

'So I guess it's up to us now,' Harry said. 'We flourish or we perish. Do you think the Holy Trinity has disappeared?'

'They could have vapourized along with Angelica and McManus but I don't think so. It is a powerful entity that is integrated into all areas of our existence. We must infiltrate it and redirect its aims and methods for the greater good.'

'So what exactly is your role as Master of Destiny?'

'I don't know really. It seems to require me to embrace my destiny and then the collective to embrace theirs. It hasn't exactly got a job description,' Dan said ruefully.

'No matter what you say, I still feel bad about trusting Angelica. Such evil but a truly horrible end,' Harry said quietly.

'She was punished for her evil as the Universal Power saw fit. Poor Anna.' Dan's face clouded.

'Yes. But remember that nothing can change your father's obvious love for you, and a father's love for his child is always a great joy, whether physical or spiritual. We have seen that things are rarely as they seem. We have to learn to think and act in a different way.'

'Quite. My love for my father has not changed. After all, he gave me this life, this adventure.' Dan smiled. 'Now, what are your plans?' he asked pulling himself back into the moment.

'I think I'll head back to Boston. There is much to be done. I left Teddy with one of the seven key documents of the Melchizedek Sacred Mysteries – a ritual of baptism and renewal that appears to be the key to unlocking our potential. What are you going to do next?' Harry asked.

'Oh, I'll just go and start preaching in the local town square. The Messiah has come again! A bit chilly at this time of year but what do you think? Does the idea have legs?' Dan joked.

Harry gave him a sideways glance. 'I think "proceed with

caution" and "remain calm at all times" are the keywords to your ministry,' he said with a laugh.

'Well, I'm seeing the Mayor tomorrow to get everything signed off. After that, I'm going home to see Mr Big and Thomas, who is struggling with his GCSE history. I suppose I should contact Douglas but I'm not going to deal with that yet.'

'I think he should know that the Holy Trinity was not, or is not, quite the shining example of a new order that he envisaged,' Harry said. 'I'm sure you'll find a way of getting that message across, maybe tell him you're going to look for ways of helping people find the right path in life and get the economy back on track. Use words he understands.' Harry glanced at Dan who seemed deep in thought. He felt proud of his friend, proud of the way he'd dealt with the recent momentous changes and challenges in his life. Strange to say it but if anyone could lead mankind to redemption then Harry realized that Dan would be the best candidate.

They arrived back at the hotel and parked the car.

'I'll just stay out here for a while,' Dan said.

'See you in the morning,' Harry punched Dan lightly on the arm and went into the hotel lobby.

Outside, Dan looked up at the stars again. There was something he had to do. Pulling his mobile phone out of his pocket he dialled a number.

'Hello,' a sleepy voice answered.

'Sorry if I've woken you Mum, just wanted to tell you I'm safe.'

'I'm so pleased. I was worried. I'm so...'

'Please don't apologize, there's been enough apologizing for the past. You're all the family I have. We must build a new beginning, a new understanding. I look forward to seeing you soon. I've got so much to tell you.'

'Please stay safe, dear Dan,' his mother said.

After the call Dan felt energized and happy. He would sleep well tonight. He walked back into the hotel and made his way to his room. As soon as his head hit the pillow he fell into a deep sleep.

The next day Dan met the mayor. She was dressed simply in a black woollen skirt, pink cashmere sweater and flat pumps. Italian style, he thought to himself. They always managed to look exactly right for every occasion. It was a bit superficial of him but he'd like to absorb some of their style. She greeted him warmly with a peck on the cheek. Obviously, he was well on the way to acceptance.

'Welcome into our community,' she said, smiling and handing him the various 'permissions' which she'd just signed. 'Marco likes to make sure everyone is treated fairly. He's very good at sorting out complex situations, and making it all... how do you say? Easily digestible?'

Dan smiled, nodded and felt at ease.

'I knew you'd come,' she continued. 'My father said it was predestined that the house would be reunited with its rightful owner. You understand that?' she said, looking into his eyes.

'I do,' Dan agreed. 'Do you have children?' he asked.

'No. Marco and I are not yet at that point.' She hesitated and a brief look of pain crossed her face.

'Oh,' he said, as images of a man driving with reckless abandon, two small children in the back seat of a car and the same car upside down in a deep gorge appeared from nowhere in his mind. These images were followed by a short, sharp headache which made him rub his temples distractedly.

Recovering her composure, she looked at him. 'You understand much but say little, it's a good quality to have.' Then she gave him a radiant smile that touched him deeply.

Before he returned to London, Dan went to visit his land again. He was surprised that he didn't see any dark images of Angelica and McManus's terrible deaths. It was as though the land had absorbed the awful incident and hidden any unpleasant residue.

He was walking back down the hill, when he noticed a shadow by one of the ancient olive trees. The shadow moved and a short rotund man came into sight. Dan grinned.

'Mr Perkins, what a pleasure. Are you just passing by?'

'Delivering, dear boy, delivering.' He handed Dan a very elegant cream envelope with an official stamp on it. Dan opened it quickly and a gold coin dropped into the palm of his hand. He looked at Mr Perkins and raised an eyebrow.

'You know the form by now,' Mr Perkins said with a grin.

'Ah yes, a message from another one of the mystical coins,' Dan said. The coins seemed to move around the universe to their own rhythm; one minute he thought he knew where they were, and the next they appeared out of nowhere.

Dan turned the coin round in his hand. He pressed the sides and the glorious, colourful hologram burst into life. He felt himself once more transported into its hidden delights, his heart filled with joy. He looked around and saw the outline of the Krak des Chevaliers. Against its luminous magnificence was written a time and date: Sunday, 3rd April 2011, at 2.22 p.m. Lord Melchizedek had told him that was the date when the Book of Eternal Wisdom would activate; it would herald his first meeting as the Master of Destiny with his Council of Elders. Dan felt himself gently drift out of the bright colours and back to earth with Mr Perkins.

'April is still a couple of months or so away,' Dan said. 'Isn't it more urgent?'

'Urgent, urgent, nothing's urgent round here, you know. It all unfolds in its own time,' Mr Perkins said briskly. 'Allow the universe to guide you. Remember you are not in the driving seat – not yet.' Then he disappeared, leaving Dan studying the gold coin, which had returned to its original state in the palm of his hand.

CHAPTER THIRTY-NINE

London

January 2011

As Dan was taking his first steps to rebuilding his life, the Judge, the Monsignor, the Politician, the Banker and the Philosopher were meeting. The Judge was pacing around the room. 'I can't understand it, Angelica and McManus have just disappeared. Where the hell are they? Beatris, what have you found out?' he snapped.

The Banker cleared her throat briefly, her fine blonde hair limp from nerves. 'Angelica and Oliver had found the whereabouts of Adams and his sidekick Harry Bakhoum, and were heading to confront them somewhere in southern Italy.'

'Then use your fine mind and your contacts to find out what's happened to them,' the Judge instructed.

'Perhaps they don't want to be found,' the Philosopher said quietly. 'Maybe they will keep the riches for themselves.'

'Then they've underestimated us,' the Judge said coldly. 'We will find them and we will discover what is going on. There is no corner of this earth where we haven't got someone who can help us. Our tentacles spread far and wide. We will know soon enough. Beatris, report to me when you've got the answers.' Then he walked to the window and looked down the Mall. Someone was lying and he was going to find out who it was, and deal with it. They hadn't come this far to fall at the last hurdle.

Behind him, the Politician studied the group. They were fools if they thought they had control over this contrary world. He knew better. He knew that you had to find the rhythm of the Universal Power and work with it – that was the key to unlocking great power and wealth. East versus West. Good versus Evil. Life versus Death. To him it was like a game of chess. Make a move, wait, move a bit more, and more and more and then surprise your opponent with a sudden crushing manoeuvre to gain victory.

'Right, we'll keep in close contact. Usual protocol and codes,' the Judge said before heading out of the door, closely followed by the others.

CHAPTER FORTY

Krak des Chevaliers, Syria

3rd April 2011

The sky was still dark as Dan drove along the road from Homs to Tartus, which was quiet after the recent unrest. He was at the wheel of his hire car, his brow furrowed in concentration. He was concerned. The recent protests by the people were increasing in intensity. Only two days ago thousands of protestors had emerged from Friday prayers and taken to the streets. The unrest had even reached Damascus where several people had been killed in the suburb of Douma. He hoped it wouldn't affect Harry or his work. He had no fear for himself, as he knew this first meeting of the new Master of Destiny and his council would be protected. But he feared that justice and fair play would not prevail as it should in this glorious country.

He turned off and followed the road up the mountain through the village of Shmiyseh, and through agricultural land until he found himself in front of the grand, pale-stoned Krak des Chevaliers.

He climbed out of the car and gazed at the imposing structure that stood as witness to so many events that had formed the land. He closed his eyes and his mind drifted back to the meeting of the Master of Destiny and the Council of Elders in 1179, and also to the events of the last couple of months.

The demise of McManus and Angelica had made the Holy Trinity more popular – 'Died in a tragic car crash', the headlines had said, for that was the way the Universal Power had presented their deaths. The other members of the inner circle had used the sympathy vote to the full and more recruits appeared each day. They were now doing house calls, carrying clever messages which weren't just about spiritual fulfilment. They were signing people up and then sending financial and careers advisers, along with personal counsellors to them, boosting their income and sense of well-being. The rich and famous were flocking to join and give away their money, knowing there was more to come, making the leaders of the Holy Trinity very wealthy.

Not a day went by when someone didn't try and convince Dan to join forces with the organization. A very persuasive lady had called to see him, Beatris de Souza, the head of one of the largest private equity groups in the world. Even Monsignor Giovanni Barbarelli, a member of the Pope's inner sanctum, had requested a meeting. Both had confessed to being leading lights in the Holy Trinity, but they'd both insisted that McManus and Angelica had acted on their own, and were nothing to do with their plans to promote good and harmony throughout the world. Dan had resisted them all. He had to form his own plan of action before he infiltrated their organization. He needed time to absorb his new status as Master of Destiny before deciding what to do about them – although he knew they'd be deciding what to do about him. He was the one person who stood between them and the infinite power of the Book of Eternal Wisdom.

There hadn't been any more huge revelations yet, he just felt more in tune with the world. He was beginning to sense things before they happened. He knew what people were thinking, or were about to say. He felt as though his talents, whatever they might be, were slowly unfolding. It would take time to get used to the changes he was experiencing in himself. He'd looked at his birth chart, but he needed to find a gifted and trustworthy astrologer to help him interpret it and that, too, would take time.

Thomas had backed away from the Holy Trinity when they had become too controlling, much to Dan's relief, so he had taken the opportunity to try and explain to his godson something about his own calling.

'Just see if you can fix it for Millwall to win the FA Cup,' Thomas had said, grinning, when Dan had tentatively said he felt he might be acquiring some unusual powers.

'Miracles can take a while!' Dan had said, laughing. That for now, had been the end of their discussion about his spiritual development.

Dan's new-found ability to read people's minds and motivations didn't seem to include the people he loved. He was rebuilding his relationship with his mother but it was without any insights into her thoughts and feelings. But they were learning to trust each other. It felt good to have a mother again.

He was still coming to terms with Anna's death, but he was beginning to accept it as part of his journey. As for Jenny, dear Jenny, she had once more become a close friend, and was slipping easily into the fabric of his life, but not in a romantic sense – not yet, anyway.

He got out of the car and turned his face up to the sun. Its gentle warmth lifted his heart as it always did, easing his anxieties about the turmoil in Syria. He breathed in deeply and smiled. The air was full of the sweet smell of jasmine. Then he turned and walked up the steep path to the entrance of the Krak des Chevaliers, feeling the warm glow of anticipation.

In the wider world, the Middle East was in flux. President

Mubarak of Egypt had stepped down on 11th of February, the second date in the hologram Dan had seen at the meeting of the Holy Trinity he'd attended with Anna. And on 22nd of February, just four days after his fortieth birthday, there had been an unexplained glitch in the world's biggest super computer – a warning of the effects of cyber terrorism. Dan had only known about it because he had read a small piece in the *Wall Street Journal*. It had made him very aware of the evil he was up against.

As he drew close to the great door it opened and he walked inside, up the old stone steps, worn and uneven with age, and on into the interior. Just as he had done previously, he walked up into the inner enclosure, through the area that had once been the stables and then along the lower ramparts and up the narrow, steep, stone stairs to the top of the castle. He felt Joshua's presence gently guiding him to his rightful place.

Dan felt a sliver of excitement. His only regret was the absence of Harry. He had hoped he would accompany him on this important journey but he'd declined Dan's invitation to travel with him, citing the civil unrest and the need to stay close to the dig, which Dan understood.

A cool breeze rustled through the trees and the upper ramparts. He walked round the old stone table and then over to the wall overlooking the plain of Al-Buqia. Ahead were the beginnings of the Lebanese and Alawiyeen mountain ranges, millions of years old, standing as a testament to the brief existence of mankind.

'Couldn't miss this grand occasion!'

Dan turned to see Harry walking towards him.

Dan gave a big grin and pulled his friend to him in a bear hug.

'So you really are here with me, fantastic, how? Why?'

'I am a member of the Council of Elders, but I couldn't tell you prior to the meeting. In any case I only found out a couple of days ago, when I had a dream about this place and then next morning found a return airline ticket on my desk. I was told to keep quiet, that the first meeting had to be spontaneous, to create a new, fresh energy that will lead us into a new age. Amazing. Incredible. I'm honoured and experiencing a rather large dose of trepidation with all that's going on in these parts,'

'I can't tell you what it means to have you with me on my journey. And you don't need to feel anxious. All will be well.' Dan was still grinning from ear to ear.

A young boy appeared and handed them cups of a sweet, red drink.

'With this cup I drink your wisdom that I might be free,' Dan whispered to himself, going back in time to the dream of the Krak he'd had previously. He still felt Joshua's presence all around him and knew the previous masters would be close to him at this his first council meeting.

He sipped the drink and considered what was to come. This was his time, he had to use it wisely. He leaned against the wall and waited.

'No sign of the Holy Trinity?' Harry asked.

'They won't be here. Today we are protected from their interference,' Dan replied, as the rustle of cloaks heralded the arrival of two new people. He turned round to see a very old Chinaman and an Arab who was wearing the formal clothes of a religious cleric. The Chinaman spoke first.

'I am Liu Shang, chief astrologer during the Han dynasty and a member of the council. I come to be with you throughout your journey.'

Harry smiled. Liu Shang was an ancient mystic who had travelled through time to be here. He had a great gift for interpreting the movement of the planets. His presence was a welcome gift, a blessing.

Dan clasped the man's hands in both of his. This man would be the key to unlocking his future through accurately interpreting his birth chart.

The young boy stepped forward and handed both men cups of the red drink.

The Arab man spoke with quiet authority. 'I am the Imam of Damascus. My ancestors have been part of the council since the beginning of time so I am continuing the ancient role which has been bestowed on us.' He smiled at Dan who embraced this eternal member of the council.

They took their places at the table. As Dan slipped into his seat opposite Harry, he saw the figure of Joshua pass along the ramparts for a fleeting moment and he felt reassured.

He glanced at his watch. It was nearly two o'clock in the afternoon. They had less than half an hour before the Board of Destiny would open and there were still three more people to arrive.

A minute later, a well-dressed man in a suit, shirt and sporting a yellow patterned cravat walked up to the group.

He greeted Dan. 'I am Jozef Guttenberg of the Mulberry Tree organization. I come to help you create and progress the ideals that will form the basis of your tenure as Master of Destiny.'

Dan raised his eyebrows in surprise. The Mulberry Tree was a secretive organization of the Jewish faith, dedicated to the promotion of harmony between East and West. It operated below the radar but Dan knew that it had a big following and achieved much in the trouble spots of the world, working hard to solve conflict. It was recognized as a force for the good of mankind.

'Welcome, please join us.' Dan indicated a spare seat.

Less than five minutes later, another man appeared in a cardinal's normal dress – black cassock with scarlet piping and buttons, a scarlet sash, pectoral cross on a chain and a scarlet zucchetto.

'I am Cardinal Blake from the United States of America. I come not in full ceremonial attire but as a man proclaiming God's faith in us, as decreed by our council. It is with the council's help that I will protect and support you,' he declared, sitting opposite Dan.

Finally, a young woman appeared, wearing a long blue silk dress and wrapped in a navy blue cloak with gold piping round the edges. She walked towards the table. Dan recognized her as the lady in the mirror at Chequers. He smiled in welcome.

'I am Jawna' of Milly descended from the line of Stephanie. Someone from the line of Milly has always been a member of the council and it is decreed that I should be here with you today. I bring the Board of Destiny.' She carefully placed the wooden ball with its intricate carvings on a polished wooden plinth in the centre of the table. Then she sat down next to Dan. The Council of Elders was in place.

Six golden coins appeared and started to spin round the table. For tonight the two that had been in the possession of the Holy Trinity were here – was the Holy Trinity losing its power? Dan wondered.

As the coins gathered speed, a seventh coin, slightly larger and brighter than the rest, appeared and started to spin in the centre of the others.

The Imam spoke. 'These golden coins represent the seven ages of enlightenment, which are the stages we must experience on our journey to full revelation. Although you have only found four coins, all seven will appear at this first meeting to bring you information about your journey as we embrace the Vitae Era. Then it will be up to you to recover the other three coins, which will return to their resting places.'

Not easy, but I never thought it would be, Dan mused,

glancing at Harry, but feeling relieved there were seven and not eight coins. He didn't feel able to handle the doubled-edged gift of what he understood from Lord Melchizedek to be an all-powerful eighth coin.

'The first coin is the Initiate,' explained the Imam. 'This is our starting point, the secret of the Initiate will be revealed tonight. After this there is the second stage of the Young Master, as we begin to understand the knowledge, then the Traveller, as we go out into the world to spread our knowledge. Then the Wilderness, where we must withdraw to contemplate the full meaning of the knowledge we have discovered. The fifth stage is Wisdom, when the knowledge we have learned will be transferred into inner wisdom. Then there is the Teacher as we become recognized worldwide as purveyors of the truth, and finally the Master of Destiny. That is the highest level in the seven heavens of wisdom, when the final secret of our destiny will be revealed to us, and when the Master of Destiny takes his place on the Universal Council.'

Dan looked up towards the heavens and saw the Archangels forming a protective circle round the group. Just as he had known. Tonight they were protected. The scene was set for the players to begin their journey.

CHAPTER FORTY-ONE

Krak des Chevaliers, Syria

3rd April 2011

Jawna' said a short, silent prayer that the darkness of her ancestor Stephanie's experience at a previous council meeting with the Book of Eternal Wisdom would not be repeated. The terrible repercussions of that night had often been told in her family. One of the council members, they'd never discovered who, had betrayed their secrets and the retribution had been terrible. It had allowed the dark power to nearly destroy their future.

The journeys of the Masters had always been challenging. Jacob had been killed in Judaea, but fortunately his spirited daughter Eschiva had brought the secrets to their destination here in Syria. For Joshua things had been worse; his son Aziz had died at the hands of his enemies as he tried to complete his long journey to the outer reaches of the known world. His mystical knowledge had lain hidden for hundreds of years, but it had still worked its magic and seen the light through collective human endeavour. It led to the period of enlightenment in the 15th, 16th and 17th centuries through great men like Isaac Newton, Galileo, the mysterious Dr John Dee, who counselled Elizabeth I, and, of course, The Royal Society. Jawna' shivered and then shook off her fears. Tonight would be different.

Dan stood up. 'I welcome you, my fellow council

members, and pray that wisdom will visit us as we embark on our journey to reveal the secrets that will lead us to fulfilment. Today we begin the Vitae Era, the era of life, and hope and optimism surround us. We are all here to participate in this ancient rite and understand the meaning of the words imparted to us here today. I wish each of you the gift of clarity and I wish for all of us the gift of benevolence.'

Harry glanced at Dan and saw a physical change in him as he officially took on the mantle of the Master of Destiny. It was a subtle change, but nevertheless a significant one. He conveyed an air of confidence and a real sense of courage and conviction; renewed vigour and optimism radiated from him.

At precisely 2.22 p.m. a group of musicians who had appeared in the background started to play their instruments and a deep, resonant beat filled the air as the wooden ball started to open. Dan's heart beat faster and an intense sense of anticipation and excitement filled his soul as the beautiful golden Board, decorated with flora and fauna from all the corners of all the worlds, appeared. Unicorns skipped across the surface, lions gambolled and eagles soared into the sky as a sweet aria filled the air.

Dan stood again and opened his arms, allowing the energy of the mysterious source to fill his mind as he spoke words alien but somehow familiar to them all. '"Let every nature in the cosmos attend the hearing of the hymn. Open, O earth; let every lock that bars the torrent open to me; trees be not shaken. I am about to sing a hymn to the lord of creation, to the universe and to the one. Let God's immortal circle attend my discourse." So says the Corpus Hermeticum, the sacred text of the Masters of Destiny.'

As the aria continued the Board opened fully, swinging into position on the stone table, its golden surface shimmering in the light and reflecting the sun's rays. As before, it was divided into twelve houses like a birth chart. The planets and the moon started to appear from the centre well, each one bringing its own special gifts and each one moving into the correct house to reflect its exact position at this time.

The ancient astrologer Liu Shang spoke softly. 'At this first meeting I will explain the movement of the planets and their relationship to each other in simple terms. But over time you, Dan Adams, as the Master of Destiny, will be expected to study astronomy and increase your knowledge, so you too will know how to harness the power of the planets, the moons and the stars, knowing when you act in an atmosphere of benevolence and when to take heed. Let me begin.

'Here we have the sun and the moon in the eighth house opposite Saturn, which is in the second house. This suggests the final struggle is about to begin for the resources both human and mineral of this planet earth.

'Both the sun and the moon are conjunct with Jupiter, indicating an expanded new world view, a brighter day in which our beliefs and our faith will gather a large following. But they are square to Pluto so this is a time of crisis. The dark power has not been vanquished, it is only dormant. History tells us that man has not yet learned to overcome his weaknesses to work for the good of the collective. We must unlock our strengths, understand the power of our minds and connect this power to the universe and learn to listen to other intelligences. Only then will the Universal Power trust us with the true wisdom of our age.' He paused and studied the Board.

'Six planets are in the eighth house of secrets, mysteries and power. Mercury is retrograde so it is a time when past secrets will be revealed. We must listen carefully, be alert. The past secrets hold the key to our power and we need to understand their meaning and how it applies to each individual.' Liu Shang gazed at each one of the council members gathered round the table. They all met his gaze, each one wondering what their individual calling would be. The mood was sombre and serious.

'We must not expect an easy journey, for negative thoughts and emotions will always be attracted to the good and seek to destroy it.' He looked at Dan. 'This time of opening today has a powerful resonance with your own birth chart. The degree of Neptune is also the degree of your sun, so it is the revelation of your life's purpose, confusing and mystifying but also a powerful message of your calling. It confirms you as Master of Destiny. It does not, though, offer you a step-by-step guide to understanding that much-discussed conundrum, your eternal myth, the blueprint of your destiny, given to you at the moment of your birth. Your life's journey is to find your own path and call on your internal and external resources to discover that which is true to you.'

Dan looked on, his mind slipping back again to the meeting of Joshua, and the Council of Elders in 1179. He closed his eyes and wished for a benevolent spirit to guide him in his words and actions.

'As our souls travel through the heavens we gather our gifts from the planets.' Liu Shang explained. 'The most prominent bring us the greatest gifts and the greatest challenges to conquer before we can fully embrace our destiny,' he paused. 'Now we wait our final three celestial planetary guests, who might not be as well known, but who are nonetheless a great influence. And here they are. Ceres, Athena and Nig-ba. Their presence brings us the important gift of trusting in the unknown and letting go of our old ways of thinking. Tonight we will receive the wisdom of the ancient masters.' He finished speaking and looked at each of them in turn.

Many emotions flowed through Dan, excitement, anticipation, trepidation, acceptance, but above all he realized he was not alone. He just had to look for the extraordinary in the ordinary, the special in the routine of everyday life. The collective would work to help him fulfil his destiny, which would help mankind to fulfil its own destiny.

Above the Board, the celestial Archangels Michael, Gabriel, Raphael, Uriel, Raguel, Sariel and Remiel continued to move slowly and gracefully in the sky, acting as protectors. Today the slate was wiped clean for a new beginning.

The sky was illuminated as the earth moved and locked itself in the centre well. The circle of infinity, the planet of human life was in place. The scene was set, the mysteries could be revealed. Dan glanced at Harry, their eyes met and they smiled at each other, anticipating the magical things that were to be revealed.

Finally, a sweet-smelling mist heralded the arrival of the Magi, their long silver cloaks shimmering with precious jewels. With them came the Book of Eternal Wisdom. It drifted slowly down to rest by the Board, its pages fanning open and changing colour as it gathered power and came to life. The seven coins spun round the Board. Dan and Harry both recognized Larvandad, Gushnasaph and Hormisdas who had appeared in Italy. They moved into the three remaining seats, and opened their arms, enfolding everyone in a warm embrace.

'Greetings, dear friends, welcome to the first day of your new dawn, your Vitae Era. We bring benevolence to your hearts, wisdom to your minds and compassion to your souls. Use your gifts wisely. We are aligned to you and redemption is once again in the hands of those who wish for the greater good. It is now up to you to ensure that the desire for the greater good wins.'

As the power of the Book of Eternal Wisdom started to activate, Neptune moved into Pisces, bringing the winds of change and the power of the new leader.

The Imam rose. 'Oh, gracious Lord Melchizedek, by your leave may we know the secret of your mysteries? The mysteries that are yours should now, through your magnificent benevolence, also become ours,' he chanted softly.

The book started to sing its message of hope, each person hearing it in their mother tongue and being enveloped in the glorious colours of the rainbow, bestowing good fortune and grace on them all.

Dan raised his eyes to heaven. Now he understood that as it was in heaven, it would be on earth. As the book sang to him in English, he felt his final transformation take place and the hidden power of his new role flow through him.

'I am awake once more, and come to serve you on earth that you may knowest that which is given to me. I contain the inner secrets of mankind, the blueprint for your future. Listen to me, for this is the last cycle of my revelations. You will, in the fullness of time, hear seven mystical secrets if you open your hearts and work as one. The coins will reveal their secrets as you make your journey of enlightenment through the heavens, until you reach the highest spiritual calling, the seventh heaven. When you reach that, heaven and earth will be as one, and you will move to the next stage of your human evolution, when you will be united with the universe and your role on the Universal Council will be revealed.

'Connect to the true meaning of the wisdom contained in the documents, which are yours to discover. However, a word of warning. If you become blinded to the guidance of those sent to help you, or you chase your own interests at the expense and hurt of others, then all will be lost.'

The council members exchanged glances, uplifted by the

book's message and also mindful of their responsibilities, which were sealing their bond as keepers of the secrets.

'My first message is to tell the Master of Destiny of his powers, and explain how he can begin to unlock the mysteries of the human race, with the guidance of his Council of Elders.

'Dan Adams, as Master of Destiny, you are already discovering your ability to see into people's souls and understand their thoughts and motivations. Know, too, that you can act as a divine guide, bringing messages to people who ask for it. But you may not force a person to take a particular action. Direct interference is not within your power.

'Most importantly, you will now be shown the sacred portals where you may pass through to communicate with other worlds, share in their knowledge and mysteries and help your own world to evolve. Your wise council will guide and advise you. But even if you will be protected, know that you are not immortal. The gift of immortality lies with the Universal Power and that has not been given to you yet.'

The singing stopped and Dan looked intently at the Book of Eternal Wisdom until it sang once more.

'You may ask me three questions.'

Dan took a deep breath and tried to think of three intelligent questions to ask out of the hundreds that were crowding his brain. He looked round at the council.

'Does anyone wish to ask a question?' he asked.

'The questions must come from the Master of Destiny,' the book sang to him.

'Where do we go when we die?' he blurted out, hoping that one day he'd be reunited with his father and Anna.

'It depends on your life's journey. As we've said, you all start your journey through the seven heavens, but you will be at different levels of evolution. You will return to earth or move on to other places in the universe until you reach the seventh heaven, then you do the work of the Universal Power.'

Dan sat silently for a while, trying to form two meaningful questions. The 'where do we go when we die?' one had been rather a waste as he didn't need to know that yet.

'How do we find the locations of the sacred portals?' he asked, suddenly finding inspiration.

'The coins will lead you to them as well as your guides. Be open to the unexpected. Both St Simeon's Basilica and Ain Dara are portals to other worlds, as you sensed while there, but others will be hidden in surroundings that will not make their inner mysteries obvious. Return to St Simeon's Basilica and Ain Dara, and the road to finding the others will be revealed to you.'

'How do I know how to help mankind fulfil its destiny?' Dan asked his third question.

'You will commune with the other worlds and learn from them. Earth is our most challenging planet, and also the one with the most divine potential. If you can harness the knowledge of your fellow travellers in space and time to your collective human potential here, then you will unlock the mystery, and in so doing release the great energy and power of your destiny,' answered the Book of Eternal Wisdom.

'But what do I do now? Live in Italy? Work? Travel? Stay in one place?' Dan suddenly found a voice to all the other questions that had been building up inside him.

But the singing from the Book of Eternal Wisdom had subsided and the pages slowly stopped turning and the colours faded into the light of the late-afternoon sun.

'Neptune has reached the top of the chart, its enigmatic presence indicates closure as the new era starts,' Liu Shang said quietly, and one by one the planets disappeared and the golden Board turned back into a wooden ball.

The Magi turned to Dan.

'You must not fill your mind with anxieties. Be open to receive our messages, which very often arrive on the breeze of ordinary life. Listen to the Universal Power which is deep within and without each of you. Use your powers well. Remember to indicate the right path rather than interfere directly in the actions of your fellow man. However, every Master of Destiny has the power to decide on the path of reincarnation for people he so chooses. And although he cannot generally interfere in the daily lives of the human race, he can summon the great universal energy three times to change the outcome of a critical situation. But once you have used that power, your own will be diminished and death will be near. You can also choose your own death in favour of one whom you wish to save. However, in following your own interests you could be condemning your fellow man to a collective demise, for that is also in your power.'

Dan hesitated but he knew he had to ask the question. 'Did my father use his powers in this way?'

The Magi answered his question without hesitation. 'Yes, he saved Angelica's mother from death in childbirth, but in so doing he released his daughter's evil on the world. Also, in exchange for his own death he saved you when fate dictated an early demise for you at the hands of a foe, the exact details of which will remain the secret of the universe.'

Dan closed his eyes and felt a wave of intense emotion pass through him. Images of his past life filled his mind. Then the sweet smell of jasmine brought him back to his senses and he was reminded of all that lay before him.

When he opened his eyes again, the Magi were gone and with them the Board of Destiny and the Book of Eternal Wisdom. Dan looked round and saw that Liu Shang, the Imam of Damascus, Jawna' of Milly, the Cardinal and Josef

Guttenberg had also disappeared, leaving him and Harry alone at the table.

Slowly, Dan rose and walked over to the ramparts and looked out into the distance. Harry joined him and they stood in silence for a long time, watching the sun bless the landscape and bring life to the world. They were each lost in their own thoughts. Finally, Dan turned to Harry.

'I'm ready to take whatever life throws at me. It is obvious that we must open our minds to a new way of thinking and a new way of interacting with our fellow humans. I guess the main test will be in uniting our disparate lives for the common good.' Dan paused, then smiled. 'I have no idea yet how to make it all work but I have absolute faith.'

'What about our fellow council members? Did they ever exist? Do they exist now?' Harry asked Dan.

'I believe the boundaries between life and death, and our lives and the lives of other beings, are limited only by our perceptions of time. I guess the question is not whether they exist in our world but what their actions do to our world.' And with that Dan and Harry walked back down the stone stairs, through the inner courtyards and stables, and out of the main entrance into the evening sun.

CHAPTER FORTY-TWO

London

Summer 2011

After the meeting at the Krak, Dan found his life returned to surprising normality, although he felt a lot more in tune with the rhythm of the universe. Time was simply the way by which the human race measured its life, but it wasn't the driving force.

Harry spent nearly all his time in Boston, working with Teddy Maitland. They were making slow but steady progress on filing and translating the sacred documents. In a couple of years the first batch of translations would be ready for the wider world. Harry had built a memorial to Mumtaz Zinohed at the dig in Syria.

Dan spent most of his time in Italy. The house was progressing well, and as it took shape he felt he was rebuilding the community spirit. Together with many of the locals, he'd celebrated Easter on the land – a giant trestle table groaning with local delicacies, and their own produce. The whole community had come together, even his mother had flown over to join them. It had been a wonderful day.

He'd set up a local school which combined traditional subjects with the more esoteric. Adults and children came to learn mathematics, architecture, and study the sciences as well as to paint, write, study astronomy and partake in the old-fashioned tradition of debate and discourse. They had created a space resembling an old Greek agora, a place of congregation. It was proving to be extremely successful.

Today he was in London, staying in his apartment, and due to meet Harry for dinner at their usual place, the In and Out Club. Dan was in London buying books and also meeting a couple of professors who wanted to come and teach at the school. Harry was in town to meet with one of his experts. It would be their first meeting since that day at the Krak des Chevaliers.

Dan stopped to buy a newspaper from the same man, Gavin, who had been selling newspapers at the end of his street for over ten years. Dan paid and was about to go when he hesitated. A strong sense of sadness suddenly engulfed him. He looked at Gavin. He was probably in his mid-thirties but he looked world weary and worn. Their eyes met and Dan noticed their lack of sparkle.

'You look a bit down on such a lovely day,' Dan commented.

Gavin buried his head further in his newspaper and Dan thought he was going to ignore his comment; after all, they'd never said much more than 'Hello' and 'Nice day, isn't it?' before now. Dan took a deep breath and with sudden clarity saw a girl of about twenty-five. She had short dark hair and was packing a suitcase. Her face was wet with tears. 'Family problems? Your sister?' Dan enquired softly. He was taking a chance, but he felt compelled to help this man.

Gavin's head jerked up. 'How did you know?' Then it all came out in a big rush. 'She's leaving soon to go to university, the first one in our family to go, and you'd think she was the blessed daughter. Mum and Dad have done nothing but go on and on about how great she is. It...' he paused, suddenly feeling self-conscious.

'Irritates you?' Dan smiled.

'Yes, especially when I'm here working twelve-hour days, seven days a week bringing in some money after Dad got laid off. I'm the main breadwinner now. Anyway, I didn't tell her that I'd been keeping a special bank account for her studies. I decided to put it on hold and keep it a secret. We had harsh words this morning before I left for work. Do you understand about families?' He stopped and blinked.

'Oh yes,' Dan replied. 'I certainly do. My family found out the hard way that withholding information leads to mistrust and heartache. I've learned to rebuild love and trust and not be so careless with the important things in life, especially for something as unworthy as pride and envy.' Dan turned to walk away.

'It won't be easy to swallow my pride,' the man said.

'Easier than taking the consequences of not swallowing it,' Dan replied.

When he looked back he saw the man quickly packing away the news stand and piling all the papers into a van that was parked nearby. He smiled. His words wouldn't change the world but it was a start. His mind drifted back again to his first meeting with his mother when he'd returned from Italy. He'd driven down to her house and found his once feisty and energetic mother had turned permanently into a frail old lady, mourning the love of her life. They'd hugged and cried together. He knew it wouldn't be easy and that the woman who often irritated him with her pretentious social climbing had not entirely disappeared. But they'd reached a new understanding. He hadn't told her about his role as Master of Destiny yet. She'd always dismissed his father's beliefs as the ramblings of a drunk.

He was walking along Charing Cross Road to Foyle's bookshop, holding a painting by Sir Claude Francis Barry which he'd just bought from well-known art restorer and historian Robert Mitchell, and which would be perfect for his study in Italy, when his mobile rang.

'Dan, been meaning to call you. How are you?' It was Douglas.

Dan felt a bolt of shock. He hadn't got round to getting in touch with Douglas again. Afterall, this was the man who'd callously pulled the rug from under his feet so he'd decided to leave it for a while.

'I know you must despise me and think me stupid and weak. I am really sorry. I was just a complete dick,' Douglas said nervously.

'Well, it wasn't the best moment in my life,' Dan said carefully.

'Look, will you meet me? I'd like to explain and... I really need to talk to you,' Douglas pleaded.

'Yes, OK,' Dan replied. He was curious about what Douglas had to say. What did he know abut Anna's death? According to the police report they couldn't find out either how she'd died or a motive, it was an ongoing investigation. The truth would never be known, of that he was sure. Also, Douglas wasn't quite the star any more. His Middle East secret talks had been outed in the press and, soon after, the Americans had shafted him yet again by announcing that foreign companies would have to pay heavier tax to trade in the USA. The Anglo-American trade agreement had been torn up in the name of protectionism.

'How about tonight?' Douglas said eagerly.

'I'm meeting Harry tonight,' Dan said firmly.

'Oh, I have to fly to Munich tomorrow morning. I really do need to see you.' Douglas sounded deflated.

'Why don't you come for a drink? I'll get there early before Harry,' Dan said on impulse.

'Love to. What time?' Douglas asked.

'Six thirty,' Dan said. It would give them an hour before Harry turned up.

Dan signed into the club as Harry's guest and informed the receptionist he'd be waiting for Mr Bakhoum in the library, but as he was walking through the hall he heard his name being called and turned round. It was Harry arriving over an hour early. He smiled, pleased to see his best friend but aware this might be a bit of a problem for Douglas who he was sure wanted a quiet chat.

'You're early. I'd better warn you that...' Dan stopped as Douglas walked into the club also early and looking unusually nervous and harrassed.

'Dan, thanks for seeing me,' Douglas said, as he and Dan shook hands. Harry looked surprised but greeted Douglas warmly.

'I'll go and read the papers,' Harry said tactfully.

'No, stay,' Douglas said, and they walked into the peaceful environs of the library, which was empty.

'I'm resigning,' Douglas said quietly.

'What?' Dan and Harry both exclaimed as they sat down.

'I'm resigning. The bullshit and compromises of remaining in this game are too much. I thought it was what I wanted but turns out it's not.' Douglas looked at Dan. 'I had to turn my back on you just to save a man I wouldn't, under normal circumstances, even allow to sort my garbage.'

'Drinks?' Harry said quickly.

'G&T for Douglas and a malt for me, doubles I think, and thanks,' Dan replied as Harry disappeared to the bar.

'And how is Brian?' Dan asked raising his eyebrows.

'As from today, he's sacked. You'll hear it on the news. Have to say you Yanks,' he looked at Dan, 'have also paid a part in my decision, after they pulled that last trick on deciding to tax British companies and making me look like an idiot when I'd just announced that we'd signed a new free trade agreement,' Douglas said ruefully.

They both sat in silence for a few minutes.

'But you can't resign,' Harry said reasonably when he returned from the bar with the drinks, breaking the silence. You can do more good fighting from inside than being on the outside.'

'I've thought it all through carefully but discussed it with no one. Have to avoid media leaks. I've got the meeting of European heads tomorrow in Munich. Have to be there, don't want my resignation overshadowing the meeting. When I return on Tuesday I will go to the Queen and tender my resignation. We'll announce that Bill Taunton, Secretary of State for the Foreign Office, is going to take over. He's a safe pair of hands and popular with the voters. The general election is two years away so it will give him time to settle in and make his mark. I was going to step down before the next election anyway. If I want there will, no doubt, be a seat in the House of Lords for me, but at the moment I'm just tired of it all. I'm tired of waking up every morning with a feeling of disgust at having to act in a way I know isn't in the interests of the people who elected me. Do you understand?' Douglas said, looking distressed. 'And more importantly do you forgive me?'

'Yes, I do. I too have learnt that the choices we make are often complex and have repercussions that we can't always see.' Dan said quietly.

'I am trying to find the truth about Anna, terrible, such a shock and for you an awful loss,' Douglas placed his hand on Dan's arm 'I won't rest until I find out exactly how and why she died, however long it takes.'

Dan smiled at Douglas 'Thanks, it was indeed a terrible shock.' At the moment, he couldn't tell Douglas about the

Holy Trinity, he had to discover who the remaining members were and where they were.

'What does Fiona think of your decision? I guess she'll be happy at the thought of possibly becoming Lady Fiona Hamilton,' Dan said changing the subject.

'Fiona...' Douglas paused. 'Fiona has left me, not officially yet, but she is spending a lot of time in America with... a new man.'

'Good grief,' Dan exclaimed. 'She was devoted to you. Surely, it's just some passing midlife crisis.'

'There have been tensions in our marriage for a while. I haven't been easy to live with. She met Jack at the end of last year. He's a billionaire socialite, penthouse in the upper east side of New York, mansion in the Hamptons, villa in the south of France, staff in each place, and a need for a wife who can organize his life. His third, very young, wife ran off with her fitness instructor, so he's been looking for a mature, charming woman to whip his life back into shape. Fiona will fit right in. We'll make it official when I've resigned, to increase the sympathy factor for the party,' Douglas said, swirling his glass so the ice cubes clinked together.

'Look, come and help Dan build his house in Italy. Thomas, Dan's godson, will be there as well. I'm flying down with them on Thursday. That's probably too soon for you but come when you can,' Harry said impetuously, warming to the new Douglas.

'I'd love to. It sounds like just the tonic I need. Facing the media is going to be draining. Here's to a new future.' Douglas raised his glass and they all smiled.

'Yes, well, enough of the dramatics,' Dan said 'It'll be hard work in Italy. I want to move in by the winter.'

As they went into dinner, Dan shivered slightly and looked behind him, but no one was there. As soon as they'd left the room, a tall, distinguished-looking, slim man stood up from the high-backed wing chair that had hidden him from view in the small adjoining room. He'd bribed the Prime Minister's driver to inform him about his movements. What he'd just heard was so much better than he'd hoped for. He ordered another drink. Time to really put the cat amongst the pigeons.

'More gravy, sir?' the waiter asked Dan and he nodded before noticing the waiter's slightly shaking hand. Dan looked up and met a pair of very dark brown eyes. They were impenetrable. Suddenly a feeling of breathlessness overcame Dan and for a moment he thought he was going to pass out. Then as swiftly as it came it left him. But he felt a strong sense of unease.

'Where do you come from?' Dan asked the waiter as Harry told Douglas all about his beloved dig and the documents they were translating.

'Albania, sir,' the waiter replied.

Dan saw in his mind's eye a middle-aged man lying on a bed. He was deathly pale and fighting for breath. By his side a young woman, hardly more than a teenager, was wiping his brow, while an older woman wept quietly and tried to get him to drink some water.

'When was the last time you spoke to your parents?' Dan said evenly, as he felt the energy drain out of his body.

'We speak every week, but not this week as my phone got stolen,' the waiter said calmly. 'Excuse me, sir, why do you ask me this?'

'I think you should call them. Take my phone and call in your break. It's important to stay in close touch with family,' was all Dan said. He handed his phone to the surprised waiter, who looked over towards his boss.

'OK, thank you,' the waiter said. Dan took deep, regular breaths to calm the panic that was rising in his throat. He knew that if he was to help people then he had to get used to this and control the feelings it invoked. He had to remember it wasn't his body having a heart attack but someone else's. See yourself as a moving, breathing message board, he told himself. In time, he hoped he'd be able to control it so he wouldn't feel things so acutely. He saw Harry give him a strange look.

A quarter of an hour later, as they were sipping their coffees, the waiter returned with Dan's phone. 'My father... he is very ill. How did you know?' he asked.

'Just a hunch. Don't worry, go to him and you'll arrive in time.' Dan gently squeezed the man's arm.

'Thank you, thank you. My boss has told me to get the first flight home,' the waiter said and hurried off.

'What was all that about?' Douglas asked.

Dan and Harry exchanged glances but said nothing.

While Douglas had a quiet word with a senior Ministry of Defence adviser who was also dining in the club, Dan and Harry walked back down the stairs.

'So the power has awoken?' Harry said.

'Yes,' Dan replied and told Harry about his conversation with Gavin the newspaper vendor. 'So far no world-changing moments.'

'I'm sure they'll come when you've got used to dealing with the strange feelings these insights must provoke in you,' Harry observed.

'Yes, it's very unnerving to feel what another person is feeling. I'm hoping I can soon start reading the minds of beautiful women!' he quipped, trying to make light of the effect this was all having on him.

'Speaking of which, how is Jenny?' Harry asked.

'Lovely as ever but we're still just friends. It feels good to be taking it slowly for once instead of diving straight in and then struggling to understand the game plan. It's part of the new me,' Dan said.

Harry raised his eyebrows but remained silent as Douglas rejoined them. They left the club together but as they walked out into the street, they were met by a barrage of flashlights.

'Prime Minister, is it true you're resigning? Why? Who will take over? Do you feel the country can take yet another change of Prime Minister in mid-term?'

The Prime Minister's bodyguards stepped forward and manhandled him back to his car. Just before he got in, he turned and glared at Dan and Harry. 'You used that bloody waiter to get revenge for last year,' he hissed before he was driven away.

Dan and Harry were left speechless on the steps. Then they turned to each other. 'The Holy Trinity,' they said in unison as Dan remembered the feeling he'd had as he'd left the library. Wordlessly, Dan walked back inside the club and headed to the library, followed by Harry.

'Was there anyone else in here when I was with the Prime Minister?' he asked the waiter.

'Yes, sir, a gentleman was sitting in the small room which leads off from the library. Very generous, he was, gave me a large tip.' He held up a wine glass which he'd just collected from the room.

'Was that the glass the man used?' Dan asked.

'Yes. Why?' The waiter looked alarmed.

'Do you know his name?' Dan asked.

'As you know, this is a members only club, and I'm new here so I didn't recognize him, but he would have had to sign in, his name will be in the book on reception,' Then he whispered, 'I could go and look at the book and get his name,'

'Thanks, that would be very helpful.' Dan took a £20 note from his wallet.

The waiter took the note and disappeared to reception, reappearing a couple of minutes later. 'His name is Roger Stowe, sir. According to the receptionist he is very rarely here, and one of the other guests who was leaving said he's a high court judge, but I didn't give you any of this information.'

'Of course not. Was his address in the book as well?'

'No, sir, all records are kept on the computer which is locked in the offices. Floor staff have no access to it,' the waiter said firmly.

'Thank you anyway. Mind if I borrow this?' Dan said taking the judge's glass with him. Then he and Harry left the club.

'Why take the glass when you have his name? And bribing a waiter isn't very noble,' Harry muttered to Dan.

'He might have given a false name. There are thousands of members, and the staff can't remember all their names. Since the alert over terrorism, our judges have their DNA and fingerprints on a special database, which very few people know about, in case they get caught up in any of it. The fight against evil isn't always noble, and until I can automatically recognize everyone's real name, if I ever can, then quick action was called for.' Dan hoped he could get some fingerprints from the glass and track the bastard down. He needed to get to whoever was behind this before the man got to him.

CHAPTER FORTY-THREE

Italy and London

Summer 2011

Dan hadn't yet found the perpetrator of Douglas's betrayal, when he left for Italy with Harry and Thomas. There wasn't a Roger Stowe registered as a high court judge, but fingerprints from the glass were being analyzed and it shouldn't be long before he had an answer.

'Hey, I've found a book,' Thomas shouted as he rummaged around in an old metal bin that had been positioned on the land ready for the grape-pickers when they arrived. He held it up and Dan walked over to him. He was holding *Growth of the Soil* by Knut Hamsun. Dan tried to recall where he'd seen it before. He smiled. Of course, Anna had raved about it at university. She'd kept badgering him to read it but he'd never got round to it. Inside was a piece of paper on which was written '*The Judge, Roger Pendleton. 16 King Street, London SW1.*'

He removed the piece of paper and quickly closed the book. He was the man who had introduced Anna to McManus. Of course, it all made sense. He'd used a false surname in the club.

'What's up, Dan?' Thomas looked at him.

'Nothing, it's just that the strangest things happen when you least expect them.' With that Dan turned and walked off, folding the paper up and putting it in his pocket. 'Thank you, Mr Perkins,' he said quietly.

'Always a pleasure, my dear chap,' whispered a voice in his ear.

The fallout from the premature announcement of Douglas's resignation had been immense. Days of media coverage had completely overshadowed the Munich conference, much to the annoyance of the other European leaders. On the day when the President of the United States had arrived to present his keynote speech and reconfirm the strength of the Anglo-American alliance, media on both sides of the Atlantic had led with Fiona's split with Douglas and her new love. It had been a disaster. Needless to say, Douglas still placed all the blame on Dan and Harry. Dan had tried to explain he was pretty certain it was the work of the Holy Trinity, but Douglas had been in no mood to listen.

That evening Dan found an email waiting for him from the forensic scientist he'd commissioned to help him. It confirmed Mr Perkins' message. 'Fingerprints belong to a man called Roger Pendleton, a very senior judge, known for his right-wing views. You can find out more about him on the internet. Quite a few of his cases have been very high profile.'

'I've got to go to London,' Dan said to Harry over dinner and told him about the email. Thomas was out exploring the town. 'Then I'll go to Boston, some unfinished business there. Back in a few days.'

'You've only just got here,' Thomas said when he heard the news later. 'I thought us teenagers had the monopoly on changing our minds constantly.'

'Yes, well, maybe I'm returning to my adolescence,' Dan said distractedly.

'I'll come with you,' Harry offered.

'No, you stay with Thomas. I won't be more than a few days. Pity to disrupt everyone,' Dan said firmly.

'Yeah, stay, Harry. We can go to the new club that's just

opened for the summer. I'll teach you to strut your stuff.'
Thomas laughed. Harry looked dubious.

'You'll be fine. Each one of us has to face his fears,' Dan
said with a grin.

Back in London the next day, Dan made his way to King Street
and buzzed the entrance phone of number 16. The door
clicked and he pushed it open. He walked up a few steps and
then into a very large hallway. 'Hello,' he shouted.

'In here,' a male voice answered.

Dan walked into an elegant drawing room which was
tastefully furnished with expensive antique furniture. The
artwork on the walls was also impressive. At least one original
Braque and a Picasso drawing.

'We meet at last. Welcome.' A tall, slim, silver-haired man
in his sixties replaced the handset of his phone on the small
mahogany table, rose from an antique chair by the fire and
handed Dan a glass of whisky on ice.

'Roger Pendleton. Member of the Holy Trinity, the people
determined to kill me, and the group who killed Anna, whom
you knew well, of course,' Dan said without emotion, placing
the glass untouched on a side table.

'Yes, Anna was a friend of mine and I am a member of the
Holy Trinity, but my intention is not to kill you, just as it wasn't
our intention to kill dear Anna,' the Judge said. And that was
true. They had wanted to weaken and keep a close eye on Dan
Adams, not kill him. And there had been no discussion about
killing Anna. None of this would have happened if someone
else had been in charge. Angelica had caused this situation.
Anyway, she was no longer alive so Adams was still the link to
their desire for power and glory.

'You were working with my half-sister and I think her
intentions were quite clear,' Dan snapped, his eyes cold.

'We had no idea she was planning on murder quite so soon. We thought she'd want to get used to her new power, but it passed her by. Pity about the car crash,' Pendleton stared at Dan.

'Cut the crap. You wanted to destroy me, and you would have been happy to see me dead if it meant you got power through Angelica. Well, it didn't work,' Dan said curtly. It was a pity he couldn't tell him how Angelica had really died. He would have enjoyed seeing the man squirm, but that would mean revealing the secrets.

'So what are you going to do about it?' Roger Pendleton asked coolly.

'I am warning you to stop meddling. The trick with Douglas didn't work.'

'Judging by the chaos it caused, it worked rather well. Douglas Hamilton is finished, and believe me, that was easy. Imagine if we start to pull our bigger tricks. We should work together, you and us. We have a huge network of contacts already in place. People in high places are members of our group – truly the great and the good. We are the new world order. You can't ignore us.'

Dan felt a hot rush of anger. 'You just want the power so you can control the banks and governments and, above all, the people. Sorry, but we're on different sides.'

'Think carefully. You don't want to regret your decision. We've regrouped since Angelica's demise. I'm in control and we're growing all the time. We won't let anyone or anything stop us.'

'I'll deal with anything you throw at me. I've survived so far and I have no intention of letting people like you perpetuate your evil,' Dan said quietly. It would be very easy to teach this idiot a lesson. He could close his eyes and summon his power to bring about a bit of destruction, ask the universal energy to get rid of Pendleton, but no, he wasn't worth it. It would be a waste and it would diminish his powers. He turned to leave the room.

'You've no idea who and what you are dealing with, Adams. Be very careful,' the Judge said.

'If you kill me, you'll lose the power,' Dan said coolly, pausing in the doorway.

'I'm sure we'll find a way round that now the power is active once again,' Pendleton hissed.

'Fuck you, Pendleton. If your partners in crime are all lowlife like you, I think I'll more than survive whatever you can conjure up.' Dan walked out.

The judge picked up the phone and hit redial. It was picked up immediately. 'Proceed as agreed.' With that he hung up the phone.

Dan was calm by the time he reached his next destination. He took a deep breath and walked towards the iron gate. A man came towards him.

'Can I help you, sir?' he asked.

'I'm here to see Douglas Hamilton,' Dan said.

'Your name?'

'Dan Adams.'

The man disappeared inside the house and emerged less than a minute later. 'I'm sorry, sir, Mr Hamilton is busy.'

Dan stood steady and impassive. 'It is imperative I see him, a matter of state business.' It was their code at university, used only in emergencies.

This time when the man reappeared, he waved Dan in through the door. Douglas was waiting in the hallway. Dan was shocked by his appearance. He seemed to have aged ten years and lost at least a stone in weight.

'Come in,' Douglas led the way to his study where bits of paper were strewn across a desk. It was the antithesis of the calm, ordered Douglas he used to know.

Dan pulled a tape recorder out of his pocket. 'Please listen
to this.' He played the bit of tape where Roger Pendleton
confessed to setting up Douglas. He was careful to leave out
the rest.

Douglas sighed. 'Roger Pendleton never forgave me for
missing out on the Lord Chancellor's job. He's a vindictive,
unpleasant but very capable man. He must have been in the
club and by chance heard our conversation. A case of me being
in the wrong place at the wrong time. I have to apologize once
again to you, my friend.' Douglas looked beaten.

'I'm not here to receive your apology. I'm here to take you
back to Italy with me. You need a rest from the relentless media
onslaught,' Dan said decisively.

'I'd love that but I need a few days to complete some
business. Fiona has filed for divorce. She wants to move on as
quickly as possible and that means eradicating all traces of me
from her life,' Douglas said sadly.

'I'm really sorry. Is there any hope she'll change her mind?
Women can be contrary creatures.'

'No, she says she's in love with her rich American. Have
you never been tempted to marry and have a family? I know
you loved Anna but you should move on. As hard as it may be,
a family is the only lasting thing you create on this earth.'

'I have moved on. Anna was my fantasy, my first love, but
in spite of my desire to make it work and for us to marry, it
was never really the same when she came back. I have learned
that love is sometimes a quiet, undramatic emotion.'

'And who is she?'

Dan smiled. 'You'll meet her soon enough. Now I have to
go to Boston for a couple of days but I'll come back to London
and we can fly to Italy together. OK?'

'More than okay,' Douglas replied.

As he left Douglas, Dan felt happy that things seemed to

be resolved. He was still shaken by the brutality of Pendleton and his cohort, but he wasn't frightened. It was all part of his life's journey.

A small, slim man with a receding hairline and olive skin was heading towards Dan, reading something from his mobile phone. As he passed Dan he bumped into him. 'Oh, I'm sorry, how rude, please forgive me. These damn things are such a distraction,' he said, holding his hand out. Dan took it, registered his accent as Iranian, and smiled.

'No problem,' he said, before hailing a passing taxi and heading off to his next port of call.

At the corner of the street, Abdullah Mustafa paused and smiled. He opened his other hand, and in his palm sat a gold coin. It was gently pulsing as though alive. It was the eighth coin, the mystical secret hidden for thousands of years and only used once to save mankind from extinction. Adams and his cronies had no idea it was back in play. He'd found it on his travels in the East, in a dusty street where the ancient language of his forefathers was still spoken. Having spent many years studying with the old mystic who held the wisdom of eternity, he knew the coin had immense power if you knew how to unlock its code. It was the Ruler. Very soon he would reach the level needed to start trying to access its secrets. He carefully wrapped the coin in a silk handkerchief, and placed it in his pocket. Before it dispensed its power it had to connect to the Master of Destiny, and he'd just achieved that by acting as a conductor of energy through the handshake. Adams hadn't had to actually touch the coin.

The game would soon be back in his control. Pendleton and the other fools were finished. He would form a new order and lead it to victory. Power, riches, and a life of glory were his destiny. He'd known it for many hundreds, if not thousands of years, through all his incarnations.

CHAPTER FORTY-FOUR

Southern Italy

Summer 2011

Three days later Dan, Douglas and Jenny, whom he had finally persuaded to come and see his house, flew to Brindisi, from where they hired a car and headed to the house. As soon as they landed Douglas sniffed the air, asked his security to keep a low profile, begun to flirt mildly with Jenny and started to look less haunted. Dan smiled and Jenny grinned as Douglas recited John Donne. *'Absence, hear thou my protestation Against they strength Distance and length: Do what thou canst for alteration For hearts of truest mettle Absence doth join and time doth settle.'*

They found Harry and Thomas digging in the garden. 'We're building a swimming pool!' Thomas exclaimed.

'Try finishing the house first. God, can't leave you for five minutes without you getting distracted.' Dan looked at his watch. 'Now, I have to go and attend to some business. See you for dinner,' he said and was gone before anyone had a chance to ask him where he was going.

Nearly an hour later he was standing high up on the cliff top at the farthest corner of his land, by an old olive tree that the locals said had been there for over five hundred years. Gently, he removed the lid of the casket he held and sprinkled his father's ashes into the wind, across the sea and into the sky beyond. Turning round, he could see his house taking shape in the distance. It was right that his father's soul should be set free on the land of his ancestors.

He knelt and wished his father's soul peace and renewal.

'The blessings of the Universal Power are with you,' the breeze whispered back to him.

He stood for hours looking out to sea, the wind ruffling his hair. Far below him, the water was calm and benevolent, the waves breaking gently over the rocks at the bottom of the cliff. He studied the rhythm of the waves and calculated the movement of the tide. He found it calming.

He accepted his vulnerabilities, knowing he had the strength to overcome them. It was part of him, just as this mystical journey was. He thought back over the past months, and did a mental review. Sometimes he despaired of the sheer selfishness and greed of his fellow man, and then seemingly out of nowhere the world could unite and show its capacity for compassion. He thought of the rescue of the Chilean miners and the enormous worldwide concern as millions of people of all cultures, creeds and languages willed thirty-three lost men back to safety. The sanctity of life was not lost in a world where celebrity often ruled over talent. If people could be transfixed for hours by the sight of a manmade capsule bringing each man to safety, then Dan held hope that the human race would grasp the chance of redemption given to it by the Universal Power. But there was a long way to go before redemption was in sight. Riots, civil unrest, continued economic instability and further uprisings in the Middle East were all swirling around as the forces of change clashed with those who clung to the old ways.

He shivered feeling the presence of a dark, dangerous entity. For a few moments tension filled the air reminding him of what he already knew – that sometime in the future his life would be threatened and at that moment he'd be entirely on his own – the outcome dependent on his own strength of character and ability to beat whatever confronted him. It was, as much of life is, unknown.

As he continued to look out to sea, thinking of Harry and hoping he was safe in the turmoil of Syria, he caught a movement out of the corner of his eye. He turned and saw Anna gliding along the clifftops, her elegant and commanding presence just as he remembered it. Then she turned towards him and he glimpsed her piercing blue eyes and her expressive mouth. Her full lips parted in a half smile as she caught his gaze. She laughed and the sound reverberated around the cliffs, filling every nook and cranny with its light tinkling sound. It was the laughter of freedom and love of life.

Then she was gone, disappeared into the ether and out of his life for good. He turned back and lifted his head feeling the wind whip round his face. He looked up at the sky and heard a voice whispering to him from the breeze,

'Embrace your journey for it is the foundation of your life, from which you can build your dreams and create your future.'

Turning, he ran down the grassy slope of the hill. At the bottom a woman stood looking up at him. Jenny. She smiled at him and wordlessly he took her face in his hands and looked at her. Lord Melchizedek's words came back to him: 'You can't read those you love, for their emotions and thoughts and feelings are on the same wavelength as yours, and are absorbed within you to be revealed only on a human level.'

Taking her by the hand, he led her back towards the house. They walked across his land, chatting and laughing, totally at ease with one another. Next week Mr Big and Juliet would arrive. Only time would tell if she was going to be a permanent part of his journey but he felt ready to take the risk, ready to include her in his future, and ready to take on the challenges, physical discomfort and pain of loss that he knew would also be part of his life's journey.

But at least for today deep in his heart, he felt the peace that surpasses all understanding as he enjoyed the gifts that life was giving him.